The Rift & The Reckoning

The Land of Nowhere Book 1

Nick Blade

The Rift and The Reckoning
Book One of *The Land of Nowhere Trilogy*
© 2025 Nick Blade

ISBN: 979-8-9927855-0-0

Cover art by Bastien Boulai
Published by EDJ Books
For more information, visit NickBlade.com
First Edition
Printed in the United States of America

DEDICATION

For my mom, who taught me how to dream.

For my beautiful wife, Emma, who listened—patiently—as I talked about this book for over a year.

And to T. Lavon Lawrence, thank you for reading as I wrote.

This is your book as much as it is mine.

Chapter 1

Theron

The cave is a tomb of shadows and whispers. Cold, wet stone presses in from every side, its surface slick with moisture. The air reeks of damp earth and mold, the scent of decay clinging to every breath. Torches sputter along the jagged walls, their flames casting distorted silhouettes that stretch and sway like ghosts reaching for the light.

No one speaks. No one dares to move.

Somewhere deeper inside, water drips slowly and steadily, creating a hollow and distant sound—like a clock counting down the moments before blood spills.

Violence hangs heavy in the air, a familiar weight. I wish it didn't have to be this way. I wish there was another path. But this is what I do. This is what I've become.

Once, I killed for a god I believed in. For a faith that guided me. Now, I kill because it is necessary. If I had my way, I'd be home, tending my fields. My wife would be alive. My son would be safe. But someone stole those choices from me. And now I am what the land demands—a blade without mercy.

The men surrounding me know that. They outnumber me seven to one, yet their fear is palpable. It clings to them like a second skin. They know my name. They know what I am. And it terrifies them.

The leader, a craggy-faced brute with a fire-red beard, steps forward, masking his unease with bravado. His leather armor is cracked and worn, his shirt stained and stinking of sour sweat. He hefts his axe with a casual ease, but I catch the tremor in his fingers.

"So," he says, his voice rough, straining for confidence. "Are we going to do this? Or do I have time to grab lunch?"

His attempt at humor falls flat. The men behind him shuffle uneasily. He doesn't want to be here. None of them do. But they're here all the same. And they won't be leaving.

"Yes," I say. The bitter word tastes bad in my mouth. The disgust seeps into my voice, and he hears it.

The big man chuckles, shifting his axe to the other shoulder. "You know there are ten of us, right?"

"Seven."

His eyes narrow. The chuckle dies on his lips. "Are you calling me a liar, boy?"

He steps closer, spittle clinging to his beard as he sneers. Anger sharpens his tone, but it's not real. It's a mask—a flimsy shield for the fear beneath.

I've seen it countless times. Fear, I've learned, is a chameleon. It wears the colors of rage to hide its true nature. A primal instinct, an animal's last defense when cornered. But anger makes men predictable. It makes them sloppy.

"No," I say, my voice calm, deliberate. "Maybe you just can't count."

For a moment, silence reigns, broken only by the rhythmic drip of water.

The man before me bristles, his bravado flickering like a dying flame. His fear isn't gone. It never left. It's simply changed its face. And I've already seen the cracks in his armor.

Men like him cling to anger like a shield, believing it will make them unbreakable. But to me, anger is a cracked mask, a brittle facade that crumbles under the pressure of real fear. Fear always reveals itself. In a glance too long. In a tremor too sharp. It slips through clenched jaws and hardened words. It's a predator that can't be caged.

I've learned to read fear as one reads a map—to follow its curves, trace its hidden paths, and find the vulnerable places it tries to obscure. In my years, I've seen both kings and killers fall victim to this alchemy of the mind. Fear leads. Anger follows.

It's a dance as old as time. And I've long since mastered its rhythm.

The man before me adjusts his grip on his axe, his knuckles whitening against the leather-wrapped handle. His anger rises to fill the silence, a desperate attempt to mask the doubt gnawing at his resolve. But I see it. I always see it.

"No," I say again, my voice steady as stone. "The answer will always be no. You won't make it out of this cave alive."

His eyes harden, his brow furrowing with false bravado as he sizes me up. I feel the weight of his gaze crawling over me—calculating, measuring, hoping to find a weakness to exploit. But he won't find one.

My height alone is unsettling enough, a towering seven feet of coiled strength and quiet menace. It isn't just my stature that makes men falter, though. It's what they sense beneath it—a force honed by years of surviving what others could not.

My body bears the proof of those years. Thick, jagged scars crisscross my skin like a forgotten map carved into stone. My arms, my shoulders, my face—each mark tells a story of battles won, of pain endured.

But it's not the scars that unsettle them most. It's my eyes. Or rather, the absence of them.

Born without sight, my eyeless face has unnerved men for as long as I can remember. They look at the space where my eyes should be and see something that defies understanding. They think it makes me blind. They couldn't be more wrong.

Sight is a crutch. It binds people to the limits of light and shadow, to what lies before them—and nothing more. But I see the world in ways others cannot. The air carries whispers of movement. Vibrations ripple through the earth beneath my feet. The faintest echoes twist and stretch, mapping every surface, every breath, every heartbeat.

I see in all directions at once. The world unfolds around me like a perfect sphere, alive with subtle shifts and hidden truths. I know when a man's hand twitches toward his blade before he's even aware of it. I hear fear in a breath held too long. I feel the weight of eyes lingering where they shouldn't. To them, I am blind. But in truth, I see more than they ever will.

The man's gaze lingers too long on my face. His expression twists with discomfort before he forces a chuckle. "You may be big," he says, resting his axe on his shoulder, "but me and my axe here have cut down bigger trees."

His bluster rings hollow, a man desperate to regain control of the moment. He mistakes my size and scars for the whole of me, failing to understand that strength isn't just muscle and bone. It's the weight of experience. The scars of survival.

I am not just what they see. I am what they can't.

"Trees don't fight back," I say softly, stepping forward. My words are calm, measured—but there's an edge beneath them, a quiet promise of what's to come.

The man stiffens, his courage wavering. The shadows on the cave walls stretch longer, darker. The flickering torchlight dances like fire over his pale, sweating skin.

He's starting to realize his mistake. I'm not a tree. I'm a storm.

I move.

Years of survival have taught me this truth: action is the difference between life and death. Hesitation kills. I've seen too many men fall because they waited for the perfect moment. The perfect moment doesn't exist. You create it—by striking first, striking hard, and striking fast.

The craggy-faced man doesn't see me coming until it's too late. My long strides devour the distance between us, my boots pounding against the stone like a war drum. His eyes widen, his mouth opens—but no sound escapes.

My fist slams into his temple, snapping his head to the side. He drops like a felled tree, his axe clattering to the ground. No hesitation. I step forward, driving my boot down on his neck. The crunch of cartilage cuts through the cavern's silence.

His chest heaves, desperate for air that will never come. The wheezing grows frantic, his body thrashing in the dirt like a fish pulled from water.

Mercy has no place here. But I give it anyway. I crouch and drive my knife deep into his eye socket, pushing until the tip hits bone. His body stills. The cavern falls silent once more.

When I rise, six pairs of eyes are locked on me—wide, terrified, disbelieving.

Good. Fear is the most powerful weapon in a fight like this.

They stand frozen, caught between fight and flight, their minds scrambling for a way out. But there is no way out. Not for them.

I scan the group. Two to my right, three to my left, one behind me.

The three on the left will move first. One of them is already reaching for his blade.

I step toward him, closing the gap in a blink. His hand is still on the hilt when I grab his wrist, twisting it hard. He cries out, the sound sharp and pitiful in the still air.

My knife finds the soft flesh beneath his jaw, sliding upward with practiced ease. Bone stops the blade's ascent, but by then, it doesn't matter. His body crumples to the ground, blood bubbling from his lips in a crimson froth.

The other two men beside him hesitate a moment too long. I don't.

I pivot, the movement smooth and fluid, and drive my blade into the first man's throat. His eyes bulge, his hands flying to the gaping wound as he gurgles for breath. He stumbles back, collapsing in a heap. The third tries to run. I catch him before he takes two steps.

A quick slash to the back of his knee sends him sprawling, and before he can scream, I silence him with a swift, clean cut across the neck. The blood sprays in an arc, dark and wet against the cavern walls.

Five seconds. Maybe less. Four men dead.

It always happens this way. I don't take pride in it. I don't feel the rush that some warriors speak of, the thrill of combat coursing through their veins. What I feel is detachment. I turn off the mind's endless chatter. I silence doubt, guilt, fear.

I let my body do what it has been trained to do. What it was made to do. Kill.

The remaining men haven't moved. They stare at the bodies sprawled across the cave floor, their expressions twisted with disbelief. The torches flicker, casting distorted shadows across the carnage. They know, now. They were dead the moment they stepped into this cave.

Now, it's three to one.

The two men to my right stare at me, their minds racing through a storm of emotions. Fear comes first—it always does. It creeps into their eyes, tightening their jaws, stealing the strength from their legs.

Then comes panic, wild and desperate. For a moment, there's hope. I see it flash across their faces as they glance at each other, silently agreeing to flee. But hope dies the instant they remember where they are.

I stand between them and the cave's mouth. There's nowhere to run.

One of them steps forward, his hands trembling as he raises them in surrender. His palms face outward, as though warding off a storm. "Look... we don't want to die here," he stammers. His voice cracks, thin and pitiful in the cold silence. "We did nothing to you. Please—just let us go."

I watch him, unmoving. His words hang in the air, heavy with the weight of a man bargaining for his life. I've heard it all before. "It's not what you did," I say quietly, each word measured. "It's what you're going to do."

His brow furrows in confusion, his lips trembling as he struggles to understand.

"Consider this judgment," I continue. "For things yet done."

In two steps, I close the distance between us. My hand moves with practiced ease, pulling the long sword from the scabbard at my back. The blade catches the torchlight, gleaming like a silver promise.

The man's eyes widen, and in that split second, I see the truth in them. He knows.

But it's too late.

I raise the sword high and bring it down with brutal precision, the blade biting into his collarbone and carving deep through flesh and bone. It cleaves downward, splitting him open almost to his navel before catching on a rib. His body crumples under the weight of the strike, folding in on itself like a ruined marionette.

Before I can pull the blade free, an arrow is loosed from behind me. I move to the right, just a breath. It's so close I feel the feathers brush my ear before it finds its mark with a sickening thud. The second man stumbles backward, clutching at the shaft embedded in his neck. Blood pours between his fingers as he gurgles, choking on his own life. His knees buckle, and he collapses to the cavern floor, his desperate attempts to stop the bleeding slowing, then ceasing.

Silence falls again. Now, there is only one.

I turn slowly, locking eyes with the man holding the bow. He's trembling, his hands shaking so violently that he nearly drops his weapon. Panic plays across his face, warring with resignation. He knows he's outmatched. He drops the bow to the ground and raises his hands in surrender.

"You don't have to do this," he pleads. His voice wavers, thick with desperation. "I can just leave."

I keep walking, each step deliberate, unhurried. The rhythm of my boots on the stone echoes through the cave, a relentless drumbeat of inevitability.

"No," I say, my voice low, steady. In one swift motion, I swing my sword. The blade arcs through the air, clean and final. His head falls from his shoulders, the body collapsing moments later with a dull thud.

Seven men lay dead around me. Blood seeps into the cracks of the cave floor, mingling with the damp earth. I stand in the silence, breathing deeply. It was necessary. It always is.

These men would have done things I couldn't allow. They would have left ruin in their wake, taken lives that weren't theirs to take. That doesn't mean I enjoy what just happened.

I've hardened myself against the world, built walls around the softer parts of me to keep them safe. But I'm not dead inside. Not yet. I feel the weight of every life I've taken. I've tried not to care. But that's not who I am.

No matter how impervious I may appear on the outside, beneath the scars and steel, I am still human. And that's the cruelest wound of all.

Then I hear it. Or rather, I don't. The birdsong is gone. It's a subtle absence, but one that grips me harder than any blade could. The air outside the cave should be alive with the chatter of sparrows, the rustle of wind through the trees. Instead, there is silence. Heavy. Stifling.

I tilt my head, tuning into the quiet, letting my other senses fill the void. There. The soft rustle of leaves beneath a shifting foot. The scrape of a boot against stone.

A throat being cleared, followed by a hissed whisper—words lost to distance, but the intent unmistakable. They're out there. Waiting.

My pulse quickens, each beat drumming against my ribs like a distant war cry. For the first time since stepping into this cave, I feel it—

an edge of unease, creeping beneath my skin like the chill of an unseen breeze.

This isn't the way it happened before. Something's changed. They're already moving. I'm out of time. My thoughts shift, narrowing to a single, burning focus. My son.

I start toward the cave's mouth, my steps measured, deliberate. The bodies around me are already forgotten—shadows of a battle that no longer matters.

What matters is out there.

I tighten my bracers, the worn leather familiar against my wrists, and draw the second sword from my back. Its weight settles into my grip like an extension of myself, steel cold and ready.

Two blades. Two hands. It won't be enough. There will be many of them. I can feel it in the stillness, in the way the forest holds its breath. I don't know how many. But there is no number high enough. No force strong enough. No army vast enough to keep me from him.

The air at the mouth of the cave tastes different—cooler, sharper. The scent of pine and earth mingles with something else. Something stale. Blood, not yet spilled.

They think they can stop me. They think they can take what little I have left.

Let them come. Let them learn what storms are made of. I won't be stopped.

Chapter 2

Jerrick

I've never cared for change. It makes me uncomfortable. Some people thrive on the unknown—on shifting tides and unexpected turns. Not me. I prefer things consistent. Steady. Where I can predict my days and know what lies ahead. But the world around me has become anything but predictable.

Over the past few weeks, the air has turned colder, far too cold for this time of year. The sky—usually bright and white—is a dull, sickly gray. The trees are bare already, their branches stretching upward like skeletal hands, clawing at that endless, empty expanse.

Everyone's talking about it. The way the light has dimmed. How the horizon looks thinner, stretched tight like worn fabric. They say winter has come early—and might never leave.

I try not to dwell on what that would mean. Not for me. Not for the farm.

But it gnaws at me all the same. A never-ending winter would spell disaster for a farmer. Preparing for it feels like admitting defeat. And I'm not ready for that.

"Things will work themselves out," I tell myself, though the words feel hollow.

My dad says I'm in my head too much. He's probably right. But I prefer my thoughts to the unpredictability of conversation. It's not that I'm standoffish—my parents raised me to be kind, to show respect. I've just never been good at talking to people. Never known what to say or how to say it without sounding awkward. So, I keep to myself.

I've convinced myself that these changes are temporary. There's no point in talking about them. People try too hard to make others see the world as they do, as if forcing a perspective makes it true. That's why I keep my thoughts to myself. At least I can control those. Most of the time.

I guide Daisy, our sturdy draft horse, along the rutted dirt road toward the City at Four Rivers. The wheels of the cart creak and groan under the weight of the apples. Unease gnaws at me, burrowing deep.

Breathe, Jerrick. Focus on what you know. You've made this trip a thousand times.

The land has changed. The trees, the sky, the very air—everything feels different. The sky is gray now, dull and endless, a smothering void. The wind presses against me, cold and constant, carrying whispers of something unseen. There's no rhythm to the light anymore. No clear sense of time. Just the gray sky above and the creeping chill that sinks deeper every day.

The abrupt surrender to winter unsettles me in ways I can't fully explain. I've always preferred the comfort of predictability. The steady rhythm of farm life. The known paths of our orchard. But I can feel it slipping away.

I pull myself from my thoughts, grounding myself in the moment. Behind Daisy and me is a cart full of apples and apple desserts. For as long as I can remember, my parents and I have made this six-hour trek to the city to sell our produce. This year, I'm alone. They stayed home. Perhaps they're trying to prepare me to take over. To show me how to run things without them. I push the thought down, refusing to let it settle. I'm not ready to think about that. Not yet.

The cart groans again, the wood protesting under the weight of the harvest. The joints are loose. I'll need to strengthen them when I get home, drive a few more nails to keep everything in place.

Our orchard, more resilient to the cold than other crops, blessed us with a modest harvest this year. "People will want to stock up," my father had said this morning, his voice tinged with both concern and hope. "With the weather turning like this, you might just sell out quickly and get back home sooner."

I hold onto that hope. Because, for now, it's the only thing keeping the unease at bay.

The road to Four Rivers is quieter than usual. The cheerful chatter and laughter of travelers has been replaced by hushed tones and hurried steps. The early winter hangs over the land like a shroud, turning lively conversations into whispers of worry.

I pass enough people, with my long strides, to catch fragments of their murmurs. The words float through the air, heavy with dread.

"It's coming..."

"The constriction..."

"The Fog..."

It's the same conversation I've overheard for weeks now, but this time there's more urgency. More pleading. They fear that the Fog will finally reach shore.

For twenty years, the Fog has crept steadily inward. Always distant, always looming, but never fast enough to cause immediate panic. Now, though, it feels different. People wouldn't be surprised if it suddenly surged forward, swallowing the coastline in a single breath. Soon, there may be no shoreline left. Only the Fog.

As I get closer to the city, the tone of the whispers changes. The unease on the road grows more tangible. People glance my way, their eyes lingering too long before skittering away, as though they've been caught in a forbidden act.

Whispers flutter through the crowd like leaves on a brisk wind.

"That's him."

"It must be."

"You think he knows?"

Their words are a chorus of uncertainty and speculation. I don't know what they're saying about me, but I feel it—like a prickling at the back of my neck, a question hanging in the air, waiting for an answer. They look at me as though I should have it.

I don't, of course. I don't even know the question.

The curiosity in their eyes itches at me. But I push it aside. I've never cared for confrontation. I find comfort in the solitude of my thoughts and the steady rhythm of the farm. It's easy to convince myself that they've confused me with someone else.

That's what I want to believe. Because if they're right, it's just one more change to worry about. And I've had enough change.

It's hard to remain invisible when you're as tall as I am. Even when I slow my pace and hug the side of the road, trying to blend in, I stand out. My mother always told me to stop slouching, but the habit stuck. I learned early that standing out isn't always a good thing.

When you're different, people notice. And when people notice, they judge. They prod. They push.

I figured that out as a kid. Rolled my shoulders forward. Bent at the waist. Anything to make myself smaller. Anything to avoid being a target. I'm twenty-one now. I'm not a kid anymore. But some habits are hard to break.

So, as the whispers grow louder, I do what I've always done when I'm the center of unwanted attention. I make myself small.

The City at Four Rivers looms ahead, breaking the endless gray horizon. Even from this distance, its towering white block walls are imposing—a fortress of pale stone stretching two hundred feet into the sky.

The city was built five centuries ago, at the end of the God Wars. They say it was meant to be the last stronghold of Lathguard and his armies. A final bastion against a world tearing itself apart. But just as the last block was laid, the gods vanished. All of them. Along with most of their human armies. No one knows how or why.

Some say the gods' disappearance is why the land has begun to shrink. Why the Fog keeps creeping inward, devouring everything in its path. Why the world feels like it's folding in on itself, collapsing toward some unseen center. But that's just speculation. Just whispers on the wind. And I've had enough of those.

As I draw closer to the city, the crowd thickens. Hundreds of people pour through the gates, their voices blending into a low murmur of conversation. The noise ebbs and flows like the tide, but there's an edge to it—a tension simmering just beneath the surface.

Up ahead, a commotion catches my eye. The crowd parts as two figures move confidently through the throng. Since I stand head and shoulders above most people, I see them before they see me. My instincts nudge me to step aside, to avoid whatever trouble they bring, but it's too late. They stop in front of me.

"Hello, Jerrick," says the younger of the two guards, offering a lopsided smile.

His face is familiar. He's about my age, with sandy blonde hair and kind eyes. We attended Civic Education together, though I can't recall his name right away. He's wiry, with a relaxed air that contrasts sharply with his companion—a shorter, stockier man with dark hair and a sour expression.

The second guard's uniform strains against his middle, his belt cinched tight to keep his sword from slipping. His eyes are too close together, his nose sharp and pointed. He looks like a man who's been interrupted mid-meal—and he's not happy about it.

"What's with the spear?" the stocky guard asks, his gaze lingering on the weapon strapped to my back. His tone is flat, but there's a weight to the question, a strain that borders on accusation.

The crowd around us slows, their conversations fading into silence. I feel the weight of dozens of eyes on me. The air thickens, heavy with unvoiced fears and unasked questions.

I shift uneasily.

This morning, before leaving the farm, I strapped the spear to my back. I'd planned to hunt on my way home. In hindsight, it was a strange choice—I could've left it in the cart. But with wild Essence warping animals into dangerous creatures, carrying a weapon isn't unusual.

It shouldn't be unusual.

So why are they asking?

The stocky guard's hand drifts to the pommel of his sword. His fingers tighten around it, knuckles whitening. "Are you going to make me repeat myself?"

I swallow hard. "No, sir."

The guard's gaze narrows. "So?"

"Oh... sorry," I stammer, forcing the words out. "I plan on hunting before heading home tomorrow."

"With a spear?" His brow arches skeptically. He doesn't let go of his sword.

"My father likes to challenge me with different weapons," I explain, keeping my voice steady. "It's... tradition."

The guard's lip curls. "Your father, huh?" He spits the word like it leaves a bad taste in his mouth.

"Yes," I say, standing a little straighter. "My father."

The guard's expression darkens, and for a moment, I think he's going to draw his sword. His hand twitches. My heart pounds.

Then, suddenly, he lunges.

Before I can react, he grabs the front of my shirt with one hand. The other hand holds a knife, its blade glinting in the pale light. The movement is quick, practiced—too quick for me to stop.

I freeze. Not from fear, but from habit.

Conflict has always made me retreat inward, pulling me into the safety of passivity.

"William!"

The younger guard—Branik, I remember now—grabs the other man's wrist, holding him back. "Let me handle this."

William hesitates. His nostrils flare, his grip tightening before he sighs and releases me. His parting glare is a silent challenge. One I'm neither prepared nor willing to answer.

"I'm sorry, Jerrick," Branik says, stepping between us. His tone is apologetic, but there's an edge to his words. "He's not a bad guy. It's just... you know who killed his brother."

Branik leans in, lowering his voice to a whisper. His gaze darts toward the crowd, wary of eavesdroppers. I blink, startled.

"I don't—"

The words die on my lips. Doubt coils in my chest, tightening like a noose.

I don't know who killed his brother. Do I?

Instead of denying it, I nod slowly, pretending to understand.

The crowd is still watching. Their collective gaze weighs heavily on me, each curious glance another link in a chain I can't escape. I reach over my shoulder for the spear.

Branik flinches.

The movement is subtle—a slight tensing of his shoulders, a shift in his stance—but I catch it. His smile fades, replaced by something wary.

What's going on?

I move slowly, deliberately, easing the spear from my back and placing it in the cart. All around me, the crowd exhales as one, like they've been holding their breath.

"Thank you, Jerrick," Branik says, his smile returning, though it doesn't quite reach his eyes. He turns to the crowd, raising his voice. "Okay, folks! Sorry for the delay. Keep moving."

The tension breaks. The crowd resumes its shuffle through the gate, their whispers fading into the background. I linger for a moment, watching them drift back into their own concerns. Turning to Daisy, I pat her neck, finding comfort in her familiar presence.

But the interaction with the guards lingers in my mind. William's glare. His scrutiny. The crowd's reaction. It all stirs a disquiet I can't shake.

I sigh, wishing I could retreat to the simplicity of the orchard. To the predictable rhythm of farm life.

But I can't. Not today. The market awaits.

With a final glance at the gate, I take Daisy's reins and guide her toward our usual spot. Whatever these whispers mean, I'll have to face them eventually.

For now, I focus on the task ahead.

But as I walk, the morning's odd encounters weigh heavy on my shoulders. The familiar streets of Four Rivers feel different now. Like a stage. And I'm an unwitting actor in an unknown play.

#

Four Rivers stands as a reminder of a time when giants walked the land alongside humans. The city's towering architecture echoes that shared history, its polished white stone buildings looming like sentinels from another era.

The doors, twenty-five feet high, stretch toward the sky—each one integrated with smaller entrances tailored for human use. Practical, imposing. The city's builders did not prioritize beauty or grandeur. They built it to endure.

Once I reach my stall in the market, I set up my display table just as my mother taught me.

"Eye appeal is buy appeal," she always says.

I arrange the apples from right to left, sorting them by type and color, creating a gradient from green to deepest red. The familiar task should calm my nerves, but it doesn't. The whispers and sideways glances from passersby gnaw at me. The market is busier than I've seen in months, but no one stops at my stall.

Voices bounce off the stone buildings—a chaotic blend of haggling merchants and curious shoppers. The smells are the best part: grilled meats, baked bread, and spiced pastries waft through the air.

But something's missing.

The back current of merriment that used to accompany the market is gone. Tension has replaced laughter. Every conversation feels hushed, secretive.

"Hi, Jerrick." The sound of my name pulls me from my thoughts.

I turn to see Elena standing behind me, her smile bright enough to banish the gloom lingering in my mind.

She touches my arm, grounding me in the moment. Elena is of average height and build, but everything else about her is striking. Her long black hair is braided down her back, and her eyes—a vibrant, impossible purple—seem to sparkle in the morning light.

"Hi," she says again, tilting her head slightly, her smile never faltering. "How are you doing this morning?"

For a moment, all my worries fade away. We've known each other our whole lives. Her family's farm borders ours, though it's a bit of a journey. We see each other most weekends at the market.

"That's your cue to speak," she teases, giggling softly.

I blink, startled out of my thoughts. "Oh—sorry. Yes, I'm okay." *Why am I such a bumbling idiot sometimes?*

"And how are you doing this morning?"

I frown, confused. "What? Umm... I'm not sure..."

She giggles again, shaking her head. "No, silly. That's what you're supposed to say."

Her laughter is light and musical, and it completely disarms me. My heart stumbles in my chest.

"Oh," I laugh nervously. "How are you doing this morning?"

She grins, her eyes sparkling. "I'm doing well, Jerrick. Thanks for asking." She ends it with a playful nod and a wink.

As usual, I have no idea what to say next.

I've always liked Elena. More than liked her. But we've always been just friends. Nothing more.

She tilts her head, studying me for a moment. Then, as if to rescue me from my own silence, she says, "I've been learning to shoot a bow."

"The bow?" I ask, perking up. "That's great! I've been shooting since I was a kid."

"I know."

There's a pause, her smile growing wider. She waits, giving me a chance to catch up.

"So... are you going to ask me?"

I blink. "Ask you?"

"To practice with you, silly."

My heart jumps. "Oh! Well, yes. Yes, of course."

Is she asking me to ask her to spend more time with me?

She laughs, shaking her head. "Are you going to ask, or do I have to do that part too?"

I clear my throat, laughing nervously again. "Would you... would you like to go shooting with me sometime?"

Her smile softens into something more sincere. "Of course I would."

Before I can say anything else, she steps forward and wraps her arms around me in a hug. Her head barely reaches my chest.

My mind screams at me to *say something*. To hug her back. To do *anything*.

But I freeze. My arms hang uselessly at my sides, stiff and awkward. I worry that I've misread her feelings. That if I react the wrong way, I'll ruin the easy friendship we've always had.

So, I stand there like a fool, letting her hug me while I do nothing.

As Elena pulls away from the hug, she looks up at me with that familiar smile. But it fades, her expression shifting into something more serious.

"What do you think about the season change" she asks quietly. "Do you think it's true?"

I hesitate, already uncomfortable with the direction of the conversation. "About the constriction?"

She nods.

"I think it makes sense," I say, choosing my words carefully. "I mean, we skipped a whole season. That can't be good."

Elena chews her bottom lip, a nervous habit I've seen countless times. There's something she wants to say, but she holds back.

"I..." she starts, then stops, shaking her head as if dismissing the thought. But after a moment, she continues.

"It's worse than that, Jerrick. Before this is all over, nothing will be the same. It will either be better because people sacrificed... or worse because people believed a lie."

Her words hang in the air between us, heavy with meaning. She looks at me, expectant, like she's waiting for something.

I shift uncomfortably. "I don't know what to say to that. But... I'm sure there are people looking into it. The Council will figure it out."

Elena tilts her head, a knowing smile tugging at her lips. "What about you?"

"Me?"

"What if you could do something about this? Would you?"

I laugh nervously. "I'm just a farmer, Elena. I'm nobody special."

Her smile softens, and this time it reaches her eyes. "You are more than what you believe, Jerrick. We all are."

She steps closer, her voice lowering as if sharing a secret.

"Each of us carries the responsibility to unearth our truths. They shape our identity, forge our legacy, and guide us on our path. Embracing them—no matter how daunting—gives our lives meaning and direction."

Her words stir something inside me.

I've always seen myself as just Jerrick—the farmer. The son of simple people, living a simple life. The idea of uncovering truths that might challenge that simplicity makes me uncomfortable.

Yet Elena sees something more. Can she be right? Elena always has a way of pulling me out of my own head, making me see beyond the horizon of my thoughts. She sees potential where I see boundaries. It's disconcerting. Intriguing.

Maybe there's more to my story—more to all our stories—than what lies on the surface. But am I ready to find out?

The answer, like the path ahead, is shrouded in mist. And when things get misty, I prefer to turn the other way.

Of course, I don't say any of that. Instead, I let her words bounce around in my head and say the only thing that comes to mind. "That's pretty deep."

Idiot.

Elena giggles, shaking her head. Then, to change the subject, I ask, "Do you know what everyone's been talking about? It feels like they all know something I don't."

Elena's expression falters, her gaze flickering toward the crowd. "Don't mind them, Jerrick. Even if it were true..."

She trails off, her attention snapping past me. Her expression hardens, her posture stiffening.

"Jerrick," she says urgently. "It's Bowen. He's coming this way."

Her voice carries a tension I haven't heard from her before. I turn, my stomach sinking.

Bowen strides toward us with a hurried, determined look on his face. His gaze locks onto me.

Great. Could this day get any worse?

Chapter 3

Jerrick

As Bowen strides toward me, I instinctively take a step back.

Elena's voice cuts through my spiraling thoughts. "We aren't kids anymore."

"I know," I murmur, though the tightening in my throat betrays my doubt.

Bowen stops in front of us, planting himself between Elena and me, far too close for comfort. His presence is suffocating, his smugness palpable.

"I know what?" he asks, his tone dripping with false curiosity.

Bowen has always been like this—prying, pressing, pushing until you break. Just over six feet tall with a stocky build, he has the look of someone used to getting what he wants. His sandy blonde hair is carefully styled, his clothes tailored and spotless. He dresses like the son of the mayor—because he is. And he never lets anyone forget it.

His smile is unsettling, a thin veil over something darker, something that hints at knowledge I don't have.

"Oh... n-nothing," I stammer, searching desperately for a way to change the subject. "Are you here to buy some apples?"

Bowen laughs, a short, sharp sound, before giving the apples on my table a cursory glance. He wrinkles his nose in mock disgust. "They're kind of scrawny, aren't they?" His sneer deepens as his gaze flicks back to me. "They remind me of someone."

Elena steps forward, her voice cutting through the tension like a blade. "You need to get new material. We aren't kids anymore, and Jerrick isn't that little boy you used to pick on. He's a head taller than you."

Bowen gasps, clutching his chest as though her words had wounded him. "Pick on? Jerrick?" He shakes his head, never breaking eye contact with me. "Jerrick and I have always been good friends. I would never pick on him."

Say something.

The words scream in my head, but my lips won't move. My throat tightens, and I have to clench my hands to keep them from trembling.

"Why are you even here, if not to buy apples?" Elena asks, her tone sharp, cutting through the awkward silence.

Bowen tilts his head slowly, as if he's only just realized she's standing there. "To catch up with an old friend," he says, dismissively waving a hand in my direction before turning back to me.

Behind him, Elena stiffens. Her jaw clenches, muscles pulsing as she grinds her teeth. She looks ready to strike him, her hands twitching at her sides. But then her expression softens—a calculated shift.

"Since when have you and Jerrick ever been friends?" she asks, her voice low and dripping with contempt.

Bowen turns to her, feigning shock once more.

I stare down at the top of his head, a realization dawning. I'm not that little boy anymore.

Standing just under seven feet tall, I tower over him. For the first time, I see him for what he is—a man who uses his father's power to hide his own insecurity.

Bowen doesn't notice the shift in me.

"Sure we are," he says with exaggerated sarcasm, flashing that unsettling smile again. "We've always been the best of friends."

Then his tone shifts, becoming more serious. "Besides, the Naming is just a few weeks away. It could change everything for us." His eyes gleam with something I can't quite place. "I want to talk to my *friend* about it."

"What about it?" I ask, my voice steadier now. I force myself to hold his gaze, hoping to draw his attention away from Elena.

Bowen smirks, satisfied that he has my attention. "See?" He turns back to Elena with a dismissive wave. "You can go now. We have serious matters to discuss—like who we might bond with and how that will shape our future."

To her credit, Elena doesn't flinch.

She doesn't say a word.

She doesn't walk away.

Instead, she stands her ground, her narrowed eyes fixed on Bowen. The tension in her jaw is back, muscles pulsing with restrained anger.

Bowen ignores her, turning back to me.

"So, Jerrick." He draws out my name, savoring the moment. "Who are you hoping to bond with at the Naming?"

In almost every encounter with Bowen, it comes down to this. Bonding.

For him, it's a way to escape his father's control. For me, it's forced servitude—a life of sacrifice with no guarantee of salvation.

"Does it really matter?" I ask, keeping my tone as neutral as I can. "Very few people bond these days. Less than five percent at last year's Naming. I heard they're expecting even fewer this year."

"It matters," Bowen says, his voice sharp. "It always matters." He leans in, his gray-blue eyes locking onto mine. "I'm just curious if you're still as selfish as you've always been. Let's imagine, for a moment, that you're one of the lucky few. Who do you bond?"

For a fleeting second, I consider lying. Just name a god and be done with it. But I can't bring myself to do it.

"None," I finally say. "I hope."

The words feel heavy, final. Just as they always have, even back in Civic Education when the instructors pushed bonding as the ultimate duty.

Bowen's sneer deepens. "Still the same old Jerrick, huh? So, you're still one of *those*, are you?" He spits the word out like a curse. "Must run in the family."

I sigh. This is how it always starts.

"It's not that," I say quietly. "I believe in the cause. It's just that... my parents are getting older. We don't have anyone else to take care of them."

"You don't owe him an explanation," Elena cuts in, her voice firm. She steps closer, standing beside me. "You have your reasons. He has his. Bowen, just leave it alone."

Bowen's jaw tightens, but he doesn't back down. "Leave it alone?" He gestures broadly to the market square. "Look around you! The land is dying. Decaying. The only thing standing between us and death is the Council. I don't understand how someone could be so selfish as to refuse to bond and be part of the solution."

I shake my head. "It's not that I don't want to be part of the solution. But if I bond, who will take care of my parents and the farm? They've sacrificed everything for me. I can't just abandon them."

Bowen shoots a glance at Elena, a cruel smile tugging at the corner of his mouth before turning back to me. His voice lowers, taking on a judgmental tone.

"More than everyone else?" he asks, nodding towards Elena. "That's just selfish, and you know it. What if your bonding would save her?"

The question hits me like a blow.

I glance at Elena. Would I want to see her hurt? No. Would I abandon my parents for her? No. I wouldn't do that for anyone. But I can't bring myself to say it.

Elena saves me from having to answer.

"Don't answer that, Jerrick," she says sharply, her gaze fixed on Bowen. "He's just trying to goad you into an argument. Bowen doesn't care about anyone but himself. He doesn't want to bond to push back the Fog. He wants an excuse to run away from his father."

Bowen's ears turn bright red, and for a moment, I think he'll lash out. But he pulls back, forcing a smile that doesn't reach his eyes.

"Funny," he says, his voice tight. "You completely missed him not answering the question. You know what that means, don't you? It means he doesn't mind seeing you dead, as long as he's safe at home with his parents."

I glance at Elena, and she meets my gaze with a tight-lipped smile. I can feel my face burning with embarrassment.

"Bowen," I finally say, breaking the silence. "You said what you came to say. Can you leave now?"

"Leave?" He laughs, a short, mocking sound. "We're not done talking."

I clench my fists at my sides. "What now?"

"You're adopted, right?"

I blink, caught off guard by the sudden shift. "You know I am."

Bowen takes a step closer, his unnerving smile returning. "Have you ever wondered why your real parents didn't want you?"

His voice is low, dripping with malice. "Do you think maybe they knew you'd be a disappointment?"

"Bowen!" Elena snaps, her voice sharp with anger.

I groan, the sound escaping my lips before I can hold it back.

"Can you just leave?" I plead, my voice strained.

Bowen's smile widens. "Ahhhhh..." He draws the sound out, savoring the moment. "So, it *must* be true, then. What everyone's been saying."

My chest tightens. "What's true?"

Bowen gestures toward the market crowd, his grin smug. "About your real father."

The air feels colder.

I shake my head. "My father?"

Bowen leans in, his eyes gleaming with cruel delight. "You don't even know, do you?"

"Know what?"

"Don't play dumb, Jerrick. You know exactly who I'm talking about!" Bowen's shout cuts through the market square, loud and sharp enough to halt conversations and turn heads. The crowd, until now absorbed in their own business, begins to gather. Bowen knows what he's doing. "Theron the Butcher!"

The name lands like a punch to the gut. The murmurs die. The crowd stills. Everyone knows that name.

Once, Theron was the Council's head enforcer—a warrior whose name commanded both respect and fear. But he turned on them. Led a rebellion that failed spectacularly. Now, he's a ghost, a cautionary tale whispered to frighten children into behaving. No one knows if he's dead or in hiding. And Bowen just said his name in connection with me.

"What?" I stammer, my voice breaking. "No. Why would you even say that?"

Bowen's smile twists into something cruel. "You don't even know who your real parents are. So, it *could* be true."

"It's not," I say defensively, but the words come out too fast, too desperate.

Bowen steps closer, his voice rising again. "That little uprising of his killed both of my uncles. What do you have to say about that?"

"I'm sorry about your uncles, but that has nothing to do with me."

It's the right answer. The logical answer. But doubt claws at me. The whispers, the stares—they've been following me all morning. What if they're right?

The thought sends a shiver down my spine. Am I connected to Theron? Am I destined to follow in his footsteps?

"It has *everything* to do with you," Bowen snaps, jabbing a finger into my chest. "We all want you to leave."

I step back, heart pounding. "Please, just—leave me alone. I don't want any trouble."

"Too late."

Bowen shoves me.

There's a gasp from the crowd, sharp and collective.

I'm not that skinny kid anymore—his shove barely moves me— but it's not about the force. It's about the message. He shoves me again, harder this time, and I'm forced to take a step back to keep from falling.

"Bowen, he asked you politely to leave." Elena's voice is steady, but I can hear the anger beneath it. She steps between us, her fists clenched at her sides.

Bowen sneers. "Oh, so he needs his *girlfriend* to protect him now? Jerrick has always been a coward." He glances back at the crowd, looking for validation. There are a few awkward chuckles, but mostly, people stay silent, watching.

"And who do you—"

"This is between you and me, Bowen." I cut him off, my voice low and firm.

Bowen's smile falters, just for a moment. Then he yells, "I agree!" and shoves me again.

In a twisted way, I'm glad he does. It means his focus is still on me. Not Elena. I should fight back. I know I should. But I can't. Confrontation unnerves me. It always has.

"Look," I say, my voice quiet. Almost pleading. "I'll just pack up and leave."

"You don't get it." Bowen steps closer, lowering his voice so only I can hear. "We want you gone from Four Rivers. For good."

I swallow hard.

"Wherever his son is," Bowen continues, "Theron will show up eventually. We don't want him here. And we don't want you here."

The crowd presses in, growing thicker. Faces blur together—some curious, others wary.

I scan the crowd, searching for help. For someone—*anyone*—who might stand up for me.

But I see only weary faces, worn down by years of hardship. People who won't risk their own safety for someone like me.

Bowen turns to the crowd, raising his arms in a theatrical gesture. His voice booms over the silence.

"Isn't that right? We all know what happened the last time Theron set foot in this city."

A nervous murmur ripples through the crowd.

"And with *junior* here"—Bowen waves toward me with a flourish—"who's to say he won't come back?"

The murmurs grow louder.

Then, from the back of the crowd, a desperate voice rings out.

"He killed my son! Maybe we should kill his!"

The words hang in the air like a thunderclap. The crowd freezes, stunned. Including me.

I can't move. It feels like my feet are rooted to the ground, as if the weight of those words has turned them to stone.

I know these people. Maybe not personally, but they've bought apples from me. They've seen me grow up. They know I'm no trouble.

But now, they look at me with suspicion. With fear. Like I'm the enemy.

The crowd shifts forward, an unconscious movement. A surge. My chest tightens. *Why isn't anyone standing up for me?*

"Stop!" Elena's voice cuts through the rising tension. "We can't condemn someone based on a rumor." She steps in front of me, her back straight, her shoulders squared. "Even if the rumor was true, we can't condemn a man for something another one did!"

The crowd wavers, their agitation softening. Faces that were twisted with anger and fear begin to shift—some embarrassed, others thoughtful.

I watch Elena in awe. There's a strength in her I've never fully seen before.

She stands between me and the crowd, as if she could take them all on by herself. As if she'd fight the entire world to protect me.

No longer rooted in place, I take a step forward.

"We should go," I whisper to her, my voice low.

I turn toward the display table, my hands trembling as I reach for the apples. I just want to pack up and leave.

That's when Bowen shoves me from behind.

The force sends me stumbling forward. My boots catch on a loose stone, and I fall hard onto my hands and knees. The rough cobblestones scrape my palms, but I barely feel it through the rush of anger surging in my chest.

"Jerrick!" Elena bends down to help me, but Bowen grabs her arm, yanking her back before she can reach me.

"He's a big boy." Bowen sneers, his grip tightening. "He can take care of himself."

"Let go of me," Elena hisses, her voice sharp and unyielding. She pulls against his grip, but Bowen holds firm, his knuckles whitening. "You have no right to put your hands on me!"

Bowen just smirks. And that's when something inside me snaps.

Maybe it's the rumors. Maybe it's the weather, pressing down like a suffocating weight. Or maybe it's this—Bowen putting his hands on Elena. Yeah. Definitely that.

The anger that's always simmered beneath my surface starts to boil. Normally, I'd shove it down. I'd retreat into silence, let the moment pass. Not this time. This time, I lean into it. I push myself to my feet, slow and deliberate, until I stand at my full height. No more slouching. No more hiding. Bowen's smirk falters as he looks up at me.

"Oh, there he is," he laughs nervously. "Are you finally ready to be a man?"

I don't answer. I just stare down at him, towering over him by nearly a foot. Not only am I taller, but I outweigh him by at least a hundred pounds.

My voice drops, low and cold. "I'm only going to say this once."

The malice in my tone makes Bowen flinch.

"Let her go. Now."

For a long, tense moment, Bowen holds his ground. His fingers twitch on Elena's arm, but then—despite himself—he lets her go.

Elena takes a step back, rubbing her wrist, her eyes darting between us.

Bowen glances over his shoulder, reminding himself of the crowd watching. When he turns back, his eyes are hard, his expression twisted with anger.

"And what if I don't, *junior*?"

He spits the word at me like a weapon, aiming for a wound he can't see.

The anger I've been holding back surges again, hot and blinding. My fists clench at my sides, shaking with the effort to keep from swinging.

I take a step forward. "Then who my father is," I spit, "will be the least of your concerns."

Bowen took a step back, his bluster faltering. His eyes darted to the crowd, seeking support. But they weren't laughing with him anymore.

For the first time, I saw it—the fear lurking beneath his sneer. The realization that he wasn't in control. Not anymore.

But Elena's hand finds my arm.

"Jerrick," she says softly, her voice steady but pleading. "This isn't you. Let's just go."

Her words cut through the red haze in my mind. I blink, taking a deep breath as the anger ebbs.

"You're right," I murmur, my voice steadier.

I unclench my fists and reach for her hand without thinking. "Let's go."

We turn to leave, but Bowen isn't done. I barely register the movement before his fist crashes into my cheek. The impact snaps my head to the side.

For a moment, everything goes quiet. The crowd, the market, even the wind—all of it fades into silence.

My cheek buzzes from the punch, but it doesn't hurt. Not really.

Instinctively, I raise a hand to my face, touching the spot where his fist landed. Bowen stands there, grinning like he's won something.

I glance at Elena. Her eyes are wide, pleading with me. *Let it go.*

So, I do.

I lower my hand and walk away. Behind me, Bowen's voice rings out, loud and taunting.

"Must not be true, anyway. You're way too much of a coward to be Theron's son!"

I pause. The words cut deeper than the punch, but I keep moving. I won't give him the satisfaction.

But Elena doesn't.

She pulls her hand free from mine and whirls around.

"Just leave him alone, Bowen!" she snaps, her voice ringing across the market square. "Not everyone is a bastard like you!"

Laughter ripples through the crowd, awkward and stifled.

Bowen's face turns red. His eyes narrow, locking onto Elena with a dangerous glint.

"Me?" His voice is sharp, trembling with barely contained rage. "*I'm* the bastard?"

He takes a step toward her, each word dripping with venom. "Do you even know who your father is?"

The crowd falls silent again. He continues, "didn't your mother sleep with half the married men in this town?"

The words hang in the air, heavy with cruelty.

Elena's face pales. Her fists clench at her sides, but she doesn't move.

The crowd murmurs, whispers spreading like wildfire. And I stand there, frozen. Elena stares at Bowen in stunned silence, her mouth slightly open. The shock in her eyes twists into something deeper—pain.

Her mother died years ago. Everyone in Four Rivers knew how close they were. Elena rarely talks about her, but I know the ache of that loss still lingers, a wound that time hasn't healed.

Bowen's words hit that wound directly. I see it in the way her gaze drops to the ground, her shoulders curling inward. Shame floods her expression, though she has nothing to be ashamed of.

And that look—*that look*—shatters something inside me.

My anger flares again, no longer a simmer. It's white-hot, burning through every restraint I've built over the years.

I don't hold it back. I don't *want* to hold it back. Without thinking, I clench my fist and swing—

The punch lands squarely on the side of Bowen's head. There's a sickening crack as my knuckles connect with his skull.

He crumples to the ground, out cold before he even hits the cobblestones.

"I told you to walk away!" I shout, my voice raw, spittle flying from my lips. "I warned you!"

But it's not enough.

The anger has nowhere to go, no outlet. It roars inside me, demanding release. I turn on the crowd, my chest heaving, my voice echoing across the square.

"I'm right here! Who else wants to make me leave?"

The crowd recoils as my words echo off the stone walls, louder than I'd intended. As soon as they left my mouth, I knew I'd gone too far. This wasn't me. This wasn't who I was supposed to be.

But a part of me—deep down, buried beneath years of restraint—felt something else. Satisfaction. Power.

And that scared me more than the crowd's reaction.

Then, Elena gasps. The sound cuts through the haze of my anger, piercing straight to my core. I instantly regret the words. This isn't me. I let my anger take over, let it consume me.

I glance down at Bowen's crumpled form. He's not moving. Guilt coils in my stomach, tight and nauseating. But another voice rises in my mind—*Why should I feel bad?*

I told him to walk away. I even tried to walk away myself. But the guilt remains, gnawing at me.

I turn toward Elena, intending to apologize, but before I can speak, I feel two pairs of hands grab my arms from behind.

Without thinking, I shove them off—hard. There's a dull thud as both guards hit the ground. Branik and William. They scramble back to their feet, more surprised than hurt.

William's face twists with anger. His hand flies to his sword, yanking it from its sheath with a metallic hiss.

"Put that back," Branik says sharply, stepping between us. "It's not needed."

William hesitates, his knuckles whitening around the hilt.

"I'm sorry," I say quickly, raising my hands. "I didn't realize who—"

"It wasn't his fault," Elena interrupts, her voice clear and steady. "Bowen—"

She falters, glancing at Bowen's unconscious form.

But William isn't listening. He steps toward me, his sword raised in a striking stance, his expression dark with fury.

Before I can react, Elena moves in front of me, arms outstretched.

"Please," she says, her voice trembling but resolute. "This isn't his fault. Bowen attacked him."

William's gaze hardens. "And he attacked *me*. Now move!"

Elena doesn't budge.

She stands her ground, defiant, her shoulders squared.

I barely register what's happening.

It's as if I've stepped outside myself, watching the scene unfold like a distant observer. The world feels distant, muted. My limbs are heavy, my mind sluggish.

Then, Branik steps forward. He places a firm hand on my arm, squeezing gently.

"Put it away, William," he says calmly. "He'll come quietly."

There's a finality to his tone that leaves no room for argument.

William hesitates for a long moment before lowering his sword with a frustrated sigh.

Branik leans in, his grip on my arm steady. His voice drops to a whisper, meant only for me. "About time."

I glance at him, confusion flickering through the fog in my mind.

But Branik says nothing more. He just gives my arm a reassuring squeeze, then turns to address the crowd, his voice ringing with authority.

"Show's over. Go about your business."

The crowd disperses, the tension slowly bleeding from the square. But I can still feel their eyes on me. Their judgment. Their fear.

And in the pit of my stomach, the guilt twists tighter.

#

The cell is colder than I expected; the chill seeping into my bones through the thin blanket draped across my shoulders. The walls, made of rough stone blocks, glisten with dampness, casting strange shadows beneath the flickering Essence Lamps mounted high above. The lamps sputter like dying embers, their glow muted and uneven, creating a dance of light and shadow that makes the small room feel even smaller.

The smell is the worst part. A stench of unwashed bodies, mildew, and something sharp—urine, maybe—clings to the air, refusing to dissipate. I breathe through my mouth, but it barely helps.

I sit on a raised slab of stone that serves as a bed, my back pressed against the wall, knees drawn to my chest. The blanket is scratchy, offering little comfort. The pillow is thin, barely more than a scrap of cloth. Everything here feels designed to make you feel small. Insignificant.

The door across from me is solid wood, banded with iron, a tiny window near the top letting in a sliver of light from the hall. There's a narrow slot midway down for food—though no one's used it yet. The silence in this place is oppressive, pressing in from all sides.

By my best guess, I've been here for six hours. Maybe longer. Time has no meaning in a cell like this.

Six hours. Six hours with nothing but my thoughts. Six hours to relive every moment of the day. Six hours to wonder why I'm here when I wasn't the one who started the fight.

My mind churns through the same questions over and over. Bowen's words. The crowd's whispers. The way they all looked at me like I was something monstrous.

I glance at the Essence Lamps again, their glow casting faint halos against the walls. Wasteful. Every bit of Essence is precious these days, with the land decaying and supplies running thin. Yet here it is, burning away to light a cell no one should linger in. A pointless indulgence. It feels like an insult—like a statement of my worth.

You're not worth conserving the light.

I close my eyes and exhale slowly, trying to push the thought away. But another creeps in to replace it. *What if it's true?* The rumor. The whispers. The name.

Theron.

I shake my head. No. It's nonsense. A desperate crowd looking for someone to blame. A lie spun by Bowen to hurt me. Still, the doubt lingers, coiling around my thoughts like smoke.

Footsteps echo down the hall, slow and deliberate, each step tightening the knot of anxiety in my chest. The clinking of keys is louder than it should be, the metallic jingle grating against my nerves. The lock clicks, loud as a judge's gavel, and the door groans open.

Branik steps inside, his familiar lopsided smile in place, though there's a heaviness in his eyes. "You know, we gotta stop meeting like this," he says lightly, trying to break the tension.

I force a laugh. "Yeah. No kidding."

The sound is hollow. Forced. There's no humor in it.

Branik glances around the cell, his nose wrinkling slightly. "This place just keeps getting worse."

"For what it's worth," he continues, his voice softer, "he deserved it."

"Yeah, he did." I hesitate. "Is he okay?"

Branik's smile shifts into something sharper. "Physically? Sure. His ego? I'm not sure that'll ever recover."

I let out a breath. "Good." Branik tilts his head, studying me for a moment. "So... how long am I here for?"

"That's actually why I'm here." He holds up a set of chains, the metal glinting in the dim light. "I'm supposed to take you to the magistrate for questioning."

My stomach tightens at the thought. "Questioning?"

"Don't worry," Branik says quickly. "There were plenty of witnesses who saw Bowen start it. You've got that going for you." He pauses, shifting the chains in his hands. "But... he *is* the mayor's kid."

The weight of that statement hangs between us.

Branik sighs and shakes his head. "We won't need these." He gestures to the chains before setting them aside. "Just follow me."

I stand slowly, the blanket slipping from my shoulders. My muscles are stiff, my movements awkward. But I'm grateful for the gesture—grateful that he trusts me enough to leave the chains behind.

As we step into the hall, I glance at him. "Branik... thanks."

He stops mid-step, turning to face me. "For what?"

"For today. You've had my back... more times than I can count."

His expression softens, and for a moment, he looks almost uncomfortable. "You're one of the good ones, Jerrick. You've always been one of the good ones."

I blink, taken aback by the unexpected sincerity in his voice.

"All those times I saw Bowen give you a hard time..." He trails off, shaking his head. "I should've said something. I should've stepped in. Today, that would've been different."

"We were kids," I say quietly. "You don't owe me anything."

"Maybe. But I wish I had."

We start walking again, the sound of our footsteps echoing off the stone walls.

"And this Theron thing?" Branik continues after a moment. "It really shouldn't matter. Even if it's true, it doesn't define who you are. People are scared. They're on edge. That's all it is."

"Maybe." I try to sound convinced, but the doubt gnaws at me. I can't shake the image of the crowd turning on me. The way they looked at me—not as a neighbor or a friend, but as a threat.

We climb two flights of stairs, each step bringing us closer to the surface, to the magistrate's hall. My legs ache, but I push through it, focusing on the steady rhythm of our ascent.

When we reach the top, the hall opens up before us—a cavernous space lined with doors and receptionist desks. Massive paintings of long-dead officials hang between each door, their eyes following us with quiet judgment. The ceiling stretches high above, adorned with light banks of Essence bulbs that bathe the room in harsh, blinding white light.

The brightness stings my eyes, making me squint.

Branik glances at me, a knowing smile playing at the corners of his mouth. "Don't let them get to you."

"Who?" I ask, my voice quiet.

He gestures toward the paintings. "Them. The ones who came before. The ones who think they know your story before you've even had a chance to tell it."

I nod, the weight of his words settling over me.

I don't know what the magistrate will ask. I don't know what the crowd will think.

But I do know one thing. This isn't over.

We stop before a door with the name *Cassian Valtor, Magistrate* etched into a polished brass plate. The letters gleam under the harsh white light of the Essence Lamps overhead.

Beside the door sits a receptionist's desk, and behind it slouches a portly man with a sour expression. His vest strains against his round middle, the buttons threatening rebellion, and his thinning hair is plastered to his scalp in a futile attempt to mask his baldness. He glances up, eyes narrowing as he takes in the sight of me.

"Jerrick Thompson to see Magistrate Valtor," Branik announces, his voice steady, almost bored, as if this is just another routine task.

The receptionist sniffs, his lips pursed like he's bitten into something sour. "Why isn't he chained?" His voice is nasally, each word drawn out like it's an effort to speak.

"I was told he wasn't a prisoner." Branik's tone remains calm, but there's a steely edge beneath it. "I didn't feel the chains were justified."

The receptionist's gaze sharpens. "The Magistrate may think differently." He heaves himself out of his chair with a grunt, the desk creaking in relief. Shuffling to the door, he raps once before slipping inside, shutting it firmly behind him.

I shift my weight from one foot to the other, the cold from the stone floor seeping into my boots. My palms are damp, but I resist the urge to wipe them on my pants. I don't know what to expect. I've never been in trouble before. I shouldn't be in trouble now. It wasn't me who started the fight.

The door opens, and Bowen steps out.

I freeze.

His face is a mess. His left eye is swollen shut, a deep purple bruise spreading across his cheek. A fresh bandage runs from his temple to his jawline. He doesn't look up right away, his gaze fixed on the floor, but when he does, our eyes lock.

For a moment, neither of us speaks.

My heart twists in my chest, not with guilt, but with something close to regret. I don't feel bad for hitting him—he deserved it—but I shouldn't have hit him that hard. My mother warned me when I was young that, because of my size, I had to be careful. I forgot that lesson today.

"Bowen," I start, but the word feels clumsy in my mouth. He flinches slightly, his good eye narrowing as he takes in my face. There's defiance there, but beneath it, something more vulnerable. Pride, wounded and bleeding.

I take a deep breath and try again. "Look, I'm sorry for how things turned out earlier. I never wanted it to go that far."

He doesn't respond, but he doesn't look away either.

"For what it's worth," I continue, forcing myself to meet his gaze steadily, "I genuinely hope you find what you're looking for. That you bond, if that's what you truly want. I know it means a lot to you."

His expression flickers—surprise, confusion, something softer—but it's gone in an instant, replaced by the familiar mask of arrogance. He opens his mouth as if to speak but closes it again, his jaw tightening. The silence stretches between us, heavy with things unsaid.

Then, he nods.

It's slight. Barely a movement at all. But it's enough.

"The Magistrate will see you now," the receptionist says, his voice cutting through the moment like a knife.

I give Bowen one last look, but he's already turning away, his shoulders hunched. Whatever war he's fighting within himself, it isn't over.

#

The office is spacious, lined with bookshelves that stretch from floor to ceiling, each shelf crammed with neatly arranged tomes. The scent of leather and parchment hangs in the air, mingling with the faint tang of Essence. Paintings of long-dead officials gaze down from the walls, their faces stern, disapproving. Everything here feels meticulously curated, from the polished desk to the perfectly aligned chairs. It's too clean. Too orderly. It feels more like a stage set than a place of work.

Magistrate Valtor stands by the window, hands clasped behind his back. He's a small man, his jacket a pale green that matches his shirt and trousers perfectly. His shoes gleam in the lamplight, polished to a mirror shine. His mustache is long and thin, meticulously groomed, and his black hair shows no sign of gray.

When he turns, his smile is quick and sharp, revealing teeth that are too perfect to be real.

"Jerrick," he says, his voice warm and practiced, like a merchant welcoming a favored customer. "It's good to meet you at last."

He crosses the room in a few quick steps, extending a hand. I shake it, his grip surprisingly firm for someone so slight.

"I knew your father growing up," he continues, his eyes gleaming with something I can't quite place. "Not Theron—the other one."

The words hit like a punch, though he says them casually, like a comment on the weather. He's watching me closely, waiting for a reaction.

I keep my face neutral. "Thom is my father," I say evenly. "He's mentioned that you were friends."

Valtor's smile widens. "Good. Very good."

He steps back, gesturing to a couch in front of his desk. "Please, Jerrick, take a seat."

I sit, the couch surprisingly soft. Valtor lowers himself into a chair opposite me, crossing one leg over the other.

"There is a resemblance," he says, studying me with a calculating gaze. "How tall are you these days?"

"Six feet ten inches."

His laugh is quick, a burst of sound that feels rehearsed. "You have almost two feet on me. Quite the presence."

I don't respond. His charm feels like a mask, and I'm not in the mood for pleasantries.

Valtor leans back, tapping his fingers against the arm of his chair. "I'm sorry to keep you waiting so long. You've had quite a day."

I nod slowly. "I have."

His expression shifts, his eyes narrowing slightly. "You made quite a mess of things."

The words land like a slap. I sit up straighter, my jaw clenching. "But I didn't—"

He raises a hand, cutting me off. "I know, Jerrick. People saw Bowen start the fight. But fear blinds them to reason."

His tone sharpens, the warmth in his voice cooling. "The land is in turmoil. The Fog is constricting, cutting us off more each day. People are desperate. And desperate people need someone to blame."

He leans forward, his gaze locking onto mine. "Your connection to Theron—whether it's real or not—makes you a convenient target."

The room feels colder, the weight of his words settling over me like a shroud.

"Fear makes people irrational," Valtor says softly. "And right now, everyone is afraid."

I open my mouth to speak, to defend myself, but Magistrate Valtor raises a hand, cutting me off mid-thought.

"Honestly, Jerrick," he says, his tone sharp and exasperated. "I could not care less if Theron is or isn't your birth father. If he is—so what? It was just something for people to gossip about. It would've blown over by morning." He pauses, his gaze pinning me in place. "But then that idiot son of the mayor picks a fight with you—and you oblige him."

"I tried to walk away. I—"

"Jerrick." His voice cracks like a whip. "Don't interrupt me again."

The warmth he carried earlier is gone, replaced by something colder, harder. I stiffen, swallowing the rest of my words. I'm not used to being spoken to like that, but I know better than to push back. Not now.

"I already told you," he continues, his tone measured but tense, "plenty of people said you didn't start it. That doesn't matter anymore."

He stops, eyes narrowing as if daring me to argue. I don't. The silence stretches, oppressive. I feel like I'm on trial, waiting for a verdict I can't predict.

Then, he sighs heavily, pressing his fingers to the bridge of his nose. When he speaks again, his tone softens.

"I'm sorry, Jerrick. That was uncalled for." He lowers his hand, meeting my gaze directly. "Look, can I level with you?"

I nod, wary but curious.

"The mayor thinks I should leave you in that cell for a few days. Let you stew. I disagree." He steps around his desk, leaning against the edge. "This is my call, not his. And I've made my decision."

Relief washes over me, but it's short-lived.

"Just go home," he says quietly. "The Naming is a little over a month away. Stay away from the city until then."

"I can do that," I say quickly, though my thoughts churn with worries about the farm, the market, and the supplies I still need to get for the winter. But I don't voice any of that. Instead, I ask, "Do you know where my cart and horse are?"

"Oh, yes." His expression softens. "Your lady friend took care of everything. Packed up your stall and took the horse to the stables."

Elena. Of course she did.

"It's getting late," Valtor adds, glancing at the Essence Lamps outside his window. "I assume you'll be staying in the city tonight?"

I nod.

"That's fine." He straightens, brushing a hand down his immaculate jacket. "But remember what I said. Stay away for a while. Normally, I'd do as the mayor asks, but since I know your father—your real father—I'm going against my better judgment."

The emphasis on *real father* makes my chest tighten, but I say nothing.

"I don't know why the mayor is suddenly so interested in you," Valtor continues, his voice dropping to a near whisper. "But he is. It's best to give it some time. Let things cool down."

His words linger as I walk out of his office, through the stark, echoing hall of the City Offices. The white light from the Essence Lamps feels harsh now, casting sharp shadows on the polished floor. My mind churns with questions I don't have answers to.

I push through the heavy front doors and step into the cool evening air. The chill is a sharp contrast to the stifling tension inside.

Then, I see him.

Bowen stands by the steps, waiting. His swollen face is half-hidden in the shadows, but there's no mistaking him. The bandage on his cheek catches the fading light, stark against the bruised skin around his eye.

I stop at the top of the steps, my heart pounding.

"I don't want any trouble," I say, my voice steady but guarded.

Bowen looks up slowly, meeting my gaze with something I don't expect—weariness. His usual smugness is gone, replaced by a hollow sort of exhaustion.

"You won't get any from me," he says quietly.

I frown, confused by his change in demeanor.

"Look," Bowen continues, glancing around to make sure no one is within earshot. "I think you should know something."

My pulse quickens.

"Today wasn't by accident." His voice is low, tense. "Something is happening. I'm not sure what, but I overheard my father talking with Rorick two nights ago. Your name came up."

I stare at him, the words hitting me like a cold wind.

"Me?" I ask, my voice barely more than a whisper. "Why would they be talking about me?"

Bowen shakes his head. "That's all I know."

He turns to leave but hesitates, looking back over his shoulder.

"Actually, one more thing."

I wait, holding my breath.

"I'm sorry."

The words hang in the air between us, unexpected and uncharacteristic. Before I can even process them, Bowen turns and walks away, disappearing into the gathering dusk.

I stand there, stunned.

His apology echoes in my mind, but it's his other words that send a shiver down my spine.

Something is happening.

The air feels heavier now, as if the shadows themselves are watching me. I wrap my arms around myself, more to ward off the growing unease than the cold.

Why would my name come up in a conversation between the mayor and Rorick? Why would the head of the SoulCasters even know who I am?

The questions swirl in my mind, each one darker than the last. And with each unanswered question, the chill in the air deepens, wrapping around me like a cloak of uncertainty.

I glance back at the City Offices, their towering walls stark against the pale sky. The Essence Lamps flicker, casting ghostly light on the cobblestones.

Something is happening. And whether or not I'm ready, I'm part of it.

Walking back through the quiet streets of Four Rivers, my thoughts spiral, replaying the day's events over and over. The confrontation at the market, my outburst of anger, the whispers about Theron, and Bowen's cryptic warning—they all feel like pieces of a puzzle I don't yet understand. There's a weight to it all, a sense that this is only the beginning of something much larger. Something that will change everything.

A shiver runs down my spine. The air is colder now, biting through my clothes as day turns into night. The magistrate's words echo in my mind—*Stay away from the city until the Naming.* It feels less like a suggestion and more like a sentence.

I think about my parents and the farm. The simplicity of that life feels distant now, like something I've already lost. And then there's Elena. Her presence has always been a comfort, but after today, I wonder if she sees me differently. She saw a side of me I've spent my whole life trying to control, trying to bury.

The road curves, and as I crest a small hill, the familiar silhouette of Daisy comes into view. She stands patiently outside the stables, her coat catching the last light of the day. But it's not just Daisy waiting for me.

Elena is there, too.

She stands with her arms crossed, a playful smirk tugging at the corners of her mouth. The sight of her eases some of the tension coiled in my chest.

"Well, well," she says as I approach. "How has your day been?"

I laugh, the sound escaping before I can stop it. "I've had better."

She giggles, a sound that feels daylight breaking through the darkness. "I figured you'd show up, eventually."

I rub the back of my neck, sheepish. "Were you waiting long?"

"No, I only just got here." She pats Daisy's side affectionately. "I thought you might be worried about her, so I took her to the stables. She's a stubborn one."

"You have no idea," I chuckle. "Thank you for taking care of her. It means a lot."

"You're welcome." Her smile softens, and she steps closer, her gaze searching mine. "About earlier…"

"I'm sorry," I cut her off, the words rushing out. "I'm sorry you had to see that. I shouldn't have lost my temper."

Elena tilts her head, her expression thoughtful. "I wanted to say thank you."

I blink, confused. "Thank you?"

"You were going to walk away. Even after he hit you, you were going to walk away." She takes another step closer, her voice quieter now. "But you stood up for me."

"You did the same for me," I remind her, my voice equally soft. "You always do. Even when no one else will."

Her lips twitch into a grin. "I thought I was going to hit him."

I laugh, the tension easing from my shoulders. "I thought you were, too."

"It would've been worse if I had," she says, her eyes twinkling with mischief. "They say he got back up after you hit him. I doubt he would've if it had been me."

We both laugh, the sound light and easy. After everything that's happened, it feels good to laugh.

Elena rises onto her toes, her braid falling over her shoulder as she tilts her head. "Can you bend down for a second?"

My heart stumbles in my chest, thudding in my ears. For a moment, I freeze, unsure what to do.

"Please?" she asks, her voice gentle. "I can't reach."

I finally get my feet to move. I lean down, bending at the waist, and as I do, Elena presses a kiss to my cheek. Her lips are soft, warm against my cold skin. She smells faintly of flowers, and the scent lingers as she pulls back.

"Thank you, Jerrick," she whispers.

My face flushes, heat creeping up my neck. I know I should say something—anything—but I can't seem to form words. Instead, I stay bent over, frozen in place like a fool.

Elena giggles, the sound light and sweet. "You can stand up now."

I straighten quickly, rubbing the back of my neck again. "Right. Sorry."

Her smile never wavers, but there's a softness to it now, a quiet understanding.

"It's getting late," she says after a moment. "I got us a couple of rooms at the Stag's Head Inn. It's too dangerous to travel at night."

Her words carry a weight that wasn't there before. It wasn't always like this. I remember camping outside the city with my parents after market days, sitting around a fire under the endless gray sky. Those were some of my fondest memories—nights filled with stories and laughter. But things have changed. Now, the stories are darker. Tales of creatures lurking in the shadows, of travelers who never make it home. The Council has all but forbidden travel after dusk.

"That makes sense," I say quietly. "I usually stay in the city on market nights, anyway. My parents won't think anything of it."

We fall into step together, walking through the winding streets toward the inn. The cobblestones are slick with moisture, glistening in the pale light of the Essence Lamps.

As we walk, I tell her everything.

I tell her about the cell, about the magistrate and his warnings. I tell her about Bowen's unexpected apology and the cryptic message he left me with.

She listens without interrupting, her expression thoughtful.

When I finish, we've reached the inn. The warm glow from inside spills out onto the street, casting long shadows.

"Something's happening," I say, my voice barely above a whisper. "Something bigger than we realize."

Elena nods, her gaze steady. "We'll figure it out. Together."

Her words settle something inside me. For the first time all day, I feel a flicker of hope.

And as we step into the warmth of the inn, leaving the cold night behind, I realize I'm not as alone as I thought.

Chapter 4

Jerrick

We leave the city just after daybreak, slipping quietly into the pale light of morning. The air is sharp, biting at my skin, though I barely notice. Overhead, the sky hangs low and gray, stretching endlessly in every direction. There's no break in the monotony—just a dull, featureless expanse that makes it hard to tell where the sky ends and the land begins.

Essence hums faintly in the distance, its invisible threads weaving through the air to push back the night. The light it brings is thin and cold, more functional than comforting. It washes over the landscape in muted tones, casting everything in shades of gray. There's no warmth in it. No life. Only a mechanical inevitability, as if the land itself is tired of living.

Mist clings to the road, curling around our feet as we walk. It moves in strange ways, almost alive, swirling into shapes that vanish before I can make sense of them. The stillness around us feels unnatural, like the land is holding its breath, waiting for something to happen.

We don't speak at first. Elena walks beside me, her presence a steadying force, but my mind is elsewhere. I replay the events of yesterday over and over—the fight, the accusations, Bowen's cryptic warning. It feels like a story I'm being dragged into, one I never agreed to be part of. A story that's bigger than me, bigger than any of us.

Elena tries to make conversation, her voice light and teasing at first. But I'm too distracted to give her more than a few distracted nods and half-hearted answers. Eventually, she falls silent.

The quiet stretches between us, and I sink deeper into my thoughts.

The mind is a strange thing. It twists and reshapes memories to fit a narrative we can live with. It's how we make sense of chaos—by forcing it into something we can control. I keep telling myself that yesterday was just an anomaly. The rumors about Theron are nothing more than wild speculation. The fight with Bowen had been brewing for years. It all makes sense, if I look at it that way.

But Bowen's parting words cling to me like a burr, sharp and unshakable.

Something is happening.

"Are you okay?" Elena's voice cuts through my thoughts, soft but insistent. There's concern in her tone—a kindness that makes me ache.

"Yes," I answer automatically. But the lie tastes bitter, and before I can stop myself, I add, "No… actually, I'm not."

She stops walking and turns to face me, her gaze steady and patient. "Go on."

I take a deep breath, the cold air burning my lungs. "It's just… everything feels like it's shifting. And I've always been more comfortable when I know where I'm going. Yesterday felt like a turning point, but I don't know what's coming next."

Elena studies me, her expression thoughtful. "Is that why you don't want to bond?"

"Partly." I sigh, the weight of my thoughts pressing down harder. "The Naming could take me far from here, into a life I don't choose. My parents are getting older. They've given everything to raise me, and they have no one else. If I leave…"

I trail off, unsure how to put it into words.

Elena's gaze softens. "You have a big heart, Jerrick. It's one of the things I've always liked about you." Her voice is gentle, but there's something unyielding beneath it—a quiet strength. "But you can't ignore what's happening to the land. Reclaiming it from the Fog will take sacrifice."

Her words linger in the air, heavy with truth.

Sacrifice. It's what everyone talks about—what they expect. But what if it's not enough? What if all the sacrifice in the world won't change anything?

"You don't think it's worth it?" Elena asks quietly, tilting her head slightly, more curious than accusing.

I hesitate. "I think the people who make that sacrifice are brave. I do. But… it's not for me." I glance away, shame prickling at the back of my neck. "I think I can do more good here, with my parents."

Elena doesn't argue. She just watches me, her gaze thoughtful.

After a long pause, she asks, "What if you had the power to do more? To push back the Fog for good? Would you?"

The question hangs between us, heavy with implication.

I scratch my head, avoiding her gaze. "I don't want to be forced into making that decision."

Elena doesn't let me off the hook. "Pretend someone forces you."

Her persistence stings, but I know she means well. "Look, Elena…" I stop walking, staring down the road. The mist winds ahead of us, curling through the trees like an unseen hand. "I'm not convinced it's working. Look at the sky." I gesture upward, where the endless gray stretches unbroken. "The seasons are unraveling. Fall didn't even happen. If the SoulCasters are making sacrifices, why hasn't anything changed?"

Elena says nothing at first. She just watches me, her expression thoughtful.

"That'll get you arrested if anyone hears you saying that," Elena says quietly, her voice laced with caution. There's no shock in her expression, though. No wide eyes or gasps of surprise. Just a calm acceptance that unsettles me more than any outburst could have.

"I know," I reply, glancing at her. She doesn't look away. Does she feel the same way? "Elena… I trust you. So, I'm going to tell you something that could get my family into trouble. But you can't tell anyone. Not a soul."

"You have my word," she says without hesitation.

I hesitate, the weight of my father's secret pressing on my chest. The words feel heavy, dangerous. But I've carried this alone for too long.

"My father has a book," I begin slowly, keeping my voice low. "It's been passed down in our family for five generations. It dates back to before the God Wars."

Elena's brows knit together in confusion, but she listens intently.

"The book talks about a vast land," I continue, my voice gaining strength. "A place where people could travel for weeks across open water and still not reach the other side. But now… it takes only a month to walk from one end of the land to the other."

Her lips part in surprise, but she doesn't speak.

"The Fog isn't retreating," I say firmly. "No matter what the Council claims, it's not slowing down. The book contradicts everything we've been taught. Everything."

She blinks, processing my words. "That's not what we learned in Civic Education."

"No, it's not."

"Are you saying…" Her voice drops to a whisper. "Are you saying we've been lied to?"

"I think we have." The words taste bitter. "Think back. Do you remember how far we were told the Fog has moved in the past two hundred years?"

Elena tilts her head, her gaze distant as she searches her memory. "A couple hundred feet. They said it's barely moved since I was born. Maybe a few inches… until recently."

"Try hundreds of miles," I say, my voice grim.

She stops walking, sucking in a breath and puffing out her cheeks before exhaling sharply. "How is that possible?"

"We're being lied to," I repeat, my tone more resolute now. "But I don't know why."

Elena bites her lip, her brow furrowed in thought. "Maybe… maybe they're trying to keep us from panicking?"

"Maybe." I shrug. "But if that's the case, where are all the SoulCasters going? If they can't push the Fog back, why are they still sending people off to fight it? And why are they telling us they're making progress?"

She doesn't answer right away. Her gaze drifts to the fog-laden horizon, the mist curling around the trees like ghostly fingers.

"Maybe they are making progress?" she suggests quietly. "Maybe that's why it slowed down."

I shake my head. "I don't know. Something doesn't add up."

Elena crosses her arms, hugging herself against the chill. "You're right," she says softly. "In fact, I know you're right."

I blink, surprised by her certainty. "How do you know?"

"It's complicated." She glances at me, wide-eyed, and then looks away quickly. "I don't even know why I said that."

It's clear she's battling something inside herself. She wants to tell me, but something is holding her back. The tension in her posture, the way her fingers twitch against her sleeve—it all screams of someone keeping a secret.

"You can trust me," I say gently, hoping to remind her that I just entrusted her with one of my family's deepest secrets.

She sighs, a sound filled with frustration and regret. "I know. It's not that."

She stops walking, facing me fully. Her gaze locks onto mine, and for a moment, I see something raw in her expression. Fear. Uncertainty. And something else—something fragile and vulnerable.

"Look, Jerrick," she says slowly. "I shouldn't have said that. I trust you. I do. But… I'm just not ready to talk about it."

Disappointment twists in my chest, but I push it down. "I understand," I say, though I'm not sure I do.

"No, you don't." She shakes her head, her voice softening. "But you will. One day. I think."

Her words hang in the air, heavy with unspoken meaning. She reaches out and squeezes my hand—a small, brief gesture that sends my heart pounding.

Her big gray eyes plead with me to let it go, to leave the questions unasked. I want to press her, to demand answers. But I don't. I can't. Not when she's looking at me like that.

My face warms, my cheeks flushing with heat. I push the feeling down, embarrassed by my own reaction. Does she know? Of course, she does. I might stumble over my words around her, but I'm not an idiot. She's not just asking me to trust her—she's trying to manipulate me into dropping the subject.

But I can't blame her for that.

She wants to tell me. I can see it in the way her shoulders tense, in the way her gaze flickers back to mine before darting away. Whatever she's holding back, it's weighing on her.

I let it go. Because that's what friends do.

"Thank you," she says softly, her fingers lingering for a moment before she pulls away.

The day stretches on, unchanged. The light remains dim, casting the landscape in muted shades of gray. The chill in the air clings to everything, settling into my bones. Even as the mist begins to lift, revealing more of the road ahead, the unease doesn't leave me. It lingers—silent, persistent.

Up ahead, a cluster of figures huddles by the roadside, gathered around something on the ground. From this distance, it looks like a small, crumpled shape lying prone in the dirt.

I stop instinctively, fingers tightening around the shaft of my spear. "What do you think's going on?" I ask, my voice low.

Elena squints toward the group. "Not sure. Maybe we should see if they need help."

"There's plenty of them," I say, reluctant. "Looks like they've got it handled."

But Elena doesn't slow. Instead, she quickens her pace, her boots crunching on the gravel road. "Come on."

I sigh and follow, though unease coils tighter in my chest. Daisy snorts in protest as I tug her lead, reluctant to pick up speed after hours of leisurely walking. It takes a few gentle pulls before she relents, but by then, Elena has already reached the group.

She halts abruptly.

Her hand flies to her mouth, her eyes wide with shock. I catch up, my heart pounding.

On the ground lies a creature I've only ever heard of in fearful whispers—a thing from cautionary tales meant to keep children from wandering too far from home.

It's no bigger than a goat, but its twisted form is anything but natural. Long, hooked claws extend from misshapen limbs. Its matted fur looks less like hair and more like a crude patchwork of soil, dead leaves, and brittle bones. Its body is malformed, grotesque, as though it were crudely shaped by hands unfamiliar with life.

The stench hits me—damp earth and rot, like a forest floor left to decay. It clings to the air, making my stomach turn.

One of the men, a wiry figure with tired eyes and a weathered face, speaks without looking up. "We found it lying here. Squirming in the dirt."

"It was whining when we first came up," adds a woman beside him, her voice thin and strained. "Kept trying to get up. Died not long after."

The group stands in a loose circle around the creature, staring down at it in silence. No one moves to touch it. No one dares to.

This isn't the first time something like this has happened. Stories have been spreading for months about strange creatures appearing near villages—beasts twisted by the wild Essence. Most don't survive long. But the ones that do? They attack.

And when they attack, the Council sends an Enforcer to deal with them.

I glance at the creature again. It's smaller than the ones I've heard about from the western settlements, but that doesn't make it any less unsettling. If anything, the way it lies there—so still, so wrong— makes my skin crawl.

The wiry man speaks again. "We passed some travelers on the road yesterday. Said they saw a live one not far from here."

Elena shifts beside me, her expression unreadable. The tension in her shoulders tells me enough—she's as unsettled as I am.

"Elena," I murmur, my voice tight with worry. "We need to go."

She doesn't argue. She knows exactly what I'm thinking.

My father is spry, but he's not young. He's in his late sixties. If one of these things finds its way to the farm… the thought twists in my chest, cold and sharp.

Elena places a hand on my arm, grounding me. Her touch is steady, but there's a flicker of unease in her eyes. "Let's go."

We exchange quick goodbyes with the group. They offer stiff nods, their attention never straying far from the twisted corpse at their feet.

As we walk away, the stench lingers in my nostrils, refusing to be forgotten.

An hour later, we reach Elena's farm. She pauses at the gate, turning to me with a small, tired smile. "Be careful, Jerrick."

"You too."

The words feel hollow, inadequate for the weight of the moment. But she nods and steps through the gate, disappearing toward her family's cottage.

The road home stretches before me, familiar and unchanged. But everything feels different now.

The fight with Bowen. The whispers about Theron. The dead creature by the road.

Things are changing too fast.

By the time I reach the farm, my thoughts are tangled with worry. I stroke Daisy's mane absently, her warm breath clouding in the cool air. The house looms ahead, sturdy and unshaken. But for how much longer?

As I walk toward the door, one thought circles endlessly in my mind.

The land is changing. And I don't know if we can stop it.

\#

The farm unfolds before me like a living memory, the rows of apple trees stretching in orderly lines down the valley. From this ridge, the world feels familiar, steady. The orchards stand in perfect quadrants, a patchwork of resilience in a changing world. Even with this year's yield reduced to half, the trees hold their quiet dignity. Their gnarled branches, stripped bare of fruit, remind me that life endures, even in scarcity.

At the center of it all sits our home. It's more than a house—it's the heart of the farm, a legacy built with care and conviction. Seven years ago, my father and I raised those walls together, every beam and nail a testament to the future we envisioned. Behind it stands the old house, now a storage shed. We'd debated tearing it down more than once, but my parents refused. *It's history,* they'd said. *A story for future generations to decide.*

As I start down the hill, leading Daisy by her worn leather halter, my father's words echo in my mind, spoken on the day we laid the first foundation stone.

Remember, son, this isn't just our home. It will be the home of the generations that come after us. It will belong to you one day, and then to your children and grandchildren. With every nail you drive and every board you place, remember the legacy you want to leave.

I've never forgotten those words. They guide me, a constant reminder of why I've chosen this life. The farm is more than land or trees. It's purpose. It's roots. It's why I've resisted the call to bond. My legacy is here. My future, my responsibility, is here.

At the bottom of the hill, my mother steps onto the porch, waving with a hand that hovers too long in the air. Her posture is tense, her smile thin. Her gaze drifts to the cart behind me, its weight giving away the truth. She knows I didn't sell a single apple. She knows something happened.

Did someone stop by the farm and tell them about yesterday? Word spreads fast in Four Rivers. I wanted to be the one to tell them— to shape the story, to soften the edges. It's not that I want to lie. I just want to be the one in control of my own narrative.

I lead Daisy to the stable, taking my time as I unhook the cart and brush her down. Her coat is rough beneath my hands, her steady breathing a balm to my restless thoughts. I make sure her water trough is full, check the hay, anything to delay the inevitable.

But there's only so long I can linger.

When I step onto the porch, both of my parents are waiting for me. They stand side by side, as they always have, a united front. Yet neither of them meets my eyes.

The knot in my chest tightens.

"You know?" I ask, my voice low, trembling with questions I'm not sure I want answered.

"Yes," my father says, his voice steady but heavy with regret. "We know. And we're sorry that you had to find out this way."

His words land like a blow.

I expected disappointment over the fight with Bowen. Maybe concern over the rumors swirling in the city. But this—*this*—is something else entirely.

"Are you saying…" The words catch in my throat. "Are you saying that Theron is my father?"

My father nods. "Yes."

The confirmation comes with the weight of finality, of secrets long kept. My mind reels, but my mother's gentle voice draws me back.

"Let's talk inside."

Her eyes are soft, filled with unspoken sorrow. There's no judgment, no anger—only love. It's that love that grounds me. I've always respected my parents. They've never given me reason not to. If they've kept this from me, they must have had their reasons.

I duck under the low doorway, stepping into the house I helped build. The windows are open, letting in the muted light of the gray sky. Despite the chill outside, the house is warm, familiar. The scent of stew drifts from the kitchen, rich and savory, making my mouth water.

We move through the front room, past handmade furniture upholstered in earthy tones of burgundy and brown, accented by bright pops of white and yellow. My mother's touch is everywhere, in the neatly folded blankets, the vase of dried flowers on the table. It's a home built on care, love, and tradition.

In the dining room, we take our usual seats around the worn wooden table. For a moment, there's only silence. I study my parents, seeing them as I always have, but also through the lens of this new truth.

My father sits straight-backed, his piercing blue eyes meeting mine without flinching. His hair is thick, streaked with silver, a testament to a life of hard work and resilience. He's a little hunched from the accident last year, but he never complains. Never shows weakness.

My mother, with her soft smile and short, bouncing curls, watches me with quiet concern. Her hair has turned completely white, a striking contrast to my father's gray. She wears her years gracefully, embodying the warmth and kindness that have always made this house feel like home.

I've always admired them—their partnership, their quiet strength. They've been together since they were kids, inseparable through every hardship and joy. Even after all these years, they still laugh together, still look at each other with the wonder of new love.

I want that someday.

Finally, my father speaks, breaking the silence. "You handled things well yesterday."

His words surprise me. There's pride in his voice.

"We got word via messenger last night," my mother adds. "Old Cassian sent him."

"It's good to have friends in high places," my father says with a knowing smile.

They've always done this—finished each other's thoughts, their conversations flowing effortlessly, like two parts of the same whole. I've always admired their bond, envied it even.

But today, their easy rhythm only sharpens the ache inside me.

"Let's get to it, then," my father says, his tone turning serious. "Theron is your birth father. We've always wanted to tell you, but we promised we wouldn't."

There it is. The truth laid bare, simple and direct.

"Who did you promise?" I ask, my voice steadier now.

"Theron."

"Just tell him, Thom," my mother cuts in, her voice firmer than usual. "We don't owe Theron anything."

My father sighs heavily, the weight of years of secrecy settling on his shoulders. "I know, Abigail. But we've been dishonest with Jerrick all these years." He meets my gaze, his eyes filled with regret. "I guess I should start at the beginning."

I nod, unable to speak. My thoughts are a whirlwind, but I hold on to the steadiness in my father's voice.

He leans back slightly, folding his hands on the table as if grounding himself. "Your mother and I were getting ready for harvest. We'd just come back to the house for lunch when we heard a knock at the door. We both got up from the table, and as soon as we rounded the corner from the kitchen, we could see who it was through the screen."

"He's the only person I've ever met taller than you, Jerrick," my mother says, her voice quiet but firm. There's a tremor in her words, as if the memory still unsettles her. "He had to be at least seven feet tall. But it wasn't just his height—it was the way he carried himself. He looked like a mountain made flesh, all hard edges and unyielding presence. And believe me when I say the rumors are true."

Her gaze locks on mine, serious and intense. "He has no eyes. None."

The image sends a shiver down my spine. I've heard stories of Theron the Butcher, of his monstrous appearance. But hearing it from my mother, a firsthand account, makes it feel real in a way it never has before.

"It's hard to believe someone like that even exists," she continues, her voice softening. "But there he was, standing at our front door."

"As you can probably imagine," my father says, taking over the story, "we didn't want to open the door. Not that it would've stopped him if he wanted to come in. Theron has a… reputation."

The understatement hangs heavy in the air.

"But when we saw him standing there," my father continues, "it became clear we couldn't just pretend we weren't home. He could see us as well as we could see him through that screen."

My father's expression darkens slightly, the memory etched deep. "So, I walked up to the door and asked him if he had the right place."

He sighs again, glancing at my mother before turning back to me. "Let me back up a bit."

I lean in, hanging on his every word.

"You know how the Naming used to be," he begins. "It was a community event—a celebration, a moment of pride for families. It was a time of joy and unity. But that changed when the Council started conscripting those who bonded to fight back the Fog. People stopped celebrating when they realized their loved ones might never return."

I nod. I've heard stories of the old ways. The Naming hasn't been a celebration in my lifetime.

"The year before you were born," my father continues, "was the last time the Naming was held publicly. That year, a young woman bonded. But her family refused to let the Council take her. They brought half a dozen men, hard men, ready to fight if necessary."

I can already tell where the story is going.

"Theron was the Council's head Enforcer then," my father says, his voice dropping lower. "He stood between the girl and her family. He tried to calm them, to de-escalate the situation. Never once did he draw his sword—until he had no choice. When he finally did, it was over in less than a minute."

The weight of the story settles over me. I've heard of that incident, though the details have always been vague. I didn't know my parents had been there, witnessed it firsthand.

"We were there," my father says, confirming my thoughts. "We saw the whole thing."

"It was terrible," my mother adds, her voice hushed. "But there's one thing most people forget—Theron didn't want what happened. He tried to stop it."

I swallow hard, trying to reconcile the monster from the stories with the man my parents are describing.

"When we saw him at our door," my father continues, "I'm man enough to admit—I was scared. I pushed your mother behind me, ready to defend our home."

"But it didn't come to that," my mother says softly. "There was something different about him that day."

"He wasn't the man we saw at the Naming," my father agrees. "There was no confidence, no authority. He looked… lost."

He pauses, his gaze distant. "He raised his hands, palms out, and said, 'My wife needs help. Can you help me?'"

There's a moment of silence, the weight of the memory filling the room.

"You know your mother," my father says, smiling faintly. "When someone says they need help, she'll do whatever she can."

My mother nods, her expression softening. "You were born in this house, Jerrick. Well, the old house, anyway. Your birth mother was in labor, and Theron didn't know what to do. I helped bring you into this world."

The warmth in her voice soothes the tension in my chest.

"We got to know Theron and his wife over the weeks that followed," she continues. "They were a delight. Not at all like the stories people tell."

I sit quietly, absorbing it all. The story my parents had told me growing up—that a stranger had dropped me off after his wife died in childbirth—was a lie. But somehow, this truth doesn't sting the way I thought it would.

I look at them, waiting for more.

"About four months later, Theron knocked on our door again," my father continues, his voice quieter now, reflective. His hands fold on the table, fingers laced tightly, a gesture that betrays his discomfort. "He wasn't the same man we met before. When we first saw him, he stood tall and proud, unshakable. But that second time…" He shakes his head. "He was slouched, shoulders weighed down like he carried the world on his back. He looked like he had nothing left."

My mother picks up the thread, her voice soft but steady. "He told us his wife had been killed. He didn't go into details, just that you needed a safe place to stay. He handed you to me—" Her voice wavers for the first time, but she presses on. "And I loved you the moment I saw you."

My father smiles, a quiet, nostalgic expression that softens his usually sharp features. "We both did."

For a brief moment, the weight of this conversation lifts, replaced by the warmth of their shared memory. But it doesn't last.

"Theron didn't stay long," my father adds, the warmth fading. "He said he'd be back one day. He gave us two rules: the first was that you had to attend the Naming, no matter what. The second was that we were never to tell you about him."

"And he left us with enough gold to last three lifetimes," my mother adds, a touch of bitterness creeping into her tone. "Which we still have."

The room falls into silence, the only sound the faint bubbling of the stew on the stove. I sit quietly, letting their words sink in. There's a strange sense of relief that the rumors are true—at least partially. It gives legitimacy to what happened yesterday. But I'm not angry. Disappointed, maybe. Conflicted, certainly. But not angry.

"Do you have questions, Jerrick?" my mother asks gently, her eyes searching my face.

I meet her gaze. "Why did you wait so long to tell me?"

"We wanted to," she admits, her voice softening further. "Many times, we started to. But we never did because…" She trails off, glancing at my father.

"Because we weren't sure how you'd take it," my father finishes. His voice carries a note of guilt, the weight of years of silence pressing down on him. "We've always taught you the importance of honesty. And there we were, being dishonest with you all these years." He exhales slowly, his shoulders slumping. "We thought we were doing the right thing."

There it is—that phrase. *We thought we were doing the right thing.* The universal balm for guilty consciences. History is full of people, both good and bad, who justified their actions with those words.

I lean forward, resting my elbows on the table. "What if he had shown up one day to take me back?"

My father sighs, rubbing a hand over his face. "We lived with that fear for years. At first, every knock at the door made us jump. But after some time… we convinced ourselves he wasn't coming back."

But I can't convince myself of that.

The Naming is five weeks away. If Theron ever planned to return for me, that's when he'll do it. Why else would he make my parents promise to send me? The thought ties my stomach into knots. Anxiety bubbling beneath the surface.

I must look as unsettled as I feel because my mother reaches across the table, placing her hand over mine. Her touch is warm, grounding. It calms me, but the unease doesn't vanish entirely.

I take a deep breath, steadying myself before I speak. "He'll be at the Naming."

My father frowns. "Now, son, you don't know that."

"I do, Dad."

A silence stretches between us, heavy with unspoken fears.

"So what?" my mother asks, her tone taking on a firmer edge. "What does that change? Nothing. You're our son. We raised you."

Her words are like a tether, pulling me back from the edge of spiraling thoughts. I nod slowly. "I know, Mom. But things are already changing." I pause, thinking back to the market, the stares, the whispers. "You should've seen how everyone looked at me yesterday."

"Bah," my father scoffs, waving a hand dismissively. "It'll blow over. You look like him, sure—but not just your size. It's your whole presence. I'm surprised it took this long, honestly. All it takes is one person noticing the resemblance and starting a rumor."

"A rumor that never would've caught fire," my mother adds, "if it weren't for everything else going on."

I sigh, leaning back in my chair. "You're right. Both of you. This changes nothing."

I don't say those words for me—I say them for them. They need to hear it. They need to believe it. Even if I don't feel reassured myself, even if the knot in my chest remains stubbornly in place. My mind won't let it go. It keeps turning over everything I've learned today, picking at the loose threads of my identity, unraveling questions that my parents simply can't answer.

Will Theron show up at the Naming? If he does, what will it mean for me? For my family?

The thought churns in my mind, coiling tighter with each passing second. His name carries too much weight, too many implications, too much history. Whether he comes or not, his presence—real or whispered—will change everything. I know it. I feel it.

And yet… I don't mention Bowen's warning. I keep quiet about his father's conversation with Rorick. What good would it do to burden my parents with more uncertainty? They've carried enough for a lifetime. But deep down, I know something is coming. I can feel it like a shift in the air, the pressure building, waiting to break.

The silence stretches until my father speaks, his voice gentle but probing. "What's going on in that head of yours? You're making this too easy. Almost *too* easy." His sharp blue eyes lock onto mine. "What aren't you telling us?"

I meet his gaze and exhale slowly. "I'm not angry," I say, though the words come out heavier than I intended. "But… I wish you'd told me sooner." My voice dips into a softer tone. "I don't think I handled yesterday very well. Even if people stop whispering about who my birth father is, they're still going to look at me differently for what I did."

My father leans back, crossing his arms over his chest. His expression shifts—something between pride and defiance. "Your mother and I couldn't be more proud of the way you handled things yesterday, Jerrick. The messenger was very thorough in explaining everything." He pauses, giving me a moment to absorb his words. "You tried walking away. More than once. Even after Bowen pushed you. Even after he hit you."

My mother nods in agreement, her eyes shining with quiet pride. "From what we heard, it wasn't until he started taunting Elena that you stood your ground."

"I don't think I could be more proud of you," my father continues. "If you ask me, Bowen had it coming."

His words lift some of the weight pressing on my chest. Their pride is unexpected, and I soak it in like warmth on a cold day. But before I can respond, my mother grins mischievously and says, "Speaking of Elena…" She winks at me, a teasing glint in her eye. "I've always liked the idea of the two of you…"

"Mom!" I groan, cutting her off.

She laughs, light and easy, the sound filling the room with warmth. "Well, I *do!*"

Her laughter is infectious, and soon my father joins in. Despite everything weighing on me, I can't help but chuckle too. The tension breaks, if only for a moment, and I'm reminded why I've never been able to stay angry at them. They've always been my best friends. They raised me with love, with care, with unwavering support.

They thought they were doing the right thing.

And that counts for something.

But no amount of laughter can shake the lingering feeling that everything is about to change. Something's coming. Something big.

And all I want to do is pretend it isn't.

I sit with them a little longer, savoring the comfort of home, the familiarity of their presence. But even as I try to ground myself in the moment, the knot inside me pulls tighter, a constant reminder that I'm standing on the edge of something vast and unknown.

Ready or not… it's coming.

#

The tunnel is suffocating, the air thick with the stench of blood and rot. Shadows flicker along the curved walls, dancing like twisted specters in the dim, flickering glow of Essence Lamps embedded in the stone. I stand motionless, disoriented, my heart thundering against my ribs. My breath comes in shallow gasps, as if I've been running—or screaming.

Bodies lie scattered across the ground in grotesque positions. Limbs bent at unnatural angles. Lifeless eyes staring into the void.

A hollow ache blossoms in my chest.

I know these people. I don't know how, but I do. And they are dead because of me.

The crushing weight of guilt bears down on me, squeezing the air from my lungs. My legs feel weak, my knees threatening to buckle under the burden of it. The tunnel echoes with my ragged breathing, the oppressive silence pressing in from all sides.

Then, a sound—low and guttural—rumbles from behind me.

A growl.

It starts as a faint rumble, reverberating through the stone like distant thunder, then rises, stretching into a menacing snarl that sends a shiver down my spine.

I turn, slowly, dread settling in my stomach like a stone.

It stands thirty feet away, but it might as well be breathing down my neck.

The creature looms over me, grotesque and towering, a twisted amalgamation of flesh and earth. Its form is a perversion of nature—a wolf's decaying body fused with stone, dead branches jutting from its shoulders like jagged antlers. Its jaw hangs open, revealing rows of jagged teeth dripping with saliva.

And its eyes—those eyes—are the most horrifying part.

They glow an unnatural red, floating in oversized sockets like embers in the darkness. They fix on me with a predatory gleam, filled with hunger.

Human-like hands, ending in claws as long as daggers, scrape together with a bone-chilling click-clack. Behind it, a thick, gnarled tail drags along the ground, leaving grooves in the dirt.

It takes a step toward me.

And another.

Despite the fear freezing my limbs, something stirs within me. A power, wild and untamed, coils in my chest—a searing force that demands to be released. It pulses through me, burning hotter with every heartbeat, whispering promises of strength, vengeance, and destruction.

But with it comes a mocking voice. "You could have saved them." The voice gnaws at the edges of my mind. "You're weak. That's why they died."

The creature charges, closing the distance in a blur of teeth and claws. It moves faster than it should, faster than anything that size should be able to.

I react on instinct, reaching for the power within me.

It surges to the surface, wild and ferocious, like a storm breaking free of its restraints. My body trembles under its weight, my vision blurring as the power threatens to overwhelm me.

For a moment, I hesitate. I'm afraid. Not of the creature, but of myself.

The force I wield feels limitless—untamed and raw. It's more terrifying than the beast charging toward me. But I have no choice. With a guttural roar, I release it.

The blast of energy sends the creature hurtling backward, slamming into the tunnel wall with a deafening crash. Stone cracks and splinters under the impact, dust billowing into the air.

But it isn't enough.

The creature shakes off the blow as if it were nothing, snarling as it scrambles to its feet. Red eyes lock onto mine, burning with rage.

It lunges.

This time, I'm too slow.

The creature barrels into me, claws tearing through the air. The impact knocks me to the ground, my back slamming against the cold stone floor.

My breath leaves me in a wheeze, pain blooming in my ribs.

I scramble to push it off, but it's too heavy. Its claws slice through my shirt, raking across my chest. Blood drips down, staining the stone beneath me.

Then, I see her. Lying on the tunnel floor.

Elena—

Her body crumpled, lifeless. Blood pools around her, dark and viscous, soaking into the dirt. Her eyes—those bright, defiant eyes—stare at me, empty and unseeing.

"No…"

The word escapes my lips as a whisper, trembling with disbelief.

"No!"

I thrash against the creature pinning me down, panic fueling my strength. But it's no use.

The beast snarls, its hot breath washing over me. It's over. Elena is gone. And it's my fault.

The creature's jaws open, descending toward me—I jolt awake with a gasp, the scream dying in my throat.

I wake with a start. My chest heaves, lungs desperate for air. Sweat drenches my skin, chilling me despite the cold night air seeping through the cracks in the window. My hands tremble as I push myself upright, my body shaking with the aftershocks of the nightmare.

It wasn't real.

It wasn't real.

But the images linger, vivid and haunting. Elena's lifeless eyes. The creature's growl, echoing in my ears. The power, raging within me.

I bury my face in my hands, trying to steady my breathing. My heart still races, thudding wildly against my ribs.

It takes several long moments to calm myself, to convince my mind that I'm safe, that it was only a dream. But even as my breathing slows, the dread remains. I can't shake the feeling that it wasn't just a nightmare. It was a warning. A glimpse of what's to come.

And I'm not sure I'll ever sleep soundly again.

Chapter 5

Jerrick

Three weeks have passed, heavy and unrelenting. Their weight presses on my mind, driving me to seek solace where I've always found it: in the woods. Spear in hand, I trade the overwhelming churn of thoughts for the primal clarity of the hunt. Elena brought word that the whispers in Four Rivers have faded to a muted hum. My father's wisdom proves true once more—time dulls even the sharpest tongues. Yet, here in the forest, the questions still echo.

The cold bites harder today, a sharpness that seeps through even my thick jacket and fur-lined boots. It mirrors the chill inside me— restless, searching. The forest, usually my sanctuary, feels different now, as if it too senses the changes creeping into our world.

I've left my bow behind, though I'd wager few in Four Rivers could match my skill with it. Instead, I carry my spear, seeking the challenge it offers. Hunting small game with such a weapon is impractical, almost absurd. But that's precisely the point. It's not about the catch. It's about testing myself, honing something deeper. Mastery of the unfamiliar. Control amidst the chaos.

The forest stretches around me, familiar yet untamed. Each rustling leaf underfoot marks my passage through an old world I know by heart, where the path shifts with the seasons but always leads back to me. This place has always been a balm, a retreat that shrinks the enormity of life to something I can hold. Today, though, the solace feels tinged with unease. My thoughts return to the Naming, and with them, the shadow of Theron's words. Why insist I attend? The question twists through my mind like the unseen trails that lace the woods.

Deeper into the trees, the forest becomes a symphony of motion and sound. The wind whispers through the bare branches, stirring the brittle leaves into a swirling, half-hearted dance. My boots crunch softly against the forest floor, the scent of damp earth rising with each step. The pine and moss lend the air a sharp freshness, edged with the lingering decay of a season unwilling to let go. Overhead, the gray light filters through the skeletal canopy, softening the world into muted tones.

A brook babbles in the distance, its song rising above the rustle of unseen creatures skittering through the underbrush. The sound grows clearer as I approach, a melody both ancient and unchanging. The water gurgles over worn rocks and fallen branches, its clarity a stark contrast to the haze in my mind. The damp air carries the aroma of wet leaves and soil, grounding me in the present moment, even as my thoughts drift.

This place feels alive, not just a collection of trees and streams, but something more—a vast, breathing entity. From the smallest insect burrowing unseen to the tallest oak standing sentinel, every part moves in harmony. Here, time slows, inviting stillness, demanding attention. The forest is patient, eternal, and yet fleeting in its seasonal rhythms. Today, its beauty feels bittersweet, as though it knows that change, profound and unstoppable, is looming just beyond the trees.

Just as my father taught me, I tune out the forest's background symphony, peeling away the layers of sound I don't need. The bubbling brook fades to a distant murmur. The birds' songs and the rustle of the wind through the trees vanish into the periphery. What's left are the subtle, deliberate noises—the heartbeat of the underbrush.

I sift through these remaining sounds, isolating them one by one: the faint crackle of dry leaves, the occasional snap of a twig, the soft, rhythmic thud of something landing and leaping again. A rabbit.

I turn toward the sound, my eyes scanning the underbrush for movement as I strip away even the noise of my breath. It takes a moment, but soon I see it—a rabbit, twenty feet away, its back turned to me. Its ears twitch slightly, oblivious to my presence.

I grip my spear, raising it over my shoulder in a throwing stance, the smooth wood steady in my hand. I could throw from here, and I'm confident I'd hit it. But confidence isn't certainty. A part of me longs for the guarantee, the perfection of a closer shot. Sliding my feet carefully beneath the carpet of leaves, I inch forward. Each step is deliberate, muffling any sound that might alert the rabbit. My heart pounds steadily in my chest, matching the tempo of my measured advance.

The closer I get, the more my instincts battle. One voice whispers to seize the moment—throw now, before something goes wrong. The other urges caution—close the gap, ensure success. The rabbit remains blissfully unaware, the wind carrying my scent safely away from it. I press forward.

One step. Then another. I'm nearly there when the wind betrays me, shifting direction. The rabbit freezes for a split second, and then, in a blur of white fur, it bolts to the left.

Instinct takes over. My arm releases the spear before I've even registered the movement, the weapon slicing through the air as I launch myself after it. The spear misses, embedding itself into the forest floor, and I reach it in three long strides, pulling it free without breaking my pace.

I know better than to think I can catch a rabbit, but that knowledge doesn't stop me from trying. My legs pump beneath me, dodging trees as I pursue the fleeting shape ahead. My lungs burn, my muscles scream, but I press on, willing my body to move faster, to close the distance. The rabbit veers left, pulling ahead with each bound. Still, I don't stop. Maybe it will make a mistake.

Just as I'm about to admit defeat, it dives beneath a massive thorn bush, disappearing into the dark tangle of branches. I skid to a halt, my chest heaving, and circle the bush. No sign of movement. Hope flickers—it might still be under there. Dropping to my knees, I peer beneath the lowest branches. The rabbit's small shape is just visible, pressed against the trunk, its body still and tense.

I glance at the thorns—long and wicked, each the size of a finger. They gleam faintly, sharp enough to pierce even thick leather. Crawling under is out of the question. My spear might reach, but the bramble is dense, the angles awkward. My best bet might be to scare it out, but what good did chasing it do before? I pause, weighing my options, as the rabbit waits, a tiny, trembling target in a fortress of thorns.

What's that? The thought flashes through my mind as I hear the faint crunch of footsteps approaching from my right. My head snaps toward the sound, and I slowly rise to my feet, clutching my spear tightly with both hands. The sound comes again, closer this time, yet the woods remain unnervingly still. I peer intently into the underbrush, my breath shallow, waiting.

Then another sound—this one to my left. My heart pounds as a chilling realization takes hold. There are two of them. My body tenses like a coiled spring, ready to flee or strike, yet I remain rooted to the spot, paralyzed by a strange mix of fear and curiosity.

And then it happens. Almost as if the forest itself births the figure, it steps into view. A Keeper.

It materializes with an eerie grace, emerging from the shadows with a presence that feels both ancient and otherworldly. The creature barely reaches five feet in height, its disproportionately large ears tapering to sharp points that seem to slice through the air.

Its skin gleams like polished stone, taut over sinewy muscles that ripple with quiet strength. A pale gray hue hints at a life spent in darkness, untouched by the vibrancy of the surface world. Hairless and unadorned, it exudes a vulnerability at odds with the power radiating from its form.

But it's the Keeper's hands and feet that draw my attention— and unnerve me. They're impossibly large, tipped with jet-black claws that seem capable of tearing through stone itself. The elongated arms, nearly brushing the forest floor, hang relaxed yet brimming with latent power. Its feet, broad and rooted, seem to anchor it to the earth, as though it's been part of this world for eons.

The Keeper raises its hands, palms outward—a universal gesture of peace. But those claws, so dark and menacing, make my heart race. The sight of them sends a wave of anger surging through me, sudden and inexplicable. The urge to strike rises within me, primal and raw, and I grip my spear so tightly that my knuckles ache.

"Back off!" I roar, the words ripping from my throat with a ferocity that surprises even me. Spittle flies from my lips, and embarrassment prickles at the edges of my mind. But my anger overrides everything, urging me forward, telling me I'm justified. It's unsettling how quickly I've unraveled—I didn't even reach this level of rage with Bowen.

The Keeper remains calm, its deep voice resonating like a stone striking the forest floor. "I know you're angry," it says, its tone measured and soothing. "My name is Brennan, and we have to talk."

The words pierce through my anger, but only slightly. I'm shaking now, not from fear but from the intensity of the emotions surging within me. They feel foreign, alien, as though they aren't truly mine. The thought terrifies me more than the creature standing before me.

"I don't want to talk to you," I snarl through clenched teeth, my voice low and venomous.

"The anger you're feeling isn't your fault," Brennan says, his voice tinged with a sadness that doesn't match his serene exterior. "It's our burden—my people's burden. But you can fight it. I need you to fight it, Jerrick."

The sound of my name jolts me. "How do you know my name?" I demand, my anger sparking anew, fueled by suspicion. If this creature knows my name, then this meeting isn't chance. It's deliberate. The weight of that realization crushes any lingering fear, replacing it with a suffocating sense of dread.

"I know your father," Brennan begins, but I cut him off, the fire in my chest flaring.

"My father? What do you know of my father?" The words erupt from me, my anger boiling over again. My grip tightens on the spear, and the weight of this moment presses heavily on my shoulders. Whatever Brennan knows, it's a thread pulling me deeper into a web I never wanted to be part of.

"I should have said Theron," Brennan corrects himself, his voice low and measured. He shakes his head slightly, as if berating himself. "Of course, you wouldn't think of him as your father."

The name strikes like a lightning bolt. "Theron?" I yell, my voice a raw edge. "Is he why you're here?" My feet move before my mind can catch up, a half-step forward driven by instinct more than thought.

Brennan's eyes widen, and his hands shoot up, palms outward in a gesture of desperate placation. "No! Drusilla, don't—"

The world tilts.

Two thoughts slam into me simultaneously: there was a second set of footsteps, and this is going to hurt.

The ground rushes up to meet me as every muscle in my body gives out. My legs crumble beneath me, my spear slipping from my grasp as though my hands have forgotten their purpose. I hit the dirt with a jarring thud, my breath forced out of me in a shallow wheeze. Panic grips me as I realize I can't move—not a finger, not a twitch. My heart races in defiance of the paralysis, pounding a frantic rhythm in my chest. Even my eyelids betray me, remaining fixed open as dirt and grit press against my cheek.

"He was going to attack you," a second voice says, female and sharp with accusation. I strain to turn my head toward her, but my body refuses to obey.

"They always do," she adds, her words cutting like a blade.

"This one is different," Brennan retorts, his voice heavy with frustration. "I know him. He wouldn't have attacked me. I told you to wait for my signal."

"It doesn't work like that, and you know it," she counters coldly.

A resigned sigh escapes Brennan as he kneels beside me. His movements are deliberate, almost gentle, as his massive hands cradle my head and tilt it so I'm lying on my cheek. Fresh air fills my lungs more easily, though the terror gripping me remains.

From the corner of my eye, I see Brennan pull a small water pouch from his belt. He tilts it carefully, dripping water onto my exposed, drying eye. The cool droplets bring a fleeting relief to the stinging dryness.

"I'm sorry, Jerrick," he says softly, his voice barely above a whisper. "I didn't want it to happen this way. I've been on the receiving end of Drusilla's ability before. The worst part is the dry eyes, isn't it?" He manages a rueful smile. "Don't worry. You'll be good as new in about five minutes."

His words are meant to soothe, but they barely penetrate the maelstrom of panic in my mind. My thoughts spiral wildly, each one louder and more frantic than the last. Why can't I move? Am I going to die here, helpless and humiliated on the cold ground? The thundering of my pulse drowns out reason as the question repeats endlessly in my mind.

"You need to hurry, Brennan," the woman—Drusilla—urges from somewhere beyond my limited view. "He's a big one. It may not last as long as you think."

Brennan leans closer, his voice dropping into a tone of urgency. "Jerrick, listen to me carefully. When you see Theron, you need to tell him everything has changed. Tell him that what happened before will not happen again." He hesitates, his eyes flickering with something between caution and resolve. "I know this sounds cryptic, but I don't know what's going to happen between now and when he finds you."

Drusilla's voice cuts through the air again, sharper this time. "Hurry, Brennan!"

Brennan exhales slowly, almost reluctantly. "If you're taken," he continues, "nobody else can know what I'm about to tell you. Say this to Theron, and only to him: 'Bring him to the place of your awakening.'" He pauses, locking his dark eyes onto mine. "Tell him that Brennan says it's urgent."

Drusilla's voice rises in pitch, laced with fear. "Brennan! We don't have time for this!"

Her panic ignites a new wave of dread within me. What could possibly frighten someone like her? And why does it feel like the answer is me?

Brennan tilts the water pouch once more, allowing a few final drops to moisten my eyes. His voice carries an unexpected warmth, almost kind. "When we meet again—and we will—I hope things will be different. I'll be looking forward to it."

His words linger in the cold air as I hear, rather than see, the two figures retreat into the northern woods. Their departure leaves an oppressive silence, as though the forest itself holds its breath. My body slowly obeys me, first with the twitch of a finger, then the blink of an eye. Relief floods through me as I sit up, my limbs regaining their strength. Yet the questions racing through my mind outpace my recovery.

Why couldn't I move? What was that anger—so primal, so foreign? And what does Brennan's cryptic message mean? Each question gives birth to another, an endless spiral pulling me deeper into uncertainty. It's then that I notice the rabbit I'd been hunting, lying motionless beside me. A small, precise wound marks the spot where its heart once beat.

The sight of the rabbit jars me. It's a stark, almost poetic reminder of how fragile life is—and how close I've just come to losing control. I reach for the rabbit, my fingers brushing its still-warm fur, and my thoughts return to Brennan's parting words. "Everything has changed…" The phrase echoes in my mind, heavy with an ominous promise.

Brennan's insistence that I deliver a message to Theron speaks to a bond I barely comprehend. Theron, a man I've never met yet whose shadow looms over my life, suddenly feels closer and more significant than ever before. What is this place of awakening Brennan mentioned, and why does it carry such urgency? The questions feel too large, too pressing, for someone who only seeks a simple life.

As I stand, the rabbit in hand, I survey the forest around me. Once a sanctuary, it now feels shrouded in unseen forces, alive with whispers I can almost hear. The leaves still dance on the wind, the brook still murmurs its ancient song, but the harmony I once found here has given way to an undercurrent of unease. The natural world seems to watch, as though it knows more than I do about what lies ahead.

I begin the walk back to the farm, my legs heavy with the weight of the morning's events. Each step is a struggle against the unanswered questions and the growing sense that the life I've known is slipping away. Brennan and Drusilla's abilities, their connection to Theron, and their interest in me—they all point to something far larger than myself. It feels like I've been caught in the pull of a current I can't escape, swept toward a destiny I never chose.

The familiar sight of the farm finally comes into view, the orchards standing in perfect rows like sentinels of the life I've worked so hard to preserve. For a moment, the sight soothes me, grounding me in the world I know and love. Yet, beneath that comfort lies a gnawing sense of inadequacy. How can I, a farmer with simple dreams, face whatever lies ahead? How can I stand against the unknown forces that Brennan and Drusilla hinted at?

I tighten my grip on the rabbit and quicken my pace. The farm reminds me of everything I hold dear: my family, my legacy, the life I crave. But it also reminds me of how far out of my depth I truly am.

Change is coming, and I can no longer ignore it. Whether I'm ready or not, my life is no longer my own.

#

The evening drapes our home in its quiet embrace, the familiar hum of the night settling around me as I linger in the doorway of the living room. Inside, the glow of the hearth flickers against the walls, casting long shadows that dance across the room. The fire's warmth does little to quell the creeping chill of the unknown, a cold that has settled deep in my bones. My parents sit waiting, their faces softened by the firelight but etched with quiet concern.

Dinner had passed mostly in silence, a meal eaten under the weight of unspoken words. They didn't push for answers, though I could tell they wanted to. They always do when they sense something gnawing at me. But they let it be. And I didn't offer. A part of me wanted to tell them about what happened in the woods, but another part—the larger part—knew it would only worry them. Would telling them ease my burden, or simply shift it onto their shoulders?

I exhale softly, then step forward. "Mom. Dad." My voice barely rises above the fire's crackle as I lower myself onto the couch. It groans under my weight, a sound as familiar as the scent of my mother's herbal tea steeping in the kitchen. The room, so often a haven, now feels like a stage set for a conversation I'm not sure I want to have.

My mother sets aside her knitting, her knowing eyes fixing on mine. She doesn't speak, just watches, waiting. My father closes his book and folds his hands in his lap, his expression steady. Encouraging. They're patient, giving me the space to say what I need to say.

"I've been thinking," I start, hesitating as I fumble for the right words. The fire crackles, a sharp contrast to the cold knot forming in my stomach. My thoughts feel tangled. Too many threads pulling in too many directions. But I push forward, even though I already know the answer to the question I'm about to ask. "Is there… any way for me to get out of the Naming?"

My mother's expression softens, her hands folding together in her lap. She can already sense the worry pressing down on me, the weight of it. I know what the law says. Everyone in their twenty-first year must attend the Naming. There's no exception. But still, I have to ask.

It's my father who answers. "I wish there were, son." His voice is quiet, heavy. "But there isn't. It's the law. If you refuse, the Council won't just come for you. They'll come for us too."

His words land like a stone in my chest. It's not just me at risk. If I don't go, my parents will suffer the consequences. The Council makes examples of those who disobey. I knew this already, but hearing my father say it aloud cements it in a way I can't ignore.

My mother reaches over, placing her hand over mine. Her touch is gentle, grounding. "You're a good son, Jerrick," she says, giving my hand a squeeze. "You've always been. We're lucky Theron chose us to raise you." There's a pause, her voice growing softer. "I know you worry. You never liked the unknown. But you're stronger than you think. No matter what happens, we will be okay. You will be okay."

I look away, my gaze drawn to the fire. The logs pop and shift, sending embers swirling upward. I think of the Keeper's words in the woods—Everything has changed. I don't know what that means, but I can feel it.

I don't tell them about Brennan. Or Drusilla. Or what they said about Theron. Not yet.

"You're right," I say instead. It's not the truth, but it's what I want them to believe. "I'm just nervous about the Naming, that's all."

"That's understandable," my father says, leaning back in his chair. "I'd be lying if I said I wasn't nervous for you too. But no matter what happens, we'll get through it. Besides, only a handful bond each year. The chances are slim."

I nod, forcing a small smile. "You're right." The words sound hollow in my own ears, but I let them stand. "I'm worrying over nothing."

I feel my mother's eyes on me, the way her fingers tighten around my hand. She knows me too well. Knows that I'm not convinced. But she doesn't press.

Instead, she asks, "What are you most afraid of?"

The answer comes without hesitation. "That I'll bond." I swallow hard. "And that I'll have to leave you and Dad."

My mother exchanges a glance with my father, a silent conversation passing between them. Then, he reaches over, placing his hand atop hers, sandwiching it between his and mine. The gesture is grounding, yet I can sense the significance of what's coming.

"I think," my mother begins, but hesitates, her expression shifting as if she's carefully choosing her next words. "I think Theron has a plan for you."

I stiffen, my pulse quickening. I open my mouth to protest, but before I can get a word out, she tightens her grip on my hand, willing me to listen. "Now, let me finish," she says gently but firmly.

She studies my face, her features softening into something wistful. "Your birth mother's name was Gwen," she says. "She was a lovely woman. You have her eyes." A small, sad smile touches her lips before she continues, as if caught between fondness and sorrow.

"When we first met them, Theron was still the Council's head Enforcer. And, Jerrick, he wasn't what the stories make him out to be. He was kind. Thoughtful. Nothing like the ruthless warlord people whisper about." She pauses, the flickering firelight catching the glint of moisture in her eyes. "But when he came back to us… when he told us Gwen had died, he wasn't the same man. He was unraveling. Lost. Angry.

"He loved you, Jerrick. That much was obvious. I don't think he wanted to leave you with us, but something pushed him forward. And then, before you even turned one, he turned against the Council."

I swallow hard. I've heard this story before. But hearing it now, from her, with this context—it feels different.

"He started the resistance," she goes on. "Sent people to Naming Ceremonies, across all of the Four Rivers and beyond, waiting for the moment they could strike. To fight back. To stop the Council from taking newly bonded SoulCasters. And when the Council refused to let them go?" She exhales, long and slow. "People died, Jerrick. A lot of people."

I already know this, but it still makes my stomach clench.

She takes a sip of water, then grips my hand again when she sees I'm about to speak. "I know you know all this," she says. "But I've been thinking about it differently lately. Theron spent years trying to keep people away from the Council. He was willing to die for that fight. So why," she asks, eyes locking onto mine, "would he tell us to make sure you're there? At the Naming? He wouldn't send you into the lion's den unless there was a reason."

The knot in my stomach twists tighter. "But nobody has heard from him in years," I say. "Who's to say he's even still alive?"

Silence stretches between us, heavy and thick. My parents look at each other, a shared understanding passing between them. Then my father stands, disappearing into the other room. I hear the shuffle of a drawer opening, the creak of wood shifting. When he returns, he's holding something small, something delicate.

"Hold out your hand," he says.

I do.

He drops a necklace into my palm. Dangling from the chain is a simple, worn ring.

"This belonged to Gwen," he says softly.

I stare down at it, brow furrowing. "How do you know?"

"Look at the inscription," my mother urges.

I turn the ring over in my fingers, tilting it toward the firelight. Inside, in elegant, worn script, is an engraving: To Gwen, with love.

My breath catches. The room feels smaller, closing in around me.

"So, he's still alive," I murmur.

My father nods. "That ring showed up this afternoon. Right on the porch."

A strange, weightless sensation grips my chest, something between dread and disbelief. "He was here?" I whisper.

"Looks like it," my father confirms. "And I think this means he's close."

I stare down at the ring, the small etching blurring at the edges as my vision clouds. The fire's glow fades from my awareness, the quiet sounds of the house dulling into nothingness. My world narrows to this single object in my palm and what it means. Theron. Here. Watching. Waiting.

The fear that's been creeping in over the past few weeks unfurls in full now, stretching its icy fingers around my ribs. This is real. No longer just rumors, just whispers. No longer something I can push aside.

A knot tightens in my gut, a hollow weight pressing against my ribs. My heart pounds. Everything is shifting beneath my feet, slipping away from familiarity.

I squeeze my eyes shut and try to breathe through it, but the words inside my head won't quiet. *To Gwen, with love.* To the mother I never knew. To a life I was never meant to have.

Then I feel them—two warm arms wrapping around me. My parents. Their embrace pulls me back, grounds me. I release a shaky breath and return their hug, gripping them tighter than I mean to.

"I'm okay," I murmur. "I'm okay. I'm okay." I repeat it like a mantra, as if saying it enough times might make it true.

My father pulls back slightly, enough to look me in the eye. "We're going to be okay," he says firmly.

Then he stands, extending a hand to me. "Come on," he says, pulling me up to my feet. He tilts his head back to meet my gaze, his expression unwavering. "Stop slouching."

I blink at him. "What?"

"You heard me." His voice sharpens just a little, but there's warmth beneath it. "Stand tall."

I straighten, my head nearly grazing the ceiling as I look down at him. He studies me, then nods. "There's greatness in you, Jerrick. You're meant for more than this farm."

The words settle deep inside me, but I shake my head.

"But this is where I want to be."

And I mean it. But as I grip the ring tighter in my palm, I can't help but wonder… does what I want even matter anymore?

"We don't always get to choose our destiny, Jerrick," my father continues, his voice steady, unwavering. His piercing blue eyes hold mine, not with force, but with a quiet conviction that sinks deep into my bones. "Sometimes, it chooses us. And when it does, we have to be brave enough to embrace it, no matter how uncertain the path forward may seem."

His grip on my hand tightens briefly—a small, silent promise of strength, of reassurance. "You've got the biggest heart I know and the spirit of a leader. Remember, it's not just about where you feel safe or comfortable; it's about where you're needed, where you can do the most good. This land, son, it's bigger than this farm, bigger than you or me, and whether you're ready or not, you have a role to play in it."

His words strike something deep inside me, a truth I've fought to ignore. I want to protest, to argue that I do get to choose, that my place is here, among the trees I know, the soil I've tilled, the family I love. But even as the words form, they crumble in my throat, because deep down, I feel it too.

Change is coming.

"I hear what you're saying, but…" The words falter, a weak attempt to hold onto the life I've envisioned for myself. A life that, even now, is slipping through my fingers. I don't want to be a part of something bigger. I want to stay here, where I belong.

But as I look between my parents, I see something in their eyes—something more powerful than fear, more resolute than love. Understanding. A quiet knowing of the road ahead, of the sacrifices that might have to be made.

"No, son," my father says, shaking his head gently. "No buts. If your destiny lies elsewhere, don't fight it. Your mother and I love you beyond words. We've always wanted the best for you, but things are changing, and there is nothing we can do to stop it." He exhales, rubbing his temple. "It's up to each one of us to rise and accept the challenges that lie ahead, even if those challenges aren't where we thought they would be."

His voice is firm, but there's sorrow there too—an ache beneath the wisdom. He doesn't want me to leave any more than I want to go, but we both know wanting won't change a damn thing.

My mother rises from her seat and gently takes the necklace from my hand. She turns to me, lifting it up. "Bend down, sweetheart."

I obey, leaning forward so she can slip it over my head. The cool metal of the ring rests against my chest, heavier than it should be, like an anchor pulling me into something inevitable. She cups my face in her hands, her thumbs tracing the curve of my cheek, just like she used to when I was a child.

"This is your home," she says softly, her voice steady, but her eyes shimmer with unshed tears. "Of course, we want you here. But if your worst fears come true—if you bond, if you have to leave—know that we will be okay." She swallows, her voice dropping to a whisper, "Know that we are proud of you."

The words pierce through me, cutting straight to the marrow.

I close my eyes, inhaling the familiar scent of my mother's embrace—the lavender she tucks into our linens, the faint aroma of the stew she made earlier, the comforting warmth that has surrounded me my entire life.

Home.

The thought of leaving it behind, of walking away from the only world I've ever known, sends an ache through my chest. I've spent my entire life believing that this farm was my future. That no matter what the world demanded, I would stay here, working the land, caring for my parents, carrying on our legacy.

But as I straighten, my fingers curling around the ring, the cold metal against my skin is a cruel reminder.

I might not have a choice.

I lift my gaze to meet my parents'. They are my foundation, my constants in a world that is shifting beneath me. Their reassurances soothe me, their love is my armor. And yet, the unease remains, lurking at the edges of my mind. The storm is coming—I can feel it.

I square my shoulders, trying to push it all down, trying to find the strength they see in me.

The fire crackles behind us, its warmth fighting against the creeping cold of night. And as I stand there, ring around my neck, home surrounding me, I realize something.

I want to believe that nothing will change. That I will wake up tomorrow and everything will be as it was. That the farm will always be my future. That my path is my own to choose.

But some part of me—the part whispering in the back of my mind, the part tied to Theron, to the Naming, to whatever the Keepers know—already understands the truth.

I'm standing at the edge of something I cannot stop.

And I don't know if I'm ready.

Chapter 6

Jerrick

Worry is woven into me as tightly as the fabric of my soul. It is not something I wear, something I can take off or set aside—it is a part of me, inseparable, inescapable. And today, it coils tighter than ever.

The past weeks have slipped away like water through my fingers, no matter how tightly I tried to hold onto them. Each daylight has brought me closer to this moment, closer to the Naming Ceremony—a presence so looming, so vast, that it has eclipsed every other thought. I've tried to prepare, steeling myself for whatever may come, but hope and dread war within me, an endless battle neither can win.

I have busied myself with the farm, clinging to the familiar rhythm of work. I pruned every tree as if shaping the future itself, cleared the fallen apples with the care of someone preserving the past, and insulated the saplings as though protecting more than just young roots from the coming winter. Our food stores are stocked and organized, our cellar packed with salted meats and smoked game. The quiet discipline of these tasks was meant to ground me. But now, with the day finally here, I feel no more prepared than when the whispers of this moment first began.

And yet, one small comfort remains. No matter what happens today, my parents will be ready for the long winter ahead—with or without me.

I lay in bed, staring at the ceiling, unwilling to rise. Not yet. Not when this may be the last time I wake in my own home, the last time I belong to this life. This farm has always been my sanctuary, the one place where I know who I am. The unknown, the endless possibilities of what today might bring, settle over me heavier than the thickest snowfall. Even the bravest souls fear the whispers of uncertainty.

A sound shatters the stillness.

A creak.

The bottom two steps of the front porch always groan under weight. I hear both of them now, in the hush of early morning. Someone—or something—is outside our door.

I sit up fast, my pulse hammering, but I push the sound of my own heartbeat to the background, pulling my focus outward, listening. The silence presses in around me. I hold my breath.

Footsteps.

Hurried, nearing my door.

I reach for the knife on my bedside table as the door swings open—too quickly. My grip tightens, my body tenses—

It's my father.

"You heard it too?" he whispers.

I nod, my voice just as hushed. "Yes."

"Your mother is still asleep. Go to her side and wait there. I'll look."

I push to my feet. "No." I stand to my full height—not as defiance, but as a silent reminder. I am no longer a child.

My father meets my gaze, reading my resolve. He nods, a small smile flickering across his face. "It's probably nothing," he murmurs, "but be careful."

I slip on my boots, grab my jacket, and move quietly past him toward the living room. My grip on the knife is firm, steady, as I reach the front door. Cautiously, I press my foot behind it and ease it open, just enough to peer into the void beyond.

Blackness.

The world beyond the threshold is pitch dark, as always. Without Essence, the night is absolute.

"Here." My father's voice is low as he presses something into my hand. An Essence lamp. Its metal casing is cool, familiar. Unlike torches or candles, it does not burn—it hums with power, drawing light from the land itself. This one has a shutter, allowing me to control its beam.

I keep the door cracked just a sliver as I open the shutter partway, sending a narrow blade of light across the porch. My breath stills. Nothing.

I push the door open a little farther, my fingers tightening around the lamp's handle. Still nothing.

Silently, I step outside, pulling the door shut behind me. The night air is crisp, biting against my exposed skin. From the other side of the door, I can hear my father shifting his weight, undecided. Whether to stay and watch over my mother, or to follow me.

I don't know what's waiting in the darkness. But I know one thing—

I am not alone.

The night is quiet. Too quiet.

The wind murmurs through the trees, a faint whisper against the silence. If someone is out there, they are hidden well. But they can see me—the thin beam of light spilling from the shuttered Essence lamp marks my position like a beacon. A mistake.

Quickly, I flick the light off and shift a step to the left, my muscles tense, my grip tightening on the knife. If they attack, they'll be striking at nothing but shadows.

The cold metal in my hand is reassuring, though I know it's no shield against what lurks unseen. I angle my head, listening intently, stripping away the sounds of the wind, the rustling leaves, my own steady breaths. I need to hear only what doesn't belong.

There.

A faint sound, the whisper of fabric shifting—someone moving. A jacket rubbing against itself as an arm bends. They are close.

I almost call out, demand to know who's there. But I don't. If they're hesitating, so will I. Somewhere in the dark, they are waiting just as I am, locked in the same silent standoff, each of us trying to gain the upper hand.

Enough. I need to end this.

With a swift motion, I flick open the shutter, directing the beam of light off to the right.

There!

A flash of brown fabric—someone is standing just beyond the edge of the porch.

I throw the shutter wide, flooding the night with light.

The man, his face caught for the briefest moment in the glow—unfamiliar, scarred—spins and bolts toward the back of the house.

Instinct takes over.

I explode into a sprint, my feet pounding against the earth as I chase after him. This is my land. My home. My legacy. And no stranger slinking in the night has the right to trespass here.

He's fast, but I am faster. Every inch of this farm is written into my bones, the land answering me as I push forward, closing the distance between us. He veers into the southern orchard, thinking the maze of trees will save him.

It won't.

I follow, my breath controlled, my steps precise. I don't need a light. He does.

Fool.

He's barely five feet ahead when he makes a misstep, catching on a root, stumbling. I lunge, seizing the collar of his jacket, dragging him to the ground with force enough to send us both crashing. His body thuds against the frozen soil. I don't hesitate. My knee slams into his chest, pinning him, my knife hovering just inches from his throat.

He gasps, his eyes wild with terror. "Look—no—I'm sorry! I was only hungry!"

I narrow my eyes. "On the porch?"

"I was—just leaving a note! With some coin for the apples." His voice shakes, but something about him is off.

I lean in, my voice cold as the night air. "You. Don't. Belong. Here."

The words scrape from my throat, raw and furious. The knife in my hand trembles—not with fear, but something deeper, something dark.

The man squirms beneath me, his scarred face twisted in desperation. "I'll go! Please! Just let me go—I won't be any trouble!"

I don't move.

Silence stretches between us, thick and suffocating. I press down harder, my knee digging into his ribs, feeling them flex beneath the pressure. I know the kind of men who leave scars like his. I know the kind of men who survive them, too. I'm no killer, but he doesn't know that. The best I can hope for is that he will feel my threats and leave.

"I'm going to let you up," I say, voice low and sharp. "But if you try anything, remember—I have a knife."

Slowly, I ease back, allowing him to scramble to his feet, my knife still poised between us.

He reaches for his satchel, and I snap, "What are you doing?"

He freezes, hands trembling as he pulls out an Essence lamp—just like mine. His fingers fumble as he flicks it on. A warm glow spills over him, making him seem smaller. Weaker. He's not as desperate-looking as he pretended to be.

He turns to leave, stumbling toward the trees.

"The road is that way," I correct, my voice like steel.

He nods wordlessly and hurries in the right direction. I watch him disappear into the night, tracking the slow fade of his light until it vanishes completely.

But the unease doesn't leave me.

Something about him gnaws at my gut—the scars, the way he moved, the way he spoke. He wasn't some starving traveler. He wasn't just here for apples. I don't need more worries, but here they are, pressing against me like an unseen hand.

I turn back toward the house, my mind buzzing.

Then I see it.

A piece of paper, folded neatly on the porch.

Frowning, I bend down and pick it up.

I unfold it, the ink sharp and deliberate, every letter carved into the paper with careful precision.

I'LL SEE YOU LATER, SON.

A threat? A promise?

Either way, it's a chilling vow I cannot ignore.

#

The dawn of our land does not ease into existence. There is no slow brightening, no gentle shift from night to morning. Instead, at precisely six each day, the world jolts awake as the sky transitions from an abyss of inky blackness to a cold, luminous expanse. Depending on the season, this shift washes the landscape in muted tones of white and gray, stark and unnatural. It is a wonder I've witnessed every morning of my life, yet it never ceases to unsettle me.

Just as predictably, at precisely six each evening, the opposite occurs. The light vanishes as if swallowed whole, leaving behind an impenetrable darkness—a void so absolute that even the strongest Essence lamps barely carve through it.

We left the farm as the world flickered to life, the daylight turning on in its usual abrupt fashion. Five hours separate us from the city, and we wanted an early start.

The day is slightly warmer than yesterday, though the air still carries an unnatural chill. The sky, while a fraction brighter, retains its heavy overcast hue—more like a dimly lit ceiling than an endless sky.

Today will be long.

The Naming Ceremony is an all-day affair, stretching late into the afternoon. In past years, I had looked forward to these events—the celebration, the music, the endless food. It was a time of joy, of gathering. But this year is different. I am different.

There was a time when the night after the Naming was something I eagerly awaited. We would either stay in the city or camp outside its walls, gathered around a roaring fire, sharing stories beneath the great dark expanse. My parents would tell me tales from their youth, their voices weaving magic into the flames. Other families would join, and for those few hours, the world was simple, safe.

But those nights are gone.

Nobody camps anymore. Not since the stories of attacks—of travelers vanishing without a trace. The Council forbids night travel now, though it hardly needs enforcing. Everyone knows the dangers.

I miss the world as it was before fear took hold.

My father sits beside my mother in the small wagon, bundled against the crisp air, while I walk ahead with Daisy. The steady rhythm of her hooves is a comforting constant in the face of my restless thoughts. Then my father speaks, pulling me back into the moment.

"So he just left? No trouble?"

"Yes," I answer, keeping my voice even. "After I pinned him down, he just pleaded with me to let him go."

I don't mention the note.

My father chuckles, shaking his head. "Look at you—I'd want no part of you either."

I force a smile, but my mind remains elsewhere. The plan is to meet Elena and her aunt and uncle before heading to the city together. But my thoughts are tangled in the note, the ring, the past month—everything I've tried to reason away.

The note was fake. It had to be.

The man I tackled wasn't Theron, so why should I believe his message? If the note was a fraud, then the ring could be, too.

And yet…

I can't stop my mind from circling back, searching for cracks in my own logic. Some things don't fit, and the more I push them aside, the more they gnaw at the edges of my thoughts. The Keepers—I saw them. That was real. I can't explain it away, and yet, I haven't thought about them as much as I should. My mind refuses to linger on them, as if instinctively recoiling from something it cannot make sense of.

The man this morning was probably just another fool who bought into the rumors, hoping to rattle me. But Brennan and his cryptic warning—that was something else entirely.

The road stretches ahead, and soon, we approach Elena's farm. Her family is already waiting. I've always liked her aunt and uncle—warm, quick to smile, good neighbors over the years.

Elena stands next to Wren, their sturdy horse, her dark hair swept back in a loose braid. It takes only a few minutes to hitch Wren beside Daisy, exchange pleasantries, and set off once more toward the city.

Elena walks beside me, and I should be grateful for her company. Yet, as usual, I find myself tongue-tied.

Then, she speaks, her voice breaking through the rhythm of our footsteps.

"You seem miles away. Are you alright?"

Her tone is light, but her gaze is sharp, searching.

I glance at her—those clear, knowing eyes, that small, playful smile that always seems to see through me.

I hesitate.

Because the truth is, I don't know.

I offer Elena a half-hearted smile. "I'm just thinking about the Naming." The words are a flimsy shield, barely concealing the storm inside me. My gaze stays fixed ahead, avoiding the quiet intensity of her concern. The familiar crunch of gravel beneath our boots fills the silence that follows.

She nods, but I can tell she isn't convinced. "It's more than that, though. Isn't it?" Her voice is soft, but there's no mistaking the insistence beneath it. She steps closer, close enough that I can feel the warmth of her presence even through the chill in the air.

I sigh, the weight of the past few weeks pressing against my ribs. "Yeah, it's... it's been a strange few weeks," I admit, feeling the first thread of my resolve loosening. I hadn't meant to say it, but the words slip out anyway, like water finding a crack in stone. Voicing it out loud makes it real.

The distance between us shrinks—not just physically, but in a way that feels deeper, unspoken. "Everything's different this year," I continue, my voice quieter. "Not just the Naming. There are things I've learned... things I don't understand." The confession hangs between us, raw and uncertain.

Elena walks in step with me, never rushing, never pushing. "Change can be terrifying," she says, her voice steady, "but it can also lead to growth. You're not alone in this."

I glance at her, and for the first time today, I feel like I'm not carrying all of this on my own. Encouraged, I go deeper, speaking of my uncertainty, the weight of expectations, and the fear of being pulled away from the only life I've ever known. And then, finally, the truth.

"It's true, you know. About my birth father." The words tumble out, and suddenly my chest feels lighter.

Elena doesn't look shocked. Instead, she smiles knowingly and squeezes my arm. "I had a feeling." She shrugs, her expression warm. "Like I said before, it changes nothing."

Her words settle in my chest like a stone dropping into still water, their ripples spreading outward. She's right. My parents were right. It changes nothing—nothing important, anyway. I am still me, despite whose blood runs through my veins. My parents are my parents. Knowing the truth of my origins doesn't rewrite the life I've lived or the choices I've made.

But what it *could* mean for my future… that's the part that gnaws at me.

"You're right," I say, looking down into her pale purple eyes. "Theron being my birth father doesn't change who I am. But my parents think he's going to be here today." My fingers drift absentmindedly to the outline of the ring beneath my jacket, the cool metal pressing against my skin.

"For your sake, I hope he is."

There's something in the way she says it, something I can't quite place.

"Why do you say that?"

"Because then you'll get some answers. You *need* answers, Jerrick."

Before I can respond, the murmur of running water reaches our ears, soft yet insistent. The small stream ahead has drawn the attention of the horses, and Daisy lets out an eager whinny, her hooves quickening. We slow our pace, and soon my parents and Elena's aunt and uncle climb down from the wagon to stretch their legs while the horses drink.

Elena and I stand apart from the others, facing each other as the moment lingers. The air between us shifts, heavier now with unspoken thoughts. I feel an impulse, a pull, an urge to tell her everything—the Keepers, the note, the encounter in the woods. But something holds me back. Not fear of her reaction, but fear of what it all *means*. Saying it out loud would make it real.

She seems to sense my hesitation. Her fingers brush lightly against mine, fleeting but deliberate. "Whatever it is, Jerrick, when you're ready, I'm here." Her voice is quiet but certain. "You don't have to carry it all by yourself."

The simplicity of her words is a balm against the weight pressing down on me. I nod, a silent promise to both of us—one day, I will tell her.

The conversation fades, but the moment between us lingers. As we resume our journey, the wagon creaking back into motion, I steal a glance at her. I like the direction our friendship is heading. She is my tether in a world that feels increasingly uncertain.

In this moment, I understand that while the future is uncertain, the bonds we forge along the way are what truly guide us. With a deep breath, I step forward, ready to face whatever lies ahead—not because I have all the answers, but because I no longer have to search for them alone.

After a while, Elena falls back into step beside me, her expression distant, contemplative. The weight of our conversation lingers in the air between us, heavy with unspoken truths and the quiet comfort of understanding.

"Elena," I say, glancing over at her. My curiosity has been gnawing at me ever since she spoke about my potential, about believing in me when I can't always believe in myself. "I've never been good with change. I find comfort in knowing what to expect, in having control over my own path. But you…" I shake my head, still unable to grasp the depth of her certainty. "You seem to think I'm capable of something more, even when I don't see it myself. Why? What makes you so sure I can handle whatever comes my way?"

She pauses, her gaze fixed on the horizon as though she's searching for the right words among the endless stretch of sky. When she finally looks back at me, her expression is unreadable. "Jerrick, do you believe in destiny? That some paths are laid out for us long before we ever take our first steps?"

I consider her question, my thoughts immediately drifting to the past weeks—the revelations, the note, the Keepers and their cryptic warnings. *Everything has changed.* Had it, though? Or had I simply been forced to see what was always waiting beneath the surface?

"I used to think we made our own destiny," I admit slowly. "But now, I'm not so sure."

A small, knowing smile tugs at the corners of her lips. "My mother—may Sylvana watch over her—had a gift," she says softly. "She saw glimpses of the future. Never full visions, just fragments, like pieces of a puzzle. Before she passed, she told me that I would bond… and that I would stand beside someone who would change the course of everything."

A shiver runs down my spine. "And you think that's… me?"

Elena doesn't answer right away. Instead, she watches me carefully, as if weighing something unseen. "I don't know for certain," she says at last, her voice quiet but firm. "But I believe you're part of

something much bigger than any of us realize. My mother's words…
they've guided me, led me to make choices I wouldn't have otherwise."

Her gaze flickers with something I can't name, an intensity that
suggests there's more she's not telling me. More she's *not ready* to tell me.

I open my mouth to press her further, to demand the missing
pieces to this ever-growing puzzle, but she reaches out, placing a hand
on my shoulder—a grounding, deliberate touch. "Not yet," she
murmurs. "When the time is right, I promise you'll know everything. For
now, just know that I'm with you. No matter what comes next, we'll face
it together."

There's something final about the way she says it, something
that tells me no amount of pushing will make her speak before she's
ready. Still, her assurance settles something deep in my chest—an
unexpected but undeniable sense of *hope.*

As we continue forward, the festival's energy begins to take
shape in the distance—the hum of the crowd, the faint strains of music
carried on the wind. The closer we get, the more I feel it—an unseen
current shifting around me, pulling me toward something I don't yet
understand.

This day, this moment—it's more than just a Naming
Ceremony.

With each step, I feel the threads of my past, present, and
uncertain future weaving together, tightening into something I can no
longer ignore. *Destiny.* Whatever it is, whatever it means, I am walking
toward it. And whatever awaits me on the other side of this day… I
know now I won't be facing it alone.

#

The city feels wrong.

During the festival, the streets of Four Rivers are usually alive
with color and sound, overflowing with laughter, music, and the mingling
scents of roasted meats and sweet confections. But as we enter, it's clear
that something has shifted. The decorations are still here, draped along
rooftops and lining the streets as they always are, yet they feel out of
place, like echoes of a past that no longer belong to the present.

The sky, heavy and gray, presses down on everything, dulling the
vibrancy that the festival is supposed to bring. The usual revelry is
missing—replaced by huddled groups speaking in hushed voices, their

eyes darting toward the walls rather than the festivities. The few musicians who have taken the stage play to a distracted audience, their melodies drifting through the air, hollow and unheeded. Vendors still man their stalls, but lines are short, and coin exchanges are sparse.

The city is full. It should be bursting with joy, with families reuniting and old friends embracing. Instead, it feels like everyone has gathered out of obligation rather than celebration. If attendance wasn't mandated, I wonder how many would have stayed home.

Then there are the guards. More than usual. Their presence is expected during the festival, but this is different. They don't watch the crowds. They barely seem to register us at all. Instead, their gazes are fixed outward, past the towering stone walls of the city, toward something unseen. The ones stationed at the gates barely spared a glance at the bow strapped across my back. I should have been stopped, questioned at least, but they were too preoccupied, their shoulders tight with tension, hands resting too readily on the pommels of their swords.

It's unsettling. The Council's rule is absolute—unyielding. There is no rebellion, no threat of an opposing force. No armies march against us. So what are they looking for?

We drop Daisy and Wren off at the stables and make our way toward the food tent, a massive temporary structure with an open front and a pitched roof, meant to shelter the crowd while still allowing the sounds and scents of the festival to spill out into the streets. The air is thick with the smell of sizzling meat, but even that seems subdued, unable to break through the unshakable quiet pressing down on the city.

"I knew it would be like this," my mother murmurs as we weave through the crowd, her voice subdued, "but seeing it... feeling it... it's worse than I imagined." She hasn't been to the city in months, and neither has my father. "I remember how much I used to look forward to the festival each year. Now, I just want to sit down and not say anything."

"That would be a first," my father quips, his grin teasing.

My mother swats him on the shoulder, but even their playful exchange is laced with a tiredness I don't like seeing in them.

"I don't know about you all," Elena's uncle chimes in, his tone lighter, almost forced, "but I'm hungry, and I see old Gallic manning the grill over there."

The food tent should be bustling—filled with the clatter of dishes, the warmth of conversation, the occasional burst of laughter from an old story retold. But as we step inside, the atmosphere is just as stifling as the streets. People sit close together at the long communal tables, heads bent over their plates, speaking in low murmurs. Their voices blend with the distant music, a soft, uneasy hum of fear and uncertainty.

I catch snippets of their conversations as I pass by.

The Fog. The decay. Winter is coming too fast. The attacks.

People are afraid.

It's the first time I truly see it, feel it—how much the world is shifting, how quickly the ground beneath us is crumbling. I've been so wrapped up in my own problems, in my own small world of the farm and my own questions, that I never stopped to consider how much this was affecting everyone else.

We gather our food and settle at a table, our group eating in silence. The tension around us is thick, pressing against our ribs like a weight that refuses to lift. The food is good, but I barely taste it. My thoughts are too tangled, my senses too attuned to the quiet that hangs over everything.

Then I hear it.

The slow, uneven shuffle of footsteps.

My mother, sitting across from me, suddenly looks up, her expression shifting, softening.

I glance over my shoulder.

An old man approaches, his gait uneven, as if the earth itself resists his every step. He leans heavily on a cane, dragging his left foot behind him as he moves. Step. Drag. Step. Drag. The sound scrapes against my nerves, something about it unsettling in a way I can't quite explain.

The hush around us deepens.

Harlan.

Even before my mother greets him, I recognize the old friend of my parents, a fixture from my childhood. He's always seemed larger than life—his presence filling whatever space he occupied. Once, he was a giant in my eyes, towering over my father with thick, powerful hands that could crush stone and a booming laugh that carried across the farm like stampeding cattle.

Now, though, time has whittled him down. His back is stooped, his once-mighty hands gnarled with age, thick fingers curled inward like the roots of an old tree. His limp is new, his steps uneven, marked by the slow drag of his left foot. It's hard to reconcile this version of him with the man I remember.

Still, his grip is firm as he places a heavy hand on my shoulder. "You've gotten bigger, Jerrick!" His voice bursts through the thick silence of the food tent like a hammer striking an anvil, unbothered by the hushed conversations and wary glances around us.

I offer a grin. "And you've gotten older."

He throws his head back and lets out a booming laugh that startles a few people nearby. They turn, their eyes flickering between us before hurriedly looking away. "That I have, my dear boy! That I have!"

He glances around the table, his sharp gaze sweeping over my father, my mother, then Elena's family. "Mind if I sit?"

At my father's nod, he eases himself into the chair beside me, his movements slower than they used to be, as if his bones ache with the weight of years lived hard. When he finally settles, his jovial expression fades, replaced with something more serious.

"How was the trip in this morning?"

"Pretty uneventful," my father replies, eyeing him curiously. "When did you get in?"

"A couple of days ago. I've been staying with my son in the market district." He pauses, his fingers absently tracing the wood grain of the table. "What about you?"

"We arrived about an hour ago," my father says. "After dropping the horses off, this was our first stop."

Harlan exhales sharply through his nose, shaking his head. "So you haven't heard?"

A quiet heaviness settles over the table.

"Haven't heard what?" my father asks, his voice cautious.

Harlan glances around, lowering his voice for the first time since he arrived. "The attacks. Those creatures people have been whispering about—they've been attacking travelers coming into the city all day."

The words hit with the force of a hammer.

"Valthrun help us." My mother covers her mouth with her hand, her voice barely above a breath.

A silence follows, thick and uneasy.

"It's the land," Harlan mutters, almost to himself. "It's turning on us." He seems embarrassed by his own words, but they strike something in me. He's not the only one who's thought it.

Because, isn't that the only explanation?

The land gives us everything—our crops, our water, the very essence that powers the lights above us. But what do we give it in return? We take. We strip it bare, expecting it to keep providing, never thinking that it might one day decide we aren't worthy of its gifts.

We were taught in Civic Education that while the land isn't sentient in the way that we are, it is conscious. It feels. It remembers. And though it has always provided for us, the Council has long warned that if we take too much, if we disrupt the balance, the land could withdraw its favor. That's why the Council was formed—to ensure that didn't happen. To regulate our use of Essence, to keep us from drawing too much and tipping the scales.

But maybe that balance is already broken.

"I know how it sounds," Harlan says, rubbing a hand down his face. "But what else could it be? It's no secret that winter is the land's time of rest. It stops growing, pulls its energy inward. But now... these creatures, these things are appearing, and they're attacking people." He looks around the table, gauging our reactions, and when nobody interrupts, he presses on. "I've been talking to people all morning. I think there's a pattern."

"What kind of pattern?" Elena's uncle asks, though his tone suggests he doesn't expect to believe the answer.

Harlan leans forward, lowering his voice further. "They're attacking people with Essence-drawing devices."

The weight of his words hangs in the air.

We all exchange glances, but it's Elena's uncle who speaks first, his voice edged with skepticism. "Are you saying it's trying to kill people who use too much Essence?" His question is more accusation than curiosity.

"I'm saying it doesn't want us channeling its Essence when it's trying to rest." Harlan's voice is calm, but there's something hard underneath it, something unwavering.

And that's what unsettles me most.

Because I think he might be right.

"What aren't you saying?" My mother's voice is calm but weighted, her sharp gaze flicking from Harlan to me. I know that look. She's thinking the same thing I am.

Harlan exhales slowly, rubbing his knotted hands together before he speaks. "I've heard stories—SoulCasters being attacked and killed. Not just this morning, but for weeks now. People are saying these creatures are going after anyone using Essence-drawing devices; lamps, water heaters, stoves, even weapons."

A heavy silence settles over our table. My father's fingers tighten around the handle of his knife, his thumb absently stroking the worn leather grip. A habit of his when he's concerned. My mother's eyes flick to his hand, and they share a brief, silent conversation.

I can't help but glance around. The tent is filled with light, each lamp feeding on the land's Essence, their glow steady but… dim. Too dim. Is it just my imagination, or is the air itself growing colder? A ripple of unease shivers down my spine.

Then I notice something else.

Other people are listening.

At the table next to us, a group of merchants has stopped eating, their eyes fixed on Harlan. They're barely trying to pretend otherwise. Not that it matters. Harlan's voice, deep and gruff, carries even when he's not trying. And now, the whispers start, spreading like ink in water, bleeding into every conversation around us.

Fog. Decay. Winter. Attacks.

The words swirl through the air, fragments of fear twisting together. Off to my left, a group of people my age has huddled closer. A young woman with bright red hair gestures wildly, her expression a mix of anger and panic. An elderly couple nearby clutches each other's hands, faces etched with something that looks like resignation.

I glance up at the nearest lamp, watching as it flickers again. It's not just dim, it's struggling.

The land is rejecting us.

A chill seeps into my bones, curling at the edges of my thoughts. The sense of unease has grown into something tangible, something thick in the air, pressing against my skin like unseen hands.

Then— a loud crash.

I spin around just in time to see a vendor's table collapse in the back of the tent, sending wooden crates and food spilling across the ground. A small commotion erupts, people rushing to help, but their movements are frantic—too frantic.

It's nothing. A simple accident. But it's enough.

The tension in the air snaps.

The whispers turn into nervous murmurs, then low, panicked voices. Someone hisses about an omen, about bad luck. Others mutter about the creatures, the land, the Council. The quiet oppression of the festival is breaking apart, cracking under the weight of collective fear.

Across from me, my father exhales and shakes his head. "Well, Harlan, you certainly know how to set fire to a room."

Harlan doesn't quite smile, but there's a ghost of something in his expression. "And here I thought I had lost my touch."

Before I can respond, a gentle touch brushes against my hand. "Jerrick?"

Elena's voice.

I turn, meeting her steady gaze. Her fingers barely graze mine before she pulls back, but the warmth lingers. "Would you walk with me for a moment?"

I nod, pushing back from the table. "Is everything okay?" I ask as we step outside, the cold air hitting my skin like a slap.

She hesitates, looking down before answering. "I don't know. Remember what I told you earlier? About my mom?" Her tone is quiet, contemplative.

I nod. "Yeah."

She swallows, her breath curling in the crisp air. "Something happened in there that reminded me of something she said…" She stops mid-sentence, her expression shifting in an instant.

Her hand shoots out, grabbing my arm.

"Jerrick, behind the bush—move!"

She yanks me backward just as a familiar figure strides past. I barely manage to stay silent, my back pressing against the rough bark of a tree.

Bowen.

He moves quickly, his head turning sharply from side to side, scanning the crowd. Looking for someone.

Looking for me.

I glance at Elena, and she nods. "Come on, I know a place where we can talk. It's not far."

She leads me through the winding side streets, away from the thick of the festival. My heart pounds in my chest—not from fear, but from the strange significance of the moment. This city, these streets, used to feel familiar. Safe. Now, every shadow seems deeper, every step carries an echo of uncertainty.

Finally, we slip into a small alcove, hidden behind a tall fence. A single stone bench overlooks a quiet garden.

"Wow," Elena murmurs, taking it in. "This place is incredible. I bet it's even more beautiful when the flowers are in bloom."

I nod. "I used to come here a lot when I was a kid. When my parents let me roam the city, I'd bring a book and read here for hours."

She turns to me then, her eyes deep and distant, filled with something I can't quite name. "Jerrick… there's something you need to know before I tell you this."

I tense. "Okay."

"My mom died when I was seven."

I nod, but she continues before I can speak. "I know you know that, but it's important to remember, because I was only seven when she told me the things she saw. That was fourteen years ago. I fight every day to hold on to those memories, but… I don't know if I'm remembering it all correctly. I just need you to know that before I say anything else."

Her voice is steady, but there's something fragile underneath, something raw.

I nod. "I understand."

She exhales, long and slow, before looking up at me. "Then listen carefully, because this might change everything."

Elena's words linger between us, heavy with an unspoken weight I can't quite define. The idea that her mother had seen glimpses of the future, entrusted those visions to her as a child, is almost too much to believe. And yet, standing here, watching the sadness in her eyes, I know she's telling the truth—at least, the truth as she knows it.

It strikes me then how heavy a burden she's carried. For fourteen years, she's held onto fragments of a future she couldn't fully understand, a puzzle missing too many pieces. And she was just a child when she received them, too young to truly grasp their meaning. How lonely that must have been. How terrifying.

But what chills me more than anything is the fact that her mother had been too afraid to write them down. What could be so dangerous about a vision that simply recording it was a risk? What had she seen that made her fear leaving behind even the smallest trace of it?

I want to know. I need to know.

Elena exhales, the sound barely audible over the distant hum of the festival. "I'm sorry, Jerrick," she says at last. "I'm having a hard time finding my words. There are… things about me you don't know. I'll always be honest with you, but there are some secrets that I can't share."

Her voice is soft, but the hesitation in it is like a blade, sharp and deliberate.

I frown. "Why not?"

"Because they aren't mine alone to share." She pauses, and I swear I see the flicker of an internal battle cross her features before she finally whispers, "I hope that when you find out—because you will—that you'll forgive me."

I don't know what unnerves me more: the fact that she's keeping secrets or the fact that she assumes I'll need to forgive her for them.

The words *I understand* rise to my lips, but I hesitate. Because the truth is, I don't. Not really.

She's always been a part of my life, steady and unwavering. And now, she's admitting there are pieces of her I don't truly know. I'd be lying if I said that didn't unsettle me.

I take a step closer, lowering my voice. "Is it something dangerous?"

She doesn't answer right away. That, in itself, is an answer.

Something flickers across her expression—doubt? Fear? Guilt? It's gone too quickly to tell.

A knot tightens in my stomach. If she won't tell me now, what does that mean for the future?

Before she can respond, I force myself to exhale, to push down the gnawing uncertainty clawing its way up my throat. I won't push her. Whatever this is, whatever she's holding back—it's bigger than just the two of us.

"I won't ask you to say more than you're ready to," I say finally, carefully choosing each word. "But understand, Elena, that whatever it is… we'll face it together."

I meet her gaze and hold it, watching for a reaction.

Her lips part slightly, and for a brief moment, I think she's going to tell me something—anything—but instead, she just exhales, a mix of relief and something else I can't quite name.

She reaches out, just barely brushing her fingers against my forearm. It's the smallest of touches, but it speaks volumes.

"Thank you, Jerrick," she murmurs.

I nod, but inside, my mind is reeling.

Because for the first time, I feel like I don't know her at all.

I mean every word. Despite the mysteries and unspoken truths between us, I feel a connection with Elena—a trust that wasn't there before, or maybe one I hadn't fully acknowledged until now. Whatever lies ahead, I know it will test us in ways we can't yet imagine.

Elena exhales, her voice softer than before. "I know there's a lot going on," she says, studying me carefully. "And we've known each other our whole lives, but your understanding means everything to me. It's like I'm getting to know you in a way I never have before."

I feel it too. I've always had a crush on Elena—admired her from afar, wondered what it would be like to be something more. But this feels different. More real. Deeper. As if something has shifted between us, allowing me to see a side of her that was always just out of reach. She was always kind, always present, but never this close. Never this vulnerable.

Things changed—for me, at least—when she stood up for me against Bowen.

"I feel the same way, Elena."

She smiles, taking a small step closer, but the warmth in her expression fades. I see it happen—the moment the impact of what she brought me here to say returns.

"Sometimes," she begins, choosing her words carefully, "I don't remember things my mother told me until something happens to bring them back. She used to say that she didn't see the future clearly. That it was like getting glimpses of puzzle pieces that didn't make sense until she saw more of them. My memories of what she told me are the same way. Scattered. Unclear. I don't always trust them."

She takes a breath, her fingers curling into fists before relaxing again. "But in there, when Harlan said, *It's the land. It's starting to turn on us*—something clicked."

I don't rush her. I can see the fear in her eyes, feel the way she's searching for the right way to say whatever it is that's clawing at her mind.

So I wait. I hold her gaze and I wait.

Finally, she speaks.

"I might be remembering this wrong, or maybe I'm putting the pieces together the wrong way. But my mom once told me that the land would rise up. That thousands would die."

A sharp chill runs down my spine.

Elena's hands start to shake, and without thinking, I reach out, wrapping mine around hers. She gives me a thin, trembling smile before squeezing my hands in return.

"She said it would start on a day of great importance." Elena hesitates, then swallows hard. "Jerrick, I can't shake the feeling that she was talking about today."

The words settle between us like an unspoken prophecy, thick and suffocating.

The land rising up? Thousands dying?

It's too big. Too terrifying. Too possible.

The city already feels off. The festival is wrong. The guards are uneasy. The land is colder, darker, and the people are whispering about attacks. Everything is out of balance.

I tighten my grip on Elena's hands, grounding her as much as myself. "Elena… that's a lot to carry with you," I say softly, the words too weak for the weight they bear. The Naming Ceremony already feels like the cusp of something bigger than me. If this—if what she's saying is true—then today isn't just about me. It's about something much, much worse.

I study her, searching for doubt, for hesitation, for anything that would tell me she isn't as certain as she sounds.

But I don't find it.

Instead, I find resolve.

"Your mother had visions," I say carefully. "You trust what she saw?"

Elena nods. "I do. She was rarely wrong."

A slow breath pushes past my lips. I want to argue. To tell her this is just a bad feeling. That it's the weight of the ceremony, the fear of change, the whisper of rumors making things seem worse than they are.

But I can't.

Not after the past few weeks. Not after the Keepers. Not after the note. Not after everything.

"Okay," I say, straightening. "If she was right, then we need to be careful. We need to stay alert and watch for anything unusual."

Elena nods, but her expression is uncertain. "I don't know what to look for, Jerrick. My mother didn't say what would happen. Just that the land would rise and that…" she hesitates, lowering her voice, "that a lot of people would die."

A sick sense of dread settles in my stomach.

This isn't just an event anymore. It's a countdown.

I nod. "Then we stick together. Keep our eyes open. If anything happens, we'll be ready."

Even as I say the words, I'm not sure I believe them.

Because how do you prepare for something you don't understand?

And what if the land is already rising?

A quiet determination settles over me. If Elena's mother was right, if today truly held some dark inevitability, then I wouldn't wait for it to come to us. I'd meet it head-on.

More than that—I'd protect my family. I'd protect her.

I squeeze Elena's hands one last time. "Thank you for telling me," I say, meaning every word. "We'll get through this, whatever *this* turns out to be."

The words are more than just reassurance—they are a promise.

Elena searches my face, her eyes flickering with uncertainty before she nods. "Do you think we should tell your parents? My aunt and uncle?"

"No," I say too quickly, my voice sharper than I intend. "Not yet."

She frowns slightly, but I press on. "Let's not worry them if we don't have to. We'll just stay close."

Her lips press together, unconvinced. "But during the ceremony, we'll be separated."

"I know," I admit, my stomach twisting at the thought. "But there will be guards everywhere. If anything happens, I'll find you."

Elena studies me, searching for the same certainty I keep giving her, but I don't know if she finds it. Still, she nods. "Alright. We should get back to the tent."

We start walking, but neither of us lets go of the other's hand.

Everything will be okay.

That's what I told her.

But even as I said it, the words rang hollow in my own ears.

I glance around at the crowd, at the faces of people who, like us, have no idea what might come next. Some are whispering, others going through the motions of the festival with forced smiles and dulled excitement. I wonder if they feel it too—the weight pressing down, the unshakable sense that something is *off*.

And yet, I told her everything will be okay.

It's a strange thing, this duality I live in—offering reassurance while being unable to accept it myself.

I think of my parents, of the quiet strength in my father's voice, the unwavering warmth in my mother's hands. I wonder how many times they've told me everything would be fine when they weren't sure of it themselves. And maybe… maybe that's what it means to be strong— not to be fearless, not to be certain, but to carry the uncertainty anyway.

I let out a slow breath.

It's a subtle but profound shift within me.

No, I don't believe that everything will be okay.

But I will face it anyway.

I stop walking, turning to Elena. She looks up at me, waiting, searching.

And in that moment, I know.

We won't be okay because of luck, or chance, or fate.

We'll be okay because we'll fight to be.

I squeeze her hand one final time. "We'll face whatever comes," I tell her. This time, my voice doesn't waver.

And this time—I mean it.

Chapter 7

Jerrick

The city is too full, too crowded, yet it feels empty. People move about in slow, uneasy currents, their murmurs hushed beneath the weight of something unspoken. The Naming Festival should be alive with laughter and music, but the air is thick with tension. I can feel it—we all can.

The food tent looms ahead, and I should be stepping inside with my family, but then—

"Jerrick!"

The voice cuts through the crowd, sharp and urgent. I turn, heart already pounding, to see Bowen hurrying toward me.

He isn't here to fight.

His usual arrogance is gone, replaced by something else—something I can't quite place. But Elena isn't fooled. She moves instantly, shifting into a fighter's stance, her right foot sliding forward, her hand already on the dagger at her waist.

Her movements are fluid, instinctive, as if she's been waiting for this moment. Her eyes narrow to silver slits, her body tensed like a bowstring ready to snap.

Bowen sees it. Feels it.

He steps back. His eyes flicker to the blade, then to her face, and for the first time in my life—Bowen looks afraid.

His hands go up, palms out. "I deserve that," he says quickly, voice tight. "But I'm not here to cause trouble."

Elena doesn't move at first. She's reading him, dissecting his stance, his breath, his posture. When she finally pulls her hand away from the dagger, I swear I see him exhale in relief.

"Alright," I say, keeping my voice steady. "Talk."

Bowen shifts uncomfortably. "Can we do this in private?"

I hesitate. Elena doesn't. She steps closer to me, a silent wall between us and him, her presence grounding me.

I glance at her, then back at Bowen. "Fine. I know a spot."

We weave through the city streets until we reach the alcove— again.

Bowen glances around, taking it in. "Huh. Never knew this was here."

I don't bother answering. "What do you want, Bowen?" My tone isn't hostile, but it isn't welcoming either.

He exhales sharply, rubbing the back of his neck. "I… look. I deserved what happened," he says, his voice tight with something I don't recognize. "I know how I treated you." He lets out a humorless laugh. "I won't apologize because I don't think you'd accept it."

I don't respond. He's right.

He clears his throat. "I'm here to warn you. Whether he is or isn't your father, I overheard mine talking about setting a trap for Theron."

Everything in me freezes.

Elena stiffens beside me. Her hand hovers near her dagger again, eyes locked onto Bowen like she can pull the truth out of him by force. This isn't the same girl from a few weeks back… or has this been her all along?

"What kind of trap?" I ask, my voice quieter now, controlled.

"I don't know," Bowen admits, jaw tightening. "But I do know that he's been talking about you. And Theron. I heard him talking to Rorick weeks ago, and now this?" He shakes his head. "Something bad is coming, and I just… I wanted to tell you."

Elena steps forward, eyes flashing. "Why?" she demands. "Why warn us?"

Bowen doesn't hesitate. "Because I hate my father." His words are flat, cold, but his eyes betray something deeper—a resentment that's been festering for years.

The weight of that hangs between us, unspoken. I've never thought about Bowen as anything other than an obstacle. But now I see the cracks in his armor.

"He kept saying 'the Awakening,'" Bowen mutters, shaking his head. "Like it was some kind of event. And you're a part of it. You're not safe, Jerrick. You should leave the city. Now."

Leave? Leave?

I almost laugh. The Naming is required—if I leave, the Council will come for my family. They'd imprison them. Or worse.

"They're going to lock the city down," Bowen says, his voice turning urgent. "I was told not to join the Naming. Whatever they're planning, it's going to happen today."

My pulse roars in my ears. I stare at Bowen, and he meets my gaze without flinching. He means this.

"I'm trying to make amends," he says. "And if ruining my father's plans does that, then even better."

I take a step forward. "Why now?" My voice is quieter now, but the question demands an answer. "Why warn me today?"

Bowen hesitates, his throat bobbing.

"…Because of what you said outside the magistrate's office." His voice is rough, almost reluctant. "You… you apologized to me. Like you were the one in the wrong. And it made me realize that just because I hate my father doesn't mean I have to act like him." His looks at his feet. "I've never been easy on you."

His jaw tightens. He looks away. "I know I don't deserve your trust, and I don't expect it. But I need you to listen. If you can get out, do it."

His words settle into my bones like cold lead.

Elena grips my arm, grounding me, but my thoughts are already racing.

If Theron really is coming today… if my father and Rorick have been planning something… and if what Elena told me earlier is true…

Then today is already set in motion.

Despite all of that. Despite everything that Elena told me, the man at the farm this morning, Theron, the Naming, and now Bowen, his words *I've never been easy on you* stick in my mind.

"Not easy on me?" The words come out before I can stop them, sharp and jagged, carrying the weight of years of torment. My hands tremble at my sides, but I don't care. I take a step toward Bowen, my voice rising, years of pent-up emotion bleeding into every syllable.

"That's putting it lightly. You made it your mission to make me hate life. You made me not care if I lived or died. Do you have any idea what your 'not being easy on me' did to me?"

I'm yelling now. My vision is hot, blurred at the edges, anger surging through my veins like a dam finally breaking.

"Jerrick…"

Elena's voice is soft, her hand pressing gently against my chest, a quiet barrier between me and whatever I'm about to do.

Bowen doesn't flinch. His expression doesn't change. Instead, he does something I never expected.

"No. Let him."

His voice is steady, lacking its usual bravado. "I deserve it."

That stops me. It douses my anger just enough for the edges to cool. I step back, but the fire still burns low in my gut.

"I just don't understand why," I say, my voice quieter now, but no less raw. "Why me? What was it about me that made you hate me?"

Bowen doesn't answer right away. For once, he doesn't look away. He holds my gaze, but I can see the battle happening behind his eyes, the war of things left unsaid.

Then he exhales shakily. "My father is a hard man. Impossible to please." His lips press together before he speaks again. "The day you and I met, he beat me because I was late for breakfast." His voice is barely above a whisper now. "I walked into that first Civic Education class, saw you with your father. Saw how he looked at you. How much he loved you. How much you loved him. And I hated you for it."

The words land like a fist to the chest.

Bowen blinks rapidly, his lips quivering slightly as he speaks. "I wanted what you had." He swallows hard, shaking his head as if he can't believe himself. "And in some twisted, messed-up way, I thought if I made you miserable, if I took away what made you happy, then maybe I wouldn't feel so alone."

I don't know what to say to that.

I thought I wanted an explanation. I thought I needed it. But now that I have it, I don't know what to do with it.

The fire inside me dies down, replaced by something more confusing. Not anger. Not relief. Something close to pity.

Bowen looks down, scuffing his boot against the ground. "I know I'm not a good person. I know what I've done. And I'm terrified of becoming my father." His voice falters slightly before he steadies himself. "But standing outside that magistrate's office… watching you apologize to me, like you were the one in the wrong… I realized I already was him."

The silence between us is heavy.

"I want to atone for that." He takes a breath, his voice quiet but firm. "That's why I'm here. That's why I think you should leave. Something is going to happen today, and it involves you."

His gaze lifts to mine, eyes shining—not with weakness, but with something painfully human.

Then, without waiting for a response, he turns and walks away.

I stand frozen, watching him go.

I should say something. But what is there to say?

Forgive him? I don't know if I can. I don't know if I want to.

I glance at Elena, unsure, unmoored. Emotions are complicated, and I've never been good at expressing mine. Bowen's confession—his warning—it leaves me feeling untethered. Was this all an act? Or was it genuine?

Does it even matter?

Elena shifts beside me, arms crossed, gaze still locked on Bowen's retreating figure. "Do you believe him?" she finally asks. Her voice is calm, but beneath it, I hear the same uncertainty I feel.

I exhale, running a hand over the back of my neck. "I don't know." I shake my head. "Bowen and I… we have history. But the fear in his eyes? That was real."

Elena nods slowly, her brows furrowed. "And this 'awakening' he mentioned? That sounds ominous, especially today of all days."

Today. The Naming Ceremony. The guards. The growing unease in the city. It all clicks into place, but the picture still isn't clear.

"Yeah," I murmur, my mind racing. "If they're planning something against Theron, then that means I'm in danger, too." My voice hardens. "And if they're locking down the city, then this isn't just about him. It's about everyone here."

Elena's eyes widen. "If the Council is preparing for something, and Bowen's father is involved, this could be bigger than we think."

I nod, tension winding in my chest. We can't just ignore this. But leaving the city now? Before the Naming? It's impossible. Isn't it?

"Jerrick," Elena's voice softens, but there's steel behind it. "Whatever you decide, I'm with you."

I look down at her, seeing the unwavering certainty in her expression. She isn't afraid.

Her faith in me is unshakable.

I swallow, forcing down my own uncertainty. "If Bowen's warning is true, leaving might be our safest option." I glance toward the festival grounds, my thoughts turning to my parents, to Elena's aunt and uncle. "But we can't leave without them."

Elena nods, squeezing my arm, grounding me. "Then we go to them now. We don't have much time."

I exhale, looking back at the path Bowen disappeared down. Something is coming.

And for the first time in my life, I feel like my fate is no longer my own.

We weave through the dense throngs of festival-goers, the air thick with tension. The weight of Bowen's warning settles over me like a shroud, each step heavier than the last. Every face I pass seems distant, muted, as if the whole city exists in an eerie limbo—waiting.

The festival is in full swing, but the mood is wrong.

The laughter is forced. The music lacks its usual vibrancy. Even the guards, normally unbothered and indifferent, stand rigid, their eyes not on the revelers, but on the walls.

Something is coming.

I spot my parents before we even reach the tent, their expressions mirroring the subdued energy of the festival. My father is standing with his arms crossed, his ever-present knife still sheathed but his hand rests on the hilt. A habit. A precaution.

Elena's family is with them, her aunt and uncle speaking in hushed tones. They sense it too.

I don't waste time.

"Mom. Dad." My voice is low but sharp enough to cut through the din of murmuring voices and distant music. "We need to talk. Now."

My mother stiffens. She knows this tone. My father's expression hardens.

"What's wrong, Jerrick?" she asks, her voice already laced with worry.

I glance at Elena, and she gives me the smallest nod, grounding me. I take a steadying breath, then drop the words like stones into a still pond.

"We just spoke with Bowen."

Their reactions are immediate. My mother's face twists in confusion, my father's frown deepens into something unreadable. Even Elena's uncle, normally quick to scoff, leans in slightly.

I keep going. "He warned us that something dangerous is going to happen today. That the city is going to be locked down. He said my name was mentioned... and Theron's."

The silence is absolute.

My father exhales sharply. "Bowen? And you believe him?"

I don't blame him for the skepticism. I barely know what to believe myself.

Elena steps forward, her voice strong, unwavering. "He looked scared, Thom. This wasn't some ploy. He overheard his father speaking to Rorick about a plan. About Theron. About Jerrick. We don't know exactly what's going to happen, but Bowen was certain of one thing—we shouldn't be here when it does."

My mother's hand flies to her mouth, her eyes wide. "But Jerrick... the Naming Ceremony. If you don't attend—"

"I know," I cut in, tension threading through my voice. "It's required. The Council doesn't just let people walk away from it. But if there's even a chance Bowen's telling the truth, if something is going to happen—do we just wait for it?"

The weight of my words settles over them, a cold realization creeping into their eyes.

My father is the first to move. His shoulders square, his jaw clenches, and when he speaks, it's final.

"We leave. Now. Discreetly. We shouldn't leave all at once."

Elena's uncle nods. "We'll gather our things. You get the horses. We'll meet outside the front gates."

We don't argue.

I take one last look at the festival grounds—at the people still lost in whispered conversations, at the guards standing stiff, at the sky above, painted in dull grays.

I can feel it in my bones. The dam is about to break.

I turn back to my family. "Let's go."

#

The urgency of our escape hums in the air like a taut wire, ready to snap. As we weave through the throngs of festival-goers, their laughter and conversations feel like a thin veil barely concealing the storm brewing beneath. They don't know. They don't realize what's coming.

We move quickly, our pace brisk but controlled, careful not to draw attention. The city is alive with subdued celebration, but to me, it feels like a trap slowly being set.

Every shout from a vendor, every distant clatter of hooves, every flicker of movement at the edge of my vision keeps my pulse hammering. My father walks ahead, his shoulders stiff, his hands clenched at his sides. The knife at his belt is no longer just a habit—it's a necessity.

My mother glances over her shoulder again and again, her breath uneven. I can't tell if she expects Bowen's warning to materialize behind us or if she's just waiting for the moment when everything falls apart.

The stables loom ahead.

The scent of hay and damp wood clings to the air as we step inside. I barely notice it—my ears are tuned for something else. Footsteps that don't belong. A sudden, hushed silence. Anything.

Nothing.

We move swiftly. My father tightens the harness around Daisy and Wren, his movements methodical, but there's a slight tremor in his fingers. My mother checks the supplies—fast, efficient, but her hands shake too.

None of us speak. Words feel too fragile. The sooner we're gone, the better.

We guide the horses back onto the main road, heading toward the city gates. The streets are even more crowded now, the revelers blissfully unaware that their celebration is about to be sealed inside stone walls.

Then, I see them. The guards.

They're standing taller, more rigid than before. Their hands rest near their weapons—not casually, but ready. They barely glance at those entering the city, but those trying to leave… they scrutinize.

My pulse quickens as we near the gates. This is it. If Bowen was lying, we'll pass through. If he was telling the truth—

A guard steps forward, blocking our path. His eyes lock onto me first.

"Where are you headed?" His voice is sharp. Too sharp. He's suspicious.

My father doesn't hesitate. "Just meeting someone outside the city," he says smoothly. "We'll be back before the Naming Ceremony starts."

The guard doesn't move. His eyes flick between us, calculating.

"The city is about to be closed down."

Everything inside me goes still.

Bowen was right.

A part of me had hoped he was lying, had hoped he was playing some twisted game. But this? This is confirmation.

The city is closing.

Which means the rest of what Bowen said… Theron. The trap. My name. It's all real.

"Closed?" My father plays along, feigning ignorance. "Why?"

The guard's face hardens. "That's city business." He waves us off as if we're nothing more than an inconvenience.

My mother isn't so easily dismissed. "When was this decision made?" Her voice is calm, measured, but I hear the edge of worry beneath it. "We had friends ahead of us—middle-aged couple, young woman. Do you know if they left?"

The guard frowns. "I've had people come and go all day. How would I know?" Then, his voice lowers, a touch more serious. "But to answer your question—you're the first people I've turned away."

The first.

As he finishes speaking, the city gates shudder.

With a deep, groaning finality, they swing shut.

BOOM.

The sound reverberates through my chest, through my bones. The gates are sealed.

We are trapped.

I exhale slowly, trying to keep my voice level. "Elena and her aunt and uncle are out there, right?"

My mother nods, her voice distant. "They left when we grabbed the horses. I would think so."

I glance at the massive doors. Stone. Heavy. Unmovable. The only way out.

My mother speaks again, softer this time. "Why do you think they closed the city?"

A cold realization seeps into my bones. Elena and her family are trapped outside the city. Vulnerable. Exposed.

My father's words echo in my head, an attempt at reassurance. "If what Harlan theorized is true, then they should be safe, Jerrick."

I want to believe him. I need to believe him.

"That's right," my mother adds, her voice softer. "They don't carry any essence channeling devices."

That knowledge should bring comfort. It doesn't.

Elena is strong. Her aunt and uncle are seasoned travelers. They know how to survive. But knowing and believing are two very different things. Belief doesn't quiet the gnawing fear in my gut. It doesn't erase the images of unseen creatures lurking just beyond the city walls, of monstrous forms lurking in the darkness. What if they're already too close?

The more I think about it, the worse it gets.

Bowen's warning. The city's sudden lockdown. Harlan's chilling theory. Elena's mother's prophecy. It all points to something catastrophic.

My hands ball into fists, my nails digging into my palms. I hate this helplessness. I hate knowing there's nothing I can do. I can't leave. I can't protect her.

But I can choose what I do next. I take a deep breath, swallowing down my unease. Focus on what you can control. Right now, that means keeping my parents safe. It means seeing this Naming Ceremony through.

I turn to my mother. "Do you trust Theron?" My voice is steadier than I expect.

She doesn't hesitate. "I do. You can trust him, no matter what others say. He's a man of principle."

That's all I need. I nod, a newfound determination settling over me. "Then we go to the Naming Ceremony. He wanted me here. Let's trust in his plan."

#

The moment I step inside, the sheer grandeur of the Naming Hall steals my breath.

The high, vaulted ceilings loom overhead, painted in intricate frescoes—depictions of history, power, sacrifice. The golden glow of essence lamps, suspended from iron fixtures, illuminates the marble floors, polished to a mirror sheen. Everything feels larger than life, a stark contrast to the simplicity of my farm, to the dirt and sweat that make up my daily routine.

But beneath the spectacle, there's something else.

The air carries the distinct scent of sage and oranges, an unmistakable attempt to invoke clarity, calm… control.

A sanctuary. That's what this place is meant to be. But I don't feel safe.

The hall is already filled, buzzing with whispered anxieties and unspoken prayers. I count just over a hundred of us—the twenty-one-year-olds who have come to face our fate.

The tiered seating ensures no one misses the central dais, where the fate of our generation will be decided.

And there, on that raised platform, stands Rorick.

He is flanked by a select few SoulCasters, each one bearing the unmistakable mark of authority, power, and control.

Their presence presses down on the room, a silent reminder that this is no festival. This is judgment.

I slide into my seat among my peers.

The air is taut with nervous energy. Some try to sit tall, forcing a facade of calm indifference, while others fidget, their eyes darting around the hall.

We all know the statistics.

Most of us will walk away unchanged. A few will be bonded. And their lives will never belong to them again.

I exhale slowly, gripping the arms of my chair as the murmurs die down. The ceremony is about to begin.

I glance down at the ceremonial robe draped over my clothes. Light blue with silver trim. The color of tranquility and unity, a symbol of our collective bond with the land and with each other.

The silver embroidery glistens under the warm glow of the essence lamps, a reflection of the ethereal link that potential SoulCasters share with the divine. Along the hem and cuffs, intricate symbols are woven in delicate, swirling patterns. Intertwining circles—a reminder that once formed, a SoulCasting bond is eternal, stretching beyond mortal lives.

But the most striking feature is the Tree of Continuity stitched over the heart. Its roots spread wide, a living testament to the sacred connection between humanity and the land. Sustenance given, sustenance taken. A never-ending cycle. It's said that those who bond become a part of that tree, woven into the very essence of the world itself.

The robe isn't just ceremonial garb—it's an invitation. A transformation waiting to happen. The fabric, though light, feels heavy with unseen significance, as if it is already weaving threads of power through me.

But I don't want to be transformed.

Across the room, the murmurs of my peers ripple like nervous currents in an unseen tide. The tension thickens as we sit in quiet rows, waiting. The weight of expectation is suffocating.

"I can't believe Rorick is here," whispers the young man beside me, his voice hushed but brimming with excitement.

He leans in, his eyes wide with awe. "He doesn't attend every Naming Ceremony, but he came to ours."

I glance toward the dais. Rorick stands with an imposing stillness, his presence takes up the whole room

"With so few people bonding these days," I reply, keeping my voice even, neutral, "it makes sense he'd come to the largest city."

The boy narrows his eyes, like I just poured water over his fire.

"Well, true," he mutters, unwilling to let go of his excitement. "But still. It's incredible, don't you think?"

I shrug. "I guess."

"You guess? Why are you even here?"

"It's required."

His expression twists, skepticism flickering in his eyes. "Why do I get the impression that you wouldn't be here if it wasn't?"

I hesitate, considering whether to lie, deflect, dismiss. But no—I owe him nothing.

"Because I wouldn't."

His curiosity deepens. "You don't want to bond?"

"Nope."

He looks at me like I just sprouted horns. "Why?"

I sigh, the weight of this conversation all too familiar.

"I'd rather choose my future than have it chosen for me," I say, keeping my voice level. "The path ahead should be mine to walk. Or not."

He exhales sharply, puffing out his cheeks before blowing the air out in one forceful breath.

"I thought I was the only one."

I turn to face him fully. Did I hear that right?

"Just a moment ago, you were excited," I point out.

Draymond chuckles, the sound tight, forced. "Yeah, well. I've been faking it so long, sometimes I fool myself."

A nervous laugh. A flicker of raw honesty beneath the bravado.

"This whole thing scares me a little," he admits after a beat of silence. Then, as if shaking off the moment, he offers his hand. "Draymond."

I take it. "Jerrick."

His brows furrow as recognition sparks in his expression. "Jerrick…" His voice trails off, then his eyes widen.

"Oh, wait. I heard a rumor about… are you Theron's son?"

I sigh again, rubbing the back of my neck. Is this how things are going to be from now on? The same question, the same stares, the same murmurs?

"Yes."

Draymond's eyes widen slightly. "Wow. How's that been?"

I exhale, the weight of it settling over me. "I wouldn't know. I've never met him. Apparently, I was the last to find out. Just learned the truth myself."

Draymond grins, shaking his head. "Well, if the rumors are to be believed, your mother was an immortal witch, and you were raised on Shardmount Isle by all manner of foul beasts."

I snort. "Close. I was raised by a little old lady on an apple farm."

He throws his head back and laughs, the sound rich and unguarded. I can't help but join in.

For a moment, just a moment, everything feels… normal.

"I needed that!" he says, still chuckling. "Nice to meet you, Jerrick."

I nod, meaning it. "You too."

A silence settles, but it's a comfortable one. For once, I don't feel like I'm under a microscope.

Draymond shifts, glancing toward the front. "What do you think the big display is going to be this year? Last year was fire."

"I don't know," I admit. "Never really thought about it. Maybe a healer? I heard a few years back they brought in someone who fell off a ladder that morning and broke their leg. He walked out of the ceremony completely healed."

Draymond's eyes light up. "The kid in me wants to see fire."

I smirk. "I got that impression."

His gaze flicks past me, landing on someone else. "Hey, if you don't mind, I see someone I want to say hello to before things start."

"Not at all." I watch as he weaves through the aisle, disappearing into the crowd.

As I sit, I finally take in the ceremony hall's splendor.

Tapestries adorn the walls, woven depictions of past bondings, their vibrant colors catching the flickering Essence light. Above, the ceiling is a celestial masterpiece, a painted expanse of the God Tree, mythical beasts, and the gods, long since dead. The entire space radiates a sense of reverence, of power, of inevitability.

I glance toward the empty balconies. Once, they were filled with families, their cheers and prayers echoing through these halls. Now, they wait in an open-air theater a few streets away, far enough that no pleas, no protests, can disrupt the ceremony's purpose. A protocol designed to handle those who would object to the law. A reminder that those who bond belong to the Council now.

The dais commands the center of the hall, a polished slab of stone that gleams under the golden lamplight. SoulCasters flank Rorick, their robes a dazzling display of colors, each signifying their bonded GodSoul. Some stand tall, their power worn like a mantle, while others move with a quiet grace, their presence a whisper of something ancient, something watching.

And there, at the center, stands Rorick himself.

The man is a relic, a force, a titan. Despite his hunched form and the cane gripped tightly in his weathered hands, his presence is undeniable. He is the closest thing this land has to a ruler. Five hundred years old, maybe more. His bond with his GodSoul allows him to endure, a living monument to an era long past.

My stomach tightens. The ceremony is about to begin.

I scan the room. Bowen isn't here.

The realization slams into me. Where is he? I search the faces around me, scanning row after row, but there's no sign of him. He warned me. Told me to leave. He had told me his father was keeping him from it. But why?

My thoughts are cut off as Rorick steps forward, his cane tapping against the stone as he moves to the podium.

Rorick's gaze sweeps over us, his presence a monolithic force in the vast hall.

"The SoulCasters," he continues, gesturing to the robed figures flanking him, "are not mere wielders of Essence. They are the custodians of our land's wellbeing, the architects of a future where harmony and balance can be restored."

He pauses, letting the weight of his words settle over the gathered initiates. His gaze lingers, searching, evaluating, imprinting his presence into our bones.

"The bond you may form today is more than a fusion of soul and Essence. It is a sacred duty, a pledge to heal our ailing land. It aches, yearning for rejuvenation, and it is through your bond that restoration will come."

His weathered hands clasp together, the motion slow, deliberate—a symbol of unity, of inevitability.

"SoulCasters have long been the cornerstone of our society. They guide us, protect us, and most importantly, they heal the very land we live upon."

His voice, already commanding, rises—stronger, fervent.

"This ceremony is not merely a rite of passage. It is the dawn of a new era. An era where the chosen few will become beacons of hope, wielding power not for themselves, but for the survival of all. Your journey will be arduous, filled with challenges and sacrifices. But remember this—" he leans forward slightly, his cane pressing into the polished stone, his voice dropping into something almost reverent "— the strength of the bond is immeasurable. Through it, you will become more. You will be the hands of the gods themselves."

His words wrap around us, sinking deep.

The hall is no longer just a grand chamber. It is a crucible, a moment suspended in time where destinies shift. I can feel it in the air, in the murmurs of those around me; an awakening, a realization.

People sit taller, eyes brighter, spines straightened. Determination blooms, cautious at first, then growing, threading itself into the fabric of the moment. Even within me, the change takes root.

The apprehension that had gripped me, the fear that had clouded my thoughts, narrowing my world to nothing but walls—

It's still there. But it's in the background now. For the first time, I see past it. If I bond today, if I walk this path, I could make a difference.

Rorick steps back, his speech finished, but the energy in the room remains taut, electric.

Another figure emerges from the ranks of the SoulCasters, gliding toward the podium.

Her robes are the color of the sky just before dawn—light blue trimmed in silver, embroidered with the sigil of Zephyra. As she moves, the air shifts around her, stirring faintly, as if drawn to her presence.

She lifts her hands, gripping the edge of her hood—slowly pulling it back.

Red hair cascades down in waves, catching the flickering light. Emerald eyes, bright and cutting as a sharpened blade, scan the gathered initiates. She is beautiful. She is dangerous.

The air responds to her presence. A faint wind spirals at her feet, lifting tiny motes of dust into the light. Then, she rises.

A whisper of wind curls beneath her, lifting her from the dais. Her robes billow, floating effortlessly as she ascends.

When she speaks, her voice isn't loud—yet it seems to reach every corner of the hall.

"My name is Aerelis. I am of the Order of the Wind."

She floats higher, until she hovers ten feet above the podium, her presence ethereal, commanding.

"I have bonded with Zephyra, the wind's goddess and master. And let me be clear—my bond allows me to do more than merely 'blow things around.'"

Without warning, she moves. Not just floating—but flying.

She glides over the gathered initiates, the wind cradling her, effortless, powerful. The entire hall watches in stunned silence.

Aerelis's voice drifts through the vast hall, deceptively soft, yet carrying an undeniable weight.

"Those of you fortunate enough to bond today will be welcomed into the Council Keep, where you will learn to wield these blessings in ways you cannot yet comprehend."

The air shifts—no, it collapses.

A crushing force presses down upon me, invisible yet suffocating, as if the very atmosphere rebels against my existence.

My lungs seize. My breath vanishes.

I try to inhale, but nothing comes. Panic claws at my throat. My vision wavers at the edges, fraying like an unraveling tapestry. Around me, others clutch at their chests, their expressions twisted in realization—

We can't breathe.

A low thrumming pressure pulses through the room, amplifying the helpless terror that grips us.

Aerelis's voice, smooth and unhurried, drifts through the chaos like a knife slicing through silk.

"I can control even the wind in your lungs. One hundred and three of you—unable to breathe. A negative vacuum, effortlessly created, collapsing your lungs."

Her tone is detached, clinical, as if she is describing a mere scientific curiosity rather than the fragile line between life and death.

Lights explode in my vision. My chest screams for air. My thoughts fragment, splintering into frantic, primal instincts.

Is this how I die?

Then—air rushes back in.

The vacuum vanishes. A desperate, gasping inhale burns my throat, leaving me reeling, shaken but alive.

Across the room, several initiates slump forward, unconscious. The ones who couldn't endure.

A door opens. Soldiers march in with cold efficiency, moving towards the fallen.

Aerelis hovers above, unbothered.

"We do not suffer weakness," she says simply.

The unconscious are lifted from their seats, carried away like discarded husks. The reality settles in—this is not a ceremony of mere selection. It is a culling.

Aerelis's feet finally touch the dais once more. Her emerald gaze sweeps across us, pausing on mine. A flicker of something—amusement, challenge—crosses her face before she speaks again.

"Our land can't breathe."

The words linger, their meaning deeper than the metaphor.

"It is decaying because it can't fill its lungs. It is suffocating. But as Rorick said, there is light on the horizon. With each new bond, we take one step closer to pushing the Fog back."

Her words should inspire hope, yet they feel more like a warning.

I sit there, gripping my knees, my chest still rising and falling too fast. The grandeur of the hall no longer impresses me. It feels smaller now, its opulence a veil for something darker.

The weight of this responsibility, of this power, presses down on me in ways I hadn't anticipated.

Aerelis turns toward the steps, leaving us with one final piece of advice.

"Be worthy."

Then, a new presence emerges from the shadows.

A figure steps forward, clad in flowing black robes. Unlike Aerelis, he does not remove his hood. The darkness clings to him, as if reluctant to let him go.

His voice is soft, a low rasp, like leather dragging across stone.

"That was... something."

He pauses, letting the silence settle uneasily between us.

"You don't need to know my name. I am of the Order of the Night, bonded with Grimlon, master of shadow."

As he speaks the word 'shadow,' a flicker of movement distorts the air—

And he is gone.

A ripple moves through the gathered initiates. Murmurs rise in uncertain whispers. Where did he go?

Then—a blur materializes beside me.

A sharp, glinting blade presses against my throat.

My muscles lock, breath hitching as the whisper of steel kisses my skin.

His voice is closer now, right beside my ear.

"I have dominion over the shadows."

His hand is steady, the pressure of the knife deliberate but not cutting.

"Even in this well-lit room, there are places even the light cannot touch. Where there is light, there is shadow. And where there is shadow..."

A pause, heavy and lingering.

"...so am I."

Then—the pressure vanishes.

The knife disappears as quickly as it came. A hand lands on my shoulder instead—steady, firm.

The figure steps back into the light, though the darkness clings to his form like an obedient pet.

His voice is no longer a whisper but a measured decree.

"The bond some of you have was formed at birth. The moment you took your first breath, a connection was made."

His shadow flickers unnaturally behind him, stretching and writhing as if alive.

"Each of us is linked to the land, to the air we breathe, to the beasts that roam. But until the god to whom your soul is bound is named, you remain powerless."

He tilts his head slightly, his hood shifting just enough to reveal the barest sliver of his face—sharp, angular, carved from shadow itself.

"Knowledge of your god's name is the key."

Could it really be that simple?

The pounding in my chest drowns out the murmurs around me.

I tell myself I don't want this. That I want to live my life as I choose. But another part of me—the part that has always wondered, the part that can't help but be curious—thrums with anticipation.

What would it mean if I bond?

I steal a glance at the others. Most are alight with excitement, their eyes eager, their breaths held in anticipation. But then there are the others—the ones who sit stiffly, their faces pale, their hands clenched into tight fists. Fear. Dread. I recognize it because it mirrors the turmoil in my own chest.

The SoulCaster in black stands before us, his voice a smooth rasp that demands attention.

"Any SoulCaster can see the god you are bonded with after a single touch. After all, we are all connected—through the link we share with the land."

The room stills, each of us caught in the gravity of what is about to unfold.

"In just a few minutes, you will form groups of five or six. There are ten of us here today, so the process will move quickly."

I shift in my seat, my hands curling against the fabric of my robe. The tension thickens as the SoulCaster continues.

"If you are bonded, you will know immediately. Once your god's name is spoken, the connection will flood through you. You will feel it— Essence filling every fiber of your being, unlocking what has always been yours."

A pause, letting the words sink in. Letting the weight of them settle into our bones.

"Some of you will be stronger than others. The strength of your bond depends on how many others share a connection with the same GodSoul. The more divided the power, the thinner it is spread."

My mind whirls. We learned about this in Civic Education, but hearing it now—moments before my fate is decided—makes it real in a way that no lesson ever could.

"There were twenty gods before the war," the SoulCaster says, his voice cutting through the silence. "All but two have bonded."

The implication is clear.

Fewer gods remain unclaimed. And fewer bonds are forming at all.

"For those of you who do not bond, and that will be the vast majority," he continues, "you must leave this hall immediately."

The finality in his tone sends a chill racing down my spine.

As the first groups are called forward, I watch.

I see the way their bodies tense when the SoulCasters reach for them. The fleeting moment where they teeter on the precipice of the unknown. Then the Name is spoken, and it is as if a door has been thrown open inside them.

Some stagger. Some weep. Some glow with exhilaration as power rushes into them, raw and unbridled.

But then there are the ones whose faces fall. The ones who step away, their shoulders rigid with disappointment as they are silently dismissed.

This isn't just a ceremony. It's a reckoning.

I feel the weight of every moment pressing down on me. The Keepers sought me out. Rorick and the mayor are conspiring against me. Theron is being hunted.

Why would any of that happen if I wouldn't bond?

A new thought settles in, slow and insidious. Do I even have a choice?

My group is called.

I rise on unsteady legs, walking toward the dais with five others. The young woman beside me is trembling.

The SoulCaster standing before us—a man draped in silver-trimmed robes, his presence calm but commanding—meets her gaze first. He places his hand on her shoulder, his fingers light but firm. Then he closes his eyes.

A breathless moment passes.

Then—his eyes snap open.

"Maelis."

The word rings through the chamber. A god's name. A fate sealed.

Maelis, the Whisperer. God of communication. Those bonded with Maelis can hear what others cannot—the voices of the land, the murmurs of beasts, the echoes of unseen forces.

The young woman gasps. Her body jolts as if struck by lightning.

A light—soft, golden—flares behind her eyes.

Her limbs go slack, her knees buckling. The SoulCaster catches her with practiced ease, lowering her gently to the ground.

"Welcome to the Council," he murmurs, his voice almost reverent.

The moment arrives.

I step forward under the gaze of the SoulCaster, his eyes dark and unreadable, as if peering into the very marrow of my being. My breath hitches, my heart pounds a frantic rhythm against my ribs. His fingers barely graze my arm, and he closes his eyes in concentration. A brief flicker—something, just for an instant—crosses his face. Fear? Uncertainty? I can't be sure.

Then, just as quickly, it vanishes. His features harden into an impassive mask.

"You have not bonded." The words fall from his lips, final and absolute.

For a moment, I feel untethered. Relief floods through me, cool and sharp—but underneath it, a strange pang of disappointment. I had braced myself for the extraordinary, for my entire life to shift in an instant. But now? Nothing. The breath I didn't realize I was holding escapes in a long exhale, carrying with it a weight I hadn't known was pressing on me.

I should be happy. This is what I wanted, right? No path chosen for me. No destiny dragging me away from my home, my parents. I'm free.

So why does it feel like something has slipped through my fingers?

I turn away from the SoulCaster, the ceremony hall suddenly stifling. The opulence, the grandeur—the murals depicting legendary SoulCasters, the glowing essence lamps—it all feels distant, like something meant for other people. I walk, my steps hollow echoes against polished stone, each one pulling me further away from the life I almost had.

The adjoining chamber is quiet. I find my gear where I left it. The familiar weight of my knife at my hip, the sturdy leather of my quiver, the smooth curve of my bow—they anchor me in something solid, something real. My fingers tighten around the bow's grip as I push through the final set of doors, stepping out into the world once more.

Cold air bites against my skin, shocking me back to reality. The muted festival sounds seem to hum at the edge of my awareness, blending into the low murmur of gathered families. My parents are waiting for me in the designated area, and for the first time, hesitation grips me. How will they react? Will they be relieved? Disappointed?

I shake my head. No. They've always accepted me, always understood. And yet... a sliver of doubt lingers.

My thoughts drift to Elena. Is she safe? Will she bond? Is she even still outside the city? The unknown gnaws at me. I tell myself she's strong. I tell myself she'll be fine. But the words, repeated in my mind like a mantra, sound thin and empty.

I push forward, weaving through the dispersing crowd, my focus set on reuniting with my family. Just as I near the waiting area, my thoughts still swirling in tangled knots, the first scream shatters the air.

It's high and raw, filled with pure, unfiltered terror.

The festival stills, a collective hush falling over the city. And then—another scream. And another.

Panic.

People freeze in place, heads whipping toward the source of the sound. The weight in my gut turns to ice.

Something is very, very wrong.

And just like that, whatever moment of reflection I had is ripped away. The Naming Ceremony is no longer the most important thing that happened today.

Because today, the world just changed.

#

Chaos explodes around me. The world turns into a writhing mass of bodies, some running in blind terror, others collapsing in pools of their own blood. The festival—once a scene of forced celebration—now resembles a slaughterhouse.

Screams fill the air, echoing off the high stone walls. The creatures, those grotesque abominations I once saw dead by the roadside, are alive now. And they are hunting. Their claws rip through flesh, their fangs tear into bone.

I can't move. I can't breathe. My feet feel rooted to the ground as I watch a child trip, only for one of the beasts to pounce—its jaws closing over her tiny frame in a sickening crunch. Decorations still flutter above in the breeze, casting streaks of color against the blood-soaked cobblestones. The absurdity of it makes my stomach twist.

Move, Jerrick. Move!

But I don't. My mind is trapped in the din of agony, the sheer impossibility of what's happening. The creatures are everywhere. I lift my gaze to the city walls—they are crawling down from above. Hundreds of them, moving with grotesque, unnatural agility. They scuttle down the stone like monstrous insects, their eyes glowing like embers in the dimming light.

Then, the crowd changes.

No longer a directionless frenzy—they are all running the same way. Away from something. A massive, unseen force.

And I know exactly where they're running from.

My heart stops. My parents are in that direction.

I break free from my paralysis, my body reacting before my mind catches up. I run. I run like my life depends on it—because it does. But more than that, theirs does. I shove past people, knocking some to the ground, but I can't stop. I won't stop.

A man bolts toward me, panic in his eyes. Then he's gone. A shadow lunges from the side, tackling him mid-stride. A creature twice the size of the others.

Before I can process what I'm seeing, it bites into his skull like an apple.

Blood sprays across my face.

I stumble, gagging, blinded by the warm wetness dripping down my cheek. Don't stop. Don't stop. I veer left to avoid the mangled corpse—

Pain explodes in my leg. I'm down.

The impact jolts through me, but I flip onto my back just in time to see the creature that took me down stalking forward. Its low, guttural hiss sends a bolt of fear through my chest.

It's watching me. Hungry.

I fumble for my knife. My fingers wrap around the hilt just as it pounces.

I roll at the last second. It misses. But barely.

I'm on my feet. My chest heaves as I hold my knife in a white-knuckled grip. The thing crouches low, snarling, its oversized fangs dripping with saliva. I can hear more dying around me. Their screams blend into the chaos.

This thing is going to kill me. Unless I kill it first.

It lunges again. I lash out. The blade sinks deep, but the creature's weight still crashes into me, slamming me to the ground.

My lungs empty.

The creature thrashes, its hot breath searing against my skin as it snaps at my throat. I twist. Its teeth sink into my shoulder instead. Agony. It rips away flesh, a fiery explosion of pain consuming my mind, but I won't stop.

I can't stop.

I drive the knife into its ribs. Once. Twice. Again. It snarls, its grip faltering. I wrench the blade free and drive it into its skull. The beast spasms. Then, it goes limp.

I shove it off me with the last of my strength, my breath coming in ragged gasps. I don't have time to think about the pain.

My parents are still waiting for me. And I don't know if they're still alive.

I groan as I force myself to my feet. My leg is in shreds, and a flap of muscle dangles uselessly from my shoulder, slick with blood. The pain is unbearable. But pain doesn't matter. Nothing matters—except reaching my parents.

I bite down hard, locking my jaw as I shove the agony aside and run.

The city is a battlefield. Guards form shield walls, driving into the monstrous tide, their swords carving through flesh and bone. Blood splatters across cobblestones. Some of the guards fall, their screams cut short as claws tear into them. SoulCasters are among them, some lying dead, others unleashing their power in dazzling bursts—flames scorching the creatures, stone walls shifting to crush them, torrents of wind sending bodies flying.

But despite the warriors and their magic, they're losing.

Hundreds lay dead and dying, their bodies tangled in rivers of blood. The screams of the wounded claw at my ears, desperate hands reach for me as I pass, pleading for help. I want to stop. I want to pull them to safety. But I can't.

I can't.

If I stop, my parents could die.

So, I run. Faster. Harder. My chest is a burning inferno, my breath ragged, my limbs screaming at me to stop. But I push forward, my entire existence narrowed to a singular purpose: get to them.

Then—impact.

A blur of movement. A wall of muscle and claws slams into me from the side.

I nearly go down, staggering, my vision a whirl of motion and noise. I regain my footing just in time to see it launch at me again, its rows of needle-like teeth snapping open. This time, I'm ready.

I catch it mid-air.

It thrashes wildly, snarling, its razor-sharp claws slashing at my arms, carving deep lines into my flesh. It's smaller than the last one—but twice as feral.

I grip its throat. Squeeze.

It writhes, its claws biting deep, drawing hot streams of blood down my forearm. I grit my teeth, squeezing harder, my fingers pressing into the corded muscle and sinew of its neck. I feel the moment its throat collapses. A shudder runs through its body before it goes limp.

I hurl it aside and keep running.

Almost there.

I reach the outdoor area where I left my parents, relief punching through the panic when I see guards holding the entrance. They are battle-ready, weapons drawn, their expressions grim.

"Hurry! Get in!" one of them shouts, stepping aside to let me pass.

I stumble inside, lungs heaving, my wounds pulsing with white-hot pain. Dozens of families are huddled together, their faces pale, eyes wide with terror. But I don't see them.

Where are they?

I spin around, frantic, my breath coming in panicked bursts. "Where are they?!" I yell, my voice raw.

No one answers.

My mind races. They should be here. They were waiting for me. They should be here.

A voice behind me: "Are you okay?"

I whirl around. A guard stands there, eyes filled with concern.

"My parents," I rasp. My voice barely works. "An older couple—sixties. Where are they?"

Recognition dawns on his face. "Oh… you're Jerrick." The confirmation hits like a hammer to my chest.

The guard points to the back gate. "They went through there. With a few others."

Relief slams into me, nearly buckling my knees. They're alive. I don't waste another second. I sprint for the small gate, shove it open, and step through.

Then, I see her. Fifteen feet ahead, my mother.

Her eyes meet mine, and all color drains from her face. Her lips part, but no words come out. A scream frozen in silence.

She isn't alone.

Two men stand beside her. One of them holds her arm. A knife gleams in his hand. My stomach plummets into a void. I know that man. He's the one I tackled this morning. The one who left the note. The one who called me son.

Without thinking, I yank my bow from my back. Fluid. Practiced. Deadly.

In the same motion, I notch an arrow, my fingers tightening around the string. The world narrows to a single point—his head.

Fifteen feet. Nothing.

I can make this shot in my sleep. My heart hammers in my chest, a wild, erratic drumbeat. Just breathe. Just—

"Whoa, whoa now, Jerrick." The man pulls my mother closer, his lips curling into a smirk as he presses the knife against her throat. Mocking me. "Is that any way to treat an old friend?"

I tighten my grip. I can do this. I've done it a thousand times before. My practice target is smaller than this. Farther than this.

Pull. Release. Straight through the eye.

But I don't fire.

Because my mother's eyes—pleading—hold me in place.

"*No,*" she mouths.

My breath catches. Why?

The pressure against her throat increases. A single drop of blood beads against the silver edge of the blade. My hands are shaking. I can't miss.

Pull. Release.

"What's going on?" My voice cracks, betraying me.

The man grins, his grip tightening as he tilts her head back, exposing more of her throat. He's enjoying this. "Put the bow down. Now."

My body refuses to comply. I can still do this. I can still save her.

"I told you I was only going to ask one more time." Then—his next words steal the air from my lungs. "I've already killed your father."

The laugh that follows is inhuman. Time stops. I see red. My mother mouths something again. But I don't understand. I lower my bow. Then I raise it again.

I won't miss.

"Let. Her. Go."

But the moment stretches too long. The knife glints. A flash of silver.

And then—

The world ends.

"I love you, Jerrick," my mother whispers—

As he slits her throat. The sound—wet, sharp, wrong. A crimson river pours from her neck, too much, too fast. Her hands fly up, instinctive, desperate, failing.

She drops to her knees. Our eyes lock. She tries to speak, but he—the monster, the murderer—kicks her.

Her head whips to the side. A sickening crack. The force of it sends her sprawling. The ground welcomes her like an old friend. And she doesn't move.

Something inside me shatters. My bow slips from my hands, falling uselessly to the dirt. So heavy now. My knees buckle. My breath stutters. My chest implodes.

It's over. She's gone.

My feet drag forward. I'm not thinking. I just— have to be near her.

Let me die next to her. That's all I ask.

A muffled roar echoes through the chaos, distant and meaningless. Someone yells my name. It barely registers. Then—impact.

A blur of movement.

Something slams into the side of my head. A loud crack. A pain so deep it doesn't even hurt. Just a sharp, shattering nothingness.

The edges of my vision go dark. My body tilts. My legs give out.

This is what falling feels like, I think.

I fight to stay awake, but—what's the point?

What's left?

I see her eyes. Still open.

Fading.

Dimming.

Telling me one last thing.

"Be brave, my child, even when the world falls apart."

The shadows close in. The world narrows to a single, agonizing point of focus—her.

Love. Loss. Regret.

A storm of emotions, raw and unchecked, surges through me. Too much. Too fast. I try to grasp them, try to hold onto something real, something solid, but they slip through my fingers like sand.

My heart splinters.

The pain is so absolute, so final, it eclipses everything else.

The laughter.

The chaos.

The death.

It all fades.

There's only her.

My anchor.
My guiding star.
Slipping away.
The ground sways beneath me. My legs give out. The sky tilts.
And as the darkness reaches for me, the last thing I see is her
eyes.
Soft.
Kind.
Begging me.
"Live, Jerrick. For me."
Her final message, etched into my soul.
And then—sweet, merciful darkness.
A cold refuge.
A world where none of this exists.
A place where I don't have to feel.

Chapter 8

Theron

As I explode from the cave's mouth, the cold air slaps against me like a wake-up call to war. The ambush is immediate—twelve figures, weapons drawn, postures rigid with purpose. Their trap is set, their advantage assumed. But they haven't cornered me.

They've provoked me.

I don't need eyes to see them. Valthrun's bond is my sight. A full, seamless awareness extends around me in all directions. No blind spots—except for the physical barriers they're banking on. Boulders scattered along the slope create the perfect obstructions for hidden enemies. And that's how I know.

A SoulCaster is near.

This is Council-planned.

I don't have the time to play by their rules. I charge.

With a single vault, I clear the two shield-bearers kneeling in defense. Mid-air, my swords are already swinging. My blades carve through both archers' throats in one fluid, efficient motion. They collapse, choking on their own blood before they even register my movement. I don't stop.

I land, already shifting.

The armored men rise to meet me—too slow. My momentum becomes a weapon. A shoulder check sends the first reeling, but the second—I see the opening. My sword drives between the exposed joint of his breastplate and pauldron. He drops instantly.

Six seconds. Four down.

I pivot—eight remain.

One more, I realize, as the shield-bearer I knocked aside staggers back to his feet. That makes nine.

They're moving together, fanning out. Standard anti-Theron tactics. They don't hesitate, don't wait for a signal. They attack. All at once.

Good.

They're predictable.

And predictability is a death sentence.

I meet them head-on. My great sword is a storm, each arc measured, deadly, relentless. The impact reverberates through my arms as I cleave through metal, bone, and flesh. One goes down, then another. I see them adjusting, shifting to cut off my escape.

And then—movement.

The archers. They're getting back up. Not possible—unless… A healer. Damn it.

They're not healing the ones fighting me, which means the SoulCaster's range is limited. I judge it at fifteen feet, maybe less. That means they're close.

I change tactics. I lure them forward, stepping out from the cover of the boulder, tempting them to push in. The fighters follow, sensing an opportunity, but I'm already moving.

A sharp pivot—I slice through the gap in a soldier's armor, severing his lifeline in a spray of crimson.

The archers react.

They loose their arrows—but I'm not there anymore.

The first shot hisses past my ribs, inches from my heart. The second I sidestep, letting it whistle past as I turn my momentum against them. They don't have time to nock another arrow.

I close the distance. One strike.

My blade finds an archer's chest, carving deep, sending him back to the ground for the second and final time.

Where are you, SoulCaster?

The thought sears through me as I prepare to finish this. Jerrick is alone. I don't have time for these games.

Then I see a handprint on the boulder next to me. It's one only I can see. It's the heat left over from the hand of the Healer. I can't let them touch me.

The remaining archer stumbles back, scrambling to nock another arrow. I lunge for him— but he's already released the shot.

I see it coming. Too fast. Too late. Ducking would take me straight into the SoulCaster's reach. A fatal mistake.

I let the arrow fly. Let it hit me.

Pain erupts as the arrow buries itself deep into my back shoulder. Flesh sears. It hurts. Gods, it hurts. But I ignore it. Turn it into fuel.

I dart behind the boulder and see the Healer with her eyes closed, concentrating. I don't give her any time to notice me. My blade finds her heart.

Her eyes fly open. She mouths a curse, but her voice dies with her. The light fades from her hands. The archer she had revived collapses behind me, lifeless once more.

She won't be healing him again.

But she could have killed me in a hundred ways.

People love healers for their gift of life, but it's their ability to take it away that makes them terrifying. If she had reached me, if she had placed even one hand on my skin, she could have ended me with a whisper.

Life Drain. A touch that leeches the very essence from your body, leaving nothing but a withered husk.

Or worse, Rejuvenation Overload. The curse that turns the body against itself. Flesh swells, organs bloat, bones splinter under the force of unnatural, ravenous growth. It's a death slow, grotesque, agonizing. A body consumed by the very force meant to heal it.

I would have died screaming. And she knew it. But she never got the chance.

The arrow lodged in my flesh throbs with every pulse of my heartbeat, a sharp and unforgiving reminder that I don't have time for this. I wrench my blade free and push forward.

Three more soldiers. That's all that stands between me and the road to the city.

I don't have time for them.

I charge.

My swords are not weapons—they are inevitability.

I strike low, fast, relentless. One sword slashes through armor, the second drives deep into exposed flesh. I barely hear their dying gasps as I move to the next, and the next.

They fall. All of them.

My breath is ragged, but I don't stop. The archer. He's the last. His fingers fumble at his quiver, but he's too slow. I dodge one arrow, deflect another. I'm already too close. One final strike.

His head snaps back as my blade splits flesh, muscle, and bone. He crumples, never to rise again. Silence.

For a moment, only the wind moves. The dead lie still, cooling beneath the open sky. The fight is over. But the war isn't.

I reach for the arrow still buried in my shoulder. My bulk makes it impossible to pull out. I do the next best thing—snap the shaft in half, leaving the arrowhead inside. The pain is white-hot, piercing. It doesn't matter. I turn to the road.

Jerrick.

That name is the only thing that matters now. I push forward, pain a distant thing compared to the fear curling in my gut. He's alone. He doesn't know what's coming. And I will burn everything to keep him safe.

With one last breath, I break into a run. The wind screams past me. Every step is a promise, a vow.

I'm coming, son.

And nothing will stand in my way.

#

As I near the western wall, a foreboding sense of dread coils in my chest. Screams—raw, terrified, dying—rip through the air. Metal clashes. Wood splinters. The unmistakable sounds of battle shake the earth beneath my feet.

Above the walls, grotesque things swarm like insects, their claws clicking against the stone as they climb—higher, faster. Below, others prowl restlessly, pacing back and forth, high-pitched mewling sounds rising from their throats, hungry, frustrated. Waiting for the wall to break.

Jerrick is in there.

A sharp, unforgiving pang of guilt twists inside me. I swore to protect him, to stand between him and horrors like these. Yet here I am, outside the gates, while he— gods help me—he might be fighting for his life.

I grit my teeth and push forward.

Just outside the walls, trade outposts, barracks, and depots stand silent, their stonework matching the fortress but lacking its sheer scale. These were built after the God Wars, in an era when there was no longer a need to accommodate giants.

I see movement—people hiding inside. They watch from the cracks in doors, from shuttered windows. Terrified. Powerless. One boy, no older than sixteen, peers out from a window, unaware that I can see him.

Then—movement ahead.

A creature crosses my path.

It moves low to the ground, sinewy, powerful. The sound of claws scraping stone reaches me even before I see the gleam of hooked talons.

It's five feet tall at the shoulder, but its head is massive, swinging from side to side as if sniffing the air. Its body is stitched together from unnatural things—catlike in shape, but made of flesh, bone, and earth. Mud and moss bind its limbs, sticks and roots knit together where sinew should be.

Its tail cracks like a whip behind it, snapping against the stone— Crack! Crack! The sound ricochets through the empty outpost like splintering wood.

I freeze.

It hasn't seen me yet. I back away slowly, careful, deliberate. No sudden movements.

Just as I slip behind a small building—

It roars.

A deep, primal, earth-shaking sound, starting as a rumble, growing, consuming, splitting the air apart. For a brief, terrifying moment, it's the only sound. The battle inside the walls? Gone. The screams, the fighting? Silenced. There is only the roar.

I press against the cold stone, every muscle wound tight, ready to flee or fight.

Crack!

The whip-like tail snaps again, louder, closer. I imagine it flexing its claws, tasting the air for my scent.

Crack!

It's just on the other side of the building now.

I inch toward the narrow alleyway between the stone walls— ten feet of open ground before I can reach another door.

Then—movement.

A second creature.

This one smaller, faster, slinking into the alley from my left. No hesitation. The moment its beady yellow eyes land on me, it screeches— a piercing, high-pitched wail that cuts through the air.

Crack!

The larger beast reacts.

No time.

I run toward the new threat, sword already swinging. A downward slash—clean, perfect. My blade cleaves through its skull, splitting it nearly in two.

Crack!

I whirl, heart hammering.

The larger creature rounds the corner.

It sees me now.

Its glowing, root-threaded eyes lock onto mine. Its massive head cocks to the side, studying me.

Then—another roar.

But this time, it doesn't charge. It waits. A hunter. Calculating. Testing.

The creature, a grotesque amalgamation of nature's fury, stirs something primal within me. In its wild, untamed eyes, I see a reflection of my own inner turmoil—the constant war between the beast I become in battle and the man I strive to remain.

How much of our humanity do we sacrifice in the name of survival? How close to the edge do I tread with every life I take?

The question lingers for less than a breath. Survival doesn't wait for philosophy.

I move.

Darting between two buildings, I press myself flat against the wall and listen.

Crack!

The tail snaps closer.

Then—silence.

I inch toward the door. Locked.

Crack!

A shadow shifts above me. My gaze flicks up—its tongue lolls from between daggered teeth, mere feet above my head. The beast stands on the roof, scanning the road. If it so much as tilts its head down, I'm dead.

The air steams with its breath, vapor curling in the frigid night.

Then—movement.

Half a dozen smaller creatures slink into view from my right. They spot me instantly, their yellow eyes flashing, bodies vibrating with excitement. They bounce on their haunches, screeching, fighting each other to be the first to reach me.

They'll be on me in seconds.

The big one above? It's watching. Calculating. Waiting.

I can take the smaller ones. Fast, vicious, but reckless. The big one? It's too powerful, too controlled.

And today isn't just about me.

Today, my life isn't the only one that matters.

I grip the door handle, steel myself—then slam my entire weight into it. The wood groans, shatters. I burst inside, kick the door shut, and brace against it just as the first creature slams into the other side.

A thunderous crash erupts behind me.

Then—the screaming.

The sound alone is a weapon. A symphony of screeches, snarls, bone-rattling howls. They slam against the door again, claws tearing at the wood, shaking the frame, trying to burrow through.

I grind my heels into the floor, arms locked, bracing. The door buckles.

Then—silence.

A silence more unsettling than the violence.

They're thinking.

I scan the room. It's small, barely furnished—a desk, some scattered papers, a cold Essence lamp hanging from the ceiling. The window to my left is barred, useless.

But—the back door.

My muscles coil. I turn to run.

Crack!

The snap of a tail—just outside.

Then—wood splinters inches from my face.

Claws. Digging. Ripping.

I lurch backward, hands already pulling two large knives from my belt. Steel sings as I ready myself.

Then—impact.

A massive head bursts through the shattered door.

The wall explodes inward, shards of wood raining around me.

The creature's eyes lock onto mine. I don't hesitate. I can't. I brace. Knives poised, ready.

It lunges. And the world slows.

My vision expands, heightens. I see everything—the beast, the room, the exact angle of every shattered piece of wood, the way the creature's weight shifts mid-air, the arc of its snapping jaws.

I know exactly where it will land before it even does. And I move.

The beast lunges—a maelstrom of claws, sinew, and fury. But I see everything.

Every twitch of muscle. Every shift in weight. Every ripple of tension before it moves.

Before its jaws snap shut where my throat should be, I sidestep—fluid, precise, inevitable. Yet my mind isn't just here. It's everywhere.

I track the fractured door behind me, calculating the timing of the smaller ones outside. They're waiting. Watching. Their collective hunger pulsing in the dark like a second heartbeat.

The creature in front of me snarls, tail whipping, claws raking the air just inches from my flesh. I counter, slashing deep with my blade—but its hide is like gnarled bark and coiled roots. Resilient. Alive. The blade sinks in, but the wound is shallow.

It doesn't bleed. It doesn't slow.

We clash again—a whirlwind of blades and claws. Its maw snaps at my face as my knife carves into its ribs. But it keeps coming.

Somewhere in the chaos, a thought tries to surface. A longing for silence. A moment without war. A place where Jerrick and I aren't running, bleeding, killing.

But peace is a luxury for dead men.

The moment shatters—its next swipe rips across my arm. I parry too slow, my knife slicing deep into its side, but the beast surges forward, knocking me to the ground. My blade stuck in it's side.

Its teeth sink into my shoulder. Pain explodes through me, sharp, tearing, primal.

I don't scream. I don't stop. I twist. My hand finds my lost blade, still buried in its ribs. I yank it free. And drive it into its throat.

Once. Twice. Again. Again.

Its body spasms, then slackens. Its head dangles from torn sinew and pulsing roots, barely attached.

With a roar of defiance, I heave the corpse off me.

I stagger to my feet. My shoulder is ruined, flesh torn away in ribbons. Blood drips in thick rivulets down my arm.

Then—movement. I lift my focus to the doorway.

The smaller ones stand there.

Watching.

Waiting.

And then—they surge forward. I raise my arm—but it won't obey. It hangs, useless. I grit my teeth. One arm. That's all I've got. It will have to be enough.

They attack in waves, relentless, efficient. Claws flash, biting into my flesh before I can counter.

I strike, blade finding purchase in slick, writhing bodies. But I can't defend my left side. I need space. I need my sword.

I spot a gap—a sliver of open ground leading back outside. I take it. They follow—faster than I expect. Smarter than I hoped.

They dart in, tear into me, then vanish before I can strike. Never lingering long enough to be killed.

Wounds open like fire across my skin. Dozens of cuts. Dozens of bites. I fight. Harder. Wilder. But they are too many. I am too slow. And I am dying.

The creatures swarm.

They circle like vultures, an ever-growing tide of gnashing teeth and snapping claws. For every one I strike down, two more take its place.

I can't hold. Not forever.

I see my failure in Jerrick's face— the memory of it, the fear of it, the reality of it.

I wasn't strong enough.

Despite everything—despite this power, this bond, these years of war— I wasn't enough to protect him.

A familiar presence stirs in the depths of my soul. A connection that has always been there, silent and unwavering.

My bond.

I reach down to it—to Valthrun, to the source of my power, the strength that has guided me for decades.

"We were close," I whisper in my mind, my knees trembling as they begin to buckle. "Thank you for being with me all these years."

I sink to one knee.

My body screams to stop, but it still fights. It won't quit. Even as logic tells me this is the end, even as my vision blurs from blood loss, I keep swinging.

And then—

Power.

A surge of searing, overwhelming warmth floods through my veins.

The wounds on my arms and chest knit closed. The deep gouges in my shoulder mend. My strength floods back as if my body was never broken.

I rise, my great sword in hand.

The creatures hesitate.

I do not.

With a single, sweeping arc, I cut through them—two, three at a time. They fall like wheat beneath a scythe, reduced to nothing but dirt, bone, and sinew.

And then—silence.

I stand alone.

My chest heaves with breath, the ground around me littered with broken bodies.

A figure steps from around building behind me. I smile.

"Hello, Theron."

I know the smile hidden at the corners of her lips.

Elena.

She saved me.

I stagger slightly, shaking off the ghosts of near-death. No time for weakness.

"Where's Jerrick?" My voice is hoarse, more demand than question.

Her expression hardens. "Gone."

A cold dread settles into my bones.

"No."

"But we don't have time," she continues, stepping closer. "Do you trust me?"

I don't hesitate.

I sweep my hand toward the bodies at my feet.

"Always."

"Thank you," she murmurs. Then, urgently: "I need you to sever your connection. Now."

The words strike me cold.

Sever my bond?

"I can't see without it."

"I know." Her voice is steady. "That's where the trust comes in. These creatures attack anything that uses Essence. Your ability keeps them coming. And when I healed you…" She pauses. "I used more Essence than you. If they were too far to sense you, they sure as hell sensed me."

I understand immediately. This is the only way.

My bond is always active. It's a part of me, like breathing. I don't summon it; it's just there. Always.

But I do sever it—every night. It's the only way I can sleep. I grip Elena's shoulder and it reminds me of growing up blind and having to rely on others. I shudder at the thought of it. But, I trust her.

I cut the connection.

The world goes black.

Nothing. No presence. No perception. No vision. Just emptiness.

A hand guides me forward.

Elena.

"Thirty minutes ago," she says, her voice low but tense, "I saw Rorick and a few others. They were flying above the treetops—heading west. They had Jerrick."

Everything stops.

"Unconscious. Covered in blood."

The words burn.

"I was too late."

My mind races. Rorick found out. But how? If they're taking him west—they're taking him to The Keep. To The Council. To dozens of SoulCasters. To their elite guards.

We can't go there. Not alone. Elena exhales sharply. "They're taking him to The Keep, aren't they?"

My jaw tightens. "Yes. But we can't go there. Not yet."

She stiffens beneath my touch. "Why not?!" There's anger there—rage and desperation.

"Because it's suicide."

I can hear the frustration in her silence.

"Jerrick is key to everything," I say, voice low, unyielding. "They won't kill him. They can't."

Her shoulders shudder with barely contained fury. But I know I'm right. I know Rorick. They need Jerrick. But for what?

Elena grits her teeth. "So what do we do?"

I exhale. "We need help."

Chapter 9

Jerrick

The first thing I notice is the sound of my own heartbeat—loud, insistent, pounding in my ears like war drums. My breath comes sharp and uneven as I try to move, but something tightens around my wrists.

Rope.

I'm tied down.

Panic surges, sharp and disorienting, as I pull against my bindings, my muscles straining. My mind scrambles for an explanation, but everything is a blur, a fragmented haze of half-formed memories. Where am I? How did I get here?

The last thing I remember… I was at home. I was in bed, dreading the Naming Ceremony.

But that was yesterday.

No.

The window across the room is open, revealing a dark sky. Not yesterday. Not home.

A soft sound shifts beside me—slow, steady breaths. Someone's here. Their form is a shadowed lump in a chair next to the bed. I can't make out their features, but the rhythmic rise and fall of their chest tells me they're asleep.

I pull again at the ropes, but they hold firm.

"Sorry about that," a voice murmurs.

The figure stirs, straightening, and then click—an essence lamp flickers to life, its soft glow illuminating deep lines and a beard that flows like silvered thread.

Rorick.

He looks at me with keen, watchful eyes, as if he's been studying me even in my unconsciousness. His gold-colored robes shimmer slightly in the lamplight as he shifts forward, using my hand for balance as he pulls himself up. He stands hunched, his body bowed by age, but there's a sharpness in him, a presence that demands attention.

"You gave us quite the scare," he says, his voice thick with something that almost sounds like amusement. "In all my years, I've never seen anything like it."

I wet my lips, my throat dry. I don't understand. "What happened?"

Rorick hums thoughtfully as he unties the knots at my wrists, his grip firm but unhurried. "It's not surprising you don't remember. When a SoulCaster discovers their bond, there's always a surge of essence as their body adjusts. But you..." He tilts his head, studying me with something close to fascination. "You didn't just draw in essence from the land, Jerrick. You pulled it from every SoulCaster in the room. Me included."

I freeze, my thoughts stalling. "I—" I shake my head. "That's not possible. I wasn't—"

"You were very much bonded," Rorick interrupts, his voice a quiet certainty. "And you took in more power than your body could handle. You collapsed, and you've been unconscious for three days."

The words barely register. Three days? Three days of my life, gone.

I try to sit up, but the motion makes my head spin. A crushing weight settles in my chest. My parents. I was supposed to go back to them. We were supposed to go home.

"But my parents," I whisper, my voice barely audible. "They need me."

Rorick squeezes my hand, the gesture oddly gentle. "You're a good son, Jerrick," he says softly. "I sent people to check on them. They won't be far if they need anything. We take care of our own."

His words should be reassuring. But something feels wrong.

"I thought once you bonded," I say slowly, carefully, "you were never allowed to see your family again."

Rorick chuckles, shaking his head. "Ah, the rumors. It's absurd, really. Hateful lies. Of course, you'll see them again. When your training is complete, they may even visit."

There's something too smooth about the way he says it.

I swallow hard, my thoughts a tangled mess. "Elena," I manage, seizing onto the one thing that might ground me. "My friend. She was supposed to go to the Naming Ceremony with me. Do you know if she bonded?"

Rorick's expression doesn't change. "Elena?"

I nod.

For the briefest moment, his gaze sharpens. The flicker of recognition. The smallest hesitation. But then he shakes his head. "No. I'm sorry, Jerrick. I don't recognize the name. She didn't bond."

Something in my gut twists. He's lying.

Before I can press him, he smiles, redirecting effortlessly. "But enough of that," he says, his tone turning almost reverent. "Would you like to know with whom you bonded?"

The room suddenly feels too small. Too quiet.

A part of me doesn't want to know. A part of me wants to reject this outright, to tell him there's been a mistake, that this isn't my path. But deep down, I already know. I can feel it—something inside me is different.

Still, my voice is steady when I say, "Yes."

Rorick steps closer, the lamplight casting long shadows across his aged face. And then, he speaks the name.

"Lathguard."

The breath leaves my lungs in a sharp exhale.

Lathguard.

The King of the gods.

He has never bonded before.

Rorick watches me, gauging my reaction, his eyes alight with something that makes my skin crawl.

"You don't have to share the bond with any other SoulCaster," he says, his voice brimming with meaning. "Your power is immense, Jerrick."

A cold shiver runs through me.

Somewhere deep in my bones, I know—everything has changed.

"How much do you know about Lathguard?" Rorick's voice is thick with reverence, as if merely saying the name holds power.

I shift against the mattress, my muscles stiff from disuse. "I know he was their leader." The words feel inadequate, given the gravity of the moment.

"That he was," Rorick nods, his pale eyes gleaming. "And the most powerful of them all. He could project force, manipulate the very air around him—he could cut through mountains."

A shiver runs through me. Can I do that now? I hesitate before asking, "Does that mean I…?"

"Essence transference works differently for us, but to some extent, yes." He tilts his head, studying me like an artifact newly unearthed. "Depending on the size of your internal reservoir—and, Jerrick, I suspect yours is vast—you are likely the most powerful SoulCaster to have ever lived."

The words land like a blow to the chest.

Part of me is thrilled by the thought. How could I not be? Bonded to the King of the Gods? The power, the possibilities—it should be exhilarating.

But the stronger part of me?

It recoils.

I don't want this. I don't want to stand out. I don't want to be more different than I already am.

I swallow hard. "I don't feel different," I admit. "Shouldn't I be able to feel it? The bond?"

"You will," Rorick assures me. "It's all inside of you. Locked away for now, waiting to be understood. In time, you'll learn how to tap into it. But, Jerrick…" His gaze sharpens, his voice dropping into something almost hushed, as if speaking aloud might shift the course of fate itself.

"You are the key to everything."

A stone drops into my stomach. "Key to what?"

He smiles, but it doesn't reach his eyes. "To pushing back the Fog."

The room suddenly feels smaller. Tighter.

What does that even mean?

Something about the way he says it—like I'm a long-awaited tool, rather than a person—unnerves me. But I don't ask. I don't want the answer. Instead, my mind latches onto my unease. I should feel… something. A shift. A connection.

I should feel different.

I close my eyes and turn my focus inward.

At first, I feel nothing. Just myself. My body. My breath. The steady drumbeat of my heart.

Then—something stirs.

A chain.

Not a physical one, but something deeper. Something tethered to me, stretching into the unseen. It feels ancient, heavy, rooted in something I don't yet understand.

Curious, I follow it.

The chain leads me into a vast, unseen ocean of power. It pulses, alive, swirling in thick, mist-like currents—substantial, endless, infinite. A force older than the land itself.

I hesitate at the edge, sensing a presence within it. It doesn't feel unkind. If anything, the energy welcomes me.

And then, beneath the overwhelming warmth of its embrace, I feel something else.

Fear.

A voice whispers through the connection.

Help me.

Barely more than a breath, but I hear it.

My stomach drops.

The voice is desperate. Ancient. Filled with the weight of a thousand unspoken struggles. It carries the echoes of something lost. Something that has endured beyond its time.

Is it… the land itself?

Or is it something else?

The sheer enormity of the voice terrifies me, but I can't pull away.

My mind grasps for a response, and without thinking, I project a thought back.

Everything will be okay.

It's the same lie I've told others. The same lie I've told myself.

A false promise, spoken in the name of hope.

And then, for the first time, I reach for the power.

The instant I do—agony explodes through me.

A scream tears from my throat as every pore in my body ignites in pain. It's like my blood has turned to acid, searing through my veins, eating me alive from the inside out. My body convulses violently, muscles seizing as fire races through me.

Somewhere in the distance, I hear Rorick's voice, urgent and commanding. But the words don't reach me.

I am burning.

Dying.

The power rejects me.

The last thing I feel before the darkness comes crashing down—

Is fear.

Not mine.

Lathguard's.

"Jerrick, can you hear me? Jerrick!"

Rorick's voice pierces the darkness, but I can barely register it. The pain drowns everything else out.

"Let it go, Jerrick! Let it go!"

Let it go?

I focus inward. My mind latches onto the chain, still tethered to that vast, raw power—the ocean of Essence. Is that what he means?

My fingers loosen their grip.

The pain vanishes.

Instantly.

I collapse back against the bed, my breath coming in ragged gasps. Sweat clings to my skin, my body trembling with lingering echoes of agony. The memory of it is still there, vivid and raw, as if my very bones recall the searing fire that coursed through me.

Rorick is holding my hand. I can feel the slight tremor in his fingers. His ancient face is lined with something I didn't expect.

Genuine concern.

"I'm sorry, Jerrick." His voice is unsteady, laced with something like regret. "I should have warned you. But I... I didn't know it would be that powerful."

I swallow hard. My throat feels raw, like I've been screaming for hours. "What was that?" My voice comes out hoarse, weak.

"You pulled directly from the source," he says, shaking his head. "You must never do that. Normally, it's just a small shock. But I should have known that your reaction would be more severe."

His words barely register past the sheer weight of my exhaustion. My body feels shaky, unstable. This is too much. All of it. The bond. The Naming. My parents.

I just want to go home.

Rorick must sense the war raging inside me, because his expression softens. "Humans were never meant to touch Essence directly," he explains. "Not like that. When we're born, we're already connected to the land. It gives us life—just like an umbilical cord sustains a child in the womb. That connection stays with us until we die. And when we do, the bond pulls whatever Essence we held back into the source."

I try to process what he's saying, but my mind is still hazy with pain. "Then… why did it hurt? Does it always feel like that when SoulCasters channel?"

Rorick shakes his head. "No. Because you're not meant to pull from the source." His gaze sharpens. "You're supposed to pull from your reserve."

Reserve?

"The connection we have to the land is always there," he continues, "but we can't touch it. Not directly. For most people, the Essence they're born with? That's all they'll ever have. But for SoulCasters, the bond with a GodSoul acts as a conduit. It allows us to draw Essence from the land indirectly."

I close my eyes, thinking back to what I felt—the chain leading downward, anchoring me to something ancient. "I don't remember seeing a reserve," I admit.

"That's because you went the wrong way."

I open my eyes. "Wrong way?"

"When you reached out, you followed the bond down." Rorick taps his chest. "You should have followed it up."

Up.

The realization clicks into place. The chain anchored me to the land itself. I had gone deeper, further than I should have. And at the other end of that chain…

Something was there.

Something ancient.

Something afraid.

Rorick watches me carefully, then continues. "Your reserve is what the GodSoul keeps full. That's why bonding with a GodSoul allows you to channel Essence. The power flows through them before reaching you. It's… filtered."

My mind spins. "So, that means… what? Each SoulCaster can only do what their GodSoul could?"

"Exactly." Rorick gives me a knowing smile. "Each god had their own abilities. They could pull from the source without fear. But humans?" He shakes his head. "We can't withstand it. Our bodies aren't strong enough. That's why the bond exists. Think of the GodSoul as a siphon. It takes the raw Essence and reshapes it before passing it to us. That's why SoulCasters from different orders wield different abilities. Their powers are shaped by the god they bonded with."

It's a lot. Too much.

I rub my temples. "What happens if I… use all of it?"

Rorick studies me for a long moment. "That's a good question," he says finally. Then, with a groan, he pushes himself up from his chair, gripping his cane. "But that's not for tonight." He gestures toward the window. "It's past midnight, and this chair is hell on my old bones."

Then, without another word, he turns and walks out. The door clicks shut behind him, leaving me alone with the thrumming silence of the room. His words linger, heavy in the stillness, sinking into the marrow of my bones.

Lathguard. The god of force. King of the gods.

And now, somehow, a part of me.

I stare at the ceiling, my heartbeat too loud in my ears. My body is still wrecked from the pain of touching the Essence source, my mind still tangled in the wreckage of the last three days. I try to force my breathing to slow, but it doesn't help. My thoughts won't quiet.

I try to remember the ceremony, the moment my life changed. But my own rebirth is a blur. Nothing but an empty space where there should be a memory. How is that possible?

I don't know what's worse—the fact that I bonded with Lathguard, or the fact that I had no say in it.

I close my eyes and think of home. Of the quiet mornings on the farm. Of the smell of freshly turned earth. Of my father's deep laugh, my mother's knowing smile.

Of the life I should be living.

A sharp pang of grief cuts through me, and for a moment, it's all I can do not to let it swallow me whole.

I was never meant for this.

I was supposed to work the land, take care of my parents as they grew old, maybe even build a family of my own one day. My life was supposed to be simple. I was supposed to have choices.

But the moment I bonded, those choices died.

I take a slow, shuddering breath and press the feeling down. Down where it won't consume me. Down where no one will see.

I have to.

Because if I let this feeling out—this ache, this rage, this resentment—I don't think I'll be able to control it.

Rorick said that past relationships aren't severed. But does he really believe that?

I don't know if I believe him. What I do know is that my parents will never truly be a part of my life again.

They are on one side of the land. I am on the other.

I close my eyes and feel for the chain again—the one that tethered me to the vast, endless ocean of Essence. I don't reach down this time. I pull up, searching for what Rorick called the reserve.

It's there.

A deep, untouched well of power, separate from the raw force I touched before. This one is cleaner, refined. It's not the chaotic storm of the land's energy.

It's mine.

The realization sends a slow, creeping chill through me. I am not just Jerrick, son of a farmer. I am Jerrick, bonded to Lathguard. A conduit of a god's power. A force that could, if Rorick is to be believed, shape the world.

The weight of it settles on my shoulders. Heavy. Suffocating. And yet, somewhere deep inside me, beneath all the fear, beneath all the grief… There is something else. Something that terrifies me even more.

Excitement.

A whispering voice in the back of my mind, hungry and thrilled at the possibilities. At the power. I don't know what that means. I don't know if it makes me something to be feared.

But I do know one thing. Come morning, a new chapter of my life will begin. And I have to be ready.

#

A thunderous knock rattles the door, jolting me upright. My pulse hammers in my ears as my eyes adjust to the bright, white glow of the Essence Lamp on the nightstand.

Another knock.

By the time I fully process the sound, the door swings open.

A man strides in without a word—sharp-featured, dressed in crisp, impeccable attire. His pinched face, pointed nose, and the precisely trimmed pencil mustache make him look like he's eternally unimpressed by the world around him. Under one arm, he carries a box—beautifully embroidered, richly ornamented.

He doesn't introduce himself.

His polished shoes click against the marble floor as he crosses the room, placing the box onto a large table beneath the far window. Next to it, an empty bowl sits waiting.

"Your robe, sir," he states flatly, then pivots on his heel toward the door. "Breakfast is in half an hour."

That's it?

"Wait."

He stops mid-step, turning only his head, raising a single impatient eyebrow. "Yes?"

"Where's breakfast?"

A sigh, almost imperceptible. "Out your door. First hallway to your left. Midway down, stairs on your right. Dining room. First floor."

He turns to leave, and just as he reaches the door, another man enters, equally silent. This one carries a large silver pitcher, his steps practiced, deliberate. Without a word, he pours clear water into the waiting bowl, filling it nearly to the brim.

Then, just as he finishes—the night breaks.

A pale, gray light floods through the floor-to-ceiling windows, washing over the room like a veil of uncertainty.

I open my mouth to thank him, but he's already leaving, closing the door softly behind him.

That was strange.

I rise from the bed, feeling the ache of muscles that are still adjusting to this new life. My eyes drift to the box.

I don't open it.

Not yet.

I just stare at it.

There's no turning back now. But that robe, whatever is inside, represents everything I never wanted.

Change.

What color will it be? Every Order has its own distinct hue—a mark of their bonded god. But Lathguard has never bonded. No Order carries his name. No robes exist for him.

What will mine look like?

I reach for the box, running my fingers over the embroidered patterns before carrying it to the bed. It's heavier than I expect.

Slowly, I lift the lid.

Inside, the robe is… unlike any I've ever seen.

A stark contrast to the solid colors worn by other Orders, this fabric is alive. Deep blue, nearly black, shifting in the dim light. Gold embroidery twists across it, forming intricate, interwoven patterns. But it's more than thread work—it moves, shimmering, almost pulsating, like a night sky teeming with little lights.

The designs change as I look at them, shifting subtly, as if responding to my very presence.

I run my fingers over the material. It's soft, but strong—like something meant to endure. It doesn't just feel new. It feels ancient.

I swallow hard. This isn't just a robe. It's a statement. A declaration.

I am bonded to Lathguard. The first to ever be. And this? This robe is a symbol of that. A mark that sets me apart. That will always set me apart.

I sigh, shaking my head as I lift it from the box.

"Great. Now I'll really stand out."

I say it to no one.

But something answers.

"That's the point."

Where did that voice come from?

I glance around the room, my breath hitching slightly. I'm alone. Unless…

"It's a robe befitting our station. I was a king among gods. We will wear nothing less than the best."

I freeze, my grip tightening on the robe. The words don't just ring in my ears—they resonate within me, as if spoken from the marrow of my bones.

I swallow hard. "Lathguard?"

"Who else would it be?"

My pulse quickens. The voice is deep, commanding, laced with expectation.

"I'm sorry, uh… sir. This is all new to me." My own words feel clumsy, like an apology to something far beyond me. Is this normal? Am I never going to be alone again?

"Never apologize." The words carry a weight, a reprimand. "It makes you look weak. Makes us look weak."

Us.

The realization slams into me like a punch to the gut.

"We'll talk later. I have a point I want to make."

And just like that, the presence recedes, leaving behind a silence far heavier than the room itself.

I stand there for a long moment, gripping the robe, feeling its weight, its significance.

I'm not alone.

Not in my mind. Not in my soul.

This is what it means to be bonded.

Not just power, not just ability—but a presence. A god woven into my very being. An entity older than time itself now sharing my thoughts.

A shiver creeps down my spine as I run my fingers over the shimmering gold embroidery again. It's more than just clothing. It's a statement. A mantle.

A cage.

I glance toward the window, searching the darkness beyond, but I already know—he's not out there. He doesn't need to be.

He's here.

How do I reconcile this? How do I hold on to myself when there's another voice, another will, threading itself into my every thought?

I set the robe down carefully, smoothing out the fabric with steady hands—as if that simple act will smooth out the turmoil within me.

I won't let this change me.

I cling to the thought like a lifeline.

I am still Jerrick.

Lathguard may be bound to me, may be inside me, but I will not let him define me.

I refuse.

As I prepare for breakfast, the quiet isn't as comforting as it once was. There's an awareness now, a lingering sensation at the edge of my thoughts—like something watching from just beyond the light.

It's going to take time to understand this. To control it. To decide if I even can.

For now, I have to step into this new world. To face the others. How will they see me?

How will they see this robe—this mark of an Order that has never existed before?

I take a deep breath, steadying myself.

This is just the beginning.

And whether this bond will be my greatest strength—or my greatest curse—only time will tell.

#

The dining hall is vast, an expanse of polished stone and structured order. Long wooden tables stretch across the room, arranged in two perfect rows of six, each seating about thirty people. A smaller, more ornate table sits at the front—elevated, expectant, a throne among the ranks.

The scent of roasted meats, baked bread, and spiced eggs fills the air, stirring something deep inside me. Hunger. A primal need. My stomach coils and twists, a sharp reminder of how long it's been since I've eaten. Days? Maybe longer.

But as I take a few steps inside, the noise dies. Conversations fade into hushed murmurs, then into complete silence.

They're staring.

Dozens of eyes locked onto me.

I feel it settle over me like a weight, heavy and suffocating. Recognition. Curiosity. Wariness. But most of all, expectation.

My instinct is to shrink. To become smaller. Less. Like I had tried to do in Civic Education class, when standing out meant ridicule rather than power. If I could just slip into a corner, grab my food, and disappear, maybe they'd stop looking.

"Stop slouching."

The voice in my head is sharp, firm.

"Take your rightful place at the head."

I flinch.

"But I—" I begin to whisper, but I don't get the chance to finish.

"Do it now."

This time, the voice growls. It's not a command. It's an expectation.

I take a slow, measured step forward. Then another.

The stares don't waver.

I move towards the front table, my steps feeling both entirely my own and entirely not. It seats five.

This is wrong. This is where Rorick sits.

"The center, Jerrick. We are second to no one."

I freeze.

"But that must be where Rorick—"

"Sat. Now sit!"

My hands tighten into fists at my sides. I don't want this. Any of it.

I just want to sit down, eat my food, and pretend—for a little while—that I can still be just Jerrick.

But Lathguard isn't told no.

I hesitate a fraction longer. Then, with a slow breath, I sit.

The door to my left swings open.

Four SoulCasters enter, their presence commanding, their robes flowing as they stride into the room.

My gaze catches on one of them—a woman in the light blue of Zephyra.

Tall. Striking. Fiery red hair. I know herm but from where?

She moves like the wind itself—gliding, effortless, the very embodiment of control.

Then, her emerald-green eyes meet mine, and she smiles.

It's not a simple smile. It's knowing. Playful. Dangerous.

I realize, too late, that I've been holding my breath.

"Did I take your breath away?" she teases, laughter bubbling up— rich, full, like she's in on a private joke that I don't understand.

I scramble for a response. Anything.

"No. Sorry, I—"

"What did I tell you?" Lathguard's voice cuts through my thoughts, sharp and disappointed.

But I barely hear him. My mind is still spinning, trying to place her.

"I just…" I shake my head. "You look familiar. I was trying to remember where I've seen you before."

She winks.

A slow, deliberate movement.

She places a hand on my shoulder, leans in slightly, and suddenly, I'm very aware of how close she is.

"Believe me," she murmurs, voice smooth as silk, "you'd remember me if we had met before."

Heat rushes to my face.

Before I can recover, the other three SoulCasters take their seats beside me, their movements deliberate, their expressions flickering between surprise and calculation. But they don't speak up.

And then, Rorick enters.

The room shifts.

Not from power, not from magic, but from presence.

He moves slowly, heavily, his cane tapping against the stone floor. His posture is hunched, his ancient form betraying the effort it takes to simply move.

But his gaze—when it settles on me—is sharp. Unwavering.

He stops beside me.

Sighs.

"Let's walk," he says.

And I already know.

This is not just a conversation.

This is a reckoning.

I rise from my chair, towering over Rorick in a way I hadn't truly registered before. He is small, frail, his frame permanently bent by time and burden. Even if he stood upright, he wouldn't be much taller than five feet.

Last night, when he had loomed over me in the dim light of my room, he had felt... larger. More substantial. But now, in the clarity of morning, he is simply old.

"Tell him I'm disappointed."

The voice slithers through my mind, coiling around my thoughts like a vice.

I hesitate, my lips parting slightly—but no. I won't say that.

I refuse.

Instead, I ignore the voice in my head and follow Rorick out of the dining hall.

We pass through the kitchen, the scents of morning meals fading behind us as we step out into the open air. Beyond the Keep, a quiet expanse stretches out—an empty courtyard dotted with simple stone benches. It's a stark contrast to the grandeur inside, a space untouched by opulence. Bare earth. Quiet. Isolated.

Rorick stops. Turns.

His back is permanently hunched, and he cannot crane his neck far enough to meet my gaze.

"Would you be kind to an old man and take a seat?" he asks. His voice is even, but there's an undertone—fatigue, maybe. Or something deeper.

"Tell him."

The voice again. Quieter. But commanding.

"Tell him, now."

I swallow hard. My body tenses.

And then, I sit.

It's not submission. Not to the voice. Just... easier.

Now seated, my head is still higher than Rorick's, but at least now he can look me in the eye.

He studies me for a moment, his gaze tracing the edges of my robe.

"It looks good on you," he muses. His voice is thoughtful. Measured. "Those were his colors."

The words land heavier than I expect.

"So it's true?" I ask cautiously. "You were around back then?"

Rorick laughs, the sound rich with amusement—but also with something else. Something older.

"It takes more than one lifetime to get wrinkles like this!" he jokes, gesturing toward his deeply lined face with an exaggerated flourish. "Yes, I'm over five hundred years old. I was the first SoulCaster. Lathguard himself told me of the bond."

Five hundred years?

I stiffen. My breath catches slightly.

He knew Lathguard.

The weight of that settles over me like an avalanche.

Five hundred years of memories. Five hundred years of watching the world change. And somehow, through it all, he still smiles.

"What was he like?" I ask, my voice quieter now.

Rorick's expression shifts.

"Powerful beyond words. Terrifying." His eyes darken, lost in the vast corridors of his past. "He was always just. Always kind—until he wasn't. His wrath was absolute. When the gods died... when Lathguard died... I was with him."

For the briefest moment, I see it—not Rorick as he is now, but as he once was. Young. Standing beside a god in his final moments.

What must it be like to carry that memory?

To be the last witness to a god's fall?

"Do as I say, Jerrick!"

The voice inside my head booms, reverberating through my very bones.

My whole body stiffens.

"Tell him he disappoints me!"

The force of it is deafening. A storm raging inside my skull, cracking through my mind like a whip.

I shake my head.

"No," I say aloud, gritted. Defiant.

"You're nothing without me!"

"I made you who you are!"

"How dare you tell me no!"

Each word lands like a hammer against my skull.

I blink. Hard. My vision flickers with pain, each syllable like a pulse of searing light behind my eyes.

"How do I make it stop?" My voice is hoarse, barely more than a whisper.

Rorick's gaze sharpens. Concern. Calculation. Understanding.

"What is he telling you?"

"He... he says that he's disappointed in you."

The moment the words leave my mouth, Rorick stills.

His face slackens, his expression blank but heavy. He doesn't respond immediately, doesn't acknowledge it—not really. Instead, his eyes shift toward the distance, gazing at something I can't see.

Then, softly—not to me, but to someone else—he murmurs, "I'm tired."

I don't understand.

I want to. But the weight in his voice—the exhaustion, the resignation—is something I can't quite grasp. And then, the voice returns.

"We've both made sacrifices."

"I have spent over five hundred years swirling in darkness."

"Now is not the time for excuses. Now is the time for action."

"Remember my promise to you, Rorick. I keep my word. Now you keep yours."

The words are cold. Final.

I repeat them aloud.

Rorick closes his eyes briefly, as if the words physically press down on him.

Then, he exhales. "Then understand that what happens next must happen."

His gaze lifts, meeting mine again.

"I'm sorry that you were in the middle of that, Jerrick."

"Weak!"

The voice snarls.

I don't repeat it.

"I don't think either of us had a choice in that," I say instead, my voice still hoarse. "Is he always like this?"

Rorick's expression is unreadable.

"Yes and no."

He studies me for a long moment, and then, softer than before, he adds: "It may not seem like it now, but he's on the right side of this." He hesitates. "You can trust him."

There's something about Rorick that makes me trust him almost immediately. His presence carries a quiet wisdom, like a kind grandfather—but beneath that warmth, there's steel. He has the look of a man who's seen things, endured things, and come out the other side still smiling.

"That's good to hear," I say.

He studies me for a moment, then his expression shifts. The fatigue vanishes. His eyes gleam with an almost childlike excitement. "How would you like your first lesson?"

The abrupt change catches me off guard, but excitement quickly replaces hesitation. I've spent the last three days unconscious, drowning in uncertainty. This is something real. Something I can control.

"Yes."

"Good!" Rorick leans forward slightly, his gnarled hands gripping the edge of the bench. "The first thing you need to master is awareness. You need to know where everything is, how to access it. Last night, you touched the Source—and if I know young men, you probably explored a little more after I left."

He's not wrong. I nod.

"I want you to do it again," he continues, "but this time, when you reach your reservoir, I want you to look for another connection. It shouldn't be too hard to find."

Tapping Into the Bond

I close my eyes and reach inward.

The chain is there, just like before—a tether that extends deep into the unknown. I follow it upward this time, to where I felt the wellspring of power before.

And then, I see it.

A sphere.

It floats in the darkness like a pulsing heart, glowing in rhythm with my own. It's unlike the raw, violent surge of the Source—this is something quieter, refined.

I reach out.

The closer my hand comes, the brighter it glows, as if it's responding to my presence.

It doesn't burn like the Source. It doesn't reject me. It's welcoming.

Curious, I sweep my hands across it. Ripples of energy dance over the surface, shimmering like the reflection of light on water. Then, something strange happens—the sphere shrinks the closer my hands move together. When I pull them apart, it expands.

I experiment, pulling it small, expanding it wide. With each shift, the Essence within shifts as well.

That's when I see it.

Another connection.

Not like the chain that links my reservoir to the Source. This one is different. It looks organic, almost like a root. It stretches outward, disappearing into a void.

Not emptiness. Something else.

The void is Lathguard.

I know it instinctively. It doesn't belong. It's severed, cut off. A foreign entity lodged into the fabric of this power.

I don't know what to make of it.

I release my hold on everything and snap back to reality.

Back on the Bench

I gasp. My breath comes fast and ragged, my heart hammering in my chest.

"Wow," I exhale. "That was... something."

Rorick smiles knowingly.

"It really is."

His expression is pleased, like a teacher watching a student take their first real step.

"Now that you know the lay of the land—so to speak—you can pull from your reservoir at will. In time, you'll learn to do it while staying fully conscious."

I blink at him.

"I was unconscious?"

"Oh, completely," he chuckles. "The moment you closed your eyes, your whole body went slack. But that's normal for beginners. With practice, you'll learn to access it while remaining aware of the physical world."

That's good to know. I'd rather not be collapsing every time I need to channel Essence.

"For now, let's take the next step," Rorick continues. "Channeling."

I straighten slightly. This is it.

"How?"

"First, you need to decide how much Essence you're pulling."

I frown. "How do I know that?"

"You may have noticed something back there—the size of your reservoir shifts depending on how you interact with it. When it's small, the Essence is concentrated. The smaller it is, the faster you'll drain it. The larger it is, the slower you'll deplete it."

I think back to what I just saw—the way the sphere grew and shrank with my movements. It makes sense.

"Make it as large as you can," Rorick instructs. "And try to remain conscious this time."

I close my eyes again.

This time, I focus on keeping my awareness split—part of me staying grounded in the real world, while the other reaches inward.

The chain. The sphere.

I widen it.

I stretch my arms as wide as they'll go, watching as the sphere expands—larger, larger, larger until it nearly blocks out everything else.

"Okay," I say, keeping my breathing steady. "I got it."

"Good."

I open my eyes. Rorick gestures toward the woods in the distance.

"Now, stand up. Face the trees. Channel your Essence. Just imagine the air hardening in front of you—and then, push it outward."

I take a slow breath.

I don't hesitate.

I command it.

The moment I reach for the power, it responds.

I feel it building inside me, a pressure coiling, waiting to be released. I focus on the air before me, imagining it hardening, taking shape—becoming something tangible.

And then, it happens.

A shimmer spreads across the space in front of me, like frost creeping over glass. The very air solidifies, a nearly invisible wall of force suspended in front of me.

I push.

A loud pop cracks through the air as the force explodes forward in a blur.

It slams into the trees at the edge of the field.

With effortless finality, three massive trunks are cleaved clean through. For a moment, they stand, as if refusing to believe they've been cut. Then, with a groaning protest, they topple, crashing into the underbrush with a series of deafening thuds.

I stare.

The Rush of Power

Incredible.

I can feel it—this force, this raw, unchecked power. The rush of energy flooding through me is intoxicating. I've never experienced anything like it. It's as if I've tapped into something primal, something ancient.

But it's also terrifying.

That blast, that force—I barely pushed and yet, three trees fell like wheat before a scythe. What happens if I lose control? If I unleash too much? If, instead of trees... it's people standing in my way?

No. I can't think like that.

This power is mine now.

I need to master it.

"Exhilarating, isn't it?"

Rorick's voice pulls me from my thoughts. I look at him, still catching my breath.

"Yes," I admit. "But also terrifying."

"There's a reason I had you channel just now, Jerrick," Rorick says, his voice calm. "Whenever a SoulCaster first bonds to a GodSoul—whether at the Naming or after severing the connection—that voice never stops until you channel through them for the first time. Some of them can be quite… demanding."

I blink. Understanding dawns.

"So you're saying… Lathguard won't be in my head anymore?"

"Not unless you let him. He won't be able to reach you unless you sever the connection willfully. It should be much quieter now."

I can't stop the wave of relief that floods me.

"Thank you," I exhale. "I don't know how much more I could have taken."

For a moment, I half-expect to hear Lathguard protest, to snarl in my mind, but... silence.

He's gone.

Finally.

A strange mix of emotions wells in my chest. Relief. Freedom. And something else. Something I don't want to name.

"I'm sorry, Rorick…" I say after a pause. "For sitting in your seat."

The old man chuckles, shaking his head.

"He's not as bad as he sounds," he says, though there's an edge of something unreadable in his voice. "When you've been a god-king for centuries, you get used to getting your way."

Maybe. But I don't know if I'll ever be comfortable with him.

"This is all so much," I admit. "To be honest, I never really wanted any of this."

Rorick's face softens. His sharp, piercing gaze is replaced with something... familiar. A look of understanding.

"I know the feeling all too well," he says quietly, and there's a note of melancholy in his voice I hadn't expected.

His gaze drifts somewhere far away, to a time long before I was even born.

"When I was about your age," he begins, "I found myself caught in a war I had no desire to fight. My dream was never to be a warrior, never to be part of something grand. All I wanted was to take care of my father."

His words hit me harder than I expect.

I see him differently now—not just as the legendary Rorick, first of the SoulCasters, but as a man. A son, just like me.

"My mother died when I was born," he continues. "It was just the two of us. My father was sick, and I joined the war effort simply to send back whatever coin I could. It wasn't about honor or duty. It was survival."

I feel a lump in my throat. I know what it's like to fight for your family. To want nothing more than to protect the ones you love.

"I remember running across battlefields," Rorick says, his voice quieter now. "Heart pounding—not from the thrill of combat, but from sheer terror. From the desperate need to survive."

I swallow hard. That sounds familiar.

"I longed to be invisible," he admits. "To be unnoticed by both friend and foe. A shadow flitting through the chaos, untouched."

His words linger in the cool morning air, and I see something in his face—a weariness. A man who has carried too much, for too long.

"But my efforts didn't go unnoticed," he says after a moment, his voice shifting. Lighter. "Lathguard saw something in me. Perhaps it was my determination. Perhaps it was my ability to move unseen. Either way, he chose me to be his eyes and ears among his generals."

A faint, almost rueful smile tugs at his lips.

"I never sought that role. I never craved power or secrets."

His eyes meet mine again, full of understanding.

"All I wanted," he says, "was to keep my father safe."

Rorick's words linger, heavy with the weight of centuries.

"I understand if this world of gods and power feels overwhelming, Jerrick," he says. "Like you, I was thrust into a life I never asked for. But sometimes, life chooses us for paths we never expected to walk."

His gaze meets mine, filled with something deeper than wisdom—understanding.

"We all carry burdens, Jerrick. Some are thrust upon us, while others we choose. But in the end, it's how we bear them that defines us."

His eyes drift past me, to the open space around us, as if looking beyond time itself. And for the first time, I see not just the legend, not just the powerful SoulCaster, but a man—one who has lived through too much. A man who, despite everything, has endured.

"I'm sorry you're caught in the middle of all this," he continues, quieter now. "But remember, every step you take on this path is a chance to define who you are and who you want to be. You have an important role to play in all of this."

I sit there, absorbing his words.

Rorick is more than a mentor. More than a guide.

He is a reflection of the choices I'll have to make. The sacrifices I'll be forced to carry. A reminder that even in a world of gods and Essence, it's the most human struggles that matter most.

There is a long silence.

Then, he smiles.

"I think we missed breakfast," he muses. "And you have class soon. Let's see if we can find something to eat."

I follow him back toward the keep, my mind still reeling. But something new settles in my chest—not certainty, not yet—but something close.

As we walk, I notice something I hadn't before.

Rorick's steps are measured, deliberate.

He moves with purpose, but there's a stiffness to him—a hesitation before shifting his weight, like every motion is a quiet negotiation with an old ache.

And yet, he never lets it show.

Never stumbles. Never falters.

The weight of centuries is carved into his form, but he carries it without complaint.

I watch him in a new light. I think of what it must be like, outliving everyone you love. Watching the world shift and change, while you remain the same. How many battles has he fought? How many people has he seen come and go?

And still, he walks forward.

Still, he endures.

When we step into the kitchen, the air is warm, alive. The scent of sizzling meat and freshly baked bread wraps around me, a stark contrast to the cold weight of the world outside.

The staff pause when Rorick enters. They don't speak, but their actions say everything.

Respect.

A quiet acknowledgment of the man who has stood against time itself.

"Can we get a quick meal for two?" Rorick asks. His voice is calm, betraying none of the exhaustion I know he must feel.

The server nods quickly and disappears.

Rorick leans slightly on his cane, his gaze drifting over the hustle of the kitchen. And for a moment, he smiles.

"This place always reminds me of my father," he says softly, almost to himself. "He loved to cook. Said it was his way of bringing a little warmth into our home. I used to watch him for hours... fascinated by how he could turn simple ingredients into something wonderful."

I say nothing.

Because this is his moment.

And I realize then that even the strongest men carry ghosts.

There's something in his eyes, a memory so distant that I doubt anyone else alive remembers it. It's the kind of memory that both hurts and heals—something fragile, yet enduring.

A lifetime trapped inside a single thought.

The server returns with our food, and Rorick thanks them with a quiet nod.

We find a table, and I watch as he lowers himself into a chair— slowly, carefully, but without hesitation. There's an art to it, a silent defiance against pain.

As I sit across from him, a thought takes root in my mind.

Rorick embodies a strength rarely spoken about.

Not the strength of Essence.
Not the strength of battle.
But the strength to endure.
To carry on despite the pain.
To wake up, day after day, and face the weight of history itself.
To still be here.

And in that moment, I understand something: His power isn't in the magic. It's in his will. A will that has weathered the storms of centuries—and still finds the courage to face each new dawn.

Chapter 10

Jerrick

The Council Keep is a colossus of stone and time, a structure older than any other. Built at the dawn of the Third Epoch, long before the God Wars, it has stood unwavering for over five centuries. Yet, its towering walls and pristine halls defy the wear of age, as though the Keep itself resists the passage of time.

Perched atop a low plateau, it overlooks the Great Plains, a sea of golden grasses that stretch endlessly beyond the horizon. The Keep itself is a sprawling fortress, a labyrinth of seven towering stories and hundreds of rooms, each one echoing with the footsteps of history.

Despite its grandeur, the Keep is no mere relic of the past—it is a living, breathing stronghold, maintained by over fifty personnel, most of them third- and fourth-generation groundskeepers, painters, maintenance workers, cooks, housekeepers, and servers. These people have spent their entire lives within these walls, tending to a place that has become both home and mystery.

I've spent the past three days wandering through the Keep's endless corridors, learning its layout, but never truly feeling at home. The other newly bonded SoulCasters keep their distance from me—and that's fine. I've always preferred my own company. Too many people means too much noise, too many expectations. And right now, I don't have answers—not for them, not even for myself.

The room I find myself in now isn't one of the Keep's grand chambers, yet it still carries a quiet elegance. Hand-carved molding, towering tapestries, and massive floor-to-ceiling windows frame the east lawn, where the first gray light of morning filters in. The scent of banana and wood polish lingers in the air—a signature aroma of the Keep, one I'm still getting used to.

The ceilings soar twenty feet above our heads, an architectural marvel designed not just for beauty, but to remind us of the power and wisdom that once ruled these halls.

There are twenty of us in the room, notebooks open, heads bent in focus as Lyrisa, our instructor, speaks from the front of the room. She is draped in the yellow robes of the Order of Light, her presence almost ethereal, her voice melodic, as though she might sing instead of speak at any moment.

"There are five main categories that pertain to the use of Essence: nurturing, protecting, projecting, binding, and revealing." Lyrisa's eyes sweep across the room, making sure we're following. "Every ability we have falls into one of these categories—or a combination of them. These categories govern everything we do and are subject so specific laws."

I take notes, trying to focus. But a part of me still wrestles with everything that's happened. The Naming, my bond with Lathguard, the sheer magnitude of what I'm supposed to become.

Lyrisa continues, "These laws are separated into two types: innate and extrinsic. Innate laws are dictated by nature itself, immutable and absolute. Extrinsic laws, however, are established by The Council, designed to prevent us from drawing too much from the land. If you wish to use Essence outside these walls, you must memorize them all."

Her words settle over us like an unspoken warning.

I glance at her robes again. The Order of Light. She is bonded with Aurilis, the Light Bringer, master of both light and illusion. Unlike Rorick, whose presence carries the weight of centuries, Lyrisa feels untouchable, effortless—as though she was born to wield her power.

She raises a hand, and a small sphere of golden light flickers into existence above her palm. "Refined Essence has many uses," she explains, sending the light floating upwards toward the ceiling. "Some known, some not. This class teaches you the basics—a foundation for you to build upon. Essence is both power and responsibility, and understanding its laws is crucial."

The orb of light shifts, growing brighter. It intensifies until I have to look away, my eyes stinging from its brilliance. Then, with a simple gesture, she dampens it, its glow softening until it is a pale, spectral white.

Then, suddenly, the room goes dark.

It's not just the absence of light. It's a void. The windows—once bright with morning light—are now blackened, as if the outside world has been erased. The air feels thicker, heavier, as if something is missing from existence itself.

Then, just as abruptly, the light returns. The warmth of the day floods back in, filling the room like a breath of relief.

"One of the innate laws of my Order is the Law of Ethereal Harmony," Lyrisa says, lowering her hand. "This law states that all uses of light and illusion magic must maintain the natural balance of light and shadow. It prohibits the creation of perpetual daylight or endless night, ensuring the cycle remains undisturbed. Should I break this law… the consequences would be severe. To defy the natural order is to risk death—or worse, the loss of my bond."

The class is silent, absorbing the weight of her words.

A mousy-faced boy beside me raises his hand hesitantly. "Do you really have the power to create perpetual daylight?"

Lyrisa smiles, but there's a trace of sadness in it. "Yes and no," she admits. "It depends on my rate of renewal and the area I wish to maintain. As you all know, your GodSoul acts as a siphon, drawing raw Essence and refining it into something we can use. But there are limits— our reservoirs can only hold so much Essence, and the rate at which we pull from them determines how quickly we drain them."

Her voice grows somber. "There's a danger in overuse. If you deplete your reservoir faster than it can renew, you won't just run out of Essence—you will begin drawing from your own life force. And if that happens…" She pauses, letting the silence speak for itself. "You could die of old age in moments."

A chill runs down my spine. The room feels heavier now.

She waits, giving us time to process her words. When no one speaks, she continues. "Your rate of renewal depends on the power of your GodSoul and how many SoulCasters they are bonded with. Some bonds are shared by many, meaning their power is divided. Others, like Jerrick's…"

I stiffen as I feel the impact of every eye in the room shift toward me. Lyrisa glances my way but doesn't call attention to it.

"Others," she repeats carefully, "stand alone."

And just like that, I realize something chilling: There's no one else like me.

I sit in silence, staring at my notes, but not really seeing them.

Lathguard has never bonded before. I'm the first. The only.

And that means no one else shares this burden.

For better or worse… this power is mine alone.

Someone from the back of the room raises their hand, prompting Lyrisa to nod in acknowledgment.

"So, our power is determined by how many SoulCasters share a bond with the same GodSoul?" the student asks.

Lyrisa inclines her head. "Partially, yes. The other factor is the density of our reservoirs. The denser it is, the harder the GodSoul must work to sustain it, and the fewer SoulCasters they can support."

She pauses, letting that sink in before shifting back to the original question. "As for the idea of creating perpetual daylight, in theory, yes, I could do it—if I maintained a rate of renewal higher than my depletion. But Essence follows its own laws, both natural and extrinsic." Her tone darkens slightly. "Which prohibits the disruption of the world's balance. Violating it carries consequences—ones that cannot be avoided. Some laws result in the severing of your bond, while others... well, they result in death."

A hush settles over the room.

"So," she continues, "if I were foolish enough to try and force daylight without end, I would likely die in the process. However, since our reservoirs are eternal, the daylight I created wouldn't just vanish with me. It would continue until the equilibrium shifted once more."

She lets that thought settle before adding, "That's where the balance of our Orders comes in. Even if someone did create perpetual daylight and perished, as their Order grew and the power was spread thin, the rate of depletion would inevitably outpace renewal, and the unnatural effect would collapse."

The logic behind it is sound, but Lyrisa's words hold a deeper, more unsettling truth for me.

Because I have no Order.

The weight of this knowledge presses into me, making my notebook suddenly feel heavier in my hands.

I am the only one bonded to Lathguard. The realization shifts something deep inside me—I am an anomaly, an outlier in a system that has existed for centuries.

The classroom, filled with students eagerly discussing their shared abilities, suddenly feels isolating. Every other SoulCaster has counterparts—others who share their burden, their strength, their weaknesses. But I am alone.

Does that mean my rate of renewal is higher than theirs? Am I stronger than all of them? If what Rorick said was true, then my power is unmatched.

The thought is exhilarating… and terrifying.

What happens if I lose control? If I overstep? If I violate an innate law, there's no one else to counterbalance me, no Order to correct my actions.

For the first time, I truly understand the burden of being the first, the only.

Lyrisa continues her lecture, but I barely hear her. I'm adrift in my thoughts, caught between the thrill of potential and the crushing weight of responsibility.

Then, without warning, my world shatters.

A colossal figure materializes before the class, so sudden, so massive, that my pulse spikes in sheer terror.

Towering at over twenty feet, the entity is a living monolith of battle-hardened armor. His hands are so large that he could crush my entire body in his grip. His eyes—deep, abyssal pools of black—stare down at us without whites, an unsettling void of expression.

Most of his body is encased in intricate battle-plate, but the exposed portions of his skin are like carapace, thick and unyielding, as if his flesh was forged from the very earth itself. His face is a brutal symphony of sharp angles and deliberate lines, each ridge carved like a statue of war.

The sheer presence of him is overwhelming.

I kick back from my chair, sending it clattering to the floor as I push away from the towering monstrosity. My instincts scream at me to run, but the only exit is behind him. I am trapped.

Then I remember—I have power now.

I reach inside myself, trying to summon it.

I search for the connection, the link to my reservoir, but panic clouds my mind. I can't find it. It's there—I know it's there—but I can't make it work.

The giant takes a step forward, his massive boot slamming into the floor with enough force to rattle my bones.

I fumble for my Essence, for anything, but I am helpless.

I am nothing.

And then—he vanishes.

Like smoke dissipating into the wind, he is gone.

I stumble backward, chest heaving, my pulse hammering against my ribs.

"Jerrick!" Lyrisa's voice snaps me back to reality. She looks horrified.

"It was just an illusion!" she gasps. "I warned everyone before I created it!"

My heart pounds against my ribs, my hands tremble. The giant is gone, and I know it wasn't real, but the fear lingers, coiled in my chest like a living thing.

I look around, feeling the weight of a hundred stares. Some of my classmates are wide-eyed with shock, but others… some are barely holding in their laughter. A few cover their mouths, shoulders shaking, their amusement poorly disguised.

Heat rushes to my face, humiliation settling like a stone in my gut. I want to disappear. To get up, walk out, find a dark corner where I can hide until this all feels like a bad dream.

But I don't.

I refuse.

Instead, I force myself to move, bending down with measured slowness to pick up my chair. I set it upright, settle back into my seat, and pretend my hands aren't still shaking.

No doubt sensing my embarrassment, Lyrisa thankfully continues as if nothing happened.

"My ability over light extends beyond mere illumination," she says smoothly. "I can shape it, change its color, its intensity, its form.

What you just saw was Aurilis, the god of light and illusion. It can appear strikingly real—especially if you weren't expecting it."

Her eyes flick toward me, full of concern. She knew. She had seen my reaction, seen my fear. But she doesn't call attention to it, and for that, I'm grateful.

Instead, she pivots, moving forward.

"This brings me to an important extrinsic law governing my Order: the Law of Benevolent Deception."

She lifts her hand, conjuring another illusion, this time a small, harmless orb of shifting light, its surface shimmering like liquid gold. "This law dictates that illusions crafted by practitioners of the Order of Light must always be used for benevolent purposes."

The orb twists, morphs, taking on different shapes—first a butterfly, then a flower, then a flickering candle.

"It forbids the use of illusions to deceive for personal gain, to harm, or to manipulate others against their will. This ensures that the power to craft illusions is wielded responsibly, in accordance with the principles of truth and guidance that Aurilis represents."

Her voice carries a quiet authority, and for the first time since the illusion of Aurilis vanished, I feel myself start to breathe normally again.

But the moment still clings to me.

I sit there, my gaze locked onto my notebook, but the words scrawled across the page feel distant. What just happened wasn't just a lesson in the laws of Essence—it was a reminder of what these laws are meant to protect us from.

Power unchecked. Fear uncontrolled. The ability to bend reality itself.

I glance at Lyrisa, at the ease with which she wields illusion, how quickly she conjures and dispels images that seem more real than thought itself.

This isn't just a classroom. This is a training ground for something much bigger.

I lift my gaze to my classmates. Some are still buzzing with excitement, whispering to one another. Others are lost in thought, digesting the weight of the lesson.

For the first time, I see them differently.

We are all part of something greater than ourselves. Something older. Larger. More powerful than any one of us individually.

This isn't just about learning how to use Essence.

This is about learning how not to abuse it.

The class ends with a hush of quiet contemplation. As I gather my things, I feel something shift inside me—not just knowledge, but understanding.

Power isn't just about strength. It's about control. Restraint. Purpose.

As I step out of the classroom, walking through the grand halls of the Council Keep, I feel the weight of history pressing in around me—but also the weight of the future pulling me forward.

There is so much to learn.

But for the first time, I don't feel like I'm running from it. I feel like I'm ready for it.

#

Seated alone in my Order's designated section of the dining room, I find solace in isolation. The room is alive with conversation, voices weaving together into a background hum, but I remain untouched by it. My thoughts are my own, and for now, that's where I'd rather be.

The long tables are meant to be shared, but with so few of us, each Order remains scattered throughout the space. There are twelve Orders in total, yet today, the room feels… emptier than yesterday.

I brush the thought aside, returning to my internal calculations.

Each day at the Keep is divided into two halves—the mornings devoted to theory, laws, and history, while afternoons are spent practicing Essence channeling within our respective Orders.

Except me.

I have no Order. No mentor, no guide beyond Rorick, and no peers who share my abilities. I'm left to figure this out on my own.

That should feel daunting. It doesn't.

If anything, I prefer it this way. I've always been better left with my own thoughts.

The problem is, we can't afford to use too much Essence right now.

The land is decaying.

The Source—the wellspring of all Essence—is finite. Just like our internal reservoirs, it needs time to recover. But its renewal rate is agonizingly slow. Too slow.

SoulCasters draw massive amounts of Essence when they channel. Ten parts raw Essence are needed to refine just one part of usable Essence. It's a process of staggering inefficiency, one that our GodSouls facilitate—but one that also drains the land.

The land mirrors our bodies. Deplete it too quickly, and it begins to wither. If its rate of depletion outstrips its renewal, the land shrinks.

And when the land shrinks, the Fog moves in.

The Fog is death. A physical manifestation of decay, spreading as the land's lifeblood runs dry.

And we—SoulCasters—are the ones bleeding it dry.

We're taught that overuse of our reservoirs leads to premature aging, even death. But what happens when the land itself succumbs to the same fate?

How much time do we have left?

My thoughts shift back to something more immediate.

If Essence can be used as an offensive force, like when I cut down those trees…

Could it also be used defensively?

If I could shape a concussive blast, why not a protective shield?

It would be the same principle. A shift in application. Instead of expelling force outward, I could reinforce the air around me, shaping it into an impenetrable barrier.

I've seen SoulCasters weaponise their abilities, but could I learn to defend with mine?

"…Jerrick?"

The voice pulls me from my thoughts. I flinch slightly, only just realizing that someone is standing beside me.

A hand lightly touches my shoulder.

I turn to see the mousy-faced boy from class earlier, the one who had asked about Aurilis. I don't think I ever caught his name.

"Oh, sorry," I say, still adjusting to the present moment. "I was… elsewhere."

He offers a hesitant smile. "I don't think we were properly introduced. My name is Eldrin."

Eldrin. The black robe of the Order of Night drapes over his slight frame. A shadow-weaver. A follower of Grimlon, master of darkness.

"Nice to meet you," I reply, sitting up slightly.

"You're from the Four Rivers, right?" he asks.

The question catches me off guard. "I am. Why?"

Eldrin hesitates.

"Don't you find it strange that you're the only bonded from the Four Rivers?"

A chill runs down my spine.

That can't be right.

Can it?

I've lost time—three whole days—but surely others bonded. Others must have been chosen.

I glance around the vast dining hall, scanning the faces at each table.

None of them are familiar.

Not a single one.

"Are you sure?" I ask, my voice quieter than before.

Eldrin nods. "Pretty sure. I've talked to almost everyone here, and no one else claims to be from the Four Rivers."

The unease in my stomach grows heavier.

Something isn't right.

"I don't know what it means," Eldrin continues. "But there's more. There are even a few of us missing."

I stiffen. "Missing?"

Eldrin nods again, this time more slowly.

"Yeah… I noticed it too. Fewer of us today than yesterday." The thought has been gnawing at me since breakfast.

"Do you know why?" I ask, my voice barely above a whisper.

Eldrin leans in. "Well… it's no secret that some just don't make it."

A cold weight settles in my chest.

"What do you mean?"

"Some don't have strong enough reservoirs. There was a kid from Sussex, same town as me. They sent him home because his density was too low. The head of my Order said he couldn't hold enough Essence to channel anything significant."

I absorb this. That makes sense—reservoir density determines our ability to cast.

But there's something off in Eldrin's tone.

There's more. I can feel it.

He hesitates. Then, his eyes flicker over my shoulder.

Something changes.

His posture stiffens. His voice drops to a whisper. "I have to go."

Before I can say anything, he turns and quickly walks away.

I don't move.

I don't breathe.

I just sit there, staring at the empty space where he stood.

And the unease in my stomach? It just turned into dread.

I turn my head, following Eldrin's gaze, my stomach tightening with unease.

Rorick.

He's watching me.

His brows are furrowed, his gaze sharp—but just as quickly as the expression appears, it vanishes. His features soften into a smile, his head dipping in a nod of acknowledgment.

I hesitate, then nod back.

The weight in my chest doesn't lift.

The realization that I might be the only bonded SoulCaster from the Four Rivers presses down on me.

It's an unsettling thought—one that suggests something more than mere coincidence.

Why me? What makes me different?

Eldrin's words about others being sent home—about people missing—only add to my growing unease. What is happening here?

The bonds. The rules. The intricacies of Essence.

They're more complicated than I expected. More dangerous, perhaps, than I've even begun to understand.

I stare down at the untouched food before me.

It feels like an afterthought, a mundane detail in a world suddenly filled with unanswered questions.

Usually, food is a comfort. A constant. But now?

I can barely bring myself to lift my fork.

My mind is somewhere else—racing with theories, tangled in uncertainties, trapped between doubt and suspicion.

Is my unique status as the only bonded of Lathguard—and possibly the only bonded from my home—a coincidence?

Or is something else at play?

Rorick's gaze lingers in my mind.

His nod, his smile—it all felt too easy. Too practiced.

Does he know? Does he know why no one else bonded in the Four Rivers? Does he know what happened to the missing SoulCasters?

I grip the table's edge, my knuckles going white.

This is more than it seems.

As lunch ends, I push back from the table, my appetite long gone.

I leave the dining hall not thinking about the lessons ahead, but about the mysteries that seem to be closing in around me.

Something is happening. And I'm in the middle of it.

#

Afternoon sessions unfold in bustling classrooms and wide open training fields, where each Order proudly passes down centuries of channeling wisdom.

Except for mine.

The Order of Force has no instructors, no ancient scrolls of forbidden knowledge, no legacy carefully passed down through generations.

There's only me.

I wander the towering halls of the library, its shelves swollen with the weight of millennia. Books on every known discipline of Essence—Nurturing, Protecting, Binding, Revealing—line the walls in meticulous order.

But Force Magic?

Nothing.

Our Order is a ghost in the records—an afterthought erased by history.

Frustrated, I seize two leather-bound journals—handwritten accounts from the God Wars, their ink faded, their pages brittle with time. If anyone ever recorded Lathguard's power, it would be here.

For a moment, I consider asking Rorick. He was alive back then. He knew Lathguard.

But something tells me he'd rather I discover the truth on my own.

Besides…

We haven't spoken since I took his seat at breakfast.

I could sit alone in the empty classroom, staring at walls that will never answer me. But that thought makes my skin crawl. Instead, I retreat to my room, away from the hushed whispers and the weight of curious stares.

The first journal is dated five years before the fall of the gods—a date confirmed by tight, slanted annotations scribbled in the margins, corrections to a history now blurred by time.

I scoff. A SoulCaster hundreds of years in the future, "fixing" firsthand knowledge through a historian's lens. The arrogance of it.

Entire sections are missing, sentences erased, as if someone deliberately smudged the truth.

The gods were not born.

They were made.

Deep beneath the surface, raw Essence fused with precious ore, forging them in the land's molten core.

The words "giant" and "giants" appear frequently, but they've been crossed out, replaced with "god" and "gods."

Someone didn't want us to know what they truly were.

The writer, awestruck, idolizes these beings, calling them saviors of humanity.

But there's mention of a forgotten war, a battle before the God Wars—one erased from history.

A powerful entity attacked. It destroyed the God Tree, the very source of balance in the world. All the gods had to unite just to banish it. My stomach knots.

How powerful must something be to challenge all the gods at once?

The Third Age was meant to be one of gods and men, but greed twisted it. Some gods, intoxicated by worship, craved more power—and turned against Lathguard.

A war ignited. Twenty years of destruction. Gods against gods. Men against men.

Lathguard stood a head taller than any other god. Unlike the others, he never wore armor.

Instead, he walked into battle clad in deep blue or royal purple, his golden hair unbound. His power was absolute.

One passage recounts him hovering above the treetops, hurling massive spheres of force that exploded on impact.

Nothing could touch him. Incoming attacks bounced off an invisible shield, as if he was wrapped in an impenetrable aura.

I sit back, exhaling slowly. This confirms my theory. If Lathguard could shield himself, then perhaps I can too.

If he could manipulate Force to fly, then maybe…

Maybe I can fly.

I grab my notebook and begin to scribble furiously.

Force Magic & Its Categories
— Nurturing: ??
— Protecting: Shields, barriers, personal armor
— Projecting: Explosive force, kinetic impact
— Binding: ???
— Revealing: ???

There's so much more to uncover.

But before I can go further—

A knock.

Loud. Insistent.

I set my notebook aside and cross the room, opening the door.

It's Aerelis. Head of the Order of Wind.

Her emerald eyes gleam with mischief, fingers idly rubbing the fabric of my robe between them.

"I need you to come with me," she declares—not a request, but a command.

Then, without waiting, she grabs my robe and pulls me into the hallway.

"Where are we going?"

She laughs—a teasing, melodic sound—and tosses over her shoulder, "Wouldn't you like to know?"

Her voice is playful, but something lingers beneath it—something calculating.

"Yes, I would," I reply, voice flat.

She sighs dramatically, rolling her eyes.

"Oh, you're no fun."

But then—

The levity vanishes.

Her playful smirk hardens. Releasing her grip, she turns to face me fully, emerald gaze piercing. "We're going to test your density."

I frown. "How do you do that?"

Her smirk returns, enigmatic. "You'll just have to wait." Now her tone is all business. "Follow me."

And so I do.

#

"How do you measure density?" I ask the man standing before me, his robe the deep brown of the Order of Earth.

We're at the back of The Keep, just a few dozen feet from the edge of the plateau. The view stretches endlessly before us—rolling plains fading into the horizon, the glimmer of the distant ocean, and beyond that…

The Fog.

It looms on the edge of the world, a suffocating wall of gray swallowing the landscape, stretching east and west for as far as I can see. A constant reminder that we are running out of time.

The man, Caelum, speaks in a measured tone, his voice deep and grounded like the earth he channels. "Every GodSoul that's ever been measured has the same rate of siphon. Given that knowledge—and the fact that we've measured every SoulCaster alive—it's just a matter of math to determine how long it takes your reservoir to fill from empty."

I frown. "That's it? Just time how long it takes me to recharge?"

He nods. "Normally, it's a bit trickier. When multiple SoulCasters share a GodSoul, we have to account for how Essence is distributed among them. But since you're the only one of your Order, we don't have to factor anyone else in. Makes things… simpler."

A sharp sigh comes from behind me.

"Can we just get on with it already, Caelum?"

Aerelis.

She stands a few feet back, arms crossed, emerald eyes filled with bored impatience. Beside her, Lyrisa watches with mild curiosity, along with a handful of other SoulCasters.

But Rorick isn't here.

"Patience, Aerelis," Caelum replies, unfazed. "We're teachers."

Aerelis snorts. "Maybe you are. I'm just bored." She flicks her wrist. "Keep going."

Caelum sighs before turning back to me.

"We'll have to empty your reservoir first, then time how long it takes to refill."

I hesitate. "I thought we were under an Essence restriction?"

"We are," he admits, "but we've been conserving Essence so we could run these density tests. We may not get through everyone this year, but…" His eyes glint with something between curiosity and expectation. "We're all very eager to see what you can do."

I shift uneasily. Once again, I'm the center of attention. I hate the feeling. But at the same time… I want to know. What am I capable of?

I swallow my nerves and nod. "What do you need me to do?"

"Well," Caelum starts, "as I said, we need to empty your reservoir." His lips curve slightly. "Which means… you're going to use all of it."

Then, without another word, he turns toward the edge of the plateau.

The ground trembles beneath my feet. A deep, low rumble rises from the earth, like something waking from its slumber.

Then—a deafening crack.

Stone erupts from the ground.

I stumble back as a massive wall of rock rises before us, groaning and grinding against itself, shifting as if it were alive. It doesn't stop until it towers over fifteen feet high and twice as wide.

I stare, jaw slack.

I've never seen such raw power.

Compared to this, my display the other day was… pathetic.

I take another step back, barely aware of myself.

"That was incredible." The words escape me before I can stop them.

Caelum chuckles, rubbing the back of his neck. "I sometimes forget what it's like to see for the first time." He gestures toward the wall. "Normally, by now, you'd have seen all your instructors channel. But with the Essence restrictions, well…" He shrugs. "You're a bit late to the show."

Then his expression hardens.

"Now, it's your turn."

I take a steadying breath. "What do I do?"

"The biggest drain on a reservoir is offensive casting." He gestures toward the wall of stone.

"I want you to hit it."

I blink. "That's it?"

"That's it." He clasps his hands behind his back. "First, focus on your Essence reservoir—make it as small as possible. That will concentrate the flow. Then, direct that force at the wall."

His voice lowers, firm.

"Hit it as hard as you can."

I exhale, shifting my stance.

The wall looms before me, solid and immovable.

Let's see if that's true.

I do as instructed, reaching for my connection to Essence.

I follow it upward, not to the source itself, but to my reservoir, shaping it down as small as possible. The sphere shrinks until it could fit in the palm of my hand, its energy compressed, dense, eager to be unleashed.

I take a slow breath and will the air in front of me to harden, just as I did before.

But this time, it's different.

"Make it bigger, Jerrick." Caelum's voice cuts through my concentration. "We need to make sure you deplete more than you renew."

I obey.

I expand the force, pouring more Essence into it. The air shimmers violently, bending light like heat rippling off stone. Shockwaves pulse outward, a deep, rhythmic pounding that syncs with my heartbeat.

Boom. Boom. Boom.

Then—I release it.

A *flash* of pure kinetic energy erupts forward.

The force collides with Caelum's wall of stone, and the result is instant devastation.

A thunderous roar explodes through the plateau as the entire structure disintegrates. Not just cracks, not just crumbles—obliterates.

The rock doesn't break—it's annihilated.

The explosion sends a shockwave ripping through the air, rattling the ground beneath our feet. Chunks of stone pulverize into dust, reducing the once-massive wall into nothing more than a swirling cloud of debris.

Then—the plateau gives way.

The land where the wall once stood is simply gone, as if some god-sized blade has sheared it clean off the edge.

The destruction is absolute.

Dust and rock billow into the air, choking out the view. When the cloud finally settles, the scale of the devastation becomes horrifyingly clear.

A massive chunk of the plateau has been torn asunder, leaving a jagged, gaping void leading into the unknown. The edge, once a sturdy boundary, now crumbles like brittle parchment.

No one speaks.

The others just stare.

Their faces are frozen in a mixture of awe and fear. I don't blame them. What I just did… wasn't supposed to be possible.

My heart pounds against my ribs. The sheer magnitude of the force I just unleashed settles heavily on me.

This isn't just power.

It's nature itself, reshaped at my will.

It's destruction incarnate.

I reach inside, checking my reservoir, expecting it to be nearly empty—but it isn't.

It's still full.

The only difference? The color. A slightly lighter shade of blue.

I exhale slowly, but my pulse refuses to slow.

Finally, Caelum speaks. His voice is breathless, almost disbelieving.

"That was incredible, Jerrick!"

He shakes his head, as if trying to process what he just witnessed. "I've never seen anything like that before. But..." His brows furrow. "You're still standing."

He hesitates. "How much Essence do you have left?"

I swallow and glance inward again. "It looks the same as before. Just… lighter."

His eyes widen. "Your density must be off the charts."

A hush falls over the group. Even Aerelis looks stunned.

Off the charts.

I don't know what that means, but I know what it *feels* like—like my connection to Essence is unlike anything they've encountered before.

Caelum exhales sharply, collecting himself. "Alright. We need you empty. Let's try a sustained blast."

I nod.

"Aim upwards this time. I already have to repair the plateau— let's not give me even more work."

A few chuckles break the tension, but my mind is focused. This time, before I unleash my power, I do something different.

I create a thin layer of Force around my body—just a test, just to see—

And then, I will myself off the ground. Not far. Just a few feet. But it works.

Aerelis laughs, shaking her head. "Now you're just showing off."

I grin. Then, I release everything.

A sustained blast of pure Force surges from me, shaking the air itself.

The space before me distorts, the atmosphere turning opaque and rippling like water, crackling with raw, untamed energy.

The force field around me vibrates, alive, pulsing with my will.

And as I hover there, suspended between the sky and the ruined land below…

I realize that I've only just begun to understand what I can do.

Essence drains rapidly from my reservoir, a sensation both exhilarating and overwhelming. The sustained blast surges forward, roaring with invisible power, a maelstrom of raw force that shakes the very air. The world around me hums, trembling under the sheer magnitude of energy pouring from my body.

At first, the rush is intoxicating. But then—the strain sets in.

My smile fades as exhaustion claws its way through me. My reservoir, though vast, is depleting faster than I expected. I push harder, forcing more Essence outward, determined to empty everything.

The effort is staggering. My vision blurs. The edges of my sight darken, flickering in and out like a candle fighting against the wind. The sensation of floating—which moments ago had been thrilling—now becomes disorienting.

I feel myself tilting, as if the entire world has started to slip sideways. I can barely hold on. Still, I refuse to stop.

I dig deeper, past the limits of reason, past the screaming protest of my body. One last push. One final effort.

A final detonation of force erupts from me—a pulse of sheer, unrestrained power.

The air cracks like thunder. The force field around me flickers—then shatters.

And then… The fall.

The ground rushes up to meet me, but I'm already gone—

Darkness swallows me whole before I even hit the earth.

#

I'm chasing someone. He's fast, but I'm faster.

The lamp in my hand swings wildly, casting flickering shadows across the ground as I sprint after him. We're on the farm, but something is wrong. The land is warped, stretched at odd angles, as if reality itself has twisted into something unrecognizable.

I close the distance, reaching out—almost there—when he turns.

His face is wrong.

Twisted. Grotesque. His eyes are deep, swirling voids of darkness. His mouth is filled with jagged, rotting teeth. And then, impossibly, it grows, stretching wider and wider, devouring the rest of his face until nothing remains but a cavernous maw of crooked fangs.

Terror grips me, cold and absolute. I try to back away, but he grabs me—his fingers like iron, digging into my shoulder. I struggle, twist, but his grip is unrelenting. His mouth moves, forming words I can't hear at first, his voice nothing but a whisper.

Then it grows.

Louder.

Louder.

"Is that a way to treat an old friend? Is that a way to treat an old friend? Isthatawaytotreatanoldfriend? IS THAT A WAY TO TREAT AN OLD FRIEND!?"

The sound is everywhere, pressing against me, inside me.

I yank myself backward, break free—fall.

The impact knocks the wind from my lungs. The world tilts as I hit the ground, my back slamming into the dirt. But I'm not alone.

A new horror looms over me, its fangs snapping inches from my face.

I thrash against it, one arm straining to keep its gaping maw at bay while my other hand fumbles for my knife. Claws sink into my shoulder, searing pain lancing through me as it presses harder, desperate to tear into my throat.

I scream, raw and unrelenting—but beneath my own voice, I hear something. A whisper, buried beneath the chaos.

"Be brave, my child… I love you, Jerrick."

I drive the blade into its throat.

Its weight collapses onto me, hot blood spilling down my chest. My breath is ragged, my body trembling, the fight still surging through my veins.

Then I see its face.

My mother.

Her lifeless eyes stare up at me, locked in a silent scream. Blood oozes from the wound in her throat—the wound I gave her.

"No, no, no," I stammer, my hands pressing against her neck, trying to stop the bleeding, trying to undo what I've done. I scoop the warm blood into my hands, trying to push it back in, as if I can put her back together, as if I can fix this—but her body is cold.

I killed her.

A sob rips through me, my entire body convulsing with grief. I cradle her against me, shaking, unraveling, my hands stained with her blood.

Then her lips move.

"Trust Theron."

I jerk upright in bed, my chest heaving.

The dream clings to me, the terror still wrapped around my lungs like a vice. But I'm not alone.

I feel it. A presence. Someone watching.

My breath catches.

"Who's there?" My voice is hoarse as I instinctively reach for my reservoir—but it's not there.

It's empty.

A whisper in the darkness. "It's me, Eldrin."

The voice is close, too close.

"I'm sorry for waking you," he says, his tone quiet, almost hesitant. "But… it looked like you were having a nightmare. You kept saying, 'I killed her.'"

My stomach drops. Was I talking in my sleep?

I exhale, steadying myself. "How did you get in here?" I mutter.

For that matter… how did I get in here?

The last thing I remember is collapsing—using up my entire reservoir. The world spinning, then nothing.

I fumble for the lamp on the bedside table, the light flickering to life.

Eldrin is standing there, cloaked in shadows, his dark robes making him almost blend into the dimly lit room.

He smirks slightly. "Order of the Night, remember? Sneaking around is kind of my thing."

I stare at him, still trying to shake the remnants of the nightmare. "Why are you here?"

His expression shifts, the smirk fading.

"We never got to finish our conversation," he says. Then, after a beat, "Besides… I did some sneaking around earlier."

Something in his tone makes my pulse quicken.

"What does that have to do with me?"

Eldrin tilts his head slightly, studying me. Then, finally, he speaks.

"You don't talk much, do you?" He half-smiles, then shrugs. "Guess not. But listen… something weird is going on here." His voice drops lower. "And a lot of it involves you."

A strange chill runs down my spine.

"We were told not to talk to you," he continues, his gaze sharp. "I got a tongue-lashing this morning for it."

Me? Why me?

Bowen's words resurface, sharp and sudden—he overheard his father and Rorick talking about me.

I tense, my fingers curling into the sheets. "What do you mean, why me?"

Eldrin shakes his head. "I don't know exactly, but they're excited that Lathguard finally bonded. I overheard Rorick and—" he smirks slightly—"the hot redheaded SoulCaster saying that it's almost time. Something about soul placement."

My stomach knots. "Soul placement? What does that even mean?"

He spreads his hands. "No idea. But after they finished talking, I followed Rorick."

"You *what?*"

Eldrin leans forward, voice dropping. "All the way down into the basement. And then *even further*—into some sort of catacombs beneath the Keep."

A chill trickles down my spine.

"There were plenty of shadows, so he didn't know I was there," Eldrin continues. "He walked for about ten minutes before he reached a door. I barely slipped through before it closed." His gaze sharpens. "And Jerrick—what I saw inside…"

He exhales, steadying himself. "It was a massive cavern, rough-hewn like it was carved straight into the earth. Empty, except for two enormous statues—built right into the wall."

I swallow hard, already dreading what comes next.

"Then Rorick pulls something out of his robe." He meets my eyes, his expression deadly serious. "A glowing orb."

Something *tightens* in my chest.

"If I didn't know any better," Eldrin says slowly, "I'd swear it was a reservoir."

The words barely register at first. Then—

"A *reservoir?*" I sit up straighter. "Are you sure?"

He hesitates. "I mean… maybe I'm wrong, but that's what it looked like. And then—" his voice drops to a near-whisper, "—he placed it into the open mouth of one of the statues."

A breath I didn't realize I was holding slips from my lips. "And then?"

Eldrin's throat bobs as he swallows. "I—I don't know if it was a trick of the light, but I swear on my GodSoul that I saw it swallow the orb."

The room feels smaller suddenly, the weight of Eldrin's words pressing in from all sides.

Rorick. A reservoir. The statues.

Every lesson I've had, every book I've read—*none of it* suggests that reservoirs can exist outside of our bodies. That they can be held. Moved. Given.

Yet…

Eldrin doesn't sound like he's making it up.

My mind races.

Why would Rorick have a reservoir? *How* would he have one? How would he even get it out of someone?

What could he possibly be doing with it?

A sick, gnawing feeling twists in my gut. Whatever is happening beneath the Keep—whatever Rorick is involved in—it's important. Maybe even…

Sinister.

I take a slow breath, forcing my thoughts to steady. *One step at a time, Jerrick.* Eldrin told me all this for a reason. But why?

My eyes narrow. "You don't know me." My voice is quiet, careful. "So why tell me all this? Why go through the trouble and risk getting caught just to warn me?"

His expression shifts, something flickering behind his eyes.

"I may not know you," he admits. Then—"but I know your father."

I freeze.

"My father?" The words leave my lips before I can stop them. Then, realization dawns. "Wait—you mean Theron?"

Eldrin nods. "Yeah. He and my aunt—"

His words cut off abruptly, his eyes widening.

I catch it immediately. "What?"

He swallows. "Jerrick… we're cousins."

The floor drops out from under me.

"What?" The word comes out almost hollow.

"My father's adopted sister," he explains quickly, "was your mother, Gwen. I don't think I ever met her—she passed when I was young. But Theron…" He hesitates. "Theron used to come around. He'd talk to my father from time to time."

I stare at him, barely breathing.

"He never once mentioned a son."

Something cold curls in my chest.

I barely recognize my own voice when I ask, "Then how did you find out?"

For the first time since he entered my room, Eldrin looks uncertain.

"Rorick told us."

Eldrin's voice is quiet, but his words hit like a hammer.

"Said you weren't to be spoken to. That you're powerful… but an unknown." His gaze sharpens. "We were explicitly told not to talk to you. Not to approach you."

I exhale slowly. "Rorick knows?"

Of course, he does.

Of course, he does.

A bitter laugh threatens to escape, but I swallow it down. "I only found out a few months ago. I may have been the last to know."

Eldrin nods grimly. "Look, something is happening. I thought we were all here to push the Fog back, but there's been no real discussion of it. It's like everyone's waiting for something. And whatever it is… not all SoulCasters are in on it."

The weight in his voice snaps me to attention.

"Rorick is, for sure," Eldrin continues. "So is that redheaded woman. And the head of my Order." His brows furrow. "But I don't think Caelum or Lyrisa are part of it."

A noise.

Just outside the door.

My body stiffens. Someone's there.

Eldrin raises a hand before I can speak, his expression calm. "Don't worry. They can't hear us. I've been dampening the sound in your room since you started screaming in your sleep—"

But before he can finish, he vanishes.

A second later, the lock turns.

I barely have time to react before the door swings open. I'm already on full alert when I see Caelum step inside. He halts immediately, eyes flicking to mine.

"Jerrick." His surprise is genuine. "I didn't think you'd be awake."

I don't move. Don't breathe. "Why are you in my room?"

He hesitates. "I… came to check on you. You passed out earlier. How do you feel?"

My mind is still reeling from everything Eldrin just told me, but I force myself to keep my expression neutral. "I feel fine."

Caelum studies me for a moment, then nods. "Good. Honestly, I didn't expect you to wake up yet. You used up a lot of Essence. Even some of your life force."

My stomach clenches. "My life force?"

That's the real danger of being a SoulCaster. We age ourselves every time we use refined Essence. If we push too far, we burn through years in moments.

"How much?" My voice is tight.

"It's hard to say," Caelum admits. "But… not much. You look the same—doesn't seem like you've aged at all. But you need to be careful. Know your limits."

I exhale through my nose, trying to settle the storm inside me. "I can't reach my reservoir," I say. "What does that mean?"

"That's normal," Caelum assures me. "Right now, it's tiny. Since you focused your reservoir before channeling and emptied it completely, it's hyper-focused. Next time you cast, you'll have to remember to increase its size first."

He tilts his head. "Actually, let's check something. How full is your reservoir now?"

I nod and reach inward, following the connection up to where my reservoir should be.

At first, I see nothing—just the emptiness where it should be.

But then, I feel it. A soft, warm tingle.

I pull on it—expanding it slowly, careful not to overdo it.

It grows to twice the size of my head. Full.

I blink. "It's full."

Caelum stills.

"…That can't be."

I frown. "Why not?"

"When a SoulCaster overextends—goes beyond their reservoir limit—they're usually unconscious for at least a day. Sometimes two." His voice grows more incredulous with every word.

"And even after they wake up," he continues, "it takes another two days just to refill their reservoir. That's three to four days total before they can even channel again."

He steps closer. "Jerrick. You've been out for twelve hours— and your reservoir is already full?"

I don't know what to say.

"Maybe my reservoir isn't as dense as we thought. Maybe I just don't need as much time to recover—"

"No way," Caelum says, cutting off my thoughts. "I saw how much power you have. It's not that your reservoir isn't dense—it's that Lathguard siphons at a higher rate than every other GodSoul."

His eyes flicker with something between fascination and awe.

"We won't be able to measure you," he mutters. "There's nothing to compare you to. My guess? Your density is in the highest tier—maybe in a tier of its own. And with Lathguard's renewal rate…"

Then, Caelum does something that completely throws me off.

He laughs.

A real, genuine, almost nervous laugh.

"Jerrick…" He smirks, rubbing the back of his neck. "We're friends, right?"

Something inside me tightens.

If Eldrin is right, and Caelum isn't involved in whatever is happening, then maybe—maybe—he can answer some of my questions.

But what if he's wrong? What if Caelum is part of it? Is there anyone I can trust?

Theron.

Both in my dream and in real life, my mother's voice said I could trust Theron.

Where is he?

Is he really dead?

What about Elena? She knows more than she's told me. But I know I can trust her.

I need to get out of here. I need to get home. I need to find Theron.

Caelum reaches out, his hand resting lightly on my arm. His touch is steady, grounding—a stark contrast to the storm raging inside me.

"Being different isn't easy," he says, his voice softer this time.

I meet his gaze. There's something there—understanding. Not just words, but something deeper. Something earned.

He repeats it, firmer now. More deliberate.

"In a world that values order and certainty, standing apart isn't just difficult—it can feel like a curse. But let me tell you something, Jerrick. Something I've learned in my many years as a SoulCaster."

He pauses, holding my attention.

"Being different? It's not just a challenge. It's an opportunity."

His fingers tighten slightly on my arm—not forceful, just anchoring me in the moment.

"When you don't fit into the mold, you see the world differently. You ask the questions no one else dares to ask. You approach problems from angles no one else even considers."

His expression hardens, but there's something warm beneath it.

"It's easy to follow the paths others have walked before you. To move where the ground is worn smooth. But those who forge new roads, those who dare to carve their own path—they're the ones who leave the deepest impact."

His hand falls away, but his words stay with me.

"You, Jerrick—you don't just have power. You have potential. A destiny that is unlike anyone else's. And yes, it's daunting. Maybe even unfair."

His lips quirk into the smallest of smirks. "But it's also a privilege."

He straightens slightly, his gaze never leaving mine. "You have the chance to reshape everything we understand about Essence. To push past the limits we once believed were absolute."

The weight of his words settles over me like a mantle.

Caelum steps back, giving me space to breathe. "Don't see your difference as a barrier, Jerrick. See it as a beacon. A light that will guide you to places no one else has ever gone. It won't be an easy road."

His smirk fades, replaced by something far more solemn. "But I promise you—it will be extraordinary."

His words linger, heavy but not crushing.

I exhale, nodding once. "Thank you… for understanding."

His knowing smile returns. "Get some sleep. And since I know you're fine, I won't be checking in every hour."

He turns for the door, hesitates for a moment as if considering saying more, but then simply nods and steps out, leaving me alone with my thoughts.

The moment he's gone, the room feels different. Still. Empty, but… not quite.

"…Eldrin?" I whisper.

Silence.

I wait, straining to hear the slightest rustle, the smallest breath, but… nothing.

He's gone.

I'll find him tomorrow.

Reaching over, I lock the door before laying back against the mattress.

Despite everything—the exhaustion, the weight of the conversation, the unsettling things I now know—sleep comes fast.

And this time, I don't dream.

#

I don't even know where to begin.

The past twenty-four hours have unraveled everything I thought I understood. I was just settling into a new normal, adjusting to the idea of life at the Keep, when yesterday happened.

That the other students were told not to talk to me gnaws at me. It's not that I mind being left alone—I've spent most of my life comfortable in solitude—but knowing I'm at the center of someone else's scheme makes my skin crawl. I've never wanted my life dictated by anyone but myself.

Yet, for months now, it feels like I've been marching down a path someone else carved for me. No matter the choices I made, they all led here. To this place. To this moment.

And worse—why haven't I questioned any of it? Why haven't I pushed back?

The Keep is a five-day journey on horseback from the City of Four Rivers, yet I was unconscious for only three. That alone doesn't add up. And how is it even possible that I'm the only bonded from the Four Rivers? The number of newly bonded dwindles every year, but statistically, it shouldn't be zero. There should have been over a hundred people waiting to be named. Where are they?

More unsettling still, I've barely thought about my parents. I haven't thought about Elena. I haven't been myself.

It's as if I've been sleepwalking through my own life, a puppet whose strings are being pulled by some unseen force. But something has shifted. A veil has lifted. I don't know why or how, but suddenly, I see it.

I don't know who I can trust, but I do know this: I will be careful. I will take control. I am part of something vast, something bigger than myself. But I refuse to be blind to it any longer.

Today, I ask questions. Today, I take my power back.

Breakfast, as always, is delicious, but I hardly taste it. I sit alone in my designated section, my isolation pressing down on me more than ever.

This isn't accidental.

I'm being kept apart—alienated. But why? What's the purpose of isolating me? Keeping me disconnected?

I look across the dining hall, my gaze locking onto Rorick. He eats quietly, his movements slow, measured. He hasn't looked my way once, but I don't let that deter me.

I push back from my chair and stand. I'm done waiting.

As I cross the room, I catch Aerelis watching me. Her expression is unreadable, but she doesn't look away. Neither do I.

I stop in front of their table. My voice is firm, unyielding.

"Rorick, we need to talk."

I don't ask. I demand.

Rorick pauses mid-bite, his spoon hovering in the air before he slowly lowers it. For a fraction of a second, something flickers in his expression—annoyance? Anger? But just as quickly, it vanishes, replaced by a practiced smile.

"Yes, we do," he says lightly. "I was going to say the same thing to you… after breakfast. But now is as good a time as any."

With a quiet grunt, he eases himself up from the table, leaning on his cane for support.

"Follow me."

We walk in silence. The clatter of dishes and quiet murmur of voices fade as he leads me down the hall, away from prying eyes.

His office is a large, cluttered space, the air thick with the scent of old books and parchment. Paintings of vast landscapes line the walls, their colors faded with time. Stacks of books cover nearly every surface, some piled so high they threaten to topple.

He gestures to a chair. "Please, sit."

I do. He settles across from me, adjusting his position with a quiet sigh. His back straightens, but there's a weariness to him I haven't noticed before.

"What's on your mind, Jerrick?"

I don't hesitate. "Why were you and the mayor of Four Rivers talking about me?"

To his credit, he doesn't look surprised.

"It wasn't about you," he says evenly. "It was about Theron. You being his son is the only reason your name came up." He pauses, his gaze steady. "You've been a pleasant surprise. I didn't know until recently that I even had a grandson."

The words land like a punch to the gut. Grandson?

I wasn't expecting that.

I stare at him, taking in his slight frame, the lines on his face, the weight of years settled in his weary eyes. Rorick… my grandfather?

I don't know if I believe it. His size alone makes no sense.

"Don't be so surprised, Jerrick," he says, reading my expression. A chuckle escapes him. "I see you sizing me up."

He shakes his head, a wry smile touching his lips.

"I adopted Theron when he was eleven. He grew up here, in these walls. You can imagine my pain when he betrayed me."

I frown. "What do you mean?"

Rorick tilts his head, studying me. "Is that really why you needed to talk? About Theron?"

"No, I... no." I shake my head. "I just found out he was my birth father. He's a stranger to me. Thom is my real father." The words come out firm, instinctual. "But that's not why I'm here. I want to know what really happened during the Naming Ceremony. A few things aren't adding up."

Rorick holds my gaze, his expression unreadable. Then, something shifts. His eyes soften, his shoulders sagging under an unseen weight.

"I knew you'd find out eventually." His voice is quieter now, more tired than I've ever heard it. "I promise I'll tell you. But there are things you need to understand first."

He leans back in his chair, exhaling deeply, his gaze drifting to the ceiling. When he speaks again, his voice carries the weight of centuries.

"The land is dying, Jerrick."

My chest tightens. I don't interrupt.

"I've known for over three hundred years, and I haven't been able to stop it. I've tried everything, but its rate of depletion is greater than its renewal. Everything draws from the Source. Every tree, every blade of grass, even the sky itself. The cycle of day and night. The turning of the seasons." His voice drops, thick with emotion. "That's why the sky is gray. Why winter has come early."

I listen in silence, the magnitude of his words sinking in.

"The Fog," he continues, "is the land's way of protecting itself. Every inch it constricts means less strain on the Source. When I was born, the world was vast—so much larger than what remains today. But over the centuries, entire towns have disappeared behind the Fog. I lost my hometown lifetimes ago."

He wipes at his eyes, his breath catching. I open my mouth to say something, but he stops me with a raised hand.

"Sorry." He forces a small, broken laugh. "A long life can be a burden. But Lathguard gave me this gift. He knew the time of gods was ending, and the time of men was beginning. He thought we would need a leader with a long memory."

His jaw tightens, his voice thick with self-loathing. "But I failed, Jerrick."

The words land heavy between us.

"We have maybe a few years left—less, if things continue as they are. Even in winter, when the land should be resting, the Fog is still advancing. The Source is still depleting. That's why Lathguard called me a disappointment. He entrusted me with protecting this land, and I haven't been able to stop its collapse."

"So... there's nothing we can do?" My own problems suddenly feel small in comparison.

"I think we have a solution," he says, leaning forward, "but we are quickly running out of time."

I brace myself for what's coming next.

"The land is trying to kill us, Jerrick." His voice is grim. "We draw from the Source, but we are not native to it. We were never meant to be here."

A chill spreads through me. "What do you mean? If we're not native, then where did we come from?"

Rorick's expression darkens. "From her. The Invader. A being who came from beyond, who destroyed the God Tree and created us in her own image."

I barely breathe as he continues.

"The God Tree was the heart of this land. It grew the world itself, from a single seed planted by the First People. They nurtured it, watched as it expanded into forests, rivers, mountains. But then she came. And she demanded worship."

His fingers tighten around the armrest of his chair. "The First People refused. They knew what she was. What she wanted. And in her anger, she created us—humanity. She gave us intelligence, but she also gave us something else."

His eyes meet mine, unflinching. "She made us hate them."

I stiffen, flashes of memory surfacing. The Keepers. The woods behind the farm. The inexplicable, seething rage I felt when I first saw them. That unnatural fury. That hatred.

It was planted inside me.

"No wonder they went into hiding," I murmur.

Rorick nods. "The land fought back," he says. "It birthed the gods—giants of stone and Essence, warriors forged to battle the Invader. You, bonded with Lathguard, know firsthand how powerful he was. But even he wasn't enough."

His voice grows distant, heavy with old grief. "It took all of them. All the gods. Only by banding together were they able to banish her."

Silence settles between us. I struggle to process the sheer enormity of what he's telling me.

"But after she was gone, peace didn't last," Rorick says, voice bitter. "We poisoned the gods. Not with weapons or war, but with our own humanity. The longer they were around us, the more they became like us. They grew greedy. Arrogant. They fought for supremacy. And then…"

A long pause.

"Then they died."

I shift in my seat, uneasy. "What does this have to do with me?"

"Everything."

Rorick's gaze hardens.

"On the eve of their deaths, Lathguard told me how to bring them back. But only as a last resort. Even he understood that gods and men were never meant to coexist. He made me promise I would not do it unless there was no other way."

A heavy breath.

"Jerrick, I don't think we have any other choice."

"Why are you telling me this?" My voice is quieter than I expect, barely above a whisper.

Rorick doesn't hesitate. "Because you're going to help bring them back."

The words land like a hammer, heavy and final. I stare at him, stunned, my mind struggling to wrap around what he just said. Bring them back? Me?

It sounds impossible, like something from the old stories—tales whispered around the fire on cold nights. Not something meant for a farm boy from the Four Rivers.

"Why me?" I ask, the disbelief thick in my voice. "I mean, I was just... I was just a normal person. How can I be part of something this big?"

Rorick meets my gaze, his expression unwavering. "Jerrick, sometimes the most unlikely individuals are chosen for the greatest tasks. You're bonded with Lathguard. That alone makes you extraordinary."

I shift in my seat, my thoughts a chaotic storm. "But my powers—I barely understand them. How am I supposed to help bring back gods?"

"It's not just about the power you wield," Rorick says gently. "It's about your character, your will to do what's right. You've shown more courage and resilience than you realize."

I take a slow, measured breath, trying to calm the pressure building in my chest. The weight of his words sits heavily on me. The idea of being at the center of this—of being part of something so much bigger than myself—is terrifying.

"What's required of me?"

"Nothing," Rorick says, "and everything all at the same time."

I frown. "I don't understand."

"You will." He leans forward slightly, resting his hands on his knees. "But first, I promised to tell you what happened at the Naming."

Something in his voice makes my stomach drop.

"Jerrick, this is going to be hard. Probably the hardest thing you'll ever hear." He hesitates, like he's weighing his words carefully. "Just know that you're stronger than you think."

A pause. Then, softly—"First, I lied to you. And even though I'm not proud of it, I had my reasons."

My pulse quickens. My chest tightens. Lied?

Rorick straightens, as if steeling himself. "There's no way to soften this, so I'm just going to say it."

Another pause.

"I'm sorry, Jerrick. But your parents are dead."

The words hit like a physical blow, knocking the air from my lungs. I don't believe him. I can't believe him. He's lying. He has to be lying.

My chest heaves, my breath shallow. My heart pounds so hard I feel it in my throat, in my ears. It's the only sound I can hear.

But somewhere, deep inside, I know it's true.

It's like I've always known, like the truth has been circling me, waiting for me to acknowledge it. This is just confirmation of something I was too afraid to face.

I stand suddenly, my body moving before my mind catches up. Anger wells up, raw and uncontrollable. "When?" I demand, my voice hoarse. "When did this happen?"

Rorick looks away, his shoulders sinking. "Just after the ceremony."

"What!?" My voice rises, my hands trembling. My legs feel unsteady, like they might give out. "You've known this whole time. Why didn't you tell me sooner?"

Rorick doesn't flinch under my anger. He exhales slowly. "Because you're a good son, Jerrick. And if I had told you, you would have left immediately."

I clench my fists. "What makes you think I won't leave now?" My lungs feel too small, my breath coming too fast. The room is closing in around me.

"You can," Rorick says simply. "I won't stop you. The difference now is that you can defend yourself. Before, you would have gotten yourself killed."

My mind goes blank at that. I feel like I'm collapsing inward, like my body can't hold the weight of his words. My knees buckle, and I fall more than sit back in my chair.

My voice is barely a whisper. "What does that mean?"

Rorick sighs, rubbing a hand through his thinning hair. His voice is heavy. "Remember when I told you the land once created giants to defend itself?"

I nod numbly.

"It's doing it again. But not giants—something worse." His face darkens. "Creatures. Foul, twisted things sent to kill us. They started appearing weeks ago, but they're getting stronger. More numerous. On the day of the Naming Ceremony, they climbed over the city walls. Thousands of people were slaughtered before we could fight them back."

His eyes meet mine. "I'm sorry, Jerrick. But your parents were among them."

I hear the words. I even understand them. But my mind refuses to process them.

"You say thousands died," I murmur. "How do you know my parents were part of them?"

Hope is all I have left, and I cling to it like a drowning man.

"They were with the other families, Jerrick." His voice is gentle but unwavering. "None of them made it. Everyone signed in when they entered the waiting area. Every name is accounted for."

His next words land like a final nail in the coffin.

"Nobody survived."

I stare at him, unblinking. "We even lost some SoulCasters," he adds, as if that matters. "You were the only newly bonded that made it."

I barely register his words. All I can see is my father's face, lined with worry as he told me to be strong. My mother's warm smile. The way she ran her fingers through my hair when I was small. The way they looked at each other, a love so steady, so solid, that I never once doubted it.

And now they're gone.

I don't realize I'm shaking until I feel the chair trembling beneath me. The room blurs, my vision swimming.

I can't breathe.

I can't think.

I can't accept this.

So, Eldrin was right. I am the only one here from the Four Rivers.

The realization sinks in like a stone in my gut. My dream—was it just that, or was it something more? A memory clawing its way to the surface? I remember seeing one of those creatures on the road with Elena. Is she dead too?

I can't stop myself from seeing it—claws tearing through flesh, my mother's screams, my father trying to fight them off with nothing but a knife, powerless to save her. I grip the arms of my chair, my knuckles white.

"What about my friend?" I ask suddenly, my voice hoarse. "The one I asked you about the other day—Elena. Did she…?"

Rorick exhales through his nose. "I don't know. She didn't bond, so she could have left early. Many died, and identifying them all will take time—if it's even possible."

"So she could be alive?" I don't expect him to say yes. I barely expect him to answer. But I ask anyway, clinging to that last, fraying thread of hope.

"I just don't know."

Rorick stands, moves toward me, and without hesitation, wraps his arms around me. His embrace is firm, steady. I should push him away—I want to push him away—but I can't. My body is too drained, my mind too fractured.

"We have to make sure this never happens again," he says, his voice thick with something I can't place. "This feeling you have right now, Jerrick? It's being felt across the land, by thousands of others. We have to stop it. And you…" He steps back, his hands gripping my shoulders. "You have to stop it."

"Me?" My voice is barely a whisper. "How?"

I can't stop seeing my mother's face, lifeless, blood pooling at her throat. My mind keeps circling back to my dream—my knife in her neck. Deep down, I know they're gone. But I also know there's something I'm missing, something just out of reach. If I could just— remember.

"What I'm about to ask of you, I've asked of others," Rorick continues. "Some have said yes. But none of them have what you have. To bring the gods back, I need to infuse their souls into specially forged bodies, crafted from a rare metal ore found deep underground."

I go still.

That's what Eldrin saw last night. The cavern. The statues. The glowing orb. Was it really what he thought it was?

"What does that have to do with me?" I ask carefully.

Rorick holds my gaze. "The reason Lathguard hasn't bonded in all these centuries is because there hasn't been a reservoir dense enough to sustain his power. Until now."

I already know what he's about to say before he says it.

"We need to transfer your bond with Lathguard to his new body."

I swallow hard. If he had told me this weeks ago, I would have agreed without hesitation. Back when this power was foreign and terrifying—before I felt it. Before I understood it.

Now?

Now, I'm not so sure.

I'm not selfish. I understand what's at stake. I know firsthand that people are dying. But this power—it's exhilarating. It's alive. And what do I have left, really? If I do this, I can finally go back to the farm, continue my family's legacy. My parents will live on through my work. But if I don't—if I can't—then it's all gone.

Not just the farm. Everything.

"I'll do it."

Rorick watches me closely, studying my face, my posture. Something about his expression shifts—regret, maybe. Or something heavier.

"Jerrick," he says slowly, "I appreciate your willingness. But I don't think you understand." He leans forward. "The bond between you and Lathguard—your reservoir—it's permanent. There's no way to remove the connection."

A pause. A beat too long.

"We'd have to remove your reservoir."

The words settle between us, and I stare at him, uncomprehending. Then, the meaning crashes down, sharp and merciless.

"But that means I would die." My throat tightens. "You're asking me to—" I can't even finish the sentence.

"To save humanity, yes." Rorick doesn't flinch. His voice is steady, but there's something behind it. Something that almost sounds like regret. "You wouldn't be the first to make this sacrifice. I've spent nearly two hundred years mining enough of the ore to create his body. Now, I finally have enough. But without you, it's useless."

I can't breathe.

Rorick's words press against me, heavy and suffocating. The room tilts. My vision narrows. Sacrifice myself to bring Lathguard back. To save humanity.

It's noble, isn't it? It's the right thing, isn't it?

Then why do I feel like I'm standing on the edge of a cliff, about to fall?

"If this is so important," I force out, my voice barely steady, "why not just force me? Why leave it up to chance?"

Rorick actually smiles, shaking his head. "First, I'm not sure there's anyone who could force you to do anything against your will. I saw what you did yesterday, Jerrick. I saw what you're capable of."

I don't respond.

"Second," he continues, "it doesn't work that way. Your reservoir is part of you. It's the very center of your being. Only you can decide what happens to it. No one can take it from you—not by trickery, not by force. Your soul can only be given." He meets my gaze. "It can never be stolen."

My thoughts spiral.

My existence, my entire being—reduced to a stepping stone for something greater. I understand the necessity of sacrifice. But am I ready to be that sacrifice? To give up everything?

But... haven't I already lost everything?

The grief is unbearable. It sits in my chest, gnawing, consuming. Losing my parents is like a festering wound, a gaping maw I can't stop staring into.

The more I look, the more I feel drawn toward it. The darkness.

Because the darkness means I don't have to feel. The darkness means this pain goes away.

Maybe—maybe this decision isn't a burden at all.

Maybe it's a release.

The thought is so vile, so shameful, that I physically recoil from it. I don't deserve to be their son. I don't deserve to carry their legacy. What would my father say if he were here? What would my mother think?

I wish I could talk to them. Ask them what to do.

But I can't. Because they're gone.

This decision is mine alone.

"I need some time," I finally manage, my voice barely above a whisper. "This is... a lot to take in."

Rorick nods, his sharp edges softening. "I understand. This isn't a decision to be made lightly. Take the day to think about it. We don't have much time, but it's important that you make this choice freely, without pressure."

His gaze holds steady, filled with something I can't quite name. Maybe it's expectation. Maybe it's hope. Maybe it's regret.

"We can talk tomorrow morning," he continues. "You'll make the right decision. Your parents raised you right."

The words hit me like a fist to the ribs. I don't trust myself to speak, so I nod. Then, slowly, I rise. My legs feel unsteady, like I've been at sea for days and only now have found solid ground.

I make it to the door, step through, and close it softly behind me. The latch clicks, and suddenly, the silence is deafening.

I am alone.

My parents are dead. And—more than likely—so is Elena.

The realization presses against me, heavy and suffocating. I walk, but I don't know where I'm going. The corridors blur. Faces pass, but I don't see them. My body moves on instinct towards my room, but my mind is far away, somewhere in the past, in a home that no longer exists, with people who are nothing but memories.

The day stretches on, each hour an eternity. My thoughts churn, a storm of questions with no answers.

What does it mean to be a hero?

Is it the grand gestures, the ultimate sacrifices? Or is it something quieter—the willingness to stand in the face of the impossible and whisper, I'll try?

As the day gets later, the weight of my decision grows heavier. This isn't just about me. It's about the legacy we leave behind, about the world we fight to save for those who come after us. It's what my parents did. They worked hard every day, loved each other deeply, and built something they hoped would last beyond them.

But my path doesn't lead back to the farm. I know that now.

Whatever choice I make, I won't get to continue their work. But maybe—just maybe—I can help others continue theirs.

Because isn't that what life is? Love. Loss. And the hope that even the smallest light can push back the darkness.

But am I ready to be that light, knowing it means extinguishing my own?

The question lingers, unanswered, as I stare up at the ceiling of my room.

Tomorrow, I'll give Rorick my answer.

But tonight—I let the weight of the world settle against my chest and close my eyes, letting my heart wrestle with a choice only I can make.

Chapter 11

Jerrick

I know I won't sleep tonight.

Rorick's words, *I'm sorry, but your parents are dead,* play on an endless loop in my mind, each repetition a fresh wound. I want nothing more than to close my eyes, to let myself sink into grief, but I don't have that luxury. Not when I have a choice to make—one that demands every ounce of my focus.

And that makes me feel like a terrible son.

Every time my thoughts drift toward my parents, I have to pull them away, force myself to think about the decision in front of me. It feels wrong, like I'm shoving their memory aside, like I'm unworthy of the love and lessons they gave me. But even as I try to focus, something gnaws at me. The things Rorick told me, the things Eldrin saw—they don't quite fit. The pieces are there, but they don't align the way they should.

I want to trust Rorick. I *should* trust Rorick. But my mind keeps rebelling, seeking order in the chaos, grasping at inconsistencies.

It's like there's a veil over my thoughts that has only just begun to lift, and now I see that I've been accepting things too easily. I don't know who I can trust. I don't know what's real. I just know that I feel *wrong.*

I think back to my father. We don't always get to choose our destinies in life, Jerrick. Sometimes destiny chooses us, and when it does, we should face it with bravery.

I wish he were here. I wish I could ask him what I should do.

Nights at the Keep are eerily silent. With nothing but miles of open land surrounding us, there's no city noise, no rustling of trees—just the quiet of hundreds of sleeping bodies. I envy them. The ease with which they must have drifted into sleep.

I focus on the stillness, trying to quiet my thoughts.

Then I hear it.

A noise at my door.

My stomach knots. I've had visitors at night before, but this is different. This time, there's no knock, no whispered conversation before entry. Instead, I hear the faint scrape of metal against metal. The telltale sound of a lock being picked.

It's careful, deliberate. But not practiced.

Whoever is outside my door isn't used to this.

I move swiftly, silently, slipping out of bed and pressing myself against the wall behind the door. The soft glow of the lamp on my bedside table casts just enough light to see without giving away my position.

A quiet *click*. The tumblers fall into place.

The door eases open. A crouched figure slips inside, slow and deliberate, taking care to shut the door behind them. I catch only a vague outline as they move toward my bed, hesitant in their approach—trying not to wake me.

Then I see it.

A blade.

The glint of dim light on metal, a knife held low at their side.

Instinct takes over. Essence flares inside me, wrapping around me like a second skin. My body ignites in a brilliant shield of energy, flooding the room with radiant light. The sudden glow is blinding, even to me, but I don't hesitate—I step forward from behind the door.

The figure recoils, staggering back under the intensity of the light, hands raised as if to ward it off.

Then—"Jerrick!"

The voice is urgent, breathless. A whisper, but desperate.

I blink through the light, forcing my eyes to adjust. The outline sharpens, the features coming into focus.

Brennen. It wasn't a blade, it was a claw.

I recognize him instantly—the Keeper from the woods. The one I nearly killed.

I expect to feel anger. I *should* feel anger. But it isn't there. Instead, I feel... nothing.

The surprise on Brennen's face mirrors my own.

Slowly, I let my shield drop, the glow around me fading into nothingness.

"What are you doing here?" I ask, my voice hushed but firm.

His shoulders rise and fall with labored breaths. His face is drawn, weary, as if he hasn't slept in days.

"For you," he says. "It's not safe here. We have to leave. *Now.*"

He glances toward the door, his eyes sharp with urgency.

"You can't trust Rorick. He has his own agenda."

Then he reaches over and pulls back the shade on the lamp, letting the dim light spill into the room. It illuminates his face fully now—worn, desperate, but certain.

I stare at him, searching for the rage I know I should feel.

But it isn't there.

Instead, I ask the only question that makes sense.

"Last time we met, I was seething." My voice is quiet, controlled. "Why am I no longer angry?"

"There is power in knowledge," Brennen says. "Somebody must have told you about the Creator, which surprises me. In doing so, they told you how she embedded inside of humans a deep hatred for us Keepers. Just by knowing that, and *believing* it, means you no longer feel its effects."

I absorb his words, and for the first time in what feels like ages, something clicks into place. *That's why my anger vanished.* The hostility that had burned inside me when I saw him in the woods—why it disappeared the moment I understood *why* it had been there to begin with.

But my mind isn't ready to settle. "Why now?" I ask, my voice tight with suspicion. "Why come for me *now*? And why can't I trust Rorick?"

Brennen's expression hardens. "Because time is running out, Jerrick. Rorick's plans... they're not about saving the world. They're about preserving *himself.* He's desperate, and desperation makes even the wise reckless."

I lean back against the wall, the weight of his warning pressing down on me. I already knew Rorick was asking too much. *Sacrificing myself for a plan that might not even work.* But Brennen's words make it worse. If Rorick's been manipulating events—not just me, but everything—then what *else* isn't real?

"How do I *know* who to believe?" I exhale sharply, forcing my swirling thoughts into words. "How do I know *this* isn't another lie?"

Brennen takes a slow step forward, his voice softer now. "Because I'm asking you to trust *yourself*, not just my words. You've *felt* that something isn't right, haven't you? I'm just confirming your suspicions, not forcing you into anything."

I look into his eyes—large, dark, and strangely earnest. I *want* to believe him.

But believing means everything I thought I knew is wrong.

I rub my face, exhausted. "And if I *do* leave with you? Then what?"

Brennen shifts uncomfortably. "First, we get you somewhere safe. Somewhere Rorick *can't* find you. Then we regroup, figure out what's next. Because this isn't just about stopping Rorick or saving the land anymore. It's about understanding *our* place in this world and how we can exist without destroying it… or each other."

His words settle deep in my chest, like a key turning inside a locked door.

All this time, I've been focused on survival—on immediate choices with immediate consequences. But this is *bigger* than that. *Bigger than me.*

I hesitate, voice barely above a whisper. "I... I need to think."

Brennen nods, his gaze steady. "I know. But we don't have much time. They're moving ahead with their plans, and every moment we delay gives them the advantage."

The air between us thickens, the weight of the decision pressing in from all sides. Every road leads to something dangerous, something I don't understand.

I rake a hand through my hair. "I'm not built for this," I admit, my voice hoarse. "If I make the wrong choice, it won't just affect me. I don't—" I swallow hard. "I don't know if I can carry that."

Brennen watches me carefully, then steps closer, his clawed hand resting on my arm.

"This burden you feel. This *guilt*. It comes from what Rorick has been doing to you." His voice is low, measured. "He isn't all that powerful, not in the way you'd think. But his *subtlety*—it's made him dangerous. He's had *centuries* to perfect it. You're not just dealing with a powerful man, Jerrick. You're dealing with *a patient* one. He's spent lifetimes shaping reality into something that suits him."

The breath leaves my lungs in a slow, shuddering exhale.

How much of my life has been *mine*? How much of what I feel is *real*?

Brennen glances toward the door. "There's more I need to tell you, but we *must* leave now. There are people waiting for us."

I narrow my eyes. "Who?"

"Theron, Drusilla, and Elena."

My heart stutters. *Everything* inside me stops.

"Elena? I thought she was…" My voice is barely audible.

Brennen hesitates, then nods. "Yes. I'm sorry I didn't lead with that. She's very much alive. I didn't realize you thought she was dead."

The world tilts beneath me.

Elena.

She's *alive.*

A choked breath escapes my lips. A single spark of hope flares to life inside my chest, wild and desperate, something I thought had been snuffed out completely.

I stare at Brennen, trying to find some reason to doubt him— but I *want* to believe him. I *need* to believe him.

"Elena…" I whisper, the name trembling on my lips.

She's a part of the life I lost. A piece of the world that was ripped away from me.

She's a reminder of everything that's been *stolen.*

And now she's waiting for me.

My voice cracks, thick with relief, disbelief, and something else I can't name.

"Elena…" I say again, breathless. "She's *alive.*"

Brennen nods, his expression solemn but unwavering. "Yes, Jerrick. She's safe—for now. But we must act quickly if we want to keep it that way. Rorick's manipulations run deeper than you know. That feeling of being out of place, the inconsistencies you've noticed? They're not coincidences. They're *deliberate*—part of his design."

His words settle over me like a weight, pressing down on my chest. I *knew* something was wrong. I've felt it since the moment I arrived, since the moment I woke up here without remembering how I even got here. But I never expected this.

Then, like a blade cutting through the fog of doubt, Elena. She's *alive.*

And she's waiting.

The thought of her—of seeing her again, of knowing she *survived*—pulls me forward, past my uncertainty and toward something solid. "If Elena's in danger because of me, I don't have a choice," I say, my voice rough with newfound resolve. "I'll go with you, Brennen. I need to see her, to make sure she's safe. And I need to know the *truth*—all of it."

Brennen squeezes my arm, his clawed hand surprisingly warm. "You're making the right choice, Jerrick. And you're not alone in this. We *all* have a part to play in what's coming. Your parents, your friends… they're part of who you are, part of who you're becoming."

A new determination floods through me. For the first time in days, I feel like I'm making a *choice*—not following someone else's path, not being swept up by forces beyond my control. This is *mine.*

"Let's go," I say firmly. "I need answers. And I need to see Elena."

Brennen nods. "We'll move quietly. The night is ours, and with me, you'll learn things about this world—and about yourself—that you never imagined."

He pauses, his brow creasing. "But before we leave, you need to understand something. Out there, things are not how you remember them. Under *no* circumstances should you channel Essence. You've been safe here, but beyond these walls, things have gotten bad. If you channel…" His voice tightens. "They will come."

A chill runs down my spine. "So it's true? Rorick said thousands died before they pushed those things out of the city."

Brennen's face darkens. He *slowly* shakes his head.

"Thousands *did* die, Jerrick." His voice is quiet, but there's a raw *ache* in it. "But those creatures weren't pushed back."

I stiffen.

Brennen looks me in the eye, holding my gaze.

"Rorick and the other SoulCasters *left* as they arrived. They abandoned the city. They left those people—*your people*—to die. You were the only one they saved."

A sickening, hollow feeling spreads through my stomach.

I can't breathe.

He just *left?*

The SoulCasters—who wield the power of gods, who claim to protect the land, who were supposed to *defend us*—they just… *left?*

The revelation rips through me like a blade to the gut. I grip the edge of the bed, trying to steady myself, but it feels like the ground beneath me is falling away.

I think of the Keep—this towering structure I've come to see as a place of knowledge, of order, of *purpose*. And now…

Now it feels like a fortress of lies.

"How?" My voice is barely a whisper. "How could he—" I stop, my throat closing around the words.

How could Rorick—who spoke of duty and sacrifice, who carried himself like a leader burdened with impossible choices—how could *he* be capable of this?

It doesn't make sense. It *can't* make sense.

And yet, the weight of it—the crushing truth of it—presses down on me with brutal clarity.

He didn't save the people of Four Rivers.

He didn't try.

He *only* saved me.

And suddenly, that's the part that feels the wrongest of all.

"Why?" I ask, my voice shaking. "Why *me?*"

Brennen doesn't answer. He doesn't have to.

Because I already know.

It wasn't out of kindness. It wasn't because of some familial bond. It was because I'm useful. Because I'm part of his *plan*.

A pawn.

A piece on his board.

And *how long* has it been this way?

Was the Naming Ceremony ever real? Was my bond with Lathguard always meant to happen? Was I even given a *choice*?

The thoughts suffocate me.

I see flashes—my parents, standing in the ceremony hall, waiting for me. *Did they know?* Did they *see* what was happening before the end?

I see the Four Rivers, my home, overrun with creatures I didn't even know existed until days ago.

I see Rorick, watching as his people burned, and walking away.

The bile rises in my throat.

I was never special. Never chosen.

I was selected.

And everyone else was left to die.

"I need to get out of here," I finally say, the words escaping like a breath I didn't realize I was holding.

Brennen nods. "We both do. But it will be harder getting *you* out. You're warded somehow—I'm sure of it. They'll know the moment you leave these grounds, so we have to hurry. I'm not without abilities of my own, so I'll keep you hidden."

I frown. "I thought we couldn't channel."

"The First People's abilities are different," Brennen explains. "We don't channel from the land. Ours is *innate*."

I think back to the woods, to the terrifying moment when I was paralyzed without warning. "Is that how I was frozen?"

"That was Drusilla." He gives a small, uncomfortable laugh. "You'll meet her soon enough."

His attempt at humor doesn't land. The memory of being helpless—of my own body betraying me—sends a shudder through me.

Brennen clears his throat. "I can become invisible. That's why I'm here and not Theron. My ability doesn't just mask me from sight—it makes people believe they *never saw me at all*. It works on sound too. As long as no one's actively looking for me, I can move freely. That's how we'll get out."

I glance toward the door, doubt gnawing at me. "Then why can't we just wait until morning? Slip out when there's more movement to blend into?"

Brennen shakes his head. "It's too risky. My ability isn't true invisibility. It *tricks the mind*. The more eyes on me, the harder it is to hold. By morning, the Keep will be busy—too many people to fool at once. It's going to be hard enough hiding both of us as it is. On the way in, I spotted a cave not far from here. I'm hoping it's just outside whatever ward they've placed on you."

I exhale sharply. There are a thousand ways this could go wrong, but staying here isn't an option.

I look down at myself. "I only have my robe." The words feel bitter in my mouth. It's the only thing we're allowed to wear, a reminder of my forced place in all of this. "I don't want to look at it, much less wear it. But it's all I've got."

"I'll see what I can do about that later," Brennen promises. "For now, grab your lamp. We need to go."

I take the lamp from my bedside and, without another word, follow him to the door.

We slip into the hallway, swallowed by the quiet of the Keep at night. Each step forward sends a pulse of apprehension through me, my senses heightened to every creak, every shift in the air. Yet beneath the anxiety, something new stirs inside me.

For the first time since I arrived, I feel like I'm choosing my own path.

Elena is alive. The lies that bound me are unraveling. I'm not just running from the Keep—I'm running toward something. Toward answers. Toward truth.

For the first time in what feels like forever, I'm stepping out of the shadows.

And I won't stop until I find out what they've been hiding from me.

#

The Keep is quiet. Too quiet.

A handful of guards patrol the halls, their armor faintly clinking in the distance. We only pass one, and he doesn't so much as glance in our direction. It's unsettling—walking in plain sight, yet being unseen.

"I came in through the kitchen," Brennen says, his voice at normal volume, not even bothering to whisper. "I noticed a few guards using that door, so I knew it was unlocked and probably not warded."

I flinch at his casual tone. Speaking out loud like this feels wrong. I still move carefully, still feel the need to tiptoe despite Brennen's confidence in his ability.

"There are more guards outside than inside," he continues. "And a few of them will be SoulCasters. We have to avoid them." His voice tightens slightly. "Not because they'll see us, but because I don't know if my ability can trick as many of them as it does normal men."

That makes me pause. Can't trick as many?

I nod, keeping my thoughts to myself.

We reach the kitchen—only to find two SoulCasters already inside, speaking to a few guards.

Brennen's hand clamps down on my arm, and he pulls me back into the shadows. His voice drops to a whisper now. "We need another way out."

He gestures for me to take the lead. I exhale slowly, steadying myself. I know another door. It's at the back of the dining room. I've never been past it, but I've seen where it leads from the outside.

We move quickly, silently. My heart pounds as we reach the door. I try the handle.

Locked.

Brennen crouches beside it, studying the mechanism. "I can pick it. Doesn't look too tricky."

I hesitate. "I heard you picking mine," I say. "Should we risk it?"

His face tightens. There's a flicker of frustration in his expression. "You did?" He sighs, rubbing his forehead. "I must have let my focus drop. That happens when I get frustrated."

"There's another door on the far side of the Keep," I offer. "Might be safer."

Brennen grimaces, considering it. "No. We're already here. You should do it."

I frown. "Do what?"

"You should be able to open it through channeling."

I narrow my eyes. "You want me to break the whole wall down?"

"No, just the door."

I scowl. "That was sarcasm."

Brennen smirks. "That wasn't lost on me."

I exhale sharply. He's serious about this.

"Look," he says, "your ability is force. If you push against the door from the other side, toward us, you should be able to break the lock without damaging anything else." He watches my hesitation, then adds, "I'll mask the sound. Let's try. I'll walk you through it."

I don't like this. But what choice do I have?

I position myself against the door. My palms press against the wood, bracing myself like Brennen instructed.

"This will help you feel how much force you're using," he explains. "Now, press against the door from the other side—towards yourself. Start with the smallest amount of pressure and slowly build up. Use only what's necessary, nothing more."

I take a slow breath. This should be easy.

So why do I feel like I'm about to lose control?

The door is solid, thicker than I expected. I push lightly to test its give—nothing. A little more pressure. Still nothing.

My heart pounds. This should be simple.

I take a slow breath and close my eyes, trying to see the lock in my mind. Visualizing its mechanisms. The force needed to break it— nothing more. I can do this. I have to.

I reach for my Essence. The familiar rush courses through me, powerful and immediate, as if my body recognizes this act, this command. I push, gently at first, just a nudge.

Nothing.

I push harder. A slow, steady increase, like pressing a weight against a stubborn door. I can feel the resistance now, the pushback of the lock and the wood itself. My Essence flows freely, like a river following its course.

But then something changes.

I don't feel like I'm pushing anymore. I feel like I am the force.

It's exhilarating. The power thrums through my veins, sharp and intoxicating, as if it's been waiting—hungry—to be unleashed. I know I should stop, that I've already reached the necessary force.

But it feels too good to stop.

I don't even realize my control is slipping until—

Boom.

The door doesn't just break. It detonates.

A violent shockwave slams into me. The air explodes with splinters and shredded wood as the force I built up releases all at once. A blast, raw and untamed.

I don't even register that I'm airborne until I hit the ground, hard. My back slams into the stone, and then the door follows.

Pain crashes through me. Pinned. Trapped. The weight crushes the air from my lungs.

My ears ring. The world tilts. For a moment, I can't move. What have I done?

Brennen's voice is distant at first. "Jerrick?" Urgency. Alarm. Then hands shove at the debris. The weight lifts slightly, enough for me to gasp in a breath.

I sit up slowly, pressing a hand to my shoulder. Sore. Aching. But not broken.

The door, however, is gone. Or rather, what's left of it is barely recognizable. Splintered chunks of wood. The metal hinges twisted. A gaping hole where it once stood. I hadn't just broken the lock. I obliterated the entire entrance.

"I... I didn't mean to," I manage, my voice hoarse. My hands shake. "I didn't think it would... I lost control for a second."

Brennen grips my arm and hauls me up. His expression is hard to read, somewhere between awe and concern. "We need to move. I masked the sound, but it won't take long before someone sees this."

I swallow hard and nod, stepping over the debris. I'd thought I understood my power. I don't.

A cold unease coils inside me. This force inside me—it's too much. Too wild. If I don't control it, I could do worse than just destroy a door.

We move quickly down a narrow hallway. Something about this place feels different. The air is heavy. The walls press inward, not in grandeur like the rest of the Keep, but with weight. With history.

I glance at the doors as we pass. They're older, thicker. Not like the others.

Cells.

A sliver of unease creeps into my gut, but we don't stop. At the end of the hall, we turn right. I lead us toward the front of the building.

Another door. This one is locked, but from our side.

I don't hesitate. Brennen slides the bolt free, and we push through.

And step into a room that does not belong here.

Five beds lined up on the right. A half dozen cribs on the left.

The air is different here. Heavy. Wrong.

The light is dim, but not enough to hide what's in front of us.

Women. Sleeping women.

In the cribs, babies.

And a feeling deep in my gut that tells me we were never meant to see this.

The room doesn't belong in the Keep.

The grandeur and structure of the corridors outside are gone— stripped away, replaced by something raw, something wrong. The walls, heavy and unadorned, seem to swallow the light. The dark gray stone presses inward, oppressive, suffocating. No tapestries. No banners. No sign that this place is part of the same world beyond that door.

The air is thick. Stale. Something lingers here, something old, forgotten. Beneath it, the sharp tang of urine and feces clings to the air, the unmistakable stench of human suffering. But there's something else too—incense. Faint, like a last-ditch effort to cover the rot. A mask for the decay.

This place is hidden. Not meant to be seen.

Brennen exhales sharply beside me. I hear his breath hitch as he steps further inside, his clawed hand covering his mouth.

"I know this place," he whispers. The words shake.

A beat of silence, then a whisper of dread:

"I didn't want to believe the rumors, but…" He swallows hard, staring at the room like it might swallow him back. "It's true."

I feel something inside me turn cold.

"What's true?"

His hesitation unnerves me. Brennen has been confident, even when sneaking into the Keep, even when facing down the unknown. But not now.

"We… we have to leave, Jerrick." His voice is urgent. "Now. We can't be here. The door on the other side will be locked—we won't be able to get through. We have to find another way out."

I barely hear him.

The weight of the room presses down on me, crushing me.

The women in the beds, the cribs—the silence. This place, this prison, is soaked in something more than sorrow.

A sickness coils in my stomach, twisting. Everything about this is wrong.

"We can't leave them." The words grind through my teeth.

Brennen flinches. "Jerrick, I understand. I don't want to leave them either, but if what I learned about these women is true, they won't come with us." His voice cracks. It's the first time I've heard real fear from him. "We have to go now, please."

He's afraid. He's afraid of this room. Of what it means.

I know we should run. I know we should escape. But the thought of walking away, of leaving them in this place, in this darkness—

No.

"What do you know about these women, Brennen?" My voice is low. Controlled. Dangerous.

"We don't have time," he pleads. "If you want to save them, live. You're the key to all of this!"

That's not an answer.

"You told me you wouldn't keep secrets from me," I snap, stepping closer. A sharp, accusing edge in my voice. "I'm calling you on it."

Brennen flinches again but nods. He looks exhausted. Defeated.

"None of this happened by chance," he finally says, voice hollow. "Before all the giants died, Lathguard made a plan to one day be resurrected. He infused four bloodlines with his mark."

The words slam into me.

"You know humans were never meant to wield Essence," he continues, voice distant. "But Lathguard found a way. He also knew no single human could ever bond him—so he created one."

The coldness inside me deepens.

"One of those bloodlines is yours, Jerrick."

I exhale sharply.

"That's why you and Theron are so massive. It's why your power is so… different."

Brennen gestures to the room, his hands trembling. "And so are these women. These children. They are your bloodline."

My stomach lurches. I don't want to hear this.

"These women give birth to babies with massive reservoirs. Rorick has been waiting for you for centuries, Jerrick. This room—this entire place—exists for that purpose."

Brennen looks away, his expression haunted.

"These babies are Named at birth," he murmurs. "And if they don't bond with Lathguard…"

He stops.

But I already know.

A dead, empty silence swallows the room.

"They don't survive."

The words hang between us like a blade at my throat.

"That's the evil we face, Jerrick," he says. The final, bitter truth. "Rorick will stop at nothing to bring Lathguard back."

I stare at him, unblinking.

A part of me had known—maybe not the details, but the shape of something horrible, lurking just beneath the surface. A part of me had felt the wrongness here from the start.

But hearing it aloud—knowing it, understanding it—

It changes everything.

Brennen's words claw at me, each revelation unraveling something inside my chest. It makes sense. That's the worst part. The pieces fit together too well.

My bloodline. Lathguard's design. This room.

I glance around again, and now—now I truly see it.

These women. These children.

They're not just prisoners. They're pieces. Numbers. Names etched in a book, ticked off as their worth is extracted. Their bodies are used, their children taken, drained, discarded if they aren't strong enough.

A slow, cold horror tightens in my gut.

This place is a slaughterhouse.

The crib nearest to me shifts slightly as a baby exhales in its sleep, oblivious to the nightmare around it.

I grit my teeth, my jaw locking so tightly it hurts.

"We can't just leave them here."

The words feel too small for the magnitude of what I'm seeing. They scrape past my throat, half a whisper, half a vow.

Brennen meets my gaze. He already knows what I'm feeling. I see it in his eyes—the sorrow, the understanding. He shakes his head.

"I know, Jerrick," he says softly. "I wish there was something we could do, but right now, we need to focus on getting you out. You're the key to stopping all of this. But we can't do anything if we're caught."

I barely hear him.

"Rorick has been working on them for generations. They won't come with us."

The words sink into me, but they don't take hold.

Because he's wrong.

They deserve the choice.

"No," I say, my voice harder, sharper.

Brennen tenses.

"We let them decide." I don't look at him. "Mask the door."

His eyes widen. "Jerrick, this isn't the time—"

"Mask the door."

He exhales sharply but doesn't argue. He knows he's lost this fight. He flicks his clawed fingers, weaving the silence around us.

I focus, but this time, I control it. I don't let it slip. I don't let my power consume.

I push.

The door doesn't shatter.

It doesn't explode.

It comes free.

Slowly, deliberately, it hovers midair—held by my will. My choice. I lower it without a sound.

Brennen exhales behind me.

I am in control.

But what I say next—that is not.

"Stop hiding me."

His voice catches.

"Jerrick—"

"Please."

He sags. I feel it more than I see it, the subtle shift as his ability drops.

I step forward into the open, exposed and unhidden.

I let them see me.

"Excuse me."

My voice breaks the silence, but nobody moves.

A heavier beat of stillness.

"Excuse me," I say again, louder this time.

A few of the women stir. One opens her eyes, blinks once. Twice. She doesn't flinch at the sight of me.

Her expression is flat, resigned.

"All but one of us are with child," she says, her voice so dull it feels wrong. Dead. "But she just gave birth yesterday. You'll have to come back in a few weeks. She'll be ready then."

She rolls to her side, pulling the covers up, as if I'm nothing.

As if this is normal.

My hands curl into fists.

No.

I refuse to be nothing.

"No," I say, my voice like iron. "I'm not here for that. I'm here to give each of you a choice." I point to the back door. "I'm leaving in a minute. If any of you want to come with me, I will clear the way."

Another silence.

Not stillness— this time, it's something heavier.

The woman who spoke slowly sits up. Her gaze narrows.

"It doesn't work like that," she says. "We cannot leave this room. We have a sacred duty that must be done in this room."

I hate the way she says it.

The way duty sounds like a sentence.

She tilts her head slightly. "Come back in a few weeks. She'll be ready for your seed then."

My stomach turns violently.

I clench my fists so tight my nails dig into my palms. "I'm not here for that." My voice is low, controlled. Stronger than I feel.

"Do any of you want to leave this place?" I force out. "If you do, we go now."

A beat.

Then another.

Nobody moves.

I feel the weight of Brennen's eyes on me.

I'm about to accept it— to turn and go, when—

A blanket shifts.

At the end of the room, one of the women moves.

She pushes her bedding aside and stands.

She is tall. Not as tall as me, but close. Too tall for a woman so broken down.

She moves slowly, deliberately, stepping toward a crib.

She reaches down, lifting a sleeping newborn.

Wraps it in a thin, worn blanket.

And turns to me.

I see her face now—gray, empty eyes. Stringy hair hanging loose around sunken cheeks.

Not old, but spent.

Used up.

She walks to me, shifting the baby in her arms, and without a word, she pushes it into my chest.

I stumble slightly, barely catching the weight of it.

Warm. Small. Fragile.

"I won't let them take her," she says. Her voice is hoarse, barely more than a breath. "Or worse. Make her do…"

Her words crack. She swallows hard. "Please help her."

I hold the baby awkwardly, stiffly.

I don't know how to hold a child.

I don't know how to do any of this.

"But… won't she… I mean, don't you…" I stammer, uncertain.

The woman grabs my arm suddenly, hard, with a strength that should be impossible.

"She has no future here."

Her eyes bore into mine, fierce, wild, desperate.

"I've lost too many," she whispers. A plea and a curse all in one. "Take her with you."

I swallow. My throat is dry, raw.

"You should come with me," I say. I mean it. "She needs her mother."

The woman doesn't hesitate.

"We can't leave this room." Her voice is flat, spoken as if it's a truth too heavy to fight against. A rule she's resigned herself to. "We're tied to this place. Even if we wanted to, we can't."

Her gaze flickers downward, something breaking in her eyes.

She shifts the baby in my arms, smoothing the blanket over its tiny face.

"I'm all dried up." Her words tremble like loose stones on a cliff. "I can't be the mother she needs."

And then—she falls.

Not out of exhaustion. Not out of weakness.

She drops to her knees and bends forward—her lips pressing against the tops of my feet.

"Please." Her voice is a wound. "Give her a future."

I stagger back, the baby jostling slightly in my arms.

The heat in my chest isn't power this time.

It's rage.

It boils, swells, chokes.

I don't know if I can live up to the faith she's placing in me, or to Brennen's desperate belief that I am somehow the key.

Key to what?

I don't know anything.

I am not ready for this.

I don't know how to do this.

I may be bonded to the most powerful of the GodSouls, but I am too indecisive, too lost, too afraid.

A real hero wouldn't let this woman beg.

A real hero would have promised her, without hesitation, that her daughter would be safe.

But I stand there, frozen, ashamed.

What would my parents say if they could see me like this?

And then—

The voices.

Distant at first, then closer.

Boots pounding down the hall.

Brennen appears beside me, sharp and urgent.

"We have to go now!" His voice is a dagger of sound against the tension. "I've hidden you and the baby."

I know the woman can't see me. She can't hear me. But she's still at my feet, still kneeling, still waiting.

I reach down, grasping her arms.

She shudders.

I pull her up, and when she stands, she shakes with silent sobs.

I do the only thing I can.

I wrap my arms around her.

She clings to me, her body racked with grief and something else—something unspoken.

Then—she rips away.

She turns, her gaze locking onto the door we entered through.

A breath, then—

"Go!" she screams.

And then, flames.

A white-blue inferno erupts from her arms, scorching the air, turning the space behind us into a column of fire.

The doors blast open.

The two SoulCasters from the kitchen step in, and in the span of a heartbeat, they are gone.

Not burned. Not reduced to corpses.

Gone.

Turned to ash, to nothing, as if they were never there at all.

The stench of charred flesh curdles in my throat.

"Move, Jerrick!" Brennen grabs me, dragging me toward the back door.

I can't move.

The baby is silent in my arms.

The woman stands, staring into the fire she has made, unmoving.

I want to call out, to reach for her.

She doesn't turn.

She doesn't look away.

Her fury is absolute.

Brennen pulls me harder. "We won't have time to hide, we have to run!"

And then—we're running.

We burst through the back door, down another hallway.

Ahead, a door— thick and iron, leading outside.

Brennen slows beside me. "It's sealed—"

I don't think.

I just act.

I raise my free hand, channeling Essence.

Not at the door.

At the wall.

A detonation of force erupts from me, not controlled, not calculated.

It's too much.

The entire wall explodes outward.

A deafening crack of stone and metal.

I stumble forward, stepping through the wreckage—

And then, Brennen doesn't follow.

I turn.

And he's on the floor.

Still.

Silent.

A massive beam lies across his body, his clothes soaked in blood.

"Brennen!" My voice splits the air.

He doesn't move.

I drop to my knees beside him, the baby shifting in my arms. Too small. Too fragile.

The beam is nothing.

It shouldn't feel heavy.

I lift it without thinking, tossing it aside.

But the weight pressing on my chest—that doesn't lift.

There's blood everywhere.

Too much blood.

The door, the explosion, the fire, the woman, the SoulCasters— it all crashes down on me.

The chaos I caused.

I let my power slip again.

And now—Brennen is dying because of it.

The weight of the beam was nothing.

But the weight of this moment is everything.

Holding the baby in one arm, I press a shaking hand to Brennen's chest, his breathing shallow, ragged.

"No, no, no," I whisper.

The battle inside me shifts.

Fear—for Brennen.

For the child I don't know how to protect.

For the unknown ahead.

And underneath it all, rage.

At myself.

At this world.

At the choices I didn't make, at the choices made for me.

Brennen's words echo, twisting like a knife.

You're the key.

I don't know what that means.

I don't know what I'm supposed to do.

But right now, Brennen is dying.

And the baby in my arms is still breathing.

I tighten my grip, a new promise forming.

I can't change what I've done.

I can't undo this damage.

But I can protect what's left.

I shift Brennen's weight carefully, lifting him.

Blood seeps into my clothes, into my hands.

The baby doesn't stir.

I don't have time to break down.

I don't have time to second guess.

I rise, each movement heavier than the last.

The night air is crisp and unmoving. The chaos behind me—the fire, the screams, the scent of ash and charred flesh—feels distant. Like it belongs to another world.

I stand in the ruins of what was once a wall, holding a life in each arm.

Brennen's weight pulls on one side, limp and heavy.

The baby's weight pulls on the other, small and fragile.

My breath steadies.

I feel it.

The shift.

Something inside me has settled.

I don't look back.

I can't.

Brennen's blood seeps into my sleeve. His breaths are shallow, but still there.

I adjust my hold on him, securing the baby closer.

I can hear them now—the shouts, the footsteps, the distant ring of metal as guards scramble.

I close my eyes.

No one is coming.

No one but me.

No SoulCasters. No warriors. No gods.

Just me and the weight of two lives.

Jerrick, the farm boy, would have hesitated.

Jerrick, the boy who only wanted to tend his land and live a quiet life, would have felt fear.

I am not that boy anymore.

I don't think.

I channel. The shield forms around us, effortless now. Force gathers beneath my feet, lifting me, lifting us.

The shouts grow distant.

The Keep—its looming walls, its cold halls, its hidden horrors—begins to shrink.

And then—the ground falls away.

I hover.

Not flying. Not soaring.

Just drifting.

Silent. Controlled.

The wind carries me forward, away from the nightmare behind me, into the unknown ahead. Into the darkness.

I don't know where I'm going.

I don't know if there's safety beyond these cliffs.

But I go anyway.

Because I have to.

Not just for me.

For us.

Chapter 12

Jerrick

If I weren't burdened with the weight of two unconscious bodies in my arms, I might have reveled in the fact that I was flying. The sensation is surreal, equal parts exhilarating and unnerving. The vastness of the plains stretches out beneath me, an endless abyss cloaked in darkness. I have no real plan—just an instinctual need to get away. Away from the Keep. Away from the things I've seen. Away from what I've done.

Brennen told me we were to meet up with Theron, Elena, and Drusilla, but he never said where. I try to rouse him, jostling his limp form in my left arm, but he remains motionless, his breathing shallow but steady. That has to be enough for now. I can't afford to stop.

I've been flying for over an hour—at least, I think it's been that long. Time feels strange up here, suspended in the dark, weightless yet burdened. There are no landmarks, no light to navigate by, just the inky blackness stretching endlessly in all directions. I could be heading straight into the Fog for all I know. I tell myself I have time before that becomes a problem.

I'm a beacon in the night. My glowing shield wraps around us like a cocoon, its soft radiance breaking the darkness. It makes me an easy target. Can they see me from the Keep? Is something else watching? I remember Brennen's warning, the creatures that hunt SoulCasters. I just hope they can't fly.

Despite the sheer weight of the two bodies in my arms, they feel light—as if my Essence is dulling their mass, dispersing the burden across my shield. But I know that isn't real. My arms burn, my grip weakens with every passing minute. How much longer before exhaustion overtakes me? How much longer before I falter?

I can't afford to falter.

My thoughts keep circling back to the room we left behind—the women, the cradles, the stench of despair. It's a sickness that clings to me, suffocating even in the open air. Their resignation haunts me, the way they looked at me like I was just another cog in a machine that has been grinding them down for generations. I struggle with the notion of choice—of how meaningless it is when the only options are to comply or to suffer.

They never even considered leaving. That terrifies me more than anything else.

I don't know what I'm doing. I don't know what comes next. I wasn't ready for this. I can fight, but can I lead? I have power, but can I protect? What good is a gift I can't even control? What happens when we land? What happens when I fail?

The image of the woman who gave me her child lingers, seared into my memory. She had no hope left for herself, but she had it for her daughter. That's what she gave me—not just a child, but her last act of defiance against Rorick's world. It wasn't just walls that trapped them—it was centuries of conditioning, of manipulation so deep it stole even the thought of freedom from them.

Rorick stole that from them.

I once saw him as a leader. A guiding force, a figure of wisdom and strength. Now, I see the truth. His twisted sense of righteousness, his belief in the greater good at any cost, has made him something worse than a tyrant. It has made him certain.

And certainty is the most dangerous thing of all.

The things I saw tonight—the things I know now—I can't turn away from them. The Keep isn't just a fortress of knowledge; it's a prison, a factory, a place where life is measured by how useful it is to Rorick's plan. How many other secrets does it hold? How many other lives have been stolen, twisted, discarded?

A cold resolve settles in my chest, heavier than the bodies in my arms. This isn't just about escaping, about saving myself. It's about burning that place to the ground.

I don't know what happens next. I don't have a plan. But I have a purpose now.

And that's enough.

For now.

I lift the baby girl in my right arm, cradling her close until our cheeks press together. She's warm. She breathes steadily, soft and rhythmic against my skin—a fragile, living thing in my arms. The sound steadies me, a reassurance that she's still here, still fighting.

But she hasn't woken up.

A dull worry gnaws at me. Shouldn't she be stirring by now? Shouldn't she be crying, hungry? A part of me fears she never will, that she'll never know the world outside of that room. That she will never know freedom.

I nudge her gently with my cheek. "You're strong, little one," I whisper. "Keep fighting. You're free now, and nobody will ever take that from you again. I promise."

I don't know if I can keep that promise. But I mean it with every fiber of my being.

Then—light.

The world around me shifts from deep, suffocating black to pale gray as night surrenders to day. It's morning. I've been flying for almost two hours. Two hours with neither Brennen nor the baby stirring. Two hours of holding them, carrying them blindly into the unknown.

I need to land.

A narrow stream comes into view below, cutting through the land like a silver thread. Just beyond it, a cluster of trees offers a semblance of shelter. I angle downward, my flight slowing, the wind rushing quieter against me. The moment my feet touch earth, I release my shield and let out the breath I was holding.

The silence is immediate. No cries. No pursuers. Just the quiet murmur of the stream and the first stirrings of dawn.

I lower Brennen and the baby gently onto the grass, then scan the horizon. Nothing. But my skin prickles as if something unseen is watching. I shake the feeling off.

I kneel beside Brennen first. Now that there's light, I can finally see him.

His face is pale, his forehead streaked with blood from a deep gash above his brow. Tiny splinters of wood are embedded in his skin. I dip the hem of my robe in the cold stream and begin wiping away the blood, working quickly but carefully. The dried streaks flake away, revealing the damage beneath.

He looks bad, but he's breathing. That has to be enough.

The baby worries me more.

I glance down at her, curled beside me on the grass, her tiny hands motionless against her swaddling. Shouldn't she have woken up by now? I don't know much about babies, but I know they cry. They stir. They need to be fed. She's too still. Too quiet.

I shouldn't be the one making this decision. I don't know how to care for her. I don't even know how to care for myself in this situation. But there's nobody else.

I adjust the blanket around her, brushing a strand of damp hair away from her forehead. She's so small. How can something this fragile be expected to survive a world as cruel as this?

And yet... here she is.

Brennen stirred in his sleep when I carried him. But she never did.

A weight presses down on me, heavier than before. I can't fail her.

A low groan breaks my thoughts. Brennen.

His eyes flutter open, dazed and glassy, confusion and pain warring on his face. He winces as he tries to sit up, hissing through his teeth as the movement pulls at his wounds.

"Where... are we?" His voice is hoarse, raw from pain and exhaustion.

Relief floods me. "Safe. For now," I answer, slipping an arm under his shoulder and easing him into a sitting position. "Far from the Keep. I flew south until daylight. We've only been here a few minutes."

His gaze sharpens, taking in our surroundings, assessing. Calculating. He still looks weak, but his mind is already working. He may be battered, but he's still Brennen.

But then his eyes snap to me, full of sudden clarity. "Did you say... fly?"

I can't help it—I laugh. The incredulous look on his face is too much. After everything that's happened, this is what surprises him?

"Oh yeah," I say, grinning despite myself. "I can fly."

The humor is short-lived. His expression twists into fear.

"Jerrick," he breathes, his voice dropping into something urgent. "I told you not to channel."

The weight of the last two hours comes crashing down on me in an instant. The exhaustion, the fear, the uncertainty—all of it.

"And what would you have had me do?" I snap, narrowing my eyes. There's an edge in my voice, sharper than I intended.

Brennen scratches at one of his long ears and gives me a tired, lopsided smile. "We're safe. That's all that matters. Thank you for saving us, Jerrick."

I shift on my heels, uncomfortable with the gratitude. I don't feel like a savior. Not when the escape was more chaos than plan, not when I barely controlled my own power.

"I'm sorry for what happened back there. I… I thought I projected the force outward."

"You did," he says, his tone gentle. "It was just bad luck." His smile falters, eyes drifting past me as if recalling something important. Then his head snaps up. "How's the baby?"

The baby. The thought sends a fresh wave of anxiety rolling through me.

"She's here, but she's still asleep," I admit, trying to keep my voice steady. "I'm worried about her."

"Hand her to me."

I hesitate. I don't know her name. I don't know anything about her except that I promised to protect her. But what does that even mean, if I can't help her wake up?

Gently, I lift her from the ground and place her into Brennen's waiting arms. His hands—large, clawed, lethal—move with careful precision. He cradles her as though she's made of spun glass, shaking her lightly, his expression tightening when she doesn't stir.

His brows furrow. "Here." He reaches into his pocket and pulls out a small piece of cloth, offering it to me. "This is still clean. Can you wet it?"

I nod and dip the cloth into the stream, squeezing out the excess before handing it back. Brennen folds it into a cone shape and presses it gently to her lips.

A flicker of relief courses through me when her tiny mouth parts, drawing in the cloth. She suckles instinctively.

"She'll eat," Brennen says after a long pause. But his voice is heavy. Too heavy. "But we have nothing to feed her."

His gaze darkens.

"I think… they did something to her," he murmurs. "To keep her like this." He swallows hard. "I don't think she'll ever wake up on her own."

My heart clenches.

That isn't an option.

"There has to be something we can do." My voice comes out sharper than I intended, but I don't care. She can't just stay like this. She can't die.

Brennen exhales slowly, his ears flattening slightly. "We were supposed to meet up with Theron, Elena, and Drusilla, but we must have flown past them miles ago." His tone shifts, more resolved now. "There's nothing we can do about that now. And as much as I wish there was another way… we need to go see my people."

I frown. "Why?"

"There's something there you need to see."

A chill runs through me. There's something in his voice—something final.

"How far?"

He tilts his head, considering. "If I'm right about where we are, we're maybe a three-day walk." He looks down at the baby, his lips pressing into a tight line. "But I don't think she has three days."

I don't hesitate. "Then we fly."

Brennen snorts, looking up at me. "Fly, huh?" His voice is dry with skepticism. "How exactly do we do that?"

I reach for the baby first, holding her close, then extend my free hand to Brennen, pulling him up. He wobbles slightly, blinking hard, but then squares his shoulders and stands firm.

I arch a brow. "I carried you before."

"I will not have you cradle me like a baby, Jerrick." His ears flick back in mock offense. "Even though I may look like one next to you." His grin is brief, but genuine.

I chuckle despite myself. "Is there another way?"

He scratches at his head, looking me over. Compared to him, I must seem like a giant. His head barely reaches my navel, his frame lean and wiry where mine is thick with muscle. But there's a grit to him, a quiet strength that has nothing to do with size.

He's people survived centuries of persecution, of being hunted by people like me. And yet… there's no bitterness in his eyes.

Why?

I watch him, the way he stands firm despite the weight of everything humans have done to his kind, and I can't stop myself from asking.

"…Why don't you hate me?"

His ears twitch. His head tilts back as he looks up at me, something flickering behind his eyes.

"What?"

I shift uncomfortably. "I know this affects all of us, but… how can you not hate me for what my people have done to yours?"

The surprise in his expression is immediate, but then it fades into something else. Something quieter.

His eyes narrow in thought. Considering.

Finally, he sighs. "The hatred your people feel… isn't your fault," he says softly. "In a way, it's our burden, not yours."

That answer rattles me.

I shake my head. "Rorick told me about our creator," I murmur. "That she destroyed the God Tree. That when the First People refused to worship her, she created man to replace them. She—" I hesitate. "She infused us with an innate hatred of your kind. I don't understand how that's your burden."

Brennen's gaze darkens, but he doesn't answer right away.

I can feel something shifting between us—like the air itself has changed.

And I'm not sure I'm ready for his answer.

Brennen sighs but doesn't answer right away. His gaze flickers up to meet mine, then shifts away, as if searching for the right words.

"That's close to the truth," he finally says. "I don't think Rorick purposely misled you—even he isn't old enough to remember what truly happened. My ancestors got our name, The Keepers, because it was our sacred duty to look after the God Tree."

I listen, enraptured. The God Tree. I've heard it spoken of in legend, but never as something so... real.

"The God Tree birthed our land, Jerrick," Brennen continues, voice laced with reverence. "It sustained everything, and in return, we sustained it. We tended to its needs, and in doing so, it provided everything we needed. It was a balance, a harmony we never questioned."

He exhales, his expression darkening. "But then, the giants rose."

A chill runs down my spine.

"They came from under the earth, powerful and awe-inspiring, and soon, my ancestors began worshiping them instead of tending to the God Tree." His voice hardens, as though the betrayal of his people still lingers after centuries. "And the God Tree... split in two."

I blink. Split?

Something cold slithers into my gut. I don't know why, but the words settle wrong.

Before I can stop myself, I blurt, "Are you saying The Creator is the God Tree?"

Brennen's eyes lock onto mine, his face unreadable. "Yes."

The world tilts.

I suddenly feel too small for the knowledge pressing down on me.

"But my ancestors didn't know that at the time," Brennen continues. "They shunned her—rejected her—because they believed she had killed the God Tree. They saw her as the destroyer, not the tree itself. That's why we view this burden as ours, and why we protect humanity instead of fighting back. When she returns, Jerrick—when she judges us—we'll prove our loyalty by how we've cared for her creation."

I stare at him.

Throughout history, humans have hunted Keepers. Killed them with impunity. I was taught they feared us.

But now...

I see the truth.

It's not fear. It's duty.

I want to say something. I need to. But my mind is still catching up to the weight of what I've just learned.

Then, Brennen's earlier words resurface in my mind.

The God Tree split in two.

I narrow my eyes. "You said the God Tree split. Where is the other part?"

Brennen's entire expression changes. His ears perk up, his tired eyes suddenly alight with something almost mischievous.

"That's a very good question, Jerrick." His lips curve into a small smile. "Would you like to meet him?"

Meet him?

My stomach knots. The other half of the God Tree is alive?

"Yes, I would," I say, honestly. "But we have to take care of this little girl first."

Brennen nods, as if expecting my answer. "Funny thing, that," he says, tilting his head. "He's the one who's going to help us."

A chill runs through me, but it isn't fear.

It's awe.

Every moment since I woke up at the Keep, I've learned something new—each revelation making my world feel bigger, more tangled, more uncertain. I used to live in my head, more comfortable with ideas than reality.

But now?

Now, I can't stop seeing.

My eyes are wide open.

And somehow, I've landed at the center of it all.

I exhale slowly. "Well… I guess we should get going, then."

Brennen chuckles. "Before you light up the sky again?"

I smirk, remembering how the last time I channeled in the dark, I turned my entire room into a glowing beacon.

"I'm going to try something different," I say. "Before, I wrapped us in a shield. This time, I want to create a platform. Something we can stand on."

Brennen hums in approval. "Smart. What do you need me to do?"

I concentrate.

The air hums with tension as I reach for the Essence, shaping it into something new. The invisible force beneath my feet solidifies into a shimmering disk—a platform of raw power.

It materializes just inches above the grass, its surface smooth and rippling like heat waves. I step onto it carefully, testing its weight.

Then, I rise.

A few feet. Then higher.

I can feel the difference. Unlike before, I'm not weightless.

The baby is heavy in my arms. The wind presses against me. It's as though the world hasn't faded away this time.

I lower myself back down beside Brennen, excitement bubbling in my chest. This works.

"I think the shield will be—"

A sharp yipping noise cuts through the morning air.

I don't even have time to finish my sentence before the treeline erupts with movement.

They come fast.

A half-dozen small creatures, moving low to the ground, sprinting toward us on two legs. Their long, gangly arms drag behind them, twisting unnaturally as they run.

Their heads are too small. Their bodies look like something stitched together by madness—flesh and bone fused with branches, vines, sinew.

The yipping grows frantic, a sick, high-pitched chorus that sends a cold shudder through my spine.

They're almost on us.

I know I should move. Do something.

But I just watch.

Because I'm still getting used to the idea that I'm the one who has to do something.

"Jerrick!" Brennen shouts. "I just hid us!"

He tugs hard on my robe, his panic infectious. Then, without hesitation, he bolts downstream.

I follow, heart hammering against my ribs.

Behind us, the creatures pour from the trees in waves, their shrill, bone-piercing yips echoing through the clearing. More and more of them come—dozens at first, then too many to count.

They're hunting us.

Brennen gasps beside me, his breath ragged. "Jerrick—there... are... too... many!"

I glance back just in time to see them turn their heads in unison. They've found us.

A guttural, collective snarl rips through the air.

Then, they charge.

A primal instinct ignites in me—a raw, desperate need to survive, to protect. Before I can even think, power surges through my core like a living thing, reaching for the air around me, bending to my will.

The Essence wrenches free.

I throw out my arms—not knowing what I'm about to do, only knowing that I must.

A pulse erupts from my chest, an invisible shockwave—no, not just a barrier.

A force. A reckoning.

The creatures slam into it full speed.

The impact is instantaneous—cataclysmic.

They don't just crash into the shield.

They cease to exist.

Their bodies explode on impact, tearing apart with a violence I've never seen, flesh and bone disintegrating into a red mist. The air becomes thick with the smell of iron and death.

I stagger back, chest heaving.

What… what did I just do?

I stare at the space where the creatures had been—where life had existed, then hadn't.

I obliterated them.

Not fought. Not defended. I unmade them.

A cold shudder rips through me.

The power—it hadn't come with effort.

It had come too easily.

Brennen grabs my arm. "Jerrick," he croaks, his voice hoarse with urgency. "We have to go. Now! More are coming!"

I snap my head up, blinking hard, and see it—another wave.

Dozens. Hundreds.

They surge toward us like a swarm, a tidal wave of claws and teeth and unnatural hunger.

I don't think. I react.

The shield condenses.

Instead of lashing outward, I pull it inward, wrapping it around us like a second skin.

The next breath I take is in open air.

Fifty feet above the ground.

Brennen grips my robe, eyes wide in disbelief. I tighten my hold on the baby, my gaze locked on the horde below.

They shriek, howl, claw at the earth where we'd stood seconds ago.

But we're gone.

Before turning south, I meet Brennen's gaze.

He nods.

Not just in gratitude, not just in relief.

In understanding.

Because no matter how much is left unsaid, we both know.

This is where the true journey begins.

Not just a flight from darkness, but a step toward something bigger. Toward a world we've yet to define.

#

Brennen has me land just a few strides from the edge of our world.

The Fog.

It looms before me like an endless, churning sea of mist, a wall of swirling gray and white that stretches from horizon to horizon. It moves like it's alive, coiling, folding in on itself, flickers of blue lightning forking deep within. The closer I stand, the more I hear it—a constant humming, low and droning, like a voice just beneath the surface, whispering something I can't quite understand.

My skin prickles.

This is the boundary of our land. The end of everything.

Brennen gestures toward it, his clawed fingers flexing. "We've tried digging under it." He lifts one of his hands, turning it over, showing me the dark crescents of his nails. "The Fog goes underground too. No matter how deep we dig, it's there."

I swallow, my throat dry.

"Nobody knows what's on the other side," Brennen continues. "The oldest of our texts say the first of us awoke to find Fog. It says the land back then was only a hundred strides in all directions. A perfect circle."

I tear my gaze from the Fog, looking at him. "Are you saying this is how the land began?"

Brennen nods. "And, perhaps, how it will end."

The words sit uneasily in my chest.

I turn back to the Fog, staring into the undulating mass. Something about it feels… wrong. Like it isn't just a wall. Like it's watching. Waiting.

Then he says the unthinkable.

"We have to pass through it."

I snap my head toward him. "What?"

Brennen grins. "What's the matter? You don't believe me?"

I scowl, setting my jaw. "It's not that. I've always heard the Fog—"

"Kills everything it touches?" he finishes. "Oh, it does. Touch it, and you die."

I exhale sharply through my nose. "And yet, you still want me to walk into it?"

He laughs. "Not the Fog. Our Fog."

I blink. "What?"

Brennen steps closer, lowering his voice slightly. "The Keepers live in a pocket within the Fog. A hidden space. It moves with the Fog itself. Centuries ago, before the God Wars, my people cast an illusion over it to keep us hidden. As long as we go in together, you'll be safe."

I look back at the mist. It still feels wrong.

But then I glance down at the tiny form in my arms.

Abby.

She breathes softly, still asleep, still helpless.

I don't have the luxury of fear anymore.

I tighten my hold on her, looking back at Brennen. "I'm ready."

Brennen nods.

"Follow close."

He strides forward, and I match his pace, step for step.

And then he vanishes.

The Fog swallows him whole.

My chest tightens.

A beat. Then another.

I clench my jaw, heart hammering, and step into the unknown.

For a moment, there is nothing.

No ground beneath my feet. No air in my lungs.

Just silence.

Then—light.

I stumble forward, gasping as I emerge onto solid ground. The oppressive hum of the Fog is gone, replaced by something softer—the rustling of leaves in a warm breeze, the distant murmur of water.

I blink, trying to adjust.

The air here is different. Lighter, more fragrant, like it's been untouched by time. The sky isn't blue or even gray, but a pale, endless white, stretching in every direction.

And then, I see it.

I suck in a sharp breath.

We stand atop a gentle hill, overlooking a sea of wildflowers that stretch as far as I can see. The colors are overwhelming—reds, yellows, blues, purples—a riot of life where there should be none.

I turn slowly, taking it all in. To my left, the land rises again, crowned by a monstrous stump.

The Stump.

It is impossibly massive, at least a hundred feet across, ancient and scarred. Even from here, I can see the rings inside—countless ages marked in its hollowed core. I can feel it, somehow. Like it is watching me. Like it is waiting.

Beyond the Stump, I spot dwellings, homes that seem to have grown from the earth itself. The walls are alive with vines, flowers blooming in windows, rooftops thick with moss and branches.

And then—the people.

At least a dozen Keepers stand before us, watching.

Their expressions are a mix of shock and awe.

Their ears twitch as they take in the sight of me—of a human emerging from the Fog.

I suddenly feel exposed, standing here, holding the baby in my arms, their wide eyes fixed on me like I'm something out of legend.

A sharp whisper breaks the silence. More voices join in, murmuring in a language I don't understand.

I glance at Brennen, who smiles at me.

"Welcome to the Stump," he says.

Brennen steps forward and speaks in their language—a fluid, lyrical sound that rolls effortlessly off his tongue.

One of the Keepers, a woman with dark, braided hair and sharp, knowing eyes, listens closely. Then, she turns to me, her gaze shifting up to the baby in my arms.

She speaks, her voice softer than Brennen's, yet firm, certain.

I don't understand the words, but there's something in her tone.

A question.

I look to Brennen for guidance.

"Mauda is asking about the child's name," he translates.

I freeze.

Her name?

I hadn't thought about it before. Did her mother ever name her? Or was she just another child meant to be used, discarded if she failed to bond?

A dull ache forms in my chest.

For a long moment, I say nothing. Then, a face flickers through my mind—my mother's.

Her warmth. Her strength.

I swallow hard, my throat tight.

"Her name is Abby," I whisper.

Brennen stiffens beside me. His jaw clenches.

For a fleeting second, there's a look in his eyes— something I can't quite place.

Pain? Gratitude?

Then, he nods, his voice low. "That's perfect, Jerrick. I think your mother would approve."

I can't speak.

I just nod, tightening my arms around the tiny girl as if she were the most precious thing in the world.

The Keeper—Mauda, as Brennen calls her—steps closer and reaches out slowly, carefully. She says something else in her language, and though I don't understand the words, I know what she's asking.

I hesitate, just for a moment, before gently placing Abby into her arms.

Mauda's hands, despite the long claws, despite the strangeness of her people, are gentle, warm, steady. She cradles Abby like she's something sacred.

I exhale.

For the first time since I fled the Keep, I don't feel alone in this.

"Thank you," I murmur. "Please, help her."

Mauda inclines her head slightly in a quiet promise before turning and walking toward the dwellings. Other Keepers move aside for her, their eyes lingering on Abby, their faces unreadable.

I watch her go, a part of me wanting to follow.

To make sure Abby will be okay.

But then Brennen touches my shoulder.

"There's someone you need to meet," he says.

I look up at him, still feeling the absence of Abby's weight in my arms.

But I nod.

And follow.

Brennen leads me down the slope, away from Mauda and Abby, deeper into the Keepers' land.

As we move, more Keepers appear.

At first, only a few peek from behind dwellings woven into the landscape. Then, more come—stepping fully into view, watching me.

Their eyes are filled with expectation.

I feel it pressing down on me like a weight.

I don't know these people. They don't know me. But there's something in the way they look at me, in the way they murmur to each other.

Like they've been waiting.

Their homes are unlike anything I've ever seen. Blended with the land itself, carved into rolling hills and tangled roots, they look as though they weren't built, but grown.

Everything here is alive.

The air feels different.

I inhale deeply. It's lighter, warmer. The scent of damp earth and blooming flowers fills my lungs.

No winter. No decay. Nothing like the land beyond the Fog.

How? How has this place survived when the rest of the world is dying?

We reach the base of the next hill. From here, I see the colossal stump sitting at its peak, a scarred monument to something ancient.

It looms above us, bigger than any structure in the Keep.

A chill runs through me.

I don't know why, but I feel like it's watching me.

We start climbing.

The whispers from the Keepers follow us. Some reach out to touch my arm, my sleeve, just the edge of my robe.

I flinch, unused to the attention.

Brennen notices.

"They're hoping," he says simply. "We all are."

Hoping for what?

I don't ask.

I already know.

We climb in silence.

The wind shifts, carrying the scent of flowers and earth up the hill. It should be soothing, but my chest feels tight.

It's the way the Keepers looked at me—the hope in their eyes. What do they expect from me?

Halfway up, I finally ask.

"What's going on, Brennen?"

His pace doesn't slow.

"We've been waiting for this moment for over seven hundred years."

I stop. Seven hundred years?

He turns back, sees my expression, and sighs. "I know how it sounds."

"No, you don't," I snap. "Because if you did, you wouldn't have said it so casually."

Brennen watches me carefully. "I didn't say it casually. I said it plainly."

I shake my head. "You don't understand. People keep acting like I'm supposed to be something. Like I'm supposed to fix everything. I don't even know what's broken."

Brennen's voice is calm, but there's something weighted in it.

"Jerrick, our land has been dying since the God Tree split. You already know that. But the decay sped up when the giants banished The Creator. That was the breaking point. Since then, we've had one purpose—to reunite what was severed."

He gestures up the hill. "That's why we protect the Stump. It's all that remains of the God Tree."

I glance up at it. Scarred. Hollow. Dead.

"And you think I can fix it?"

"We think you can reunite it."

I exhale sharply. "I'm not who you think I am."

Brennen grins. "None of us are. But I have it on good authority that you're Jerrick."

I roll my eyes. "You know what I mean."

His expression turns serious. He takes a step closer, his grip suddenly firm on my wrist.

"Every soul harbors depths untold, potential untouched." His voice lowers, but there's a force behind it, something almost ancient in the way he speaks. "We wander through life blind to the power that slumbers within us, greatness veiled by time until the destined moment awakens it. Jerrick, you stand unaware on the threshold of your own vastness. It is not I who must recognize who you are—it is you."

The weight of his words settles on me like a stone in my gut.

How can he believe this?

How can they?

How am I supposed to?

For my whole life, I was just a boy from the Four Rivers. A boy who worked his father's farm, who had no bigger worries than tending fields, who dreamed of a life that felt safe. Simple.

Now, I'm here. A land hidden in the Fog. A people waiting for something. A prophecy I never agreed to.

I've been chosen.

But I never got to choose.

Brennen releases my wrist, his expression softening. He's said his piece. Now, it's up to me whether or not I listen.

I don't move.

The path ahead feels heavier than the one behind. Seven hundred years have been leading to this moment. To me. But I'm still the same person I was yesterday—a boy trying to survive. Not a savior. Not a legend. Just Jerrick.

Brennen waits, his sharp eyes studying me. I don't know if he's waiting for me to run or step forward. Maybe he doesn't know either.

I glance at the Keepers down the hill, the people who looked at me like I was an answered prayer. What happens if I turn around? What happens if I say no?

I already know the answer. Nothing changes. I take a step. Then another. Brennen nods, then turns and walks ahead.

I follow.

The climb is steeper than I expected, the ground uneven beneath my feet. It's not a mountain, but it feels like one. Maybe it's the responsibility of what's waiting for me at the top.

The Stump looms above us, its surface massive, each scarred ring telling a history I don't know.

A tree that once birthed the world.

A tree that was torn in two.

Brennen says the Keepers have spent centuries trying to fix it. And now, somehow, I'm part of that.

We reach the top, and the air shifts.

The sky, which was so white and bright before, dims slightly. The breeze carries something else now, something I can't quite name.

It's like the land is watching me.

Brennen stops just short of the Stump and turns. His voice is quiet.

"Before we go further, I need to ask you something, Jerrick."

I wipe my palms on my robe. Here it comes.

"Go ahead."

Brennen studies me, like he's searching for something. Then he asks, "Why did you choose to save that baby?"

I blink. That's not what I expected.

The words stick in my throat.

I don't know what to say. I don't even know if there's an answer.

Because I couldn't leave her? Because it was the right thing to do? Because if I left her behind, I wouldn't be able to live with myself?

Because my mother would have done the same?

I don't know which answer to give.

So I just say the truth.

"Because she deserved a chance."

Brennen watches me for a long moment, then smiles. Not a smirk or a knowing grin. Just something small. Something real. "I thought so."

Then he turns and walks toward the Stump.

I don't ask what that means.

I just follow.

#

As we crest the final hill, my breath catches in my throat.

The Stump.

I've heard the stories. The towering God Tree that once stretched beyond the sky. The roots that shaped the land itself. The heart of creation, the source of life, wisdom, and power.

Now, all that remains is this.

It stands only as tall as I do, but its sheer vastness is staggering. The jagged edges at its top are a battlefield frozen in time, as if the tree had been ripped apart from the inside out. Each crack and crevice feels like an old scar, whispering of a violent, unnatural end.

The colors of the Stump are a testament to time itself. Deep, earthen browns fade into ashen grays, the mark of centuries exposed to wind and decay. Yet life refuses to yield—moss, lichen, and tiny white flowers have begun their slow reclaiming, growing defiantly in the cracks.

The ground trembles beneath me. Not a violent shake—more like a pulse. A heartbeat. The hum of something waiting.

I look at Brennen. He only nods.

This is normal.

Then—the rings of the Stump begin to glow.

Not bright. Not blinding.

Just enough.

Faint threads of green light pulse through the rings, like veins awakening after a long slumber. The air shifts, thick with something ancient. Something watching.

Then, a voice.

"Jerrick, I'm glad we finally get to meet."

I freeze.

The voice doesn't come from outside. It comes from within.

Not like Lathguard, whose voice was thunder and fire, an overwhelming presence crashing through my mind. This voice is woven into me. Gentle but unyielding. As if it had always been there, waiting for me to listen.

I glance at Brennen again.

He nods once more.

He knows this voice.

I swallow. My throat is dry. "I… it's nice to meet you too?"

It comes out like a question, because how else do you greet something that is older than time itself?

"What I say to you is for your ears alone. There is no need to speak aloud. Direct your thoughts to me, and I will understand."

A private conversation. A choice. I can share it later, or keep it for myself.

I nod. I understand.

"My name has been many things to many people. In the old tongue, I am called Aethelwyrdverdan, the Primordial Sentinel. But you may call me Aethel."

Aethel.

I know that name. The God Tree. The beginning of everything.

I take a slow breath, steadying myself. It's real. It's real. It's real.

"I am not whole, Jerrick."

The voice grows heavier, carrying something I can't quite grasp.

"I have not been whole for a thousand years. My mind and body were torn apart. A part of me wished to pass on, to follow the natural order. Another part refused. The war within myself was so great… that I broke."

How can something so powerful just break? Not just mentally, but physically?

Aethel's voice returns, softer this time.

"Since my other half was banished from this world, our land has been decaying. And now, something is coming."

Something is coming?

"I don't know what it is. But just before I was split, we received a signal. A message telling us to open a rift and prepare for arrival."

A signal? From what? From who?

Aethel doesn't answer.

But I can feel something beneath the silence.

Fear.

Even something as old and powerful as Aethel… is afraid.

Aethel's voice carries weight, but beneath it, I sense something else. Hesitation.

A flicker of fear woven into the words, a buried urgency pressing at the edges of my thoughts.

And then the images come. Not like a vision, but a memory. Aethel's memory.

The God Tree as it once was.

Its branches pierce the sky, its trunk so wide it could hold a kingdom. The roots extend into the very bones of the land, each one a lifeline that pulses with Essence. It is both creator and caretaker, standing apart from the world, yet shaping every part of it.

Until—

The split.

A rending, an explosion of sound so loud it has no noise. The trunk bursts outward, bark and sap spraying in all directions. Essence hemorrhages into the world, flooding it in a final cry of creation.

And when the chaos settles, something remains.

A woman.

She sits upon the shattered stump, steam rising from her bare skin. Her bark-textured flesh is cracked and raw, seeping golden sap. Her tangled hair falls in sheets around her, dark as soil, curling at the edges like withering leaves. And her eyes—

Green.

Deep. Glowing.

She stares at me.

Not at the memory, not at the vision.

At me.

She moves, standing to her full towering height, her form shifting with the creaks and groans of ancient wood. Yet she is graceful, a thing not quite of flesh, not quite of tree.

She reaches out a hand. Not to help. Not to harm.

To ask.

"Help me."

A shudder rolls through me. The words don't stop.

"Help me. Help me. Help me."

The plea echoes in my very marrow. I've heard this before. At the Source. This is her. This is who I felt reaching out in the void, calling to me before I even knew who I was.

I feel myself reaching toward her, compelled beyond reason. My fingertips graze hers—

Shock.

My entire body seizes. The world fractures.

"My own children banished me from our land. They stole Essence from the Source itself, forging a weapon— the Wellspring Syphon —to trap me beyond the veil. I need you to find the Syphon. I need you to open the gate."

Her presence floods me.

Not a command. A plea.

The weight of it is unbearable. The God Tree, the Primordial Sentinel, the creator of our world… is asking me for help.

And yet…

Why me?

I find my voice—or maybe just my thoughts, woven into the silence between us. Why am I special?

Aethel does not hesitate.

"Your bond with Lathguard gives you access to his power. His power is the key to opening the gate. The gate that holds her. The gate that must be opened."

Aethel's words come like stone crashing down:

"Without the Syphon, opening the gate would kill you."

I freeze. Kill me?

I barely get the thought out before Aethel continues.

"That is why we made a bargain with Theron."

Theron.

The name flares through me like a brand.

I know it, though I've never met him. His name follows me like a shadow, whispering through the cracks of my life.

Why?

"We urged Theron to bring you here, to ask you to make this sacrifice."

Sacrifice.

"He refused. Not until we found the Syphon. Because of his refusal, the land has decayed at an accelerated rate."

I shake my head, trying to grasp the full weight of what I'm hearing.

Sacrifice me? Again?

"The Wellspring Syphon will let you channel from the Source safely. But it was lost to time. Until recently."

My mind sharpens like a blade. Then who found it?

A pause.

"That is not important."

I narrow my thoughts. Why isn't it?

"I made a promise."

Something hardens inside me.

Another secret. Another layer of manipulation. Who did you promise?

"Theron."

His name again. Always, always Theron.

"Will you retrieve the Syphon and open the gate?"

I barely hear the question.

Everything inside me boils.

I have been used. Lied to. Pushed, pulled, shaped like a piece on a board. I am done. No.

The word lands like stone. For the first time, Aethel hesitates.

"No?"

The voice is softer now, the whisper of a forest bending in a storm.

storm.

"You understand, if you do not do this, everyone will die? You will die."

The words hold weight. Real weight. But I do not bend. Rorick told me the same thing. I fire back the name like a weapon. He said the only way to stop the decay was to bring the gods back.

Aethel's answer is immediate.

"Rorick is an evil man. He does not seek salvation—only power. His way will not prevent the land's decay. It will accelerate it."

A deep certainty burns beneath the words. But I refuse to let go. Then tell me who found the Syphon.

A pause.

"I gave my word."

So, you understand that if you don't do this, everyone will die?

"HOW DARE YOU USE MY OWN WORDS AGAINST ME!"

A shockwave rips through my mind.

I collapse to my knees, clutching my head as a flood of images crash into me—

The land decaying.

The rivers drying, cracking. The sky burning. The earth collapsing inwards, curling into itself like a dying thing.

I see faces. People I love. Burning. Screaming. Turning to dust. The land implodes, a black void where existence once stood.

And at its center—

Me. My failure. The weight of it is unbearable. I can't breathe. I can't move. But in the storm, I find myself. I find my soul. I push back.

No! I force the word through the storm, through the agony, through the illusion of my own failure. What I want is for people to stop keeping things from me. Is this what you want, Aethel? Because if you keep playing these games, this is what will happen.

Silence.

A stillness settles over everything.

The green glow dims—then dies.

The connection breaks. For the first time since I stepped into this place, I feel alone. I exhale, shaking. Did I just doom us all?

Then—

The glow returns.

"You are right."

The voice is quieter now. Humbled.

"What does it matter anymore? Jerrick, you found the Syphon."

The words hit like a hammer. Me? I found the Wellspring Syphon?

The statement is so impossible that my mind refuses to process it. The pieces don't fit. They can't. I've never—

Then Aethel continues, and the ground beneath me is ripped away.

"If I had my way, Theron would have taken you to the gate and opened it. Your life is a small price to pay to stop the decay."

I stagger back, but the words keep coming.

"But he refused. He hid you away from us so we would never have this conversation with you. He said he would only help if you and he could find the Syphon."

I can't breathe. The world around me feels far away. Distant. Like I'm fading.

"So, we accepted his bargain. And upon your death, we allowed time to restart itself. You forget, but he remembers."

A silence crashes over my thoughts, heavier than any noise.

Then, like a knife to the gut:

"Jerrick, you've died five times trying to find the Syphon."

A hollow void opens in my chest. Cold. Vast. Infinite.

I feel myself reaching for something solid, something real, something true—

But what's real now?

Not me. Not my life. Not my death.

Because none of it is real. None of it stuck.

I'm just a ghost on repeat, a loop of existence running until I get it right.

And I never knew.

The weight of it is suffocating. I have died. And I didn't even know.

The very idea fractures me.

How many times have I stood right here? How many times have I heard these words? How many times have I fought and bled and broken—only to wake up, ignorant, and start again?

And Theron. Theron knew.

He has watched me die over and over, has carried the weight of every failed life so I wouldn't have to. My jaw clenches.

I don't know if I should feel grateful or betrayed.

Theron kept me from this truth. But he also fought for my choice. He refused to hand me over like a lamb to the slaughter.

Unlike Aethel. Unlike Rorick. Unlike everyone else. Five lives.

Gone. Erased.

Each one a wound I cannot remember.

Each one a sacrifice I never got to choose.

And this time? Aethel's voice cuts through my spiraling thoughts.

"That was part of the bargain. Theron carries each memory of your death with him. That way both of you don't have to start over."

The truth twists like a knife in my gut.

I stare into nothing, trying to comprehend the sheer gravity of what's been done to me.

"Everyone outside of this place loses all memory of their past lives and resets along with the land. It takes massive amounts of Essence. I don't think there is enough left to do it again."

The words are spoken with finality. No more resets. No more second chances. The next time I die, I stay dead. The next time the land collapses, it stays gone. I lift my head, my voice raw in my mind.

"Now that I told you, Jerrick. Will you open the gate?"

I understand now.

Not just the words. Not just the logic. The weight of my past lives, the cycle of sacrifice I never knew I was a part of, settles over me like a second skin.

This knowledge—the truth of my own deaths—fractures the foundation of everything I thought I understood.

And yet…

Something stirs within me.

A flicker of something unshaken, unwavering.

These repeated endings—orchestrated, erased, reset—were not empty. They were echoes of my determination. A testament to my resilience.

I have died five times.

And yet—I'm still here.

Theron has carried each of my deaths within him. A silent burden, a private grief. He has fought, over and over, to protect not just my life, but my choice.

That realization is both a comfort and a curse. He kept this truth from me—but was it for my sake? Or his? Was it love? Or guilt? I don't know. But I do know this:

There will be no more resets. This is the last chance. The last life. And I am both the key and the lock.

That knowledge presses down on me, but I do not break beneath its weight. I straighten my back. The decision before me is not just about saving this land. It is about defying fate itself.

This is the moment where my will collides with the preordained.

I take a slow breath. My mind is clear. My pulse is steady. I choose. I will.

A simple thought. A simple answer.

But in the fabric of existence, it is the single most important choice I have ever make. I don't just think it this time; I say it aloud as a testament to my will. "I will open the gate. Not because I was told to. Not because destiny demands it. I choose this because I believe in something better."

I don't know if I made the right choice. But I do know that it is mine. I lift my chin. I own this decision. Whatever comes next—I will face it standing tall.

Aethel's voice, now softer, resonates through my thoughts.

"Thank you, Jerrick. You will not be alone. This time has been different. You have never been Named this early. And I believe that will make all the difference."

A pause.

"You're different this time. More sure of yourself. I don't think the you of a few lives ago would have stood up to me like that."

A final whisper, fading with the last glow of the stump's rings:

"You will save us all."

The hum of the Essence dies.

I stand there in silence. The space where Aethel's voice once filled me feels empty, as though something ancient and powerful has stepped away, leaving behind only its expectations.

I turn my head, meeting Brennen's gaze.

His chin is firm. His eyes sharp. He knows.

"You know, don't you?" He asks quietly.

I nod. "I do." A beat. "And I'm okay with it."

My voice is steady, but there's a weight behind it. He understands more than I do.

"But I will have questions," I add, and I smirk despite myself.

He nods

"When will everybody be here?"

"Tomorrow," He says. "I contacted Drusilla through our link. They'll meet us here."

Tomorrow.

Tomorrow it all changes.

And for the first time in all of my lives…

I see exactly where I fit in.

Chapter 13

Jerrick

For the past couple of hours, Brennen and I have talked about nothing and everything all at once. It's the first time since I arrived at the Keep that I haven't felt like I was being steered toward some unseen outcome. For once, I'm on the path of my own choosing. That doesn't mean I picked the easier road—if anything, I made things harder for myself—but at least the decision was mine.

"There's something you need to know, Jerrick." Brennen sits across from me, the small fire between us flickering weakly. The sky has darkened completely, but here, within the confines of the Fog, everything is bathed in an eerie blue glow from the shifting light inside it.

I hesitate before responding, unsure if I even want to hear what he has to say. "What is it?"

"I think Rorick lied to you about your parents." His voice is quiet, careful. "I'm sorry to bring this up, but… he may still have his hooks in you, even now."

My breath catches, my chest tightening as if the words have wrapped around my ribs and squeezed. My mind jumps to the only thing that could make sense of his statement. "Are my parents alive?"

Brennen's eyes widen, his face falling in regret. "No, I—Jerrick, I'm sorry. That's not what I meant. I don't think they died the way Rorick told you they did."

The world feels suddenly unsteady beneath me. I try to speak, but my mouth is dry, my head tingling like something is trying to surface—something I should remember but can't. Since the moment Rorick told me how they died, an unbearable weight of guilt has settled in my chest, a grief that feels strangely familiar, as if I already knew, deep down. But something about it never fit.

I force myself to meet Brennen's gaze. "What do you know?"

He hesitates, his mouth opening, then closing. His long ears twitch slightly, his eyes locked onto mine, searching for something—permission, maybe, or courage to say what he's been holding back.

"It's not what I know about their deaths," he finally says, his voice low, "but what I know about Rorick… and what he can do."

I wait, but he doesn't continue. He's struggling with something, weighing his next words carefully. I don't push. The fire between us is dying, the embers pulsing like a slowing heartbeat, its dim light casting eerie shadows across his face. Smoke curls lazily into the night, stinging my eyes, filling my lungs with the acrid scent of burning hardwood. Neither of us moves to stoke the flames.

Brennen exhales sharply and looks away, his gaze lost in the night. Then, just as suddenly, he turns back to me, something firm settling in his expression. "I thought it was the right thing to tell you about Rorick," he admits. "But now I wonder… maybe it's better this way. You seem like you've adjusted to what he told you."

"But I haven't," I say, the words rushing out. "It feels like I'm holding two versions of the same truth in my head. The one Rorick told me… and the one I can't remember. I can't make them fit together."

Brennen nods as if he expected this. "Rorick's power doesn't come from raw force, Jerrick. His real strength—his most dangerous gift—is persuasion. And not just the kind that convinces you to trust him in the moment. His words linger. They take root, shape your thoughts until they feel like they were always yours. He doesn't need to control people outright—he only needs them to believe his version of the truth. And he's had centuries to perfect this. He knows exactly how to make you doubt yourself."

"So this feeling I have—the one where I can't reconcile what Rorick told me with what I can't remember—that's his persuasion?" My voice is tight, skepticism laced with frustration. "That doesn't make sense. You said he isn't powerful. Yet, he made me forget what happened to my parents?"

Brennen exhales, rubbing his hands together as if weighing his words carefully. "I have you at a disadvantage, Jerrick. As Aethel told you, this isn't your first life. That means I've known you longer than you've known me. No, we didn't meet in every one of your past lives, but in the last one… we were friends. I got to know you. And I know how much you loved your parents."

My breath hitches. My heart pounds in my chest. "Did they die then too?" I cut him off, barely aware of the sharpness in my voice. I need to know.

Brennen shakes his head. "No. Things are different this time. That's what I was trying to tell you back in the woods behind your farm. Something has changed. We can't rely on what we thought we knew." He stops, giving me space to process. I don't speak. I can't. "For Rorick's power to work so completely, there must have been something so traumatic that you wanted to forget it. And once that door was cracked open… all he had to do was help you forget completely."

The words land like a stone sinking into a deep, still lake, sending ripples of unease through my thoughts. A part of me recoils from the suggestion, while another part—one I can't quite name—leans into it, desperate for something that makes sense. The possibility that Rorick didn't just lie about my parents' deaths but altered my very memory of them, plants a deep, festering seed of betrayal in my chest.

This isn't just about them anymore. It's about me.

It's about whether anything I feel—grief, guilt, even my own sense of self—has been real or if it's all just another one of Rorick's manipulations. The duality inside me—the version of events Rorick gave me, and the void in my mind where my real memories should be—stretches wide, like a chasm threatening to swallow me whole.

I stare into the dying fire, watching the embers pulse like a weakening heartbeat. The flickering light carves sharp shadows across Brennen's face, his features etched with quiet patience. The air smells of burned wood and damp earth, heavy with the weight of the conversation hanging between us.

"I'm tired of being manipulated, Brennen." My voice is raw, barely above a whisper. "Ever since I was cursed with this bond, all I've known is heartache. Everywhere I turn, I hear half-truths. First from Rorick, then from Aethel. My life is no longer my own. My parents are dead, and I'm still being influenced by a man I thought I could trust." I meet Brennen's eyes, a sharp, desperate edge to my next words. "How do I stop his influence over me?"

Brennen sighs deeply, as if he's been waiting for this question. "Remember what I told you when you asked why you no longer felt anger toward me?"

I blink. "You said… that there's power in knowledge. That just by knowing and believing—"

The moment he confirms it with a small nod, something inside me cracks wide open.

And then it hits me.

Like a flood breaking through a dam, the memories come rushing back, drowning me in their relentless tide.

The morning of the Naming.

The scarred man lurking outside, watching.

The moment they told me I wasn't bonded.

The attack on the city, the fire, the screams.

The desperation in my chest as I ran, knowing I had to reach my parents.

And then— *him*. The scarred man again, a blade pressed to my mother's throat.

I see him. I see *her*. I see *me*.

I remember the moment I could have saved her.

The moment I failed.

I see my hands shaking, my breath ragged, the bowstring taut between my fingers. I had the shot. I *had* the shot. And I froze. I didn't release the arrow.

I could have saved her.

But I didn't.

A choked breath escapes me, but I barely hear it. The world is spinning, my chest tightening like a vice. I don't need Rorick to tell me it was my fault.

I already know.

Then, another memory crashes into me.

I remember waking in a dark room. My limbs are heavy, my mind sluggish, as if I've been floating in a sea of fog. I try to move, but I can't—I'm strapped down.

And then, Rorick's voice.

He stands over me, his face a mask of barely contained rage, but not at me—at someone else. Someone unseen.

"Why didn't you stop it?" he snarls, his voice cutting through the haze like a blade.

I try to speak, but my throat is raw. My lips form the words It's my fault. I say it again. And again.

Rorick looks down at me then, something softer—almost sad—behind his eyes. His hand presses against my forehead, and his voice lowers.

"It's not your fault, Jerrick," he murmurs. "Forget the pain. Let it go."

I don't want to let it go. My mother's face is burned into my mind, her final breath, the light leaving her eyes. The scarred man. The bow in my hands, my fingers frozen on the string. The moment I could have saved her, and I didn't.

Rorick's voice becomes soothing, coaxing. "It wasn't your fault. It was out of your hands. It will be easier if you just forget."

He's right.

The pain is unbearable. It's everything. It's crushing, suffocating, filling every inch of my soul.

And I want it to stop.

I want to forget.

Movement stirs around me, shadows shifting beyond the dim candlelight. Rorick turns away, speaking to someone just beyond my field of vision.

"It's a disaster," he says, voice sharp with frustration. "We need to make sure that no one speaks to him. He can't know what happened. He's not strong enough to do what needs to be done. Not like this."

The pain. The weight of my failure. The memory of my mother's face.

And then… nothing.

I forgot. Because I wanted to.

Even now, the pain is overwhelming. It claws at me, trying to crush me under its weight. I could have taken the shot. I could have saved her.

And I didn't.

The dream I had a few days ago—it wasn't a dream. It was a warning. My mind had been trying to tell me the truth. Trying to break free.

Now that I remember, I'm not sure I want to.

"Jerrick."

Brennen's voice is quiet, cautious. I wasn't aware he had moved, but now he's sitting beside me. He doesn't touch me, doesn't press—he just waits.

I don't look at him. I can't. "You knew, didn't you?" My voice is hoarse.

His silence is answer enough.

"I could have stopped it," I whisper, my throat tightening around the words. "I don't know what happened to my father, but I could have saved my mother. I had the shot. And I didn't take it."

Brennen inhales slowly, as if choosing his next words carefully. "I'm sorry. Maybe I shouldn't have—"

"No." I cut him off, shaking my head. "You did the right thing."

I needed to know.

But Rorick was wrong.

I am strong enough.

I try to shove my feelings aside, to bury them under the weight of everything else pressing down on me. But my thoughts refuse to quiet.

Rorick's anger.

His demand—why didn't you stop it?

That wasn't meant for me. He wasn't angry at me.

Then who was he angry at?

If Rorick didn't send the scarred man, then who did?

Why was he there that morning? Why did he kill my parents?

The questions churn inside me, fighting against the crushing guilt, against the image of my mother's face, her last breath.

Finally, I force the words out, trying to ease Brennen's guilt instead of my own. "I'm glad you told me," I say, even though the truth is a blade cutting deep. "I'd rather know."

But would I?

I chose to forget once.

Because it was easier than living with this.

The guilt is suffocating. Paralyzing.

I always promised to protect them. To keep them safe.

And when it mattered most, I failed.

I don't even realize I've gone silent until Brennen speaks again. His voice is quiet, steady. "… I don't know what happened, but from our time together, I feel like I've gotten a pretty good measure of your character. The blame isn't yours to shoulder. If you need to talk, I'll listen."

I swallow hard. The words are appreciated, but they won't change what happened.

"Thank you," I say, though my voice sounds hollow in my own ears. "But not tonight. I need sleep."

Brennen doesn't argue. "I understand. Sorry you have to sleep out here. There's no room inside for someone your size."

I force a faint smirk. "I'd rather be alone, anyway."

He hesitates, then nods. "Alright. Good night, Jerrick."

"You too."

I watch as Brennen walks away, his figure fading into the soft blue glow of the Fog.

I try to focus on anything else. But my mind won't let go. The memories replay over and over, my mother's final moments burned into my vision.

And just when I think I won't find sleep, it finds me.

But there's no peace in it.

Only ghosts.

#

Waking with a sharp intake of breath, I find myself lying on my side, facing the hill where Aethel stands, silent and immovable. The weight of my dreams, of memories I can no longer ignore, still lingers like a dull ache beneath my ribs. But something else is off—I'm not alone.

The moment I roll over, I see him.

Theron.

He sits opposite the smoldering remains of last night's fire, his massive frame casting shadows in the dim morning light. The stories never quite prepared me for the reality of him. They always seemed exaggerated, but seeing him now? The stories weren't enough.

He's impossibly large, every part of him built for war—his sheer presence is something to contend with. Broad shoulders like stone cliffs, thick arms corded with muscle and scar tissue, a frame that speaks of both power and endurance. He's clad in worn leather armor, not ornamental but practical, built for movement and function. Two massive swords rest on his back, their hilts well-worn from use. A belt of knives circles his waist, some nearly as long as short swords. Each weapon, each scar, tells a story of battles fought and survived.

Yet, it's his face that holds me still.

His features are sharp, defined—and eerily familiar. The slope of his nose, the cut of his jaw, the shape of his mouth. They mirror my own.

But where my eyes hold light, his hold only darkness. Or rather, they don't exist at all. He's face is void of both eyes and eye sockets.

His face is marked by deep, old scars—not just where his eyes should be, but across his brow, his cheeks, his temple. As if someone, long ago, stole his sight from him with fire and steel.

And yet, I do not fear him.

The world fears Theron. His name is whispered with reverence and warning alike, a ghost in the dark, a warrior of legend. He's the man people pray never comes for them.

But I remember my mother's words. Trust him. No matter the stories, no matter what I've been told, that trust holds.

I push myself upright, still unsure how to approach this moment.

I feel the weight of his gaze—even without eyes, I can feel it. He doesn't move, doesn't speak. Just waits.

And not for the first time in my life, I don't know what to say.

A joke? A demand? An accusation? Should I even be the first to speak? This is my father. The realization lands like a hammer to the chest.

I should say something.

But instead, I just sit there.

Finally, he breaks the silence.

"Hi, Jerrick."

His voice is deep, layered, a contradiction of rough and smooth, like gravel shifting beneath silk. It's a voice that has commanded armies, told stories by firelight, whispered both threats and comforts.

"I should have been there," he continues, voice steady. Unapologetic. "I wanted to be there."

His words twist something deep inside me, unlocking a door I didn't know was there.

They're simple words, but they hold weight. The weight of years lost, of choices made without me, of a life where he was nothing more than a name and a shadow. A stranger.

I should feel anger. Maybe I do. I don't know yet.

All I know is that his words split something open in me, something raw and unresolved.

He is not just Theron, the legend.

He is my father.

And I don't know what to do with that.

"I don't know how to respond to that," I finally admit, my voice quieter than I intend. What's wrong with me? Why am I always so awkward in moments like this?

Theron doesn't seem surprised by my fumbling.

"It's okay," he says. "You don't have to."

He exhales, a sound like a man carrying too much.

"When you were born, your mother—Gwen—and I didn't want you to be part of this." His voice is steady, but there's something beneath it. Regret. Resignation. "But things happened. And I had to make a choice. I had to hide you somewhere. When I look back now… I'm not so sure I'd make the same ones again."

His words hit like a fist to the gut.

My life—mine—has never felt like it belonged entirely to me. But hearing it so plainly, hearing that my very existence has been dictated by his choices before I was even old enough to understand?

It changes something.

I thought I was just me. A boy from the Four Rivers. A farmer's son. A nobody.

But I was never just that.

I was hidden.

I was placed somewhere, tucked away like a secret because Theron made a choice.

And now, I have to live with the weight of that choice, just like him.

It binds us together—but it also sets us apart.

I don't know how to feel about that.

But I do know one thing.

This meeting isn't just about him. It's about me.

And for the first time, I realize… I'm not just meeting Theron. He's meeting me.

I know he's waiting for me to respond.

But I can't.

The words are there—I can feel them, clawing their way up, reaching for my mouth—but they won't come. My mind jealously guards them, locking them behind the wall I've spent years unknowingly building. So instead, I stand there, silent, staring, making everything awkward.

Finally, I force something out.

"I've lived a good life. My parents…"

I pause. It hits me mid-sentence—I spoke about them in the present tense. As if they're still alive. As if I could go back to them.

"…They were good people."

Theron says something, but I don't hear him.

Because I'm fighting it—the rising tide of emotion, the grief waiting to swallow me whole. I can't think about them right now. I won't.

I love you both, but I can't mourn you yet.

Not here. Not now.

I force a breath. Swallow the lump in my throat. Push it down.

"The Wellspring Syphon," I say abruptly, shoving away everything else. "I heard we found it?"

Theron moves instantly.

For someone his size, he shouldn't be able to move that fast— but he does, leaping to his feet as if burned. His entire demeanor shifts, face hardening, his muscles flexing as his hands clench into fists.

"Who told you?"

The words snap out, low and sharp, charged with something I can't quite place. Anger? Fear? Something deeper?

I rise as well, refusing to let him loom over me. It's strange—for the first time in my life, I'm looking at someone at eye level.

No, not just eye level. He's taller.

Only by a couple of inches, but it's jarring.

I lift my chin. "If you want to be angry at someone," I say evenly, "be angry at me. I forced Aethel to tell me."

Something shifts in Theron's stance.

He exhales slowly, the tension in his shoulders loosening—not entirely, but just enough for me to see past the initial reaction. There's something else beneath it, something more complicated.

His fists relax. When he speaks, there's a hint of something unexpected in his voice.

Pride.

"You've grown up," he says, tilting his head slightly. "There's something different about you. Something… stronger."

I smirk, trying to break the tension. "It's the robe," I say, holding out my arms. "Fancy, isn't it?"

Theron lets out a breath of laughter, small but real.

"It's something."

He shakes his head, a slow chuckle escaping him. "Looks like Drusilla was right. I coddled you too much."

Coddled me?

We just met. How—

Oh. Right.

Five lives.

This is going to take some getting used to.

"How so?" I ask, wary.

Theron crosses his arms, looking more thoughtful now than defensive.

"I know Thom and Abigail raised you," he says. "But you're still my blood. Your safety is my burden to bear."

My stomach twists at that.

Burden.

The word lands wrong. It stings, even though I don't think he meant it that way.

"My burden," I repeat, my voice tightening. "I can take care of myself. I'm nobody's burden."

Theron winces.

He doesn't argue. Doesn't push back. Just sighs, lowering his head slightly.

"You're right, of course." His voice is quieter now. "I didn't mean it that way. But your safety was always the priority. So much so that I… I never let you grow into your own. I never let you be strong enough."

His next words land heavier than all the rest.

"I've watched you die five times."

My breath catches.

He says it so plainly. So matter-of-factly.

I've known for a while now. That I've died before. But to hear him say it, to hear the weight of it in his voice—

Each time he lost me, he lost a son.

Each time he watched me fall, he had to wonder if it would be the last.

Each time, he was left behind, wondering if the world would reset or if this was the time it wouldn't.

I don't know what that must feel like.

But I can imagine.

And suddenly, he doesn't feel like a stranger anymore.

"I can only imagine," I say at last, voice quieter now. Not softer—just more real.

Theron exhales, running a hand through his graying hair.

"This gets no easier," he admits. "I've met you for the first time six times now. And every time, I never really know what to say."

Maybe that's where I get it.

I smirk, just a little. Just enough.

"I know that feeling," I tell him. "You're doing alright."

And for the first time, it doesn't feel so awkward anymore.

Theron's laugh rumbles through the air, starting as a small chuckle before rolling into something deeper, something genuine.

But just as quickly as it begins, it dies.

His expression hardens, and the humor drains from his voice.

"Before I sat down to wait for you to wake up, I spoke with Aethel." He shifts slightly, his fingers tightening into a fist. "He doesn't think there's enough Essence left to reset things again."

He lets that sink in.

"This is it."

I feel the weight of those words settle over me like a stone.

No more do-overs. No more second chances.

Before, when I failed, time would reset. I never knew it was happening, but it happened. Now? If I fail, if I die—that's it.

Theron continues, voice low and measured.

"Before, we didn't have to contend with the land hunting us. That's changed. We're going to limit how and when we channel. We can't take any risks."

I think back to yesterday morning by the stream.

One moment, Brennen and I had been alone—the next, dozens of creatures were upon us. I still don't know where they came from, or how they always seem to be there.

I hesitate.

Is the land adapting?

I used my abilities to fly across the plains, to escape the swarm. I know I'm not the only SoulCaster who can fly—Aerelis could at the Naming Ceremony. But did the land learn from me? Did it change its strategies because of what I did?

That thought is daunting.

"I can fly us to where the Syphon is," I say, grasping for something solid, something I can control.

Theron's fists tighten again. He's angry—but not at me.

"That would come in handy." His voice is clipped. He's trying to keep his emotions in check. "Sounds like you learned a few things at the Keep."

He says the word Keep through clenched teeth.

I file that reaction away for later.

"But the land is adapting," he continues. "We saw a few flying creatures this morning. They were massive. We have to go the slow way."

My stomach twists.

I don't know why, but that statement hits harder than it should.

The land is adapting. The creatures are changing. I am the constant in all of this.

The weight of expectation presses down on me—the Keepers, Aethel, Theron, even my parents' memory. Everyone sees something in me. A key, a leader, a warrior.

But what if I can't use my abilities?

If I can't channel, if I can't fly, if I can't be the hero they expect—then what good am I?

Am I truly what they believe me to be?

Or am I simply playing a role in a story written by fate?

I glance at Theron. There are so many things I want to ask him.

Rorick claimed to be my grandfather. Was that true?

Why did Theron turn against him?

His reaction to the Keep… the way his teeth clenched at the mere mention of it—what happened there?

I hesitate. Time is running out.

The questions can wait.

"We don't have a lot of time," Theron says suddenly, as if reading my mind. "We need to form a plan with the others and leave as soon as possible."

Elena.

I almost forgot—she's here.

My heart flutters at the thought of her, a sensation that catches me off guard, unsettling in its intensity.

"Of course," I say quickly. "We should get moving."

As if summoned by my thoughts, she appears.

Elena moves swiftly toward me, her form a beacon against the encroaching dawn. There's something deliberate in her steps, a quiet resolve that mirrors my own internal battle. Yet, beneath that resolve, I sense something else—hesitation.

Her gaze locks onto mine.

Sorrow. Empathy. Understanding.

It's all there, an unspoken storm raging between us.

"Jerrick," she breathes, her voice barely above a whisper. "I am so sorry about your parents."

The words, though expected, slice through me.

It's as if she's peeled back the fragile veneer of strength I've been clinging to, exposing the raw ache beneath.

Before I can respond, her arms encircle me.

It's warm.

She presses herself against me, her embrace something solid amidst the chaos of my mind. The chill of the morning and the weight of my revelations feel distant compared to the warmth of her body.

I close my eyes for a second, inhaling the faint scent of her—lavender and rain-soaked earth.

For a brief moment, it's just us.

Elena buries her face in my chest.

Her body trembles, her grief for me so palpable it shatters something inside me.

"You had enough time with him for now," she murmurs, a soft but firm rebuke to Theron.

Tears slip down her cheeks, one after another, their silent path speaking volumes. She mourns with me, for me.

And in that instant, something within me shifts.

It's a tectonic movement—a fault line breaking, revealing something underneath.

The realization dawns, sharp and sudden.

I love her.

The thought is terrifying. But it's also undeniable.

I gently push her back, just enough to see her face.

Her eyes search mine. I see my own vulnerability reflected back at me, as if she's holding a mirror to my soul.

My hand rises, almost without thought, to wipe away her tears.

But before I can, she swats my hand away.

"I'm here to console you, not the other way around," she says, her voice wobbly but teasing.

But she doesn't let go.

If anything, she pulls me closer.

A single tear escapes down my cheek, a quiet betrayal of everything I'm trying to hold together.

I let it fall.

I let her hold me.

In this moment, beneath the soft blue glow of the Fog, surrounded by the dying embers of the fire and the weight of what's to come, I let myself be held.

Not as the hero they expect me to be.

Not as the pawn in a war I never asked to fight.

But simply as Jerrick.

And Elena is here.

She sees me.

And for now, that is enough.

#

The Keepers have set a long wooden table before their dwellings, its surface laden with a feast so rich it contrasts starkly with the decaying land outside the Fog.

Around the table sit Elena, Theron, Brennen, Drusilla, myself… and, surprisingly, Eldrin.

The aroma of freshly baked bread mingles with the scent of roasted root vegetables and grilled fish, its crispy skin glistening in the firelight. The porridge, thick and creamy, is swirled with golden honey and jeweled berries. Jars of preserves sit next to aged cheeses, while pitchers of clear water, dark spiced brew, and a vibrant golden fruit juice offer refreshment. The flavors of the land, cultivated even in hardship, are displayed in full abundance.

This is more than a meal—it is a celebration, a testament to the Keepers' resilience and their reverence for life. A moment of defiance against the decay creeping at the edges of our world.

I barely have time to take my seat before Mauda appears beside me, her face lit with a broad smile. In her arms, Abby, awake.

She hands the baby to me.

The moment hits me like a force of nature—my ears burn, my throat tightens, and an emotion I refuse to name surges through me.

Not now.

I blink rapidly, forcing back a sob that threatens to break free.

She's so small in my hands, so fragile, and yet—she's here. Alive.

A life I carried out of the shadows of the Keep, away from a fate too horrible to contemplate.

She is a reminder.

Of what needs protecting.

Of what's at stake.

If she is to have a future beyond what she was born into—then we cannot fail.

"Who is that?"

Elena's voice breaks through my reverie, soft yet inquisitive.

I glance up, meeting her deep brown eyes, and suddenly, everything feels real again.

"This is Abby," I say, my voice cracking despite myself. "She came with us from The Keep."

"Don't be coy, Jerrick."

Brennen, seated across from me, places down his bread with a pointed expression.

A long, clawed finger levels at me.

"You saved that little girl. If not for you, she would either be dead right now, or worse."

The table falls silent.

All eyes are on me.

I feel the weight of their gazes.

My face flushes with heat.

I look down, away, anywhere but at them.

What's wrong with me?

I did a good thing.

So why does praise feel like a burden?

Wouldn't anyone else have done the same?

"You found them, didn't you?"

Theron's voice, gravel-rough, pulls my attention. He sits to my right, his presence a steady force in the growing storm of my thoughts.

"I found a room with five women," I admit, my voice quieter than I intended. "Three babies."

I pause, shifting Abby slightly in my arms.

"I tried to get them to come with me, but none of them would. One of them… insisted I take her baby. She…"

I trail off.

Something dawns on me.

Theron knew about them.

How?

"I know what you're thinking," he says, reading my hesitation. "And the answer is no. I didn't know about them until…"

He stops.

Clears his throat.

"…until after I left the Keep."

His fingers clench around a piece of crusty bread.

"Gwen told me about them."

Gwen.

My mother.

He doesn't look at me when he says it, but I can feel the weight of it in his voice.

"Your mother was one of them," he continues, voice low but firm, "before Rorick introduced us."

The words hit like a hammer.

A storm rages inside me—a whirlwind of emotions I can't even begin to unravel.

Confusion.

Curiosity.

A strange, aching sense of loss—for a connection I never knew existed.

Theron's words shatter the already fragile foundation of my understanding.

My mother.

One of them.

My thoughts race, trying to piece together the fragmented truth of my own existence.

I was never meant to know. A lineage hidden in shadow.

"How did she end up being among them?"

My voice is quieter now.

"Was she… like them?"

Theron inhales sharply. His expression hardens.

"I will not talk about her in front of others."

His tone leaves no room for argument.

"You deserve to know the truth, and I will tell you. But not right now."

Finality. A door closed before it could even be opened. He takes a bite of bread, as if that's the end of it. A few moments pass in silence. The weight of his words settles in my chest, a heavy thing I don't know how to carry.

Then, at the far end of the table, a chair scrapes against the wood.

Drusilla stands, rising to her feet, and the flickering firelight catches the sharp glint of her clawed hands.

Unlike the other Keepers—whose skin is a soft shade of gray— hers is green, deep as moss-covered stone. Where Brennen and the others are sinewy and wiry, Drusilla is built for war. Thick muscles coil under her armor, her every movement a reminder that she is a fighter first, everything else second.

Her eyes, dark as the depths of the earth, sweep over the table as she speaks.

"Enough of this," she says.

Her voice isn't loud, but it doesn't need to be. There is something about it—soft, yet unyielding. Like iron wrapped in silk.

She turns her attention to Theron, who continues to eat as if nothing has changed.

"Theron," she presses. "Where are we going?"

Theron doesn't look up.

Instead, he takes his time, finishing his bite of fish, chewing thoughtfully. His fingers brush against the rim of his cup before he takes a slow sip.

Finally, he speaks.

"Shardmount Isle."

The table erupts.

Everyone speaks at once—outrage, disbelief, fear.

Shardmount Isle.

The name alone summons dread.

A wasteland.

A scar on the world.

A place where nothing grows—where the very air is said to devour the breath from your lungs.

Once, it was the heart of creation. Now, it is a grave.

Jagged mountains of stone slice into the sky, cruel and unyielding, their peaks blackened by time. The land beneath them is worse. Some say the rocks there are cursed—once living things, now turned to lifeless husks by the land's hunger.

No one who steps foot there ever returns.

Brennen's voice breaks through the chaos.

"Nobody goes there," he says. His claws curl into his palms. "Once, it was the center of life. Now, it's a place better left to itself."

Theron nods.

"All true," he says. "But it's where we must go. It being there makes sense. I didn't want to believe it, but I've looked everywhere else."

His hands rest on the wood of the table, his fingers tapping a slow rhythm.

"I found a text. An old one. Unaltered. It spoke of the Syphon. How it drinks Essence from the very bones of the land. How it turns trees to dust, rock into midnight. Now tell me—where else does that sound like?"

Silence.

It is Drusilla who speaks first.

"Then we go."

Her words land like stone. Unshakable. Final.

Eldrin is not as convinced.

"Are you all mad?" he demands, looking at each of us in turn. His knuckles are white against the table's edge. "Is nobody going to say it? That place will devour us. There's a reason no one ever comes back."

Theron shrugs.

"You're welcome to stay behind," he says between bites. "But it's where we must go."

Elena's voice cuts through the tension.

"Brennen," she says, eyes sharp, "you said it was once the center of life. What does that mean?"

Brennen hesitates. His ears flick, his lip curls slightly as he searches for the right words.

"The history you know," he says slowly, "is not the history that is. Rorick has spent centuries rewriting your past to fit his own narrative. The giants weren't gods. Aethel created them of the land. They grew underground, their bodies shaped from a special ore—an ore found in only one place."

Shardmount.

But it wasn't always Shardmount.

It was something else, once.

Deep beneath the Southern Sea, hidden in the blackness, waiting.

Then one day, they rose.

"When they were powerful enough, they exploded from the earth," Brennen continues. "Tore through the ocean floor, sending molten stone and fire into the sky. The land ripped open, stone shattered, and when the sea settled, Shardmount was all that remained."

Drusilla scoffs.

"You people," she spits the words out, her lips curling in disdain, "used to worship that place. You called it holy. You bowed to the giants and named them gods."

Her fingers drum against the hilts of her knives.

"Now," she finishes, her voice sharp as her blades, "it's as dead as your deities."

Brennen's ears flatten.

His voice rises.

"Drusilla," he says warningly, "you forget yourself! It wasn't just the humans who worshipped them."

Drusilla snarls.

"We haven't worshipped them since before their fall."

She turns to the others, her eyes burning.

"These humans still do."

Silence. A heavy, suffocating silence. I sit with it. I sit with all of it. The weight of the past. The weight of the island. The weight of my own death.

Theron said I died retrieving the Syphon.

Did I die there?

The thought latches onto me, sinking its hooks deep into my mind.

Was that where I fell? Was that the place I lost everything? Was that the moment that doomed us? I look down. Abby stirs in my arms, her tiny fingers curling against my sleeve.

Her chest rises and falls.

Alive.

This is the path I chose. For her. For all of them. I breathe in. And then, I speak.

"If the Syphon is there," I say, "then that's where we must go."

The words sound more certain than I feel.

But I say them anyway.

Because they need to be said.

Because they are true.

Elena's hand finds mine. A quiet squeeze.

I turn my head, and she's smiling. It calms me. It terrifies me.

I told her once I wouldn't get involved. That the fate of the land wasn't my concern.

And yet…

Here I am. Here she is.

Theron nods, his mouth set in a firm line.

"Jerrick," he says, "when you and I were there, we docked on the western side of the island, at the rear of the mountains, because that's where the cliffs are the shortest."

His voice lowers.

"The whole island is on a slant, with the back reaching over a thousand feet high. The front is at sea level, but there's only a quarter mile before you hit the Shardmount range."

"Then it's settled," Drusilla says, her voice edged with finality. "We land in the same place. I assume we're heading for the ruins at the back of the island?"

"Yes, but landing in the same place isn't a good idea." Theron turns his sightless face toward me, though I can feel his attention settle like the weight of a blade at my throat. I still don't know how he perceives the world around him, but the gesture is for my benefit, not his. "Not long after we made landfall and began our trek inland, we were attacked."

Brennen stiffens. "So, the rumors are true."

"Yes," Theron affirms, his voice grim. "I saw them myself."

I glance around the table, catching the same puzzled expression on Elena's face that I know is mirrored in my own. I've heard plenty of myths and half-truths on this journey, and I'm not in the mood for another vague threat shrouded in mystery. "What rumors?" I ask, directing my question at Brennen.

He takes a breath, his sharp, clawed fingers tapping absently against the table's surface. "Shadowghast Wraiths," he says finally. "They've existed since before man, from the days when the giants first emerged from beneath the sea. The great upheaval that created Shardmount didn't just shape the land—it tore something loose from the Essence itself. The scholars believe the wraiths were born from the raw magic that bled into the earth that day, creatures of wild, untamed power."

My stomach knots. "And they're still there?"

Brennen nods. "For centuries, they fed on the Essence that seeped from vents in the Shardmount, living off the land like parasites. But the day the giants fell, everything changed. When the Syphon was used, it drained the island completely, stripping it of all Essence, turning trees to dust and rock into midnight. With nothing left to consume, the wraiths were driven mad. They have been starving for over five hundred years."

A chill creeps over me. My father once told me there is no man more dangerous than a starving one. If that was true, then what does that make a creature that has spent half a millennium in hunger?

I turn back to Theron. "Is that how I died?"

He exhales sharply, his expression unreadable. "No. Well, not immediately," he corrects. "We had been on the island for maybe half an hour when one attacked us. I tried to fight it, but my blade was useless. I could feel the impact of every strike, but it was like cutting into stone—solid, unyielding, indifferent to pain. It just kept coming." His jaw tightens. "You saved us, Jerrick. Where steel failed, your power tore it apart. You unraveled it with ribbons of force." His voice darkens. "But then we met three more."

The table is silent. The weight of his words settles over us like a shroud.

"They didn't hesitate," Theron continues. "They ignored me completely. They went straight for you, as if they knew you were the greater threat." He shakes his head. "You held them off, but there were too many. We both died that day."

The air feels thick with unspoken fears. I glance at Brennen, Elena, Drusilla—none of them speak. No one dares to ask the question lingering in all our minds.

How do we fight an enemy that can't be fought?

Mauda, who had been quietly listening from the edge of the gathering, suddenly steps forward. "I know." Her accent is thick, and she pronounces the word like *nah*. Her large, luminescent eyes flick toward Brennen as she begins speaking in her own language, her voice a soft melody of consonants and breath.

Brennen listens intently, nodding as she speaks, then turns to us. "Mauda says there's another way onto the island." His voice takes on a measured, careful tone. "She's one of our scholars and has spent years studying it. Before the fall, humans used to treat Shardmount as a holy site, a place of pilgrimage to honor the giants. There was a small settlement at the back of the island, near the cliffs. Pilgrims would travel through the mountains to prove their worthiness. The wraiths had plenty to feed on back then, so they kept to themselves."

Brennen pauses, his expression clouded. "She says there's a way up from the back of the island—a natural staircase carved into the rock. It leads straight to the ruins you're looking for."

Theron nods once. "That's where the Syphon is. That's where it's always been."

I swallow hard. The Syphon. The key to opening the gate without me dying. The key to bringing back the Creator. The key to ending all of this. And to retrieving it, I must walk into a place where I've already died.

"What then?" I ask aloud, my voice steady despite the storm inside me.

"Then," Theron says, "we travel north across the land to another island, where you will use the Syphon to open the gate and release the Creator."

Drusilla rises sharply, her chair scraping against the stone. "Enough talking," she declares, her claws flexing at her sides. "We leave now. It's almost noon, and we have to move."

Theron stands as well, towering over us all, his presence filling the space. He turns his scarred, sightless face toward each of us in turn. "This is it," he says, his voice grave. "There are no more resets. No more second chances. If we fail, we all die. The land is decaying, and it is trying to kill us." His hands clench into fists. "We have to get Jerrick to the gate. Nothing else matters."

The air crackles with tension.

Theron draws a slow breath, then delivers the words that seal our fates. "None of us are as important as he is. Our lives mean nothing if Jerrick doesn't survive."

His words ring like iron striking iron, a statement that is both an order and a challenge. He looks at each of us in turn. "I want your word that you will protect his life with yours."

The weight of Theron's words settles over me like a heavy cloak—both a shield and a burden. To have my life defined as the linchpin for the survival of an entire land is overwhelming. I've always thought I was nothing special, but now, for the thousandth time, I question that belief. Slowly, I begin to see my role more clearly, and with that understanding comes a reluctant acceptance. This acceptance doesn't erase the fear or the crushing expectations—it transforms them into a quiet resolve to face what comes, not as an unbearable load, but as a purpose that I must embrace.

Elena is the first to rise. "You have my word. I'll protect you with my life," she declares. One by one, the others follow suit. Eldrin is the last; he hesitates, searching my eyes as if weighing my worth, then finally speaks the vow. I nod, not only accepting their commitment but also affirming the path that now lies before me—a silent promise to myself and to those who trust in me: I will not falter. I will confront whatever challenges arise, not because I am fearless, but because I refuse to be ruled by fear.

Standing slowly, I meet the eyes of each person around the table, just as Theron had. "I never wanted any of this," I confess, my voice steady despite the storm inside me. "I always saw myself as someone who kept to the shadows, never meant to be involved. But a wise woman once told me that we each bear the duty to unearth our own truths. And when we do, no matter how daunting they seem, we must embrace them—because that's what gives our lives meaning and direction."

Elena's cheeks warm as she looks away, and I pull her close, I bend down and press a soft kiss to her lips. "Smart and beautiful," I whisper just for her, a private promise amidst our gathering.

When I turn back to the others, they're all staring. Some in surprise, others with knowing smirks. Brennen is grinning, Drusilla looks unimpressed, and Theron just shakes his head with the weariness of a father who has seen too much.

I let them stare. For the first time in my life, I'm not searching for words.

Instead, I lift my arms and glance down at myself, at the robe still hanging from my shoulders, heavy with the weight of everything I've been through. "Now," I say, a wry grin playing at my lips. "Does anyone around here have something that actually fits me? Because I need to get out of this robe."

Chapter 14

Jerrick

Almost two hours ago, we said our goodbyes, and I left little Abby with Mauda. Now, we move east, the coastline stretching ahead like a silent promise. We'll hug the shore for a few days before reaching a small town where we'll charter a boat, slipping around the back of Shardmount Island like ghosts in the fog.

I'm no longer wearing that ridiculous robe. The padded leather armor feels foreign against my skin, yet it settles over me like a second skin—fitting in a way the robe never did. The weight of the bow slung across my shoulder and the knives at my hip is strangely reassuring. Even Elena has a sword strapped to her waist, though I'm not convinced she knows how to use it. But in a world unraveling, the mere presence of a weapon is power.

The cold air bites deeper after the warmth of the pocket, but something inside me has changed. For the first time in my life, I feel grounded—not in the safety of the farm or the familiar rhythms of routine, but in purpose. Direction. I've spent too long drifting, clinging to the illusion that I could resist the tide. But now, even if this isn't the path I would have chosen, it gives my life meaning. There's a goal ahead, a destination, and with that, a reason to keep moving.

When I first woke in the Keep, I felt utterly alone. Now, there are six of us, bound by a common goal. We march toward danger, but I no longer feel isolated in the weight of it.

Ahead, Theron and Eldrin walk side by side, their familiarity unspoken but evident. Behind me, Brennan and Drusilla take up the rear, watchful, steady. Then, without a word, Eldrin drifts away from Theron and falls into step beside me. He's still wearing his black robe, an odd contrast to the rest of us.

I glance at him. "How did you get here?"

Eldrin chuckles, the sound dry. "Funny thing—I followed you through the Keep. Couldn't see you when you went invisible, but you left enough destroyed doors in your wake that tracking you wasn't exactly difficult. After you and Brennan flew off, I knew Theron wasn't far. With all the noise you made leaving, it was easy enough to slip away."

I groan, shaking my head. "So much for subtlety." The joke is meant to be light, but a realization crashes into me like cold water. I turn to him, my voice quieter now. "Wait—you followed me through the room with the women and their babies?"

Eldrin's expression shifts. His easy amusement vanishes, his face paling. His throat works, but at first, no words come. Then, he nods.

A cold weight settles in my stomach. "The woman who gave me her baby… do you know what happened to her?"

Eldrin's jaw tightens. "Yes." He hesitates, as if part of him doesn't want to say more. But then, with a reluctant breath, he does. "I almost didn't make it. When she incinerated those SoulCasters, I was just to the side of the door."

A shiver works its way down my spine. "Are you okay?"

He nods, but his face says otherwise. "It's not that… it's what happened after." His voice lowers, as if speaking the words aloud makes them more real. "She turned on the other women. One moment they were standing there, the next… ash. They didn't scream. They didn't run. It was like they…" He stops, searching for the right word. "Like they welcomed it. Like they were relieved."

Elena gasps beside me, clasping a hand over her mouth. "And the babies?"

Eldrin shakes his head, the memory hollowing his voice. "Gone." His breath shudders as he continues. "She kept screaming *no more* over and over. More SoulCasters came, but she threw fire at them like she had an endless supply of Essence. I've never seen someone use that much power and still stand." He swallows hard. "But then… the head of my order appeared behind her. He sliced her throat." He exhales slowly, staring at the ground. "She fell instantly. And as she lay there, she whispered something. I couldn't make it out at the time. But now?" He meets my eyes. "I think she said… *thank you.*"

Elena's voice is barely above a whisper. "She wanted to die."

"Maybe." Eldrin's gaze turns distant. "But when she said it, she turned toward the door you left through, Jerrick. I think she was thanking *you.*" His voice cracks, and he wipes at his eyes with the back of his hand.

You're welcome. I think it, but the words feel hollow. I just wish she had come with me.

"I don't know if we would have made it if she hadn't… sacrificed herself," I murmur. "I should be thanking her."

Eldrin watches me, something shifting in his expression. It's almost like he's *seeing* me for the first time, as if some hesitation within him has been resolved. His shoulders square, and then, with a sense of finality, he stops and grabs my arm, locking eyes with me.

"You before me," he says solemnly. "I promise to protect your life with mine."

Before I can say anything, Eldrin turns and strides back toward Theron. A moment later, Elena's hand finds my arm, her fingers warm despite the chill.

"Keep walking," Drusilla hisses from behind. "We still have a long way to go."

And so we do. The hours stretch on, filled with the rhythm of footsteps and hushed conversations. Twilight bleeds into the horizon, the sky bruising into deeper shades of blue. Then, just as the first hints of nightfall creep in, Theron and Eldrin drop back, falling in beside Elena and me. Theron gestures sharply for Brennan and Drusilla to catch up.

"We're being followed." His voice is low, urgent. "A quarter mile back—one man, on horseback. Likely a forward scout."

Drusilla stiffens. "SoulCaster?"

"No. Council Guard. But if they sent a scout, they won't be far behind." Theron's gaze flickers toward the darkening landscape. "They're tracking us. Somehow."

A knot tightens in my stomach. "What do we do?"

"We can't outrun them," Theron says. "Not if they're all on horseback. And since we can't channel…"

"You're channeling right now," I cut in. "Maybe we're safe out here?"

Theron exhales sharply. "Mine works differently. I still have to be careful, but those things have to be close to sniff me out. You three, though…"

I frown. "Three? It's just Eldrin and me."

Elena lifts her chin. "Three." Her voice is steady. "I was honest with you about my secrets. I bonded Eirwen. I'm of the Order of Life."

A rush of thoughts crashes through me, but there's no time to sort them. I *knew* she kept things from me—she told me as much—but hearing it now makes something twist deep in my chest. What else don't I know? *Later*, I tell myself. *Later.*

"But you weren't at the Naming," I murmur, confusion flickering through my voice. "When did—"

Drusilla cuts me off with a sharp hiss. "We don't have time for this. We strike first."

"I agree," Theron says, nodding. "But we bring *them* to *us*. Jerrick, they must be tracking *you*. You were at the Keep. They must have tagged you there."

I stare at him. "How would I even know?"

"Your link," Brennan says suddenly, his excitement barely masked by urgency. "Check your chain. Follow it down to the source— see if anything feels… *wrong*."

The idea is ridiculous—how could I possibly *feel* something hidden in my own Essence chain? But there's no time to argue. I close my eyes and reach for the invisible tether linking me to the Source. It stretches before me, an ethereal chain connecting me to something vast, something ancient. I run my fingers along its length, searching. Nothing. Just when I'm about to give up, my fingertips brush something small, something smooth and out of place.

It's wedged beneath two links, tucked away where I wouldn't notice. It feels foreign, wrong—round and polished against the chain's usual rough texture.

I dig my fingers in, prying at it. It won't budge at first, but I grit my teeth and force it loose. It's no bigger than my pinky nail, cold against my palm. Instinct flares, telling me exactly what to do. I follow the chain down to the Source and throw the object in. The second it makes contact, a soft *sizzle* fills my ears—then a sharp *pop*.

I open my eyes. "It's gone."

"Good," Theron says, his expression grim. "But that means they'll be coming fast. They know we won't wait around. There's nowhere to hide out here, but I have an idea." He turns to me. "Jerrick, how many arrows do you have?"

I glance at my quiver. "Fourteen."

"Brennan," Theron orders, "you and Jerrick take that ridge." He points to a small rise in the land to our left. Then his face find mine. "Jerrick, listen to me. You will hesitate. I know you well enough to know that killing doesn't come easy to you. But I need you to take out as many as you can *before* they reach us."

My stomach tightens, but I nod.

"Drusilla, you and I take them head-on. Elena, stay back but close enough to Jerrick—he's their target. Eldrin, you're fast with that blade. Pick off any stragglers. *And no matter what, no one channels.* The last thing we need is to be swarmed."

My pulse pounds in my ears as Brennan and I jog toward the small hill—if it can even be called that. He slows just before we reach the crest, turning to me with a grim expression.

"I'll hide us for as long as I can," he mutters. "But if too many of them are looking our way, they'll see through it. How good are you with that bow?"

"Pretty good," I say, my voice steady, though my stomach churns. "But I've never shot at people before."

The thought alone sickens me, but I'm not naive. This is a fight for survival.

I slide my quiver off my back, placing it in front of me for quick access. With a steadying breath, I tighten my bowstring. This longbow is heavier than what I'm used to, but it's powerful. I test the pull—*strong,* but manageable.

A distant rumble pricks my ears. Then, I see them.

A dozen riders crest the ridge, galloping full-speed down the incline toward us. The earth trembles beneath their charge, dust curling up behind them like a storm. They bear down on Theron and Drusilla, who stand motionless, unshaken, waiting for impact. Just below our hill,

Elena crouches into a ready stance, sword gripped tight, knees bent. Eldrin stands beside her, daggers glinting in both hands.

I taste something acrid, but swallow it down. My fingers find the shaft of an arrow, nocking it in one fluid motion. The broadhead is heavy, made for tearing through armor and flesh alike. I level the bow, sighting down the shaft, heart hammering in my chest. *Two hundred feet.*

I loose the arrow before I can overthink it—*miss.*

No time to dwell. My fingers find another arrow. Nock. Draw. Breathe. *Loose.*

This time, my shot lands true. The lead rider jerks backward, an arrow buried deep in his chest. He topples from his horse, the impact a sickening *thud.*

My hands tremble. I shove down the feeling. Later. I'll deal with it later.

Another arrow. Another shot. The bowstring *twangs* as I let it fly. Then another. Two more riders crumple to the earth, trampled by the hooves of those behind them.

Below, Theron finally moves. His shoulders relax—an almost imperceptible shift—as the next rider closes in. I draw back another arrow, aiming for the charging figure, but at the last second, my shot lands—not on the rider, but the horse.

The beast screams, rears violently, sending its rider crashing to the ground. A second later, the horse collapses beside him, twitching, dust billowing from its fall.

The battlefield erupts in chaos.

Drusilla is already moving. She weaves between the riders, twin knives flashing. Two men cry out as they're struck, tumbling from their saddles, their bodies limp before they hit the ground.

Theron—*still* motionless—waits. Calculates.

Then, with a single, effortless step, he dodges a galloping horse. His sword sings through the air.

The rider barely has time to scream before he's sliced nearly in half. His torso dangles from the saddle, arms dragging through the dirt as the terrified horse flees into the distance.

I wrench my gaze away. More riders. Six. Charging straight at them.

I reach for another arrow, but hesitate. Too close. If I shoot now, I might hit Theron or Drusilla. I search the battlefield for another target—Eldrin. He's moving up, ready to intercept stragglers, his blades flashing under the dimming light.

Then I see her.

Elena.

My breath catches as I spot a rider closing in—the man whose horse I killed. He's on foot now, but fast, his sword gleaming as he rushes at her from behind.

"Elena!" I swing my bow toward him, readying a shot—*too late.* She doesn't hear me.

I lurch forward. "Brennen, drop it!" I shout, but the illusion masking me has already flickered away. My feet pound against the earth as I race toward her, but the rider is already swinging.

Elena ducks. The sword whizzes past, inches from her head.

Her counterstrike is swift, a controlled thrust—but the rider's bracer catches the blade, deflecting it harmlessly. His eyes glint with savage satisfaction. He's already preparing his next strike.

Elena doesn't give him the chance.

Her sword arcs upward—quick, precise—a diagonal slash that rips across his face. Eye. Nose. Lip. Blood sprays.

Three things happen in the next heartbeat.

The man screams.

His hands snap to his ruined face.

Elena runs him through.

He crumples.

"Go back!" she shouts at me, not even sparing me a glance.

For a moment, I can't move. Can't think.

The ground *shudders* beneath my feet.

My head jerks toward the incline—more riders.

And they are coming.

I sprint back up the hill, nocking another arrow as I move. The bowstring hums as I let loose—one hits, one misses. I don't have time to dwell on it. Nine arrows left.

I fire again. And again.

The battlefield is a storm of chaos, steel flashing through the dimming light. Seven arrows.

A rider crumples mid-gallop, my arrow buried in his chest. Six.

Another shot—the broadhead punches through a man's throat. He gargles, toppling from his saddle. Five.

I keep firing, numbing myself to the bodies falling below, to the screams, the carnage. I don't count the kills. I don't want to. But when I reach for another arrow, I find only one left.

Breathing hard, I lower my bow. The battlefield is strewn with bodies, the air thick with the copper stench of blood. Riderless horses scream and rear, their eyes rolling in terror as they trample the fallen beneath their hooves.

Beside me, Brennen remains locked in concentration, his illusion still masking our position.

Below, Theron and Drusilla dance with death.

Drusilla is a blur, her small frame weaving effortlessly between soldiers. Knives flash—two, three, four men fall before their swords even fully swing. She moves with a predator's grace, her claws carving through armor like parchment.

Theron is… something else entirely.

He moves not like a warrior, but like a force of nature.

Each swing of his massive sword cleaves limbs, heads, lives. He fights with the eerie precision of a man who sees his opponent's next move before they even make it.

I force my gaze elsewhere. Eldrin.

He's holding his own, daggers flickering in quick, brutal strikes. He doesn't have Theron's deadly efficiency or Drusilla's speed, but he fights with tenacity, weaving through attackers, surviving.

Then, the new wave arrives.

A fresh wave of Council Guards pour down the incline, dismounting mid-gallop to join the fray. The noise is deafening—metal on metal, the wet gurgle of dying men, the frantic whinnies of terrified horses.

My stomach churns. Blood pools in the dirt, glistening, thick. Severed limbs twitch where they've fallen, as if they haven't quite accepted death yet. The stench of spilled intestines nearly makes me gag.

But beneath the horror, a pulse of something else burns in my chest.

We're winning.

We're winning.

Then, the ground shakes.

More hooves. More war cries.

I turn toward the sound and feel my stomach plummet.

A final charge, bigger than all the rest combined, surges toward us. Too many to count.

I stare at my single remaining arrow.

A whisper of hopelessness coils in my chest. This is it.

Then—something inside me shifts. A raw, visceral feeling surges up, a knowledge deeper than fear.

I have the power to end this.

Yes, there will be consequences. But none greater than the finality of death.

I take a step forward, hands tightening around my bow.

Brennen grabs my arm. "Don't." His voice is sharp, urgent. "We still have time. If you do this, they won't stop coming. Not ever. Once they have your scent, they'll hunt you to the ends of the earth."

He's right.

But I can't be persuaded.

I won't stand here and watch my friends die when I have the power to stop it.

I jerk my arm free. Brennen's claws scrape against my wrist, drawing blood. A slow trickle rolls down my arm. I barely notice.

Then—movement.

A flicker at the edge of my vision.

I whip my head around just in time to see two large men closing in on Eldrin.

He lashes out, dagger slashing, but the first man batters him aside with a powerful blow.

The second drives his blade into Eldrin's shoulder, tearing deep.

Eldrin staggers back, bleeding, struggling for space. But they don't give him any. They rush in for the kill.

Everything slows.

One of the men lunges—sword aimed for Eldrin's gut.

I nock my final arrow.

I don't think. I don't breathe.

I release.

The arrow slams into the attacker's face, sinking deep into his skull. His head snaps back—but his blade keeps going.

A sickening, wet schlck.

The steel buries itself in Eldrin's stomach, the tip punching through his back.

Eldrin drops to one knee, blood soaking his tunic.

The second man raises his sword for the final strike.

Then—Elena is there.

Her blade is merciless, slicing through the man's throat in one clean motion.

He drops without a sound.

I barely have time to breathe before—the next wave crashes toward us.

"Run!" Eldrin yells, his voice raw with pain.

A shadow spreads over the battlefield.

Theron echoes Eldrin's cry, already sprinting toward me. Drusilla is right behind him.

In seconds, we're all at the top of the hill—except for Eldrin.

He stands alone, his hands raised.

A thick, oily black fog begins to swirl around him, rolling out in unnatural waves.

Theron doesn't hesitate. "East! Run!"

We run.

But it feels like leaving my own heart behind.

We flee, feet pounding, lungs burning, leaving Eldrin to his fate.

Behind us, the screams begin.

At first, they are battle cries.

Then, terror.

Then—silence.

I chance a look back, but there is only swirling, living darkness, roiling over the battlefield, consuming all.

Then I see them.

Creatures. Large, winged beasts swoop down from the sky. They dive into the blackness and reemerge with riders and horses clutched in their talons.

Then, from the south, a swarm of smaller creatures converges on the battlefield.

And they vanish into the black.

Nothing gives chase.

The battle is behind us, swallowed by the land, the screams already fading into memory. The terrain slopes downward, forcing our momentum forward even as exhaustion claws at our limbs. Every breath is fire in my lungs, every step heavy with the weight of what we left behind.

Eldrin did what he said he would.

His sacrifice bought us this moment—this narrow escape, this fragile chance to keep fighting.

But there is nothing noble in survival.

Not when it means leaving him behind.

My fists clench as I run, the blood on my wrist already drying. The cut from Brennen's claws stings, but it's nothing compared to the burn inside me—a rage so deep it threatens to consume me whole.

Rorick. The Council.

How *dare* they?

How *dare* they come at us when we all want the same thing? When we all want to *live*?

Their greed, their control, their twisted grasp over the world— it's killing us just as surely as the decay.

I grit my teeth. No more.

No more running. No more waiting. No more hoping the world will fix itself.

I make a vow.

Not just to myself.

To Eldrin, who fought until his last breath.

To little Abby, innocent and helpless in a dying world.

To Elena, who trusts me more than I trust myself.

To Theron, Drusilla, and Brennen, warriors who still have a chance to fight.

I will see this through.

I will not stop.

I will not hesitate.

I will open the gate.

I will stop the decay.

And if it costs me my life?

So be it.

My life is second to theirs.

And I will stop at nothing to do what must be done.

#

Night swallows us whole.

The thick curtain of darkness is absolute, a void that strips the world of form and direction. Only Theron can see through it, his unnatural vision cutting through the black as easily as daylight. He leads us onward without hesitation, knowing that distance is our only ally. None of us argue. None of us slow. We just move.

We hold on to one another as we snake through the unseen landscape, tethered by touch rather than sight. My fingers grip Elena's shoulders, grounding me in something tangible. Behind me, Brennen's presence is steady, and Drusilla lingers at the rear, silent as a shadow.

No one speaks. The weight of the day presses down on us all, crushing, suffocating.

Eldrin's sacrifice still echoes in my mind, a raw and unshakable wound. He should be here. I should hear his footsteps, his breath, the quiet mutterings he always made under his breath when he was thinking too hard. Instead, he is gone, his life spent so that we could keep running.

His death wasn't meaningless. It was the only reason we lived.

And yet… it does not feel like a victory.

It feels like a warning.

The cost of this journey is measured in lives, and today we paid a toll that can never be undone.

But it's not just Eldrin's absence that claws at me. It's the lives I took—those men, those riders, the ones who fell to my arrows.

I tell myself it was necessary. Kill or be killed.

But the words ring hollow.

I see their faces in my mind—the ones I struck down, the ones who crumpled, lifeless, before I had even registered their deaths. Who were they? Fathers? Brothers? Husbands? Did they believe, as I once did, that they were fighting for something worth dying for?

Were they just pawns, like us?

The thought coils around my chest, cold and unrelenting. The lands isn't made of heroes and villains. It's a battlefield of the desperate. And today, I was the one who survived.

I envy the ones untouched by war, their hands unbloodied, their souls unstained.

But I am not one of them anymore.

I clutch onto that truth like a lifeline. Because as much as I hate what I've done, I fear what would happen if it no longer bothered me.

This war is not just about survival. It's about who I will become when it's over.

As we move forward through the dark, I realize that this—this—is the real journey. Not the miles we cross. Not the battles we fight. But the war within myself.

The silence around us is its own kind of mourning, thick with shared grief and unspoken vows. Every step forward carries me further from today's horrors, yet they cling to me like a second skin.

I try to shove them away, lock them in the same place I've buried all the other things I refuse to face.

But I'm running out of space.

I can feel it—the door inside me splintering, buckling under the weight of all I've refused to feel.

You can do this, Jerrick.

I repeat it in my mind, over and over, a whispered command against the rising tide.

There are people counting on you.

But how much of myself will be left when I finally get them where they need to go?

The fatigue is more than just exhaustion of the body—it's a weariness of the soul. And yet, we cannot stop. Not here. Not now.

Not with the weight of the dead at our backs and the weight of the future pressing on our shoulders.

Time becomes shapeless. Distance meaningless. The only measure of our journey is the ache in our bones and the heaviness in our hearts.

Then—at last—Theron halts.

"We rest here tonight," he says, his voice low but firm.

I exhale.

For now, we stop.

But the battle inside me rages on.

Making camp—even in this oppressive, suffocating darkness—is a necessary concession to our limits. We are exhausted, bodies fraying at the edges, minds worn thin from the day's horrors.

We need this. A moment.

A chance to breathe, to process, to prepare for whatever comes next.

"None of you can see where we are," Theron whispers, his voice barely carrying over the wind. "But we're about thirty minutes from the coast. Ahead of us, there are large rocks—we'll keep them at our backs while we sleep. We're at the southernmost end of the Emberfall Mountains, so we're protected from the north and the east."

One by one, Theron guides us down, ensuring no one trips or stumbles in the unseen terrain. His movements are careful, deliberate, as if his awareness extends beyond sight—as if he feels the shape of the night itself.

Then, after settling the others, his voice finds me.

"Jerrick," he says, still hushed. "I need to speak with you."

He doesn't wait for me to answer. He just pulls me to my feet.

We walk for a while, my footsteps uneven as the unseen ground shifts beneath me. The silence between us stretches, thick with unspoken words. When he finally stops, he places a firm hand on my shoulder and lowers me onto what feels like a rock.

"You did good back there," he says, his voice steady. "But you took an unnecessary risk."

I stiffen.

"I made it clear," he continues, his tone sharpening, "that your life is more important than ours."

His words feel like a slap.

Theron leans in, his next words deadly quiet, but unyielding.

"Your life is more important than Elena's."

Something inside me recoils. No.

"When you became visible and rushed down that hill, you put us all at risk," he says. "Do you understand?"

I do. But I don't want to.

He's right. Of course, he's right. I don't want to think of my life in comparison to theirs—especially not Elena's. But logically, I know what's at stake.

I know my role in all of this.

I must open the gate. Release The Creator. Reunite the two halves of the God Tree.

That's the mission. That's my purpose.

But how do I separate that? How do I tell myself that saving the land matters more than saving the people standing right next to me?

Even now, away from battle, I can't imagine putting strangers before Elena. Or before myself.

That doesn't mean I don't know what must be done.

It just means that when the moment comes, it won't be easy to go against my instincts.

Theron exhales, the sharp edge in his voice softening. "Look," he says, "I have the advantage of spending thirty-six days with you. Just you and me, hunting down the Syphon, studying, preparing for this. That means I know you better than you know me."

He pauses, then places a hand on my shoulder.

"From your perspective, we just met this morning. But trust me—I know exactly who you are."

He lets those words settle before continuing.

"Every time you died—every single time—it was because you either hesitated or put someone else first."

I stiffen.

"You've always been physically strong enough, Jerrick. But you lack the ability to understand your own importance."

His words hit hard.

Because he isn't wrong.

I've never thought of myself as important. As anything more than ordinary.

Bullied kids don't grow up thinking they matter.

I've spent my life existing on the edges, never feeling strong enough, smart enough, *worthy enough* to do anything but work the orchard.

An apple farmer.

That's who I am.

Even now, sitting here in the dark with blood on my hands, I can't reconcile what I did on that hill with the person I feel I am inside.

An apple farmer doesn't kill people.

An apple farmer feeds people.

"I know who I am," I say, my voice quieter than I mean it to be. "I know what has to be done. But when I saw that man moving toward Elena…" My throat tightens. "It wasn't a decision. It was instinct."

The worst part? She didn't even need me.

Theron doesn't respond right away. I can feel his gaze in the dark, studying me, weighing my words.

Finally, I exhale, shaking my head. "How did she learn to fight like that?"

Theron is quiet for a moment, then he speaks, his voice unreadable.

"That's something you'll have to ask her." A pause. Then, softer, "That's not my story to tell."

"So, you know?"

"That's not my story to tell."

Silence stretches between us, thick and weighted with unspoken truths.

Fifteen seconds? A lifetime? I can't tell.

Then, quietly, I say, "Eldrin… it was almost me that channeled back there. He saved us. He saved *me*."

Theron exhales through his nose, his grip on my shoulder steady. "He was a good kid." A pause. "His actions saved us. But so did yours." His fingers tighten briefly. "What I said about you hesitating before? I didn't see that today."

I let the words sink in, uncertain how to respond.

I don't know who I was before. Not really.

But I do know this—I'm not the same man I was a few months ago.

I've seen too much. Felt too much.

The horrors of men and the horrors of this land, both intent on devouring us.

I've felt Lathguard's presence, the weight of his will pressing down, and I have no desire to live under his rule.

"Maybe it's because I've finally seen enough to decide for myself," I say, my voice quiet but firm. "Instead of being told how to feel, or what to do."

Theron doesn't interrupt. He just listens.

I let the words spill out.

"I've seen a town overrun by those creatures. Watched people run for their lives—only to be ripped apart." My throat tightens. "I watched my mother die and did nothing to stop it."

My fingers curl into my palms.

"I was lied to. Fed half-truths. And then, in the Keep, I saw women give birth, only to have their children's souls stolen—fed to a false god in some perverse resurrection." My voice falters, but I push through.

"And then—Eldrin. I watched him die for this cause. Because he *believed* in it. Because he believed in *me*."

The weight of it all presses down, but I don't let it crush me.

Instead, I let it forge me.

"If you want to know what's different, Theron, it's my outlook." I lift my chin. "I've been blind my whole life. I thought I wasn't enough to change anything.

But when everything you love is taken from you…

You can't help but be different."

The silence that follows isn't empty. It's heavy.

Then, I feel Theron's hand tremble against my shoulder. It slackens… then tightens again.

When he speaks, his voice is hoarse, barely above a whisper.

"Jerrick, I… I'm sorry." A sharp breath. "Losing Gwen set me on this path. I know what it does to you. Losing someone you love." His voice cracks, and for the first time since I've known him, Theron falters.

Something shifts between us.

Maybe it's the blood that ties us together.

Maybe it's the pain we both carry.

Or maybe it's simply this: I understand him now.

"Tell me about her," I say softly.

For a long moment, he doesn't answer.

Then, finally, he exhales.

"I wish you could have known her." His voice is filled with something rare—a longing so deep it threatens to swallow him whole. "I'm *angry* that she was taken from me. From you."

He pauses, as if forcing himself to piece the words together.

"Rorick introduced us—not long after I turned twenty-one. She was… vibrant. So *full of life*. And smart." A small, broken laugh escapes him. "I could never keep up with her."

I can hear the smile in his voice. But it fades quickly.

"I know now," he continues, "but I didn't know then—that Rorick put us together for a reason. He wanted us to have a child—one that would bond to Lathguard."

I go still.

"She was part of the deception, Jerrick. Born into it. Just like little Abby." His voice turns hollow. "Raised to be subservient to Rorick. Raised to believe in *his cause*."

Something cold settles in my gut.

Theron keeps going, voice distant, as if caught in memories he can't escape.

"When she became pregnant, after a couple of years… she told me *everything*." His breath hitches slightly. "Or at least… *everything she thought was true*."

I hear the betrayal in his tone. The pain that lingers, even after all this time.

"She feared what might happen to you. And even though I felt betrayed by what she'd been a part of, I…" He stops. Swallows. "I loved her. And I wanted to keep you both safe."

The wind shifts around us, carrying the distant sound of the waves.

"So we kept her pregnancy a secret. And we ran." His voice drops lower. "We never stayed anywhere long enough to call it home. But… I felt at home with *her*."

Then, softer—almost too soft to hear.

"Far from Rorick's influence… I finally saw the truth of what I'd done."

Theron stops talking.

But I don't say a word.

I want him to continue.

The silence between us stretches, heavy and raw, filled with things he isn't sure he wants to say and things I'm not sure I'm ready to hear.

Eventually, his voice returns, quieter now. More fragile.

"They found us in the middle of the night."

A pause. A breath. A memory.

"We were asleep in an old, abandoned farmstead. Just up the coast from Sussex. I don't know how they tracked us—maybe we stayed too long, maybe they were always close—but I woke to the sound of boots, armor, blades drawn."

He exhales, slow and controlled.

"They didn't send a squad, Jerrick. They sent a small army."

My chest tightens.

"I fought like a madman," Theron says. "So did your mother. She never bonded, but she was ferocious. She fought as if the world itself had no right to take you from her."

He stops, his breath catching.

I know what comes next.

"When she went down…"

His voice thickens, the words heavy and slow, as if he's forcing them out against his will.

"I tried to get to her." His jaw tightens. "But there were too many."

Silence.

"I killed them all," he says finally.

Not boastful. Not triumphant.

Just a fact.

"They even brought a SoulCaster from the Order of Fire. If he could've used his full power, I'd be dead instead of him. But they made a mistake—they came inside. Too many walls. Too many flammable things. He couldn't risk it. So I killed him, too."

His voice turns rough. Ragged.

"Before she died, Gwen made me promise something."

I feel my throat close.

"She made me swear I wouldn't seek revenge. She said… you needed a father. That I should focus on raising you." His voice drops lower. "And I intended to keep that promise."

The air around us feels smaller, the night pressing in, wrapping around his words like a shroud.

"For the next month, it was just you and me," he continues. "I didn't walk away from that fight unscathed—most of my scars came from that night. But that wasn't the pain that mattered.

There are worse pains than wounds.

And I felt them all."

He pauses, as if summoning the strength to finish.

"I finally broke," he says simply. "That's when I brought you to Thom and Abigail. Asked them to raise you. I knew you bonded. I knew who you bonded with. And I knew… the only way you'd ever be safe was if Rorick was dead. I've been trying to make that happen ever since."

We sit in silence.

Not because there's nothing left to say.

But because some things don't need words.

I remember something my mother used to say—that words weren't always required.

So I don't speak.

Instead, I move forward, hesitating only for a moment, and wrap my arms around Theron.

At first, he doesn't move.

His body is rigid, his breath uneven, a sharp contrast to the ironclad strength he always carries.

Then, slowly, I feel it.

The shift.

His chest rises. Falls.

And then his arms come around me.

The embrace is strong. Solid.

And somehow, familiar.

Neither of us speaks.

For a few breaths, we just hold onto something we both thought we had lost.

Then, Theron pulls back first.

The air between us is different now. The space smaller.

"Jerrick," he says, voice measured, "I've made choices. Hard ones. Each step I took was for the greater good, but the path was… darker than I ever expected."

I listen, hearing years of weight in his tone.

"I've walked a road paved with loss and sacrifice," he continues. His voice catches, just slightly, but enough for me to hear the truth in it. "Seeing Gwen die. Then leaving you. It was the hardest decision I ever made."

His breath shudders.

"But back then, it felt like the only way to protect you. The only way to give you a life free from Rorick's grasp."

I hear it in his voice—the scars he carries aren't just on his body.

They're in his soul.

And it hits me, hard, because I understand it now.

I feel the weight of it in myself—the cost of survival. The guilt of choices made.

Theron exhales, softer now.

"Looking back…" He hesitates, voice barely above a whisper. "I wonder if I could have chosen differently. Could I have been stronger? Smarter?"

He shakes his head, answering himself.

"But the past is a shadow we can't outrun."

His eyes meet mine.

"We can only learn from it."

Theron's honesty, the raw openness of his reflection, offers me a glimpse into the depths of his struggle.

It's a mirror of my own.

Only his burden carries the weight of years, the consequences of a life entangled with Rorick, with war, with the fate of this land.

He shifts beside me, and though I cannot see through the darkness, I sense him turning toward me.

When he speaks again, his voice is quieter now, but no less firm.

"I see so much of her in you, Jerrick."

Something in my chest tightens.

"Your strength. Your resilience. It's what gives me hope that we can end this. That we can break the cycle of suffering." He pauses, then exhales slowly. "But you need to understand… your life—it's the key to all of this."

I swallow, my throat dry.

"My battles, my sacrifices… they were all to ensure you could be here, now. To finish what was started."

The air between us shifts, charged with understanding, something unspoken bridging the years of separation.

Theron's voice lowers, soft, almost a whisper.

"Your journey… it's not just about surviving." He pauses, then shakes his head. "It's not just about defeating Rorick."

I turn slightly toward him, listening.

"It's about healing. About mending the fractures—in this world, and within ourselves."

A breath. A hesitation. Then—

"I wish I could shield you from the pain, from the choices you'll have to make." His voice carries a weight I recognize—one I've felt in my own chest, in my own bones. "But I know… I've always known… you're stronger than you realize."

I close my eyes.

"And when the time comes," he says, "you'll make the right decisions. Not just for the land. But for yourself."

Something shifts inside me.

A piece of doubt, of fear, softens—not gone, but no longer unbearable.

Theron's words are a balm to the raw edges of my thoughts, easing wounds I hadn't realized were bleeding.

I don't respond. I don't have to. Some things don't need words.

Together, we rise.

As we step away from our conversation, he places a hand on my shoulder—a gesture of solidarity, of understanding.

"We're more alike than you know, Jerrick," he says, voice steady. "And whatever comes, I want you to know you're not alone."

The words settle over me like armor.

Then, without another word, he leads me back to the others.

He sits me down beside Elena. I want to talk to her, to say something, but as I listen to her soft, even breathing, I realize—she's already asleep.

The night around me still feels vast. But somehow, the darkness is a little less suffocating.

The weight of the journey ahead doesn't feel like a burden.

It feels like a purpose.
And in that quiet certainty—sleep finds me, too.

Chapter 15

Jerrick

Just as Theron had said, we reached the coast exactly thirty minutes after leaving camp. We took our time leaving the camp; we didn't want to reach the village during daylight. The sea stretched before us, restless and unending, as we followed its curve north, skirting the rugged shoreline.

By the time we reached the small fishing village, the Shardmount Island loomed in the distance. Slick and black, it rose from the sea like a jagged claw raking at the sky.

For two days, we traveled without incident. Without seeing another soul.

Theron surveyed the village from our position, his expression unreadable. "We'll wait till nightfall," he said finally. "I have a contact here, but I can't go in until dark. Can't risk anyone recognizing me."

No one argued.

We withdrew into the treeline, a mile or so south of the village. Close enough to keep an eye on the road, but far enough that we wouldn't be seen.

The days were growing colder, but tonight, for the first time in what felt like forever, we risked a fire.

Not seeing a single living soul in days had given us a false sense of security—or maybe we just needed the warmth.

The sea air was crisp, fresher than the thick dampness of the mainland, but as we sat in the fire's glow, the island loomed ahead like a silent threat.

A feeling settled over me.

Unease. Dread.

And judging by the quiet around the flames, I wasn't the only one who felt it.

I sat between Theron and Elena, watching the fire flicker. Across from me, Drusilla's eyes were on me. Unblinking. Studying.

Next to her, Brennen tended the fire, poking at the embers before tossing on more wood.

She didn't look away.

"Drusilla?" I finally said.

She kept staring, her head tilting slightly, as if examining something she couldn't quite place.

"I was just wondering," she said abruptly, her voice sharp. A challenge.

"Why are you here?"

I frowned. Was she serious?

I wanted to snap, *Are you crazy? You know why I'm here!*—but instead, I exhaled and said, "What do you mean?"

Her gaze hardened, her sharp features illuminated by the fire's glow. It felt like she was looking into my soul.

I didn't like it.

"We've met before," she said. "A few of your past lives." Her expression didn't change. "You've always been… *meek*. Uncommitted. Your heart was never *in it*."

She leaned forward slightly.

"What's different this time?"

I swallowed, feeling the weight of a thousand past versions of myself pressing down.

"I don't remember those previous lives," I said. "But if I had to guess, it's because I just wanted to go *home*." I hesitated, then added, "I've never been the type to get involved in other people's—"

Drusilla's expression snapped into anger.

"Other people's *business*?" she repeated, her voice cutting through the night like a blade.

She leaned in, her eyes flashing.

"This *is* your business, Jerrick. This *affects* you."

I exhaled slowly, trying to keep my voice even. "I've always felt inadequate. I'm nobody special—"

Drusilla lunged forward, pointing a clawed finger at me. "Nobody special?"

Her voice rose, frustration evident.

"You're the special one here!"

I clenched my jaw. "Are you going to let me finish or just keep interrupting me?"

Her muscles tensed, her teeth grinding together.

"You can finish," she said flatly, "but I'll cut you off every time you say something stupid."

I glared at her, a heat rising in my chest.

"When I was a kid," I started, forcing my voice steady, "I got picked on. A lot. It made me want to be alone. I never—"

"You're *doing it again*," she snapped.

I inhaled sharply, fighting back my temper.

"You're not some wimpy kid anymore, Jerrick." She was glaring now, firelight reflecting in her eyes.

"Stop making excuses for your choices!"

Something inside me snapped.

"Damn it, Drusilla!" I surged to my feet, anger igniting in my chest like a spark catching dry tinder.

I jabbed a finger at her, my voice rising with every word.

"What do you want from me?!"

She smirked.

"That."

I blinked, heart hammering.

"What?"

"That," she said again, more calmly this time. "*Fire.*"

I stared, breath still coming hard.

"You've always second-guessed yourself," she said, voice leveling out, though the intensity never left her eyes. "And it's *killed* you. Repeatedly."

I swallowed.

"We can't do this again," she continued. "This is the last time."

The words sent a chill through me.

"So I'll ask you again," she said.

Her voice was softer now, but the weight of it was crushing.

"Why are you here?"

I clenched my fists. "Because I'm the only one—"

"Stupid."

My anger surged.

I explode, stepping toward her, jabbing my finger at her with every word.

"I'm here to save your life."

My voice shook, but not with fear. With fury. With conviction.

"Everybody's life. Because without me, the Fog will kill you. Or Rorick will get his wish and bring Lathguard back, and you'll *still* die."

I didn't stop.

"I'm here because I want to be."

My breath came hot, words tumbling out faster, fiercer.

"I'm here because I have the power and the will to see this through."

The fire crackled.

"I'm here because I don't want to die."

A lump formed in my throat.

"I don't want Elena to die. Or Theron. Or Brennen."

My hands shook.

"I don't want to see one more person die because I made the wrong choice."

My voice broke on the last sentence.

I swallowed hard, forcing it back, and exhaled shakily.

Then, quieter—almost reluctant, but still resolute—

"I don't even want you to die."

A moment of silence.

Then, Drusilla smirked.

"Well, good."

She leaned back, arms crossing over her chest.

"I don't want to die either."

A tear wells in my eye, burning hot, threatening to spill over. But I don't look away.

"Why are *you* here?" I ask, my voice tight.

Drusilla steps closer.

She doesn't hesitate, doesn't flinch as she moves around the fire and stops right in front of me.

I tower over her, but it doesn't feel that way.

Not when she looks up at me with those piercing, unyielding eyes.

I hold her gaze, but it's everything I can do to endure its intensity.

"Because I, too, am tired of people *dying*," she says.

Her voice is sharp. Fierce.

"Your people kill my people *every day*. You've driven us underground. And yes, you *hate* us for our folly, but that doesn't give you the right to exterminate us."

Her hands clench into fists.

"We don't even *fight back*."

A pang of shame washes over me.

What do I even say to something like that?

"I'm sorry, I—"

She lifts a clawed hand, cutting me off.

"Don't."

Her voice softens. Almost a whisper.

"Don't take our sacrifice away by apologizing."

I fall silent.

She takes a breath, and when she speaks again, her voice is steady.

"I'm here because it's time we work together. It's time we step out of the shadows."

Her gaze flickers toward Brennen, something unspoken passing between them before she turns back to me.

"We're stronger together," she says. "You may be what stands between us and death, but I am here to stand with you."

A pause.

"I'm here for what comes after you set her free."

The words hang in the air, heavy with meaning.

I swallow.

"Your contribution to this is only the beginning," she continues. "We have a long road ahead, Jerrick. We need you to know why you're doing this. We need you to understand what's at stake. And we need you to understand what will happen if we fail."

I meet her gaze, holding it this time.

"I *do* know, Drusilla." My voice is firm.

She watches me. Waiting. Expecting more.

I take a deep breath.

"You want to know why I'm here?" I say.

The fire flickers between us.

"I'm here because I choose to be."

A small smile twitches at the corner of her mouth.

I press on.

"I'm here because this land is worth saving."

I glance at Theron, at Elena, at Brennen. At Drusilla.

"It may have taken me *dying* a couple of times to realize it, but—
"

"Five times."

Elena's voice cuts in smoothly.

I blink.

She smirks. "*Five* times."

A laugh escapes me, shaking my head.

"Thank you, Elena."

"You're welcome."

I exhale, rubbing a hand across my jaw.

"It may have taken me five times," I say, shaking my head, a wry smile tugging at my lips.

"But now, I understand something profound."

I let my gaze drift across all of them.

"None of us are islands unto ourselves. We're *all* threads in a grand tapestry, woven together. Our fates are intertwined."

I pause, my throat thick.

"I was selfish before," I admit. "I thought only of *my* survival. Of the *legacy* of my farm. But now, I see the value of action. The necessity of looking out for one another. And the legacy of this land."

I inhale slowly.

"Every life is a part of something greater. Something that binds us all. I fight not just for myself, but for every soul—human or Keeper— who shares this land with me. It's in our unity, in our collective strength, that we'll find the power to push back the Fog."

The words leave me before I can even process them.

I blink, glancing around the fire, and realize—

They're all staring at me. Theron is beaming. Elena wipes away a stray tear, her expression soft.

Brennen watches me with an intensity I haven't seen before. Like he's seeing me for the first time.

I shift slightly.

"…What?" I ask hesitantly.

Drusilla nods.

"Now, you're ready."

I frown. "For what?"

"For what comes next."

She sits back down, arms resting on her knees, the firelight dancing in her sharp, calculating eyes.

"You've changed for the better, I think," she says simply.

Then, more seriously—

"It's important to understand where you stand when faced with difficult decisions. If you lack passion for what you're doing, a stiff breeze will throw you off course."

She's right. And deep down, I know it. I lower myself back to the ground, my thoughts swirling. Drusilla knew exactly what she was doing. There's more to her than she's letting on. But despite that, I feel like… I know her a little better.

And maybe… I know myself better, too.

My mind has always been jumbled. Unsure.

But when Drusilla challenged me—when she forced me to *fight for my purpose*—

It made things clearer.

The silence that follows is comfortable.

No forced words. No need to fill the space.

Just quiet understanding.

The fire crackles.

Then, finally, Theron breaks the silence.

"It's almost dark." His voice is quiet, his presence steady. "I'm going to leave, but I should be back in a few hours. Try to get some sleep."

We nod. No one argues.

We eat silently—dried fruit, cheese, crusty bread.

But the silence doesn't feel empty. It isn't awkward. It's comfortable. It speaks for itself.

Besides—I have something else on my mind.

I glance at Elena. She's asleep, her breaths slow and steady.

I want to ask her where she learned to wield a sword like that.

It's not that I worry she won't tell me.

I worry that I'll see her differently when she does.

I know she has secrets. She told me as much. And part of me feels like… I don't need to know. That I love her, regardless. But another part of me… Another part wants to know everything.

Do you really need to know? I ask myself the question over and over, my thoughts circling like vultures over a dying certainty. I finally decide that I don't.

And then Elena breaks the silence.

"Jerrick, we should talk."

Her voice is quiet. Thoughtful.

I'd mistaken her silence for sleep, but when I turn to her, she's already watching me, her gaze steady in the dim firelight.

I push up on one elbow. "Do you want privacy?"

She shakes her head.

"Here is fine. What I have to say can be said in front of Brennen and Drusilla."

At her words, the Keepers exchange glances, then both nod in silent appreciation.

A strange way to start a conversation. It feels important. Before I can speak, Elena fixes me with a look—serious, unwavering.

"But before we start," she says carefully, "I need you to promise me you won't jump to any conclusions."

That makes me pause. I frown. "You have my word."

She nods, exhaling slightly, then blurts it out quickly—as if saying it faster will make it easier. "My mother was part of Theron's uprising."

The words land like a stone in my chest.

"She brought me into the resistance at a very young age," Elena continues. "When I told you she used to share her visions with me, it wasn't just to bond with me—it was to make me *valuable* to them. She wanted them to take care of me."

I promised I wouldn't jump to conclusions. But I do. I can't help it. My mind races, connecting the pieces.

Elena… part of the resistance?

She knew about the uprising? Was raised in it?

And then I remember what she said the day I was arrested. It makes too much sense. And if she was part of the resistance, that means…

Did she know Theron before all of this? Did she know he was my father?

She reaches out, her hand settling over mine. "You're doing it, aren't you?"

Her voice is soft, amused, but knowing.

I blink, pulling myself out of my spiraling thoughts.

I sigh. "Yes. I'm sorry. It's… kind of what I do."

She laughs, and the sound loosens something tight in my chest.

"I know," she says, smiling. "So instead of doing *that*, just ask me what you're thinking."

I exhale slowly.

"Did you know Theron was my father?"

Her expression shifts.

"No," she says, shaking her head. "He never told me. I'm upset with myself that I never figured it out."

She sighs. "Not until that day in the city."

Her gaze softens. "The resemblance is there. I just… I couldn't make it make sense."

I laugh, shaking my head.

"It's okay. I know how I am. We may *look* alike, but we don't act alike." I smirk. "He's a man of action. I'm a man of jumping to conclusions."

She grins, nudging me slightly.

"Ask me anything," she says. "I don't want things to be weird between us."

I hesitate, but then I just ask.

"Did Theron teach you how to fight?"

"Yes."

"When did you know about your bond?"

"Young," she says simply. "My mom told me early on."

That makes me frown.

"But we were going to the Naming *together*. Why?"

Elena tilts her head slightly.

"I was going to be a spy."

The words hit like a punch to the gut.

She continues before I can react. "The idea was to pretend that I didn't know I bonded. Eirwen knows."

My breath stills.

"She was part of the resistance that tried to overthrow Lathguard."

That stops me cold. My thoughts stumble, processing what she just said. *Eirwen—the Giant?*

That… actually makes sense.

She can communicate with us. If she wasn't part of the resistance, she could have easily given up their plans to the SoulCasters. I take a moment. Let the realization settle. Then, I find my next question.

"Then why did you decide to leave with me?"

I look at her, searching for something—truth, clarity.

She lifts her chin slightly, holding my gaze.

Her smile melts me. Melts everything.

"Isn't it obvious?"

I suddenly forget how to breathe.

My chest tightens, my pulse kicking hard against my ribs.

I don't look away. I can't. I swallow, feeling warmth rise to my face. "I… so, you feel how I feel?" I finally manage.

She tilts her head slightly, her expression turning coy.

"I don't know…" she murmurs, glancing at me from the corner of her eye.

Her voice lowers just enough to make my stomach flip.

"How do you feel?"

Thump thump.

Thump thump.

My heart is loud. Too loud. I try to speak, but the words get stuck in my throat. I take a breath, gathering what little courage I have left—

And blurt it out.

"I love you, Elena."

The words tumble out, unpolished, unfiltered.

"I have for a while," I confess. "But I convinced myself that you were just being nice to me because you were my neighbor."

And then—silence.

The fire crackles.

Elena watches me.

And I hold my breath, waiting for what she'll say next.

Elena laughs, the sound light but tinged with something deeper.

"Oh, Jerrick," she murmurs, shaking her head. "There's a lot you don't know about me."

Her gaze softens.

"I'm not as *nice* as you think," she admits. "I was nice to you because… you've always had such a good heart."

I swallow, my chest tightening.

"I love the way you love your parents," she continues. "And I… I needed someone like you in my life."

Her voice drops lower, almost like a confession.

"You've always been my safe place."

And then—

"Yes, Jerrick," she says, her lips curling into a soft smile. "I feel the same way."

Thump. Thump.

Thump. Thump.

My heart hammers in my chest.

And then—

"Isn't that sweet?"

A voice. A voice I don't recognize. We both jump to our feet, my pulse spiking as Elena draws her sword in one fluid motion.

We spin, facing the intruder. He stands ten feet away, just outside the fire's glow. A big man, with a big beard and a large, puckered scar pulling at his cheek.

A traveler's cloak drapes over broad shoulders, the hilt of a longsword visible at his side.

He carries himself like someone who knows how to fight—but there's an ease in his posture, a genuine enough smile that doesn't quite reach his eyes.

By his feet, a travel bag rests on the ground.

His hands are up, palms out.

"You'll get no trouble from me," he says, his voice like broken glass—rough, jagged, dangerous.

He nods toward the fire.

"I'm just hoping to share some warmth before night falls. Been traveling all day."

His gaze flickers between us. "Is it just the two of you?"

The two of us?

Brennen must have hidden Drusilla and himself. Good. We don't need this turning into a bigger problem.

"We don't have the room," Elena says, her voice firm. "Keep moving."

The smile vanishes from his face, leaving only hardness.

"That's no way to treat a fellow traveler," he says, his voice edging into something dangerous.

I step in, hoping to diffuse the tension. "What she meant was—"

"I meant what I said," Elena interrupts.

She doesn't take her eyes off him. "We don't know you. You don't know us. Times are crazy, and it's best if we all keep to our own."

The man tilts his head, considering her words. Then—

"The name's Garanth."

His voice is calm, but too deliberate.

"There. Now we're not strangers."

He gestures toward the fire again.

"Mind if I sit?"

"We do," Elena replies, unwavering.

Garanth exhales through his nose, then turns to me.

"We?" he repeats, raising an eyebrow. "What about *you*, big fella? Does she speak for you, too?"

Elena doesn't look away from him. She also doesn't answer for me. I hold Garanth's gaze and repeat Elena's words.

"Keep moving."

Something shifts in him.

A flicker of something exhausted. He sighs, shaking his head, muttering to himself. "Why does it always have to be this way?"

His voice has softened, but there's something underneath—something broken.

"Been on the road longer than I care to remember," he says. His eyes drift toward the fire, his expression unreadable.

"Rorick's promise of order…" he murmurs.

A pause. And then—

"It's *tempting*, you know."

His gaze lifts to us again, sharp now. "For a man who's seen chaos *up close*."

A shadow of something flickers across his face—regret? Resignation?

But he shrugs it off, and the hardness returns.

"Rorick has an offer for you."

Rorick. Of course. It's always Rorick. My stomach knots as questions slam into me—how did he find us? Who else knows we're here?

It doesn't matter. I already know my answer. No.

"No," I say aloud, my voice firm, final. "I have nothing left to say to him."

The shift is instant. Garanth moves—fast. Steel flashes.

His sword clears its sheath in a blur, and he charges. No more words. No more pretense. Just death coming for us.

With a two-handed grip, he raises his blade high, bringing it down toward Elena's skull. She dodges, twisting aside with an ease that makes it seem effortless.

But he's quicker than I expected. With unnatural speed, his sword whips through the air, aiming to cut her in half. The firelight catches on steel, burning against the blackness.

I reach for my knife—but it feels laughable in the face of his blade.

I'm not prepared for this. Elena catches his next strike, steel meeting steel in a brutal clang—

But the force of his blow knocks her sword from her hands. She stumbles back, eyes wide as the blade spins into the darkness. Garanth laughs.

His sword rises again for the killing blow. And I move. I don't think. I step in front of Elena. Knife raised, body braced—

And I know, in that instant—

This is how I die. The thought slams into me with terrifying clarity.

This is it.

I tighten my grip, ready to block the impossible.

But before Garanth's blade can fall—

His body goes limp.

His arms drop uselessly to his sides. His sword clatters to the ground. And then—he collapses. A look of panic flickers across his face.

His mouth moves, trying to form words, but nothing comes out. His eyes dart wildly, as if searching for something.

And I realize—

He can't move.

"Don't just stand there," Drusilla's voice cuts through the firelight, sharp and unyielding.

She's suddenly visible, stepping forward from wherever she had been watching in the shadows. "Tie him up."

I hesitate, still caught between the violence of moments ago and the unnerving stillness now. "With what?" I ask. "We have nothing to tie him up with."

Drusilla smirks, tilting her head toward Garanth's travel bag. "Check his bag." Her voice is too certain. "I bet he has shackles in there."

A cold pit settles in my stomach at her confidence, but I kneel down and rummage through Garanth's belongings. Sure enough—

Iron shackles.

The kind that bind the wrists and ankles together. What kind of messenger carries these? I don't ask. I just lock them into place. As I snap the final clasp, the light around us fades—

And then—

Total darkness.

Garanth can't move. But it won't last forever.

I grab him by the arm and drag him closer to the fire for a better look. His eyes are wild, darting back and forth—panicked.

I know how he must feel. It seems like a lifetime ago when it happened to me. "What now?" I ask, exhaling.

Drusilla crosses her arms, her expression unreadable.

"We wait," she says simply. "When he can move again, we hear what he has to say."

A pause.

"If we don't like it—"

Her eyes flick down to Garanth, her voice cold—merciless.

"We kill him."

The words send a chill through me. I turn to look at her, really look at her. She means it. I can see it in the calm certainty in her stance, in the hardness in her gaze.

Would she actually kill him? Yes. I have no doubt. I glance toward Brennen, but he says nothing.

Elena, her sword back in her hand, watches Garanth with a wary eye.

Drusilla stands rigid, her expression somewhere between annoyance and expectation.

Brennen remains silent, his gaze shifting toward the treeline as if he's expecting more unwanted company.

The fire crackles, casting long shadows that dance against the trees.

And suddenly—I feel the weight of it all.

We're not just fighting for our lives. We're fighting against Rorick's reach.

He's everywhere, his influence stretching beyond the cities, beyond the SoulCasters, beyond the Council.

Even here. Even now.

I let out a slow breath, staring down at Garanth's motionless body.

"I didn't want any of this," I whisper, more to myself than to anyone else.

The words feel small, fragile against the vastness of the night. The fire's warmth does nothing to shake the chill in my bones. Not from the night air. From the knowledge of the path that lies ahead.

Then—

Garanth stirs.

A sharp inhale, a twitch of his fingers, a shift in his bound legs.

I step closer, standing over him as he regains control of his body.

"We'll hear what you have to say," I tell him, my voice steady now.

"But remember this—"

I crouch down slightly, meeting his gaze.

"Our path is our own. No one—not Rorick, not you, not anyone—can dictate our direction."

The fire crackles, filling the space between us. A silent witness. A reminder.

Then—

Garanth gasps. His eyes widen in horror. He writhes, struggling against his bindings.

"My eyes!" he chokes out, voice raw with panic.

Then—rage.

"What did you do to me, you disgusting tunnel rat?!"

Drusilla moves like a whip-crack. One moment she's standing still—

The next, she's on him. Her claws slash across his face.

Not deep—but deep enough to bleed. The red lines blossom instantly, stark against his rough skin. Garanth grits his teeth, biting back a sound of pain.

"Drusilla!"

Brennen's voice rings out, sharp and commanding.

"To harm a human in self-defense is one thing—"

His expression darkens.

"But harming an unarmed man?"

His voice lowers.

"That's another thing entirely."

Drusilla turns her head slowly, her gaze locking onto Brennen.

A dangerous stillness fills the air. Her voice, when she speaks, is lethal. "You forget your place, old man."

Brennen stiffens. Something flickers in his expression—something I don't understand. His lips part, but no words come.

Then—

His eyes drop to the ground. And he says nothing. I put that away. I'll ask him about that later.

Drusilla turns back to Garanth, dismissing Brennen entirely. She crouches beside him, eyes gleaming in the firelight. And then—just one word.

"Speak."

Garanth scowls, his chest rising and falling with uneven breaths.

"What do you want me to say?" he spits.

Drusilla tilts her head, her smirk sharp as a knife.

"Whatever you think is valuable."

A pause.

Then—

Her voice drops lower, colder. "But I will be the judge of whether it is—"

She leans in slightly.

"Or whether it isn't." The firelight glints off her claws. "If it isn't—"

She flicks her fingers toward the bloody scratches on his face. "Then that little scratch I gave you? It won't be so little next time."

Garanth sighs, his chest rising and falling as if this were all just an inconvenience to him.

"No need for all that," he mutters. "I told you—I came to talk."

Elena scoffs, her grip tightening on her sword.

"Do you always talk with your sword?" she spits.

Even bound and prone, the man looks dangerous. Now that I take a better look at him, I see what Elena saw the moment she laid eyes on him. A killer. Not just a soldier. Not just a fighter. A seasoned, bloodied, ruthless killer.

Scars line his face, his arms, his hands. His palms are thick with callouses, hardened by years of swinging that blade at men who never got back up.

Garanth watches me, expression unreadable.

"When words fail me," he says finally, "my sword won't."

Drusilla smirks.

"It failed you this time," she says, stepping closer, her voice dropping into something sharper. A warning. A challenge. Garanth's smile widens.

"Unshackle me," he taunts, "and try again."

Then, mockingly, he makes a kissing sound with his lips. I tense, fully expecting Drusilla to lash out, but—

She doesn't. Instead, she takes a step back, tilting her head. "No," she says simply. "Unlike you, we'll use our words."

Garanth laughs. It's a deep, amused sound, but there's something calculating behind it.

"Oh, I don't think you much like words," he muses. His eyes flick over her, studying her like a puzzle he's trying to solve. "You're not like the others, are you?" he says slowly.

A pause.

Then, a grin.

"Oh, I bet you could teach me a thing or two."

Drusilla doesn't react.

But I see it—the flicker of something dangerous in her eyes. Garanth leans his head back, sighing theatrically.

"Before all this is over, you and I are going to have some words."

That's it. I step forward. "Enough."

He lifts a brow, looking pleased that he got a reaction.

"Let's hear what you have to say," I say.

Garanth exhales, almost lazily.

"Ahhh, if it isn't the prodigal son." His eyes gleam as he studies me. "Sit me up so we can talk like men."

"You're fine where you are," Drusilla hisses.

Garanth chuckles again, but his eyes—they're colder now.

His gaze settles on me.

"Do you always let women speak for you?"

I don't bite.

I keep my voice even, controlled.

"Get on with it."

Garanth's amusement doesn't fade entirely, but something shifts in him.

"Very well," he says, exhaling like this is all so beneath him.

"Let's get down to business, then, shall we?"

Then—

His next words hit like a punch to the gut.

"Rorick wants to make a trade."

I frown.

"A trade?" What could Rorick possibly have that I want? Garanth smirks.

"Your father… for you."

Everything stops. For a brief moment, my heart slams in my chest.

And then— Laughter.

It bubbles out of me, harsh and sharp.

"I don't believe you."

Garanth shrugs.

"You don't have Theron."

His smirk widens.

"Who said anything about Theron?"

His next words are a hammer to my ribs. "I'm talking about Thom." The world blurs. My thoughts scatter, shatter, reform in jagged pieces.

Dad is alive? No. He can't be. I don't believe it. This is a trick. It has to be.

But—

What if it isn't? I think back to the ceremony.

The man holding my mother, knife pressed to her throat. I remember him saying—

He's already dead.

But my mother— She mouthed something. A single word. No.

At the time, I thought she was telling me not to shoot. But… what if she wasn't?

What if she was trying to say—

He's not dead. My breath feels tight.

"I don't believe you," I say again, my voice quieter now. Garanth shrugs.

"I wouldn't believe me either," he says easily.

A pause.

Then—

"But I have proof, Sprout."

My stomach drops.

That word—

That damn word.

Sprout. My father used to call me that when I was young.

"You're shooting up like a sprout."

I always hated it.

But now—

I'd give anything to hear my father call me that again. And that's the real question, isn't it? What would I give? Would I give my life? Would I trade myself to Rorick—so he can bring Lathguard back?

Would I risk everything—for the *chance* that my father is alive? Garanth watches me, something unreadable in his expression. He shifts, his chains clinking in the silence.

"I've made my choice, Jerrick," he says, voice calm but weighted. "Rorick found me when I was nothing but a mercenary, lost to the wind." His lips twitch. "He offered me a purpose."

His gaze darkens. "…Something you're *clearly* still searching for."

My teeth clench.

That's where you're wrong, Garanth. "I have a purpose."

The words leave me fast—maybe too fast.

Was I trying to convince him? Or myself?

Then—

Garanth frowns. His expression shifts. His eyes dart around.

"Where did you go?" he asks suddenly. His voice has changed— not mocking, not smug.

Confused. Uneasy. And then I realize—

He can't see me.

Pulled from my spiraling thoughts, I glance toward Brennen. His stance is rigid, his furred ears flat against his head. His eyes, wide and serious, lift to mine.

"You're not considering it… are you, Jerrick?" His voice is low, barely above a whisper. And for the first time—

I don't know the answer.

"You can't believe a thing this man says," Drusilla mutters, her voice edged with certainty.

I know I can't. But… what if? What if it's true? What if my father is alive, and it's in my power to save him? What kind of son would I be if I didn't at least consider the possibility?

"Are you just going to let your father die?"

Garanth's voice slithers through the firelight.

And then— A sharp kick to his ribs.

Drusilla's boot connects hard, silencing him with a grunted exhale.

To his credit, he doesn't speak again. He understands the meaning of the kick.

"Jerrick." Elena's voice pulls me back, grounding me.

She reaches for my hand, her fingers warm against my skin. "I can only imagine what's going on in that head of yours," she says softly. "But I want you to know—I'll back your move."

Her gaze is steady, unwavering. "I'll be with you," she says, her voice a quiet promise. "No matter what you decide."

A pause. "But, Jerrick—" She squeezes my hand. "You know that what we're doing now is right."

Her voice lowers. "Releasing the Creator is our only hope. Without the God Tree whole, none of us live."

Do I believe that? What if Aethel is wrong? What if they can't fix the decay? How do I know Rorick is wrong? What if Lathguard can fix this? What if I'm wrong?

Then, I see it. My father's face. Smiling. Calm. He doesn't judge me. He never did. His eyes tell me what they always did. Follow your heart. Do what you know to be right. I take a slow breath.

Then—

"Okay, Brennen," I say. "I'm ready to talk to him."

Brennen hesitates. His ears flatten slightly, uncertainty flickering in his expression.

He looks at me—then at Drusilla. He doesn't trust me to make the right choice. That stings more than I expect.

I step closer, placing a hand on his shoulder. Brennen searches my face. Then, finally—he nods. And just like that— Garanth sees us again.

His gaze lifts to me, that smirk creeping back onto his face. "Ah," he drawls. "There you are." He tilts his head. "So, what will it be?"

I don't hesitate.

I meet his gaze, my voice firm. "My father once told me— We don't always get to choose our destiny. Sometimes, destiny chooses us. And when it does, follow it bravely."

I swallow, but I don't falter. "If what you say is true, then my father will understand why I'm saying no."

My voice cracks on the last word. But I stand firm. Did I just condemn my father to death? The thought hits me like a fist, but—

No. I know I'm on the right path. If I trade myself for him, Rorick wins. Rorick's path means we all die—

Eventually.

The Creator is the only one who can push back the Fog. I have to believe that. Garanth's face twists with fury.

"Fool!" he spits, his voice venomous. "You are killing us all!"

He struggles against his shackles, rage burning in his eyes.

"You're the only one who can end this, and you choose these— these creatures?!" His voice breaks with raw betrayal. "You're a traitor to your kind!"

I don't flinch.

I take a slow breath, my voice barely above a whisper—

But steady.

"You're wrong," I say. "You're wrapped up in Rorick's lies so tightly that you can't see the truth."

I exhale. "If I go with you, we all die." My hands tremble, but I keep my gaze locked on his. "If I don't—" A pause. "We have a chance."

My throat tightens, but I force the words out. "My father will understand that."

But will I? Garanth stares at me. Then, he laughs. It's a bitter, hollow sound.

"You think you're the first ones to try changing the world?" He scoffs, shaking his head. "I once thought as you do."

His eyes darken. "But life—life teaches you the cost of ideals." A pause. "Rorick, at least, offers a clear vision."

His gaze narrows on me. "What do you have, Sprout?" He tilts his head. "Besides hope?"

Drusilla moves before I can. A wad of fabric is suddenly stuffed into his mouth. "Much better," she mutters.

Elena exhales, looking between us.

"What are we going to do with him?" she asks.

Drusilla shrugs. "Dump him in the sea?"

Then—a wink.

I blink.

Did she just—

Did Drusilla just make a joke?

Elena turns back to me, stepping closer. She places her arms gently around my waist, tilting her head up to meet my eyes.

"Are you okay?" she asks.

Am I? I take a moment before answering. I always want to be honest with her.

"I don't know," I finally say, forcing my mouth to move. "If not—"

I exhale.

"I will be."

Brennen steps toward me. "He can't see or hear us," he says. "If you want to talk about it, Jerrick."

I shake my head. "I don't."

But I force a small smile. "We should figure out what to do with him."

I glance at Drusilla.

"And we're not dumping him in the sea."

She deadpans.

"Okay, fine."

"In the morning," I continue, "we'll drop him off on the road to the village. If we do it before daylight, we won't be seen, and he won't know which direction we go. We'll leave him shackled."

"He won't be found for hours."

The fire crackles.

My thoughts drift back—

To the morning of The Naming. To the man I let go. To my mother's death. I've changed since then.

But I haven't changed so much that I'll kill an unarmed man. I settle into a warm spot by the fire. Sleep finds me faster than I expected.

#

The water is like glass, eerily still as we sail across its placid surface toward the back of the island. It looms ahead, dark and foreboding, its jagged peaks rising like the teeth of some great beast, ready to swallow us whole.

We've all heard the tales—of those who ventured here and were never seen again. A place where nightmares take form. A place where the unlucky vanish and the lucky return broken. As the island grows larger, I feel its presence—not just as a place, but as a force.

Untamed. Wild. Relentless.

And yet, despite its threatening silhouette, there's a beauty to it. Stark. Raw. Uncompromising.

It speaks of power and mystery, of something ancient and waiting. The wind bites hard, cold enough to sink into my bones. I pull my cloak tight, but it's not enough. The chill seeps in, relentless. We all stand in silence on the creaking wooden boat, listening to the rhythmic groan of old wood meeting restless sea.

At the helm, the fisherman guides us forward. An old codger, weathered and grizzled, but one of us—one of the resistance. Until recently, I didn't even know the resistance existed.

A quiet rebellion, growing beneath the Council's nose, working to bring back the Creator and undo the decay. Theron is their leader. And in some way, I suppose… I'm part of them now, too.

"This place," Theron speaks at last, breaking the silence.

His voice is low, nearly swallowed by the wind in the sails. "…isn't just some old legend to scare children."

His gaze remains locked on the island. "It's a reminder." A pause. "A reminder of the hubris of the past, and the very real danger we face in the present if we fail."

His words feel heavier than the wind. He turns to us, eyes sharp. "Don't take what I'm about to say lightly." His voice drops, deadly serious. "This place will kill you. And the moment you think otherwise—"

His gaze sweeps over us, locking onto each of us in turn.

"…is the moment just before it happens."

I glance down at Elena, and she squeezes my hand. A silent vow of unity. Of courage. I don't see fear in her eyes. I see determination. A reflection of my own.

I smirk. Then, looking at Theron, I raise an eyebrow.

"That was a rousing speech."

Theron gives me a look.

"It's because we could die," he says, voice edged. Then, he realizes I'm messing with him.

He snorts, shaking his head. "Funny, Jerrick," he mutters. "Let's see what *you* got."

I blink. Wait. What? I glance at Elena, hoping for help.

She just stares back, her expression clear: You did this to yourself. Brennen smirks, barely hiding his amusement. Drusilla looks bored.

Fantastic. I clear my throat.

"I…" I stop. Why do I never know what to say? Come on, Jerrick. You big oaf. Just speak. I inhale.

"I don't have the experience that any of you have."

I let my gaze linger on each of them—

Drusilla. Brennen. Elena. Theron.

Letting my admission sink in.

"I've been thrust into this, and I'm still figuring it all out."

A pause.

"But what I do know is this—" My grip tightens on the railing. "Greatness doesn't wait for perfect moments. It finds us in our darkest hours, when we have nothing left but the will to push forward."

I let the words settle.

"We may be stepping into the unknown, facing dangers we can't predict…" I exhale. "…but together, we are more than our fears."

I glance at the island. "This place may try to break us…" My voice steadies. "But it's in facing the impossible that we discover who we truly are."

A beat of silence. The island looms closer. I exhale.

"What awaits us may be shrouded in darkness, but we carry with us a light."

I meet their gazes. "A light forged from our bonds, our hopes, and the unwavering belief in our cause."

Silence. Total, stunned silence.

Even the captain, who I didn't think was listening, wipes a tear from his eye. "Well said," he says, his voice straining. He clears his throat. "We've lost so many friends on this journey," he murmurs, pausing. "It brings me great peace knowing it's almost at an end. We're really doing this, aren't we?"

Elena's voice cuts through the quiet, soft but strong.

She smiles, looking at me. "If he can put that many words together at once…"

She grins. "Then we *can* bring the Creator back."

I can't help it. I laugh. The sound spreads, Brennen chuckling, Elena giggling, and even Theron letting out a deep, amused exhale. Drusilla just shakes her head, but there's something almost approving in her expression.

Then, Theron steps forward. He places a heavy hand on my shoulder. "I believe in you."

I hold his gaze. Then, with a slow breath, I shake my head.

"I believe in us." A pause. "None of us got here alone."

I let my words linger, the truth of them settling in.

"We've all made sacrifices." My throat tightens, but I push forward. "Sacrifices that have changed us in ways we don't fully grasp."

I take in a deep breath. "In ways we may never grasp."

A belief that led me to forsake my father. The thought cuts through me, but I don't speak it aloud. Guilt claws at my ribs, pressing against the edges of my mind.

I try to push it down, shove it into the same dark place as all the other things I don't want to feel. But this time—

It pushes back. The wind howls around us. The cliffs of Shardmount Island loom above, jagged and waiting. This is more than just a journey. More than just an island, no matter how dangerous. This is a passage through the veil of our own fears and doubts.

A test of who we are. Of what we believe. And of what we're willing to risk—

For the fate of everything.

Elena's hand tightens on my arm. I turn to her, and in the dim firelight of the ship's lanterns, I see it—

Sadness. Understanding. She knows of the sacrifices I speak of. She doesn't know their full weight, but she carries some of it with me.

I exhale, thankful I'm not alone in this. The island, with all its legends and nightmares, does not know the strength of determined hearts.

And as we draw closer, I feel it—

A shift. A readiness inside me. We may face the unknown, but we do so together. Like bearers of light stepping into the dark.

Then—

Movement. A blur of practiced motion as the crew drops sail in one swift motion. "Anchor!"

The captain's voice rings across the deck. His crew moves like clockwork, ropes coiling, wood groaning, the ship settling into the swelling sea.

Stepping away from the helm, the captain moves wordlessly to Theron.

And then—

He embraces him. It's not just a farewell. It's something more. A shared understanding. A silent wish for survival.

Then—

He turns. And walks toward me. Up close, the captain looks exactly as I'd expect—

A weathered man of the sea. A messy gray beard, a big floppy hat, and a face lined deep from years beneath the sky and salt. But his eyes… They aren't as hardened as the rest of him. They hold hope. He stops before me.

"Thank you," he says. His voice is deep, raspy—like rocks tumbling in a barrel. "You give me hope."

He swallows, then nods. "You give us all hope."

And then—

He embraces me. The same way he embraced Theron. The same way he embraces Elena. Then Brennen. Then, to my utter shock—

Even Drusilla.

And even more shocking—

She lets him. We're led to a rope ladder, its wooden rungs slick with sea spray.

Below, bobbing against the hull, is a small boat that will take us the last few hundred feet to shore. Theron and I wordlessly grab oars and begin to row. The water is black glass beneath us. Silent. Still.

As if the sea itself is holding its breath. But as we draw closer—

A scent reaches me. It's faint at first, just beneath the briny sea air. Then, stronger. A bitter, pungent aroma. Like sweat-drenched fabric left too long outside. Like fruit, overripe and rotting on the vine. It's not overpowering, but it lingers—

Just beneath the breeze.

At the back of the island, a landing comes into view. The rock juts out from the cliffs, a narrow strip of dark, uneven stone. The boat scrapes against it as we come ashore. Without a word, Theron leaps out first, boots hitting stone.

Then, grabbing the rim of the boat, he drags it further onto land—

Pulling us with it. I step out. And immediately, my gaze is drawn upward. The cliffs. Rising over us. Vast. Ominous. Watching. The sheer scale of them steals my breath.

Dark rock, streaked with veins of white stone, stretching toward the storm-heavy sky. They are both awe-inspiring and terrifying. They dwarf us. Make us small. Insignificant. And then—

I see it. The path. A series of crude steps claw their way up the cliff side, uneven and weathered by time. Some are mere indentations, barely more than toe-holds.

Others are larger, but slick—dangerously smooth from centuries of wind and rain. The climb will not be easy. One misstep, and we plunge to the rocks below. And yet—

As I stare up at this natural staircase, it strikes me. This isn't just a path. This is a metaphor. For us. For this journey.

Unpredictable. Dangerous. Unforgiving.

A path not given but taken. A path that demands perseverance, faith, and strength. A path that tests us. Breaks us. But—

If we survive it, we reach the summit. We become something more. The cliff face looms, whispering of secrets lost to time. Of ancient things waiting to be awakened. Of dangers yet unseen. And still—

I feel something else. Not just the weight of what's to come—

But the weight of being watched. A prickle runs down my spine. I glance behind me. Nothing. Just the shifting mist curling over the water. And yet—

I know we are not alone. I take a deep breath, feeling the air thicken in my lungs. I steel myself. Because whatever awaits us atop these cliffs—

Will shape the fate of our world. And it begins now.

We begin our climb. At first, it's simple. A steady pull upward, step by step. But quickly—

It becomes grueling. Some steps rise over seven feet high, forcing me to hoist Elena and Brennen up. Drusilla refuses help of any kind. Her short claws dig easily into the rock, making her climbing look effortless. Most impressive, though, is Theron. At seven feet tall and nearly four hundred pounds of sheer muscle, he hauls himself up with brutal efficiency. He climbs almost as easily as Drusilla—

A man his size shouldn't be able to move like that. We crest the top of the cliff. And what awaits us is—

Nothing. A vast expanse of black stone, stretching in all directions. Lifeless. Barren. Everything is hard, cold, and unforgiving. In the distance—

The ruins. A small town, just as Brennen had described. Broken silhouettes of abandoned buildings, skeletal remains of a place forgotten by time. And the smell. The scent that had been just beneath the breeze before—

Now it's everywhere. It clings to the very air. A putrid, decaying stench, as if the land itself is rotting. I grimace.

"The island is cut off from the Source," Brennen says.

His voice carries a mix of awe and something close to reverence. I turn to him. "What do you mean?"

"The power pulled through the Syphon all those years ago—" Brennen gestures around us. "It cauterized the connection."

His ears flick as he sniffs the air. "I bet you can channel here without worrying about being attacked by those things on the mainland."

A pause. "Which also means—" He turns his golden eyes to me. "You'll only have access to what's in your reservoir."

Elena nods. "Then we'll be careful." She meets my gaze. "If we drain ourselves, we'll have to be carried out of here." Her lips curl into a smirk. "And some of us will be harder to carry."

I chuckle. Then look at Theron. "Yes, some of us."

"Haha, you two," Theron grumbles. Then his voice hardens. "But remember where we are." His gaze sweeps over us. "And what I said." His grip tightens on his sword. "This place will kill you if you're not careful."

"Way to kill the joy, Dad," Drusilla quips.

I blink. Still not used to her joking. But… I like it. She catches me watching her, then winks. I don't think I'll ever understand her. Then—

"Left!" Theron's shout cuts the air. And in one swift motion—

His sword is drawn. I spin. And in the distance, I see it. A blur of motion, moving fast. The same color as the blackened land, almost blending into the desolation.

But it's coming. Fast. "Wraiths!"

Theron's voice is sharp, commanding.

"Two of them. Coming fast."

I don't think—

I just move. Quickly, I unshoulder my bow, tighten the string, and—

Loose. The arrow flies true.

Straight into the skull of the first wraith.

But—

It doesn't stop. It doesn't even slow. I nock another arrow. Draw. Release.

This one slams into the front shoulder, embedding deep. And still—

Nothing. No reaction. No pain. No stopping.

Elena pulls her sword, stepping forward. But—

Drusilla stops her.

"You're a healer," she says, voice firm.

"You may be a capable enough fighter, but you're best used as a healer." Drusilla's eyes narrow. "We may go down." She tilts her head. "It's your job to see we get back up."

Elena's jaw tightens, but—

She sheathes her sword. Takes a step back. Reluctant, but resolute. Then—

The wraiths reach Theron. And I see them clearly for the first time.

They are a mass of sinew and boils. Teeth and claws. Black as night. Skin stretched too tight over bulging muscle and thick veins. Their movements are erratic, frenzied by hunger.

And Theron moves. With effortless precision. A dance of death.

Dodge. Thrust.

Sidestep. Slash.

Duck. Shoulder check.

Steel flashes. Blood spills. But—

The wraiths don't slow. They don't react. They just keep coming. Then—

Drusilla leaps in. Faster than Theron. Sharper. Her knives flash. She climbs onto the wraith's back. And drives her blade down.

Once.

Twice.

Three times.

But the wraith doesn't even acknowledge her. Its hunger is locked onto Theron. The bigger prize. I'm frozen.

I can channel, but—

Theron and Drusilla are too close.

I don't want to hit them.

I need to do something, but—

The wraiths don't feel pain. They don't tire.

Even with Theron's powerful swings, his sword barely bites deep.

These things are all muscle and fury.

Then—

A shift. A mistake.

One wraith notices Drusilla.

And it swipes.

She doesn't see it coming.

It catches her across the side, sending her flying ten feet back.

She lands hard. Gasps for air.

Tries to get up—

And in one powerful leap—

The wraith is on top of her.

It howls in delight, pinning her face down against the black rock. A second too slow—

And she'll be torn apart.

Blood. Too much blood.

A lake of red spreads beneath Drusilla, staining the black rock.

Her breathing is shallow. Her limbs twitch, her body failing. I have to do something. Now. I don't think. I don't hesitate. I act.

The air ripples before me, bending under my will.

A blade takes shape—

A crescent of pure force. I fling it forward.

It screams through the air—

Sharp. Silent. Deadly.

Before my heart even beats again—

The wraith is severed in two.

Its body collapses soundlessly, the two halves falling away from each other.

The black ichor that spills onto the rock hisses, evaporating into nothing.

The second wraith freezes. Just for a moment. Then, its head snaps toward me.

Its body tenses—

And it charges. I brace.

It moves faster than I expected—

A black blur of hunger and rage. But I'm ready. I throw out my hands.

A wall of force slams forward—

Colliding with the wraith in midair.

A sickening crack shatters the silence.

Bones snap.

The creature folds inward—

Its back end meeting its front, crushed into a mangled heap of skin, pulverized bone, and thick black blood.

Silence. Total. Complete.

I exhale, my breath loud in my ears.

I turn. They're all staring at me.

Even Drusilla, who—

Is now standing. Completely healed. Theron is the first to speak.

"That was…"

He takes a breath, still catching it from the fight.

"…something."

A pause. His gaze locks onto mine. "The last time I saw you do that—"

He shakes his head. "It was nothing like that."

He exhales. "You saved our lives, Jerrick."

A rare, genuine smile touches his lips. "Thank you."

Drusilla steps forward. She moves slowly, deliberately.

I watch her, searching her face—

But for once, she's completely unreadable. "Drusilla?" I swallow. "Are you okay?"

She stops in front of me. Holds my gaze for a single moment. Then—

She drops to one knee. And bows her head.

Her voice is steady, but there's weight behind every word.

"I, Drusilla Thalrassia. First-born daughter of King and Queen Thalrassia, Thank you for saving my life." She lifts her chin slightly. "My people will forever be in your debt."

A princess? It clicks. Last night. What she said to Brennen. The way he lowered his gaze. The way she spoke with authority. I look at Brennen now. He's grinning.

I look back at Drusilla. She's still kneeling, head bowed.

Waiting. Expecting something.

"Tell her she may stand," Brennen whispers.

I clear my throat. "You may stand."

The words come out hesitant, unsure. But Drusilla obeys without hesitation.

She nods once, then—

Turns toward the ruins.

"So," she says casually. "Are we just going to stand here?"

Then—

A howl cuts through the silence.

Distant. Echoing. More are coming.

Theron's sword is up again in an instant. "More are coming!"

His voice is sharp. I don't wait. "Everyone behind me!"

No hesitation. They move. Theron. Elena. Brennen. Drusilla.

They all fall in behind me. I channel.

A wall of force erupts before us—

A half-circle barrier, curved like a shield. Solid. Unbreakable. I scan the horizon. Something moves. Fast.

But not clearly visible yet.

"There are six of them," Theron mutters.

His eyes cut through the darkness, seeing what I can't yet.

Then, I hear them. A high-pitched mewling sound. Sharp. Unnatural. Like a thousand screaming voices tangled into one. They're fighting each other to get to us. Each one snapping at the legs of another.

Clawing. Tearing. Trying to be the first to reach us. Then—

Something else moves.

From the direction of the ruins. Something bigger. Something different. A figure sits up. Then—

It stands. My blood runs cold. It's huge. Towering. A dark silhouette against the dead sky. Is that… a giant?

For the second time, Theron reads my mind. "I think that's a giant."

His voice is quiet. Almost uncertain. And then—

It moves. Not toward us. Toward them. Its massive strides eat up the distance in seconds. It reaches the wraiths before they reach us. Without breaking pace, it bends down—

And swipes. Two wraiths go flying. Their twisted forms tumbling end over end into the darkness. The rest scatter, shrieking, vanishing into the shadows. My hands shake as I reshape my wall—

Pulling it into a dome. The giant runs toward us. Faster than it should be able to. The rock trembles beneath its pounding steps. My breath hitches. I try not to panic—

But my hands won't stop shaking. It gets closer. And closer. And then—

It stops. For the first time, I see it clearly. A male giant. Easily twenty feet tall.

Muscle and scale-like skin, eyes glowing like embers.

Ancient. And then—

It speaks. A voice like thunder rolling over mountains. "Lathguard…" It tilts its head. Eyes narrowing. "How did you get so small?"

Chapter 16

Jerrick

The giant is massive. More than just his size—

It's the way he carries himself. The sheer weight of his presence. Standing just over twenty feet tall, that's not even the most impressive thing about him. It's his arms. Too long. Too thick. And covered in metal scales—

Each one a different shade of blue, shifting like a living kaleidoscope of steel. Beautiful. Almost.

His face is sunken, dominated by a flat, oversized nose, too large for his features. He wears nothing except a massive black apron, thick and scorched, hanging from his chest down to just below his knees. A smith's apron. The kind worn by a forge master.

He crouches. And when he does, his size becomes even more overwhelming. The ground shifts beneath his weight. And then—

His dark, sunken eyes settle on me.

"Nah, nah." His voice rumbles, thick and gravelly. Like metal scraping stone. He leans in—

And stares directly into my eyes. "You're not Lathguard."

He shakes his massive head. "Valkrum killed Lathguard. Valkrum killed them all."

His brow furrows, and he mutters, almost to himself—

"You can't trick old Valkrum. Valkrum is smart. Yes, he is. Brodan said so—"

A pause. "Right before Valkrum killed him. Before Valkrum killed them all."

I go still. My breath catches in my throat. This is Valkrum. The Forge Master. God of metal and fire.

And he's still alive.

But something is wrong. The way he speaks—

Pausing between words, as if each one is a puzzle he must piece together before speaking. There's a hesitation, an uncertainty, almost… childlike. My fear is real. A giant stands before me. The last of his kind. And I have only a fraction of the power Lathguard had. If he attacks—

I can't protect them. My hands shake. But still—

I step forward. What are you doing, Jerrick? I take another step. Stop. But my legs won't listen. You're not strong enough. You'll get them all killed. I inhale. And—

"You're right." My voice is steady. "I'm not him. My name is Jerrick. I've bonded Lathguard."

The words spill out before I can stop them. Words have never been my strong suit.

But right now—

They're all I have. Just in case, I keep the shield over us. Valkrum's head tilts. He squints, thinking. Then—

"Ahhh, Valkrum was told you'd come." A deep inhale. "Not Jerrick. But Lathguard's bond. Because—Lathguard is dead."

A pause. His voice drops. "Valkrum killed him. Valkrum killed them all."

And suddenly—

Fear. His massive body recoils, leaning back slightly.

"Are you here to kill Valkrum?"

"No," I say gently. My fear is still there, but I tuck it away. "I would never do that."

I study his face. "Why do you think I'd kill you?"

He points at me, a finger larger than my entire arm. "So, you're the good one, then? Not the bad one?"

His voice, for all its thunderous power, carries a childlike uncertainty. Something instinctual in me recognizes it. I soften. Speaking to him feels like speaking to a child. A dangerous, immensely powerful child. But a child nonetheless.

"Yes." I nod. "I'd never hurt you."

Another step forward. "What do you mean by 'bad one'?"

Valkrum's giant shoulders hunch. His voice lowers, as if sharing a secret.

"Brodan told Valkrum that one day, Lathguard's bond would come."

A pause. "That he would kill Valkrum." His fingers twitch. "For what Valkrum did."

His voice drops even lower. "But… but there might be a good one." A long pause. "Are you the good one?"

"Yes." I say it without hesitation. Even though I'm not sure about any of this. Even though my four companions remain utterly silent—

Watching. Waiting. Like statues.

Valkrum leans closer. His breath is hot, metallic. "Good. Valkrum doesn't want to die."

His voice drops to a whisper. "Valkrum is scared. Valkrum is lonely." His eyes darken. "There are only bad things here."

His lips pull back, baring massive teeth. "They bite at Valkrum when Valkrum sleeps." His massive fists clench. "Valkrum smashes them." A pause. "But they keep being reborn."

Reborn? Something clicks in my mind. I want to ask—

But I force myself to focus. Stay on target, Jerrick. "I came here for the Wellspring Syphon." I keep my voice calm. "Do you know where it is?"

His face twitches. "The Syphon?"

A slow nod. "Yes. Yes. Valkrum made it. Valkrum made many things."

His massive hands flex. "But not anymore."

His tone shifts—

Something darker seeps in.

"Valkrum can't access the Source anymore." He pauses, there is afar away look in his eyes. "Valkrum was master of fire. Master of metal."

Another twitch. "Valkrum made things of death."

His voice turns soft, almost regretful. "Valkrum doesn't like death."

A beat. His eyes flicker back to me. "Are you here to kill Valkrum?"

I exhale.

Patiently—

"No. I'm the good one."

Relief washes over his face.

"Oh, that's right."

His tone brightens.

"Valkrum forgot."

And then—

He reaches for me. A massive hand extends. A single finger moving toward my chest. Every instinct screams. Move. Attack. Run. But I stand my ground.

Then—

He jerks back. Like something bit him.

My shield shimmers.

"OWWW!" His roar shakes the earth. His massive face twists into rage. "YOU HURT VALKRUM!"

He rises to his full height. Hands interlacing. Muscles bulging. And with all his strength—

He brings them down on my shield.

"What do I do?" I yell, my voice barely rising above the sound of stone trembling beneath us.

Valkrum's massive fists continue to hammer down, each strike a thunderclap that rattles my bones. "He's like a child," Elena says, suddenly at my side. Her hand finds my arm, grounding me. "He's scared."

And she's right. Even as he pounds his fists against my shield, his own screams mix with the pain of his strikes. He thinks I'm hurting him on purpose. I grit my teeth. Think, Jerrick. Then—

An idea. "Elena, heal him." She blinks. "Heal him?"

"Yes. He needs to know we're not here to hurt him." I glance at her, urgency filling my voice. "Make him feel good."

She doesn't question me. She channels. Almost immediately—

Valkrum halts mid-swing. His breathing is ragged, his massive shoulders heaving.

Then, slowly—

He sits down. Right in front of us. I lower my hands, letting my shield dissipate.

"Are you okay?" I ask, cautiously.

Valkrum's lower lip juts out. "You hurt Valkrum."

A deep, rumbling pout.

"Not on purpose," I say gently. "I got scared. I was trying to protect my friends."

His massive eyes squint at me. "Is Valkrum your friend?"

The question startles me. I hesitate. Then—

"Yes. Valkrum is my friend."

His expression shifts. Something vulnerable flickers across his weathered, massive face. "You'll protect Valkrum like you protected your friends?"

His voice drops, barely above a whisper. "Valkrum is always afraid."

My chest tightens. He is a child. Trapped in a giant's body, drowning in guilt and fear. His sheer size is overwhelming—

But it's the sadness in his eyes that hits the hardest.

How long has he been here? Alone? Haunted?

Valkrum's childlike innocence, tangled with regret, only adds layers to my growing unease. He is immensely powerful—

Yet so visibly broken.

A reminder of what unchecked power can do. A reminder that even gods can be casualties of war. Part of me wants to back away. To protect myself. But another part—

The part that bonded Lathguard—

Pushes me forward. There's a connection here. A shared history. One terrifying. One tragic. Valkrum pouts, his massive hands resting in his lap. The rage is gone. All that's left is a lonely, forgotten god. And in that moment—

I realize something. We're here to stop the Fog. To save the world. But this? This is more than a mission. This is about recognizing pain in others.

Even those we might consider monsters. Even those we think are beyond saving. I step forward. And—

I reach out. My fingers brush against his massive hand. The surface is metallic, rough like forged steel, but somehow alive. A texture both man-made and natural. "You are my friend," I say softly. "And I am here to protect you."

He stares at me. Then, his eyes drift—

Towards the Fog in the distance. His voice drops to a whisper.

"It eats everything." His massive body shudders. "It will eat Valkrum one day."

He's afraid. I tighten my grip on his hand.

"I'm here to stop it." I let the words sink in before I continue. "But I need my friends' help." I meet his eyes. "I need your help."

Valkrum's face tightens. He chews his lower lip.

"My help?" He looks away. "Valkrum is a bad friend. Valkrum… killed his friends."

"Not all." My voice is gentle. I squeeze his massive fingers. "I'm here." A small smile. "I'm your friend."

His breath hitches. "Y-you are?"

"I am." I nod. "And I need your help."

A long pause. Then—

"Do you need the Syphon?" His voice is small, uncertain.

"I do." I swallow.

"Do you know where it is?"

His massive shoulders hunch. "Yes." He hesitates. "Valkrum threw it down the well."

I blink. "The well?"

He nods. "The Syphon is scary."

His hands tremble. "It connects to the Source. All the Essence you want, without it going through you." His voice drops. "Brodan had Valkrum make it."

He wrings his fingers, as if trying to squeeze the memories away. "He made Valkrum use it." His next words barely escape his lips. "To stop Valkrum's friends… from opening a portal."

My blood runs cold.

"A portal?" Valkrum's entire body tenses. "Valkrum doesn't want to talk about it." His lower lip sticks out. "What do you need it for?" "I need to open a gate."

His eyes widen. Then—

Recognition.

"A gate?"

A slow nod.

"Ohhhh." His voice softens with wonder. "You mean her." A pause. "Yes, Brodan said the good you would set her free."

His tone turns childlike again, almost excited. "You are Valkrum's friend."

A small, exhausted laugh escapes me. "I told you I was." I inhale. "Where is the well?"

Valkrum's eyes dart toward the ruined city. "It's in the center." A deep breath. "After Valkrum used the Syphon… Valkrum threw it away."

"I need to get to it." I keep my voice steady. "Can you show me?"

He bites his lower lip, hesitation written across his giant features.

"Yes… but it's not safe." A shudder. "I hear sounds from the well at night."

His voice drops to a whisper. "Scratching. Biting."

His massive fingers twitch. "Like something is… digging." A deep breath.

"And sometimes… I see light coming up from the well." His body visibly tenses. "And voices." A small, fearful whisper. "They frighten Valkrum."

I turn to Brennen. He knows more about this place than the rest of us. "Do you know what that could be?"

"No," Brennen says, shaking his head. His voice carries a thoughtful edge, as if he's piecing together a puzzle aloud. "There's got to be more here than just those wraiths."

He crosses his arms, his eyes narrowing as he works through the logic. "They can take most physical attacks, but Jerrick took them out too easily. This place kills SoulCasters—that's why no one comes here anymore. Sure, those wraiths could take out a SoulCaster… if there were enough of them." He pauses, considering something, then continues. "Maybe… maybe they drain Essence. If there's enough of them, a SoulCaster might exhaust their reservoir just trying to stay alive."

His gaze shifts toward Valkrum, his brow furrowing. "What else is on this island?"

Valkrum stiffens. For the first time, hesitation clouds his expression. His massive shoulders bunch as he glances toward the Fog in the distance, then back to Brennen. He doesn't speak right away, as if weighing whether or not to answer.

"Valkrum's fire was hot," he finally says, his deep voice quieter than before. "Hotter than Dravion's. Even though his fire was bigger."

His jaw tightens. "Valkrum's fire could melt ore. Shape metal. Make weapons. Valkrum used that fire with the Syphon… to draw even more Essence." His words slow, becoming heavier, like each syllable carries a weight that drags him deeper into his own past. "Valkrum burned up his friends."

The quiet that follows is absolute.

No one breathes.

Valkrum lifts a shaking hand and presses it to his chest, his massive fingers curling into his apron. "It burned up my connection to the Source," he murmurs. "It took part of… me… with it." His voice drops, and for the first time, he sounds small. "Valkrum has never been the same since. Valkrum is always scared."

His breath shudders as he exhales. I can tell that he is concentrating heavily on his words. "It took my mind. It took my power."

I glance at Theron, then Elena. Neither of them speaks. How do you respond to something like that? This is a being that once forged the world itself, and now he's sitting in front of us, broken, afraid of his own past.

Valkrum continues, his voice tightening as if the memory itself is constricting around him. "When it happened—there was an explosion. In here." He taps his chest again, then lets out a bitter laugh. "Essence poured from me… and it changed things."

He lifts his head, his jaw clenching. "There were humans here." A deep, measured breath. "Some of them turned into… scary things. Some animals too. They hunted each other." He shudders. "Most are dead. But not all."

His eyes flick toward the ruins, and a shadow crosses his face. "Some still remain. Others escaped to the mainland." He swallows hard. "They are powerful. They devour anything that comes here."

For the first time since we met him, I see real fear in Valkrum's massive eyes. He looks at me, and his voice barely rises above a whisper. "Valkrum thinks his friend should leave."

I step forward and place a hand on his enormous fingers. They're solid and rough, metal and flesh intertwined, but beneath all that, I can feel a slight tremor.

"You're a good friend," I tell him, giving his fingers a reassuring squeeze. "But we need the Syphon, remember?"

He hesitates. His lips press together, brows pulling tight in conflict. "Oh yeah," he mutters, voice tinged with guilt. "Valkrum forgets a lot."

"Can you show me where it is?"

Another hesitation, then a slow nod. "Yes. But we have to be quick." His body tenses as he glances at the sky. "You don't want to be here at night."

Valkrum rises to his full height. Even after everything, his size still takes my breath away. Each step he takes vibrates through the rock beneath us like a distant earthquake.

Then, before I can even think about it, the words slip from my mouth.

"I'll go down the well alone."

A beat of silence.

Then—

"No!"

Elena and Theron speak in unison, stepping forward.

Theron's voice is sharp. "We can use my vision. I can see things you can't."

Elena tightens her jaw. "If we're attacked, I can heal you."

I shake my head. "I appreciate both of you. But this is my burden to bear."

I take a steadying breath, searching for the right words. "I'll have my shield on the whole time."

"I'll go with you," Brennen interjects.

Theron and Elena glare at him, but he simply shrugs. "I can keep us hidden."

Drusilla folds her arms. "Why can't we all go?"

I exhale, already knowing this will be a fight. "We've made it this far together. We all know I wouldn't have made it here without you." I look each of them in the eyes, letting the weight of my words settle. "But me going down alone is the safest option."

I glance at Brennen. "He knows what my power can do. He knows what happens in tight spaces." My voice hardens. "If there's danger down there—and we all suspect there is—I stand the best chance of surviving it. But not if any of you are with me. I'll hesitate. And that could get us all killed."

Theron steps toward me, his expression hard. "Still not happening. We're better together."

Elena moves closer, placing a hand on his arm. "He's right."

I don't reply, I just stare at them with intensity.

Theron clenches his jaw, exhales sharply, then relents. "Fine. But you have twenty minutes, or I'm coming down after you."

"Understood."

I turn to Valkrum. "Where is this well?"

We follow him through the ruins. The silence is eerie, broken only by the sound of our footsteps on the hard black rock.

In the distance, wraiths watch us. Still. Waiting.

Valkrum rumbles, "Don't worry about them. They are afraid of Valkrum."

Then, we reach it.

The mouth of the well.

No stonework. No rope. No covering.

Just a gaping abyss, waiting.

Theron crosses his arms. "How are you going to see down there?"

I tighten my shoulders and channel a shield of force around me. The energy hums, glowing faintly, illuminating the darkness. Then, I let it drop again.

Turning to Elena, I offer a small smile. "Thank you for believing in me."

Then, before I can stop myself—

I bend down.

And kiss her.

What has gotten into me?

"Be careful," Elena whispers, her arms tightening around me.

I can feel her warmth, the way her breath brushes against my neck. My heart pounds in my chest, an insistent rhythm that drowns out the world for just a moment.

How long have I wanted this?

Why did it take so long?

Before I can linger in the moment, Theron steps forward, wrapping his strong arms around both of us, his voice low.

"Twenty minutes."

I nod. "Twenty minutes."

With a final glance at Elena, I turn, wrap myself in a shield, and step to the edge of the well. The gaping darkness yawns beneath me, its depth unknown, its secrets buried in shadow.

Then, I step over.

The descent is slow, the air thick and still.

Above me, the faint glow of daylight shrinks to a pinprick, swallowed by the black.

The silence here is absolute, broken only by my own breathing and the occasional scrape of my shield against the jagged walls.

Every inch I drop, the air grows denser, heavier, as if pressing against me, testing me. The very atmosphere seems to carry a weight, a presence that whispers at the edges of my mind.

Dust and loose pebbles break free from the rough stone as I descend, rattling down around me before vanishing into the abyss below. I have no idea how deep this well goes, only that I must keep going.

I pass a widening—what was once the original bottom—but I do not stop. A large crack splits through the stone, revealing the path deeper. My shield scrapes along the jagged rock as I slip through, carefully searching for any sign of the Syphon.

Nothing.

Only darkness and the faint, steady drip of water.

The deeper I go, the more I feel the weight of everything.

The choices I've made. The people I've lost.

I tell myself that I'm not the same person I was, that I'm stronger now, that I belong here. But I also know the truth.

I am still afraid.

And maybe that's okay.

Because courage isn't about the absence of fear—it's about what you do in spite of it.

The silence stretches on, pressing against my ears like a suffocating weight.

This place feels forgotten. Left to time and decay.

I should focus, should keep my mind sharp, but my thoughts threaten to spiral. Memories surface—my mother's final scream, the betrayal at the Keep, the moment I turned my back on my father's only chance at freedom.

My chest tightens.

Not now, Jerrick.

Not now.

My voice cuts through the stillness, but there is no reply. Only the echo of my own defiance, fading into the dark.

Then—

A glow.

Faint.

Somewhere far below me.

A trick of the light? My own reflection?

No…

I lower myself further, and as I descend, the glow sharpens. It dances against the wet stone walls, shifting and flickering.

As my feet touch solid ground, I realize I am standing in shallow, flowing water. It brushes over my boots, cool and slow-moving, its current flowing away from me through a narrow opening in the rock.

The smell is overwhelming—the same pungent, decayed scent from the island above, but stronger. It clings to the damp air, making it harder to breathe.

I take a slow step forward, scanning my surroundings.

The cavern is narrow, barely twelve feet across, its walls slick with condensation. Water flows gently downhill, disappearing into a small opening in the shaft's side.

The Syphon has to be here.

I close my eyes for a brief moment, centering myself. I don't know what it looks like, but I trust myself to recognize it when I see it.

I conjure a sphere of force, letting it hover beside me. Its glow is weak, nothing compared to Lyrisa's brilliant light back at the Keep, but it's enough.

I scan the uneven stone, searching.

Nothing.

Not here.

A minute passes. Then two.

If it's not here, then…

I follow the stream.

The shaft narrows.

At first, I only need to duck, but then the walls begin closing in, forcing me into a low crouch. My footfalls echo unnervingly ahead of me, and the air feels stagnant, trapped.

Still, I push forward.

I see a light ahead.

A real light.

Faint, flickering, not like my shield.

I move faster, the passage squeezing around me as I reach the final bend.

Then—

I stop.

Hard.

The tunnel ends.

Water flows past my boots, vanishing through a narrow, six-inch crack in the base of the wall.

Beyond it—

The light shimmers.

At first, I think it's just a reflection. A trick of my shield.

But then—

The glow shifts.

Moves.

The water stills.

The light stabilizes.

And I see—

People.

Figures.

Standing in a vast room beyond the crack.

For a heartbeat, my mind refuses to process what I'm seeing.

They are tall, almost Keeper-like, yet… not.

They lack claws.

Their bodies are covered in strange clothing, different from anything I've ever seen.

They move with purpose, gesturing toward large metal boxes, their hands emphasizing some unseen conversation. The air around them glows unnaturally, bathed in a white radiance that comes from long, hanging tubes of light.

I stare.

They don't see me.

They don't even seem to know I'm here.

I lean closer, straining to hear—

But the crack is too narrow, the sound too muffled.

They are arguing, that much is clear. Their gestures are frustrated, urgent.

And then, without thinking—

I speak.

"Hello?"

One of the figures looks up.

Our eyes lock.

Her expression shifts instantly, from curiosity to alarm.

She gestures wildly to the others, her movements frantic as she points directly at me. Then, she runs forward, her excitement clear—but I flinch back, instinct telling me to retreat.

She pulls something small and metallic from her pocket. It looks like a cube, its surface smooth and strange, with faint etchings glowing along its edges.

She presses something on it.

A faint click.

Then—

Sound.

Their voices fill the space, a sudden flood of words in a language I don't understand. They're talking—fast, urgent, overlapping—their gestures sharp and commanding. Some are pointing at me, others are flipping switches, adjusting knobs on the glowing metal devices that surround them.

They're reacting to me.

It's not just curiosity.

They know who I am.

The realization washes over me like a slow, creeping chill. I can feel it, deep in my gut. It's not rational, not something I can explain, but I know.

They recognize me.

Then, an explosion.

Not from my side of the wall—from theirs.

The room erupts into chaos.

The figures shout in alarm, their heads snapping toward the sound. Smoke and debris billow from somewhere beyond my view. Their movements become frenzied, desperate.

Another explosion rocks the space, shaking their strange metal structures. A section of ceiling collapses, crashing down onto one of them.

The others barely have time to react.

They run—scattering like insects—panic etched across their faces.

The woman with the cube turns back to me, her face taut with urgency. Her hands shake as she presses another button, then another. Her gaze locks onto mine, willing me to understand.

And then—

I hear my name.

"Jerrick."

Her voice is strained, desperate.

"Help us. Don't let the Creator free. Please!"

I freeze.

The words hit me like a physical blow.

Don't let the Creator free?

Go back?

Back where? The Keep? The mainland? What does she mean?

The very core of my mission wavers, just for a moment.

I've spent weeks fighting, running, pushing forward with every fiber of my being to see this through. I've sacrificed, lost, bled, killed— and now, at the bottom of a forgotten well, through a crack in reality, I'm being told…

To stop?

Another explosion rips through their world, drowning out my thoughts. A massive section of wall collapses inward, sending shrapnel flying. The woman jerks around, eyes wide.

Then—

A shadow moves.

Something metallic.

Something inhuman.

A massive arm—silver and black, covered in shifting plates of metal—lashes out, striking the woman hard across the back. She crumples to the ground with a ragged gasp.

My breath catches.

From the gaping hole in their world, it steps forward.

A man made of metal.

It sees me.

And it sneers.

I barely have time to register its shape, the impossible speed of its movement, before the room erupts into carnage.

The metal man lunges, ripping through them like paper.

Limbs are torn free, bodies shattered against walls. The air is thick with the sound of rending flesh, metal grinding against metal, screaming, screaming, screaming—

It doesn't kill like a man.

It disassembles.

Every motion precise, calculating, efficient.

I can't move.

I can't breathe.

The woman coughs.

She lifts her head, blood smeared across her mouth. She's still alive.

She stumbles forward, reaching for me.

"Help us!"

I open my mouth, but—

The metal man is already on her.

"Behind you!" I yell.

She barely turns.

A hand like a vice clamps around her throat, lifting her off the ground like a rag doll.

Then—

She's thrown backward, her body slamming into the console with a sickening crack.

I watch in horror as the metal man turns its attention to me.

Our eyes lock.

It reaches for me—

And then—

Everything blinks out.

The room vanishes.

The figures.

The machines.

The bodies.

All of it—gone.

Except—

The arm.

It lands in the water with a wet slap, severed just below the shoulder. The metal plates are still whirring, twitching, the fingers clenching and unclenching as if searching for something to crush.

I stumble backward, my pulse roaring in my ears.

What just happened?

My gaze snaps downward—

And there, at my feet—

The Syphon.

I don't think.

I snatch it up, turning on my heel, my body already moving, running, fleeing.

My feet pound against the wet stone, the walls of the shaft blurring past me. The water splashes violently as I push forward, my breaths coming in short, gasping bursts.

Everything inside of me screams to get out.

I reach the well.

I don't hesitate.

I launch myself upward, flying fast, my shield humming around me.

The cavern walls rush past, the darkness peeling away as I ascend, back toward the world I know.

My heart hammers.

My mind races.

The woman's plea rings in my head, over and over, an echo I can't shake.

Don't let the Creator free.

Please.

But why?

What am I missing?

What did I just witness?

One thing is certain.

The stakes are far greater than I ever imagined.

Not just our world.

Something bigger.

Something older.

Something that does not want the Creator to return.

And I just made my choice.

The fear that gripped me in the depths morphs into a steely resolve as the well's entrance grows brighter above me, a beacon in the oppressive darkness. I clutch the Syphon tightly, its weight no longer just physical—it's a reminder of the burden now resting on my shoulders.

The woman's words haunt me.

"Don't let the Creator free."

What could it mean?

Why would freeing the Creator spell disaster, as she seemed to imply?

Am I missing something?

The first breath of open air fills my lungs as I break through the mouth of the well, the sudden shift from darkness to light blinding me. For a moment, my senses reel, my body instinctively recoiling from the sheer contrast. The air is crisp, briny with the scent of the sea, carrying the untamed wildness of the island.

I barely register the figures rushing toward me before Elena throws her arms around me, her warmth grounding me, pulling me back to reality.

I'm safe. I made it back.

But my mind doesn't stay here.

It lingers in the well.

In the darkness.

With them.

The ones who begged me to turn back.

As I stand among my friends, their faces mirrors of relief and concern, I know I have to speak.

So, I tell them everything.

Their reactions are immediate.

Theron's brow furrows, his grip tightening on his sword. Drusilla crosses her arms, watching me with an unreadable expression. Brennen listens quietly, his face hard. Elena stays close, her presence solid and unwavering.

But it's Brennen who speaks first, his voice calm, but firm.

"I don't know what you saw down there," he says, eyes locked on mine, "but we are doing the right thing."

Am I?

The question rises unbidden, pressing against my ribs.

I almost say it aloud, but the words catch in my throat. Instead, what comes out is a single, hesitant reply.

"…I know."

Drusilla's gaze sharpens.

"Do you?"

The challenge in her voice cuts through the night like a blade.

I hesitate.

Then, the truth spills out.

"No. Not really." My voice is quieter than I intended.

I look at each of them, letting them see my doubt.

"It's not that I'm questioning my decision. It's just… I don't know what freeing the Creator will actually mean. It has to be better than bringing Lathguard back, but that doesn't mean it's the best thing for any of us. It's just the better of the two choices.

I pause, trying to put the weight in my chest into words.

"I keep wondering… if maybe there's a third option."

Brennen exhales sharply, shaking his head.

"We're lost without her." He gestures around us, around the dying world. "We've been spiraling for over seven hundred years. We've made a mess of everything. We lack direction. There is no better option, Jerrick. We need her guidance."

I hear the conviction in his voice, but I can't ignore the gnawing feeling in my gut.

"Maybe." I admit. "We need guidance, that's for certain. But who's saying it has to be hers? The Creator turned humanity against your people just because you failed to worship her."

For the first time, Brennen's carefully composed mask cracks.

His fist clenches, his voice rising with an anger I've never heard from him before.

"The alternatives are Lathguard or death." His eyes burn into mine. "Actually—just death and death. Is that what you want?"

I sigh.

"Of course not, Brennen. That's not what I'm saying at all."

I step forward, lowering myself to one knee so I can look him in the eye, my hand resting gently on his shoulder.

"I'm not second-guessing my decision to free the Creator," I say, making sure he hears me. "I just think there's a bigger picture we don't fully understand yet. Maybe there's another path. One that isn't dictated by a god."

Something in Brennen shifts.

For the first time, I see doubt in his eyes.

Not doubt in me—but in the certainty of the path he's followed for centuries.

His voice drops to a whisper, just loud enough for me to hear.

"I hear you."

He exhales slowly, his eyes searching mine.

"It's easy for me to follow this path. My people have spent generations working toward this. We've waited lifetimes for the Creator's return. And I forget… humans haven't carried that same burden. I forget… you're still trying to figure this all out."

He doesn't get to finish.

A scream rips through the night.

Not just any scream.

Something inhuman.

Something starving.

The sound is wrong—high-pitched, guttural, hungry.

It makes my blood run cold.

Valkrum shifts uneasily, his massive form tense.

"You must leave this place." His voice trembles, something I never thought I'd hear. "It's almost dark. They… they are coming."

I do not want to see what makes a giant afraid.

I turn to him, giving him a firm nod.

"Thank you for your help, Valkrum." I hesitate, then add, "When this is over, I'll come back and see you."

His massive eyes widen.

"Promise?"

"I promise."

The moment is fleeting, lost to the urgency pressing in around us.

We move—fast, hurried—our footsteps pounding toward the edge of the cliff. The descent looms before us, steep and unforgiving.

Then, an idea strikes.

I grin.

Turning to the others, I spread my arms wide and say, "Who wants to fly down?"

Chapter 17

Jerrick

For the past two days, we've been traveling due north, skirting around Abyssmere Lake before finally making our way to the town of Windthorn. The journey has been surprisingly lighthearted, a stark contrast to what lies ahead. Conversation flows easily, kept deliberately shallow, as if none of us are ready to dive too deep into what awaits us at our final destination—the Rock of Echomire.

I've been there before.

As a child.

Back then, it was nothing more than a tourist destination, a place of wonder wrapped in myth and mystery. The Rock of Echomire is exactly as it sounds—a massive island of sheer stone and labyrinthine caves, a place where voices from the past still whisper through the tunnels, echoing from days long gone. Nobody knows why or how. The echoes can be from a day ago or a century past, repeating words forever captured in time.

Scholars spent lifetimes trying to decipher their meanings.

But now?

Now, the Fog has crept to the island's northern edge, and the echoes are all that remain of the people who once visited.

Brennen walks beside me, his tone thoughtful as he shares the island's deeper history.

"Athel used to live here, back before the split."

His words linger in the cool air, the weight of history pressing down.

"Echomire Island used to be part of the mainland," he continues. "But after the giants banished the Creator, the ground shook for three days and two nights. On the third day, the land cracked. The rock dropped into the sea."

I picture it—a cataclysmic rupture, an entire landmass torn away, as if the earth itself sought to erase what had happened there.

"Nobody knows why," Brennen adds, "and Athel isn't saying. But somehow, the stump transplanted himself to where he is now."

Elena tilts her head, considering. "And that's why the gate is there?"

Brennen nods.

"That's where it happened."

His voice is quiet, but the truth of it rings louder than any echo in those caves.

"That's why the echoes exist," he explains. "A massive amount of Essence was used that day to seal the Creator away. So much, in fact, that it left a scar on the land itself. The caves still drink in whispers of the past. And the gate?" He exhales. "It remains locked by that same Essence, constantly drawing from the Source to keep her imprisoned."

I look down at the Syphon in my hands.

For the hundredth time, I wonder:

How am I even supposed to use this thing?

The Syphon is about three feet long, its surface a strange white metal that looks carved, almost like wood. It's deceptively light, cylindrical, its runes curling around its body in intricate, delicate lines.

It was made by Valkrum, that much I know.

But it was never meant for human hands.

When I grip it, my middle finger just touches my thumb, but I can tell—Valkrum could have held this easily, curling his entire fist around it like a child would a pebble. The sheer size of the forge master's hands makes the delicate carvings all the more impressive.

I run a finger along the etched runes, feeling the grooves beneath my touch.

Did Valkrum carve this with his massive fingers?

Or was it made another way?

Brennen watches me closely.

"Our scholars believe the Syphon works the same way a GodSoul does."

I glance up, waiting for him to elaborate.

"Essence, in its raw form, can't be used to channel," he explains. "It's just inert energy, useless until it's shaped."

I nod. I already know this. SoulCasters like me can only access Essence that's been activated, filtered, through something designed to shape it into a usable form.

That's what a GodSoul does.

It takes raw Essence and transforms it into one specific element—whether that be Force, Fire, Light, Healing, Shadow, Metal, or more.

"That's why Lathguard could only use Force," Brennen continues. "Each giant was bound to a single element. But the Creator?"

He watches my face, letting the weight of his next words settle before speaking them.

"The Creator can use them all."

I freeze.

I grip the Syphon tighter, my heartbeat quicker now.

"…And this?" I hold up the Syphon, studying the runes. "This can do the same?"

Brennen nods. "Those runes mimic the filter needed to harness the true power of raw Essence."

The words hit differently this time.

I turn the Syphon over in my hands, staring at it like I'm seeing it for the first time.

"So, you're telling me…" I begin slowly, "…that whoever holds the Syphon has the power of the Creator?"

Brennen doesn't hesitate.

"That's exactly what I'm saying."

Silence.

The implications settle on my chest like a weight I wasn't prepared to carry.

Brennen keeps his gaze on me, unblinking. "It's overkill for what we need it for," he finally adds. "You just need it to amplify your Force ability—so you can unlock the gate without destroying yourself in the process."

His voice drops. "Without the Syphon… you'd do irreparable harm to your reservoir. You could die."

I swallow hard.

The Syphon feels heavier now.

Not because of its physical weight, but because of what it represents.

Because of what it can do.

Because of what it means if I use it.

And for the first time, a new question enters my mind.

Not how to use it.

Not if I can use it.

But should I?

The weight of what I carry is crushing.

The Syphon hums softly in my grip, but its true weight isn't in its metallic form—it's in what it represents.

The power of a god, resting in my hands.

Would I be able to heal the land without releasing the Creator?

Could I end Rorick and his machinations on my own? Is there another path, one beyond the two I've been given?

And those people I saw in the well—the desperate figures, the woman who pleaded with me—can I save them? Should I?

The questions swirl faster than I can chase them.

Each one tightens the coiling dread in my chest.

This is too much for me.

What if someone takes it from me?

What if I use it for the wrong reasons?

I think of Aethel—even when shattered, the stump could restart time itself. What happens when they're whole? When they're power is fully restored?

And now, in my hands, I hold a relic that grants me that same potential.

A terrifying thought creeps in.

A whisper of temptation, curling around my resolve like a shadow in the dark.

Could I use it to save my father?

Could I bring my mother back?

Eldrin?

Would it be so wrong?

Wouldn't I deserve that much?

"I don't want it."

The words slip out before I fully realize them. The Syphon feels foreign in my grip now, something too dangerous, too consuming.

I push it toward Brennen. "This is too much. If it can create Force, then you don't need me to use it. You take it."

Brennen doesn't move. He watches me carefully, his eyes unreadable. "I can't."

I frown. "Why not?"

"Keepers don't channel Essence. Someone can only use it with a connection to the Source." His voice is calm, but there's a depth to it—a certainty that only fuels my unease.

"Also, it takes more than just Force," he continues. "If it were that simple, the Creator could have broken free on her own. It takes Lathguard's unique signature to unlock it."

He meets my eyes, his gaze steady.

"You're the right choice, Jerrick."

I scoff, my hands tightening around the Syphon.

"What makes you say that?"

Brennen doesn't hesitate.

"Because even though you hold the power of a god in your hands, your first instinct was to give it away."

My breath catches.

I want to argue, to deny the truth in his words, but... he's right.

"What if I lose it?" I press. "Or worse—what if it's taken from me?"

"It won't matter," Brennen replies. "The Syphon can only be used by someone who was given it freely by its previous owner. Valkrum wanted you to have it. Unless you willingly pass it on, no one else can wield its power."

I stare at him. "And how do you know that?"

For the first time, Brennen hesitates.

It's brief, a flicker of something unsaid, but I catch it.

"Valkrum didn't make the Syphon alone," he admits. "He had help." A cold chill runs down my spine. "Who?"

Brennen doesn't blink.

"Who do you think carved those runes into it?"

The truth crashes into me.

"A Keeper."

Brennen nods. "Yes."

He lets it settle, waiting for the implications to sink in.

"My people have been working toward reunification for centuries," he says. "It only makes sense that we had a hand in killing the giants, doesn't it?"

I feel sick.

I look between Brennen and Drusilla, suddenly seeing them in a new light.

The Keepers have always been there—hidden, waiting, pulling the strings just out of sight.

And then it clicks.

How did Rorick find out about the time loop?

Theron was ambushed on his way to the Naming—how, when he had lived this life multiple times before?

How did Rorick get the upper hand?

Why did my mother have to die?

I stop walking.

My pulse pounds in my ears.

Slowly, I turn to Brennen, my voice low, seething.

"It was you, wasn't it?"

Brennen takes a step back.

I see panic flash across his face, his eyes darting toward Drusilla, but she doesn't move.

She doesn't even look surprised.

She just looks bored.

"Wh… what do you mean?"

His voice wavers—not in fear, but in hesitation.

He knows exactly what I mean.

And suddenly, I know the truth.

"Don't lie to me."

My voice is razor-sharp, cutting through the air like a blade. My chest heaves with the effort of keeping my anger contained, but I can feel it boiling beneath the surface, threatening to burst free.

"How did Rorick find out about the time loop? How did everyone know that Theron was my father? Keepers have been manipulating us for centuries. For centuries! Your only goal is to reunite the Stump and the Creator—everything and everyone else be damned!"

My face burns, my fists shake, and my vision tunnels in on Brennen, who stands before me with his jaw set, his shoulders squared.

Did I make the wrong choice?

Did Rorick have it right all along?

Am I taking us all down the wrong path?

Brennen lifts his chin. His voice is firm, but I hear the strain beneath it. "I did what I did for all of us. I did the right thing."

The right thing?

The white-hot rage inside me explodes.

I step forward, fists clenched. "The right thing?" My voice shakes. "Was the right thing getting my mother killed? Is that what you're saying, Brennen? Is it?"

From the corner of my eye, I see Theron tense, like he wants to step between us, but I shake my head, warning him off.

He steps back.

Elena stands beside me, a quiet pillar of support, but she says nothing.

Drusilla still looks bored—or maybe she's just waiting.

Waiting to see how far this goes.

Brennen's head sags.

"No, Jerrick. Of course not." His voice is quieter now, but there's a hardness in it, a justification. He lifts his eyes to Theron, then back to me.

"He's a stubborn man. We begged him to bring you to Echomire, but he wouldn't. You died over and over, and each time, the land grew weaker. Yet, Aethel gave their word—this was the only way. We had to change things up."

He pauses, watching me carefully.

"We got word to Rorick about the time loop."

The ground feels like it shifts beneath me.

"We took a gamble."

He stares into me, unwavering.

"And it paid off. Here we are."

I laugh—a bitter, hollow sound.

"Just like that, huh? 'Here we are.'"

I take another step forward, voice low, but every word drips venom.

"Jerrick, the witless human who watched his mother get murdered and chose this path over his father. Is that the part that 'paid off?'"

Brennen's eyes go wide.

For the first time, he looks afraid.

And I realize that I want him to be.

"I never meant for that to happen," he rushes to say. His voice is urgent now, a mix of fear and sadness. "My intentions were good. We all want the same thing. We want to heal this land. We just disagree on how to go about it."

The anger pulses in my chest, but it's Elena's voice that cuts through it.

Soft. Barely above a whisper. "No matter the consequences?"

Brennen closes his eyes for a brief moment, as if steadying himself.

"If I could change it, I would." He looks at me, his eyes wet. "But we all knew Jerrick was the only way."

Then he says something that cuts deeper than anything else. "You always lacked the fortitude to do what needed to be done."

I freeze.

"We told Rorick because we knew he would come for you. We trusted you enough to see him for what he really was. We figured that would be enough to strengthen your resolve."

He takes a slow breath. "It worked."

I see red.

My anger swells, pressing against my ribs like something alive, something dangerous.

He just admitted it.

He just admitted that my mother's death was acceptable as long as it got me here.

I feel Elena's hand on my arm.

But when I look down… it's not her hand at all.

It's Drusilla's.

She doesn't pull away.

She speaks, her voice softer than I've ever heard it.

"My people have a habit of meddling in the affairs of man."

She finally looks at Brennen, and for the first time, her usual bored amusement is gone.

She's disappointed.

"Even when our desires align," she says, "we still move behind the scenes instead of communicating directly with you."

Her golden eyes flick back to mine, sharp with something that almost looks like regret.

"While we didn't kill your mother, it was our actions that led to it."

The words hit me like a hammer to the chest.

She continues, unwavering. "We can never do enough to equal the pain of losing a parent. But I can give you my word that, as long as I live, my people will try."

I don't know what to say.

I feel betrayed.

I feel furious.

I feel tired.

But I know one thing for certain.

I look at Brennen.

His expression is shame.

Good.

I let the words settle before I finally speak.

"Drusilla, I won't pretend to understand the full weight of the decisions your people have made, nor will I ignore the pain those decisions have caused."

The lump in my throat threatens to choke me, but I swallow it down. "It's clear now, more than ever, that the path we're on is fraught with sacrifices and actions that, from the outside, might seem unforgivable."

I turn my gaze back to Brennen, staring right into him. He looks away. Good.

"Your admission doesn't erase the loss. It doesn't erase the manipulation. But it does shed light on the enormity of our shared burden."

My people killed theirs, yet here they are—willing to work with us.

I let that sink in for a moment, gathering my thoughts, trying to steady the storm inside me.

I glance between Brennen and Drusilla, two Keepers who have played their own parts in shaping my path—one with manipulation, the other with unexpected honesty.

I square my shoulders and speak, voice steady.

"But here, at this crossroads, I choose to focus on what lies ahead."

The words come naturally, yet they feel like they belong to someone stronger than me, someone I want to become. I gesture toward Brennen, then Drusilla, acknowledging them both.

"We're entangled in this together, and it's my plan to see it through."

I turn back to Brennen, locking eyes with him.

"I…"

I hesitate.

For the briefest moment, I see her—my mother—and wonder what she would say.

What would she want me to do?

And then, I know.

I take a slow breath and steady myself.

"I forgive you."

Brennen flinches, as if I'd struck him.

His mouth opens slightly, but he doesn't speak.

"When this is done, you and I need a long talk."

His only response is a small nod, barely perceptible, as if he's afraid that any more movement might shatter whatever fragile bridge remains between us.

Then, I turn to Drusilla. Her golden eyes meet mine, sharp, searching. I match her intensity. "I'll hold on to your word, Drusilla."

She doesn't blink.

She doesn't look away.

And so, I continue.

"Not as a promise for retribution or a remedy for past wounds, but as a beacon—guiding us toward a future where such decisions no longer weigh us down."

I take a slow breath, making sure they all hear me.

"Where we—all of us—can move beyond the shadows of manipulation and sacrifice. Let's not allow the past to dictate our future any longer. We have a land to save. And we can only do it together."

A silence settles over the group, thick and heavy—not awkward, not tense, but charged.

I can feel their eyes on me.

Are they as shocked as I am by what I just said?

Because I meant every word.

Yet, despite it all, the pain remains.

I'm hurting.

I trusted Brennen.

Even if we haven't known each other long, I trusted him.

I stand behind my choice, but I know now—I will never trust him the same way again.

Then, Theron steps forward.

He places a heavy hand on my shoulder, his grip firm, grounding.

"I'm proud of you, son."

His voice is warm, filled with something I haven't heard from him before—a father's pride.

"That took a lot of courage. Not sure if I could have done that."

Elena nods, her eyes soft.

"I agree." She gives me a small smile. "You've really grown a lot in the last couple of months."

Drusilla tilts her head, watching me with something close to admiration. "I couldn't have said that and meant it." She pauses, then adds softly—

"Thank you."

I turn my gaze back to Brennen.

His lips are tight, his eyes downcast, shifting as if he's searching for the right words but coming up empty.

Finally, he shuffles forward, closing the space between us. "I won't apologize for doing what needed to be done to get you here."

I feel Elena stiffen beside me. Theron's jaw tightens. Even Drusilla narrows her eyes slightly. But Brennen isn't done.

His voice lowers.

Softer.

Almost pleading.

"But…" he swallows, as if the words are hard to say. "I will say that if I had known your mother would be killed, I would have found another way."

His eyes lift to mine, hesitant. "For that, I will be forever sorry."

I take a long, steadying breath.

And then I say the words that I know will stay with him forever.

"I said I forgive you, Brennen. But I don't think I'll ever be able to trust you again."

The words hit their mark.

Brennen flinches, his face twisting for a brief second into something pained, raw. Then, just as quickly, he shuts it down. He nods once, looking away. "I understand."

I should feel relief, but instead, I feel heavier than before.

I have no more space left to push things down.

I feel as if I'm about to burst from the inside.

Each step I take, my guilt threatens to crush me.

But I had to forgive him.

Not for him.

For me.

If I hadn't, the weight of it would have kept me from taking even one more step forward.

Now…

If I could just forgive myself.

That's the real test.

#

We boarded another fishing vessel, nearly identical to the last, helmed by a man who looked just as worn by the sea and time as the one before him.

It was a mirror of the past, yet everything was different.

The island, like Shardmount, loomed ahead, but unlike its jagged, forsaken twin, this place wasn't infamous for death.

It was smaller, a massive rock crowned by a sparse jungle, its labyrinth of caves stretching through the stone like veins in a dying body.

I've been here before.

Not all over, but enough to know its face—yet I found myself puzzling over one question.

Where is the gate?

As if reading my mind, Brennen answered in a voice that lacked its usual passion, as if repeating something he'd said a thousand times before.

"The gate isn't physical."

I looked at him.

His big, sad eyes barely met mine.

His voice was mechanical, hollow.

"It's more of a hole in our world—one that leads to another. The only way to find it is to use force to reveal it. Once it's visible, you'll have to use the Syphon to channel enough Essence to break the seal."

Elena's voice cut through the tension.

"Wouldn't that send those creatures after us?"

Brennen nodded.

"Yes, so we'll have to be quick. From what I've researched, the gate should be near the island's center."

He swallowed hard, forcing himself to continue.

"Jerrick, you should be able to send out small pulses of force, but your range will be limited. Theron can channel without worry because his Essence use is so low that the creatures don't sense him unless they're already close."

I exhaled sharply.

"Understood."

That was all I said.

We sailed in silence.

When the captain finally called for anchor, his crew lowered a smaller boat into the water, and just like before, Theron and I took up the oars.

But this time, there was a pier.

The island looked exactly as I remembered it—rocky but lined with well-worn paths for hikers, fishermen, and tourists.

The air was crisp, fresh—a welcome contrast to the stench of Shardmount.

Yet, something wasn't right.

It was too quiet.

The absence of life was almost louder than the howling winds of Shardmount.

No birds.

No rustling leaves.

No distant murmur of travelers.

Just silence.

Theron's low, commanding voice broke through the eerie stillness.

"We go inland."

His hand rested on the hilt of his sword.

"Toward the center. If the gate isn't there, we'll work our way out."

I nodded.

My fingers curled around the Syphon, the weight of it unnatural in my grasp.

Brennen met my gaze.

His voice was firm, but lacking its usual certainty.

"When Jerrick channels, we need to be careful. I'll keep us hidden when he does."

Theron nodded in silent agreement, and with that, we pressed forward.

Each step felt heavier than the last.

The closer we got, the more I could feel the weight of expectation pressing down on my chest.

My hands trembled at my sides.

We're almost done.

Yet, something felt off.

This is too easy.

I wanted easy.

I needed easy.

But something inside me whispered:

It won't be.

I clenched my fists, trying to still the shaking.

Get a hold of yourself, Jerrick.

You can break down later.

Not now.

Not here.

You have a job to do.

A gentle hand slipped into mine.

I turned.

Elena's eyes searched my face, her concern unspoken but unmistakable.

"Are you okay?"

I forced a smile—small, weak.

"I will be."

She didn't look convinced.

"I'm just… thinking about my mom. You know me. Always in my head."

I let out a pathetic laugh, shifting my hands behind my back— hiding the tremors.

Elena didn't press.

Instead, she simply squeezed my hand tighter.

"When this is done, we'll do it right."

Her voice was soft, certain.

"We'll hold a remembrance for her."

She always knew what to say.

I swallowed hard, nodding.

"I'd like that."

I hesitated, then added—

"But first, I'm heading to the Keep to get my father, if they haven't—"

I never got to finish.

Theron went rigid.

His voice was low, sharp.

"Down."

My breath caught.

"There are a dozen SoulCasters just around the bend."

His gritted teeth made his words barely audible.

"And about three times as many guards waiting for us."

My heart pounded.

My lungs burned, like they'd forgotten how to work.

I remember playing here as a child.

I know these caves.

I know how they connect.

A realization snapped into place.

I barely breathed the words—

"We should go underground."

Theron's eyes flicked to mine, and in a single moment, he understood.

I continued quickly, voice low.

"These caves are marked. We can use them to get around them."

A slow nod.

Then, he motioned for me to take the lead.

We backtracked.

Took another path.

One I knew.

One I used to love.

The mouth of the cave yawned before us. Massive. Like a gaping wound in the earth, stretching thirty feet wide, twenty feet tall.

I knew this place.

This was my favorite cave as a child.

Just inside was a large, glassy pool of water, where I once swam without fear.

Now, the water was still.

The air felt different.

I swallowed hard.

The past and present blurred together.

This island—my childhood refuge—was about to become something else entirely.

When we enter the cave, Theron takes the lead, grabbing Brennen's hand. Elena takes his other. I grab hers. Drusilla grips mine last. A fragile chain of trust, each of us tethered together, stepping into the abyss.

Instantly, the darkness consumes us.

The cave swallows all light, thick and oppressive, like stepping into a void. No light, no sky, no horizon—just blackness.

There used to be Essence lamps lining these tunnels, guiding explorers, tourists, children like me who once played here without fear. Now, only shadows remain.

"I see light up ahead," Theron whispers. His voice barely carries in the thick air. "Looks like… glowing cracks in the stone?"

I swallow, forcing my voice steady. "Veins of Essence. They're all over."

And then—

You can't do this!

The words slam into the cavern walls, crashing over us like a sudden storm.

A voice, a man's voice.

They are coming, and you won't survive without me!

This time, it's a woman.

The echoes shake the stone around us. Not just noise. Not just a trick. This is different. This is real.

We knew the voices would come. We expected them. But knowing does nothing to prepare us for the suddenness of it, for the way the words seem to claw at the back of my mind.

We press forward, but our footsteps are cautious now.

Turn back! Turn back! Turn back!

A new voice, frantic, repeating itself in waves.

But something is… wrong.

The voice changes mid-echo, twisting, reshaping— becoming something else entirely.

"Jerrick, run!"

My stomach lurches.

No.

"Jerrick, please! RUN!"

Not here. Not now.

The cave isn't just repeating the past. It's repeating mine.

"Don't let them take you."

My mother's voice.

No.

I clench my fists, but it's too late. The memories surge forward, dragging me back—

The Naming.

The knife.

Her eyes locking on mine.

The silent plea.

The choking gasp.

The way her body jerked, then sagged.

The blood.

The moment everything in my world was torn away.

And what had I done?

Nothing.

Nothing.

Nothing.

Nothing.

"Jerrick, move!"

Theron's voice this time. Urgent. Commanding.

But I can't move. I can't breathe.

The weight of everything crashes over me all at once. Then I hear the growls; the nails scratching on stone. It sounds like there are dozens of them.

I brought us to this cave. I did this.

Now here we are, standing at the edge of death, because I thought we could hide, because I thought we could outmaneuver them.

I have killed us.

"Jerrick, are you okay?"

A hand tugs hard on my arm.

Elena.

Her voice is frantic, desperate—but real.

Not an echo.

Not a memory.

Reality slams back into me. The cavern. The others.

The creature.

The growl builds.

A low, throaty vibration that rattles my bones.

Then, from behind us, a screech.

A sound that makes every hair on my body stand on end.

We turn just in time to see it emerge from the darkness—

A monstrosity of flesh and bone, wood and stone, twisted together in a grotesque mockery of life.

A wolf's face, but wrong.

Too long. Too many teeth.

Red flame burns in the pits of its skull, not eyes, but something worse. Something hungry.

It scrapes against the walls, claws dragging, sending up sparks.

The tail of a tree trunk, swinging wildly, splintering stone.

It moves toward us.

It remembers me.

Because I've seen it before.

In a dream.

This is where we die.

"Run!" Theron yells.

But the word doesn't make sense anymore.

The cave has already whispered my fate.

I am frozen, drowning in a sea of grief and guilt.

"Move, damn you!" Theron roars.

Something claws inside me, screaming for me to break free.

But the voices in the cave hold me still.

I stood frozen before. I watched my mother die.

And now, I am doing it again.

Letting them die.

Letting it happen.

Again. Again. Again.

Elena's grip tightens.

"Jerrick, please!"

The desperation in her voice cuts through me.

This is different.

I am not that boy anymore.

I am not helpless.

I will not stand here and watch them die.

I force a breath into my burning lungs.

My hands stop shaking.

My vision clears.

And then—

I move.

I shake my head hard, trying to banish the weight of my guilt, but it clings like a parasite, digging into my ribs, poisoning my thoughts. My throat is dry, my voice almost gone.

"*Yes,*" I croak, but the word feels empty.

Ahead of me, Theron is fighting for his life.

The creature attacks in a frenzy— snapping jaws, clawed hands, a whipping tail that cracks against the cavern walls, sending shards of stone flying. Theron moves like liquid steel, a dance of precision and brute force. He dodges in inches, counterstrikes in moments. A master of war.

But this is not just another fight.

Not just another battle he'll walk away from.

Drusilla lunges in, blades flashing. I flinch as she moves—a blur of strikes, in and out, like a shadow. But the creature doesn't even seem to notice. It's fixated on Theron.

I feel useless.

I can't channel—not here, not now. Not without bringing more of them.

My bow.

I fumble for it, hands shaking. Draw. Tighten. Knock. Breathe.

I let the arrow fly.

The shaft punches through the creature's eye socket, sinking deep. It screams— a sound so terrible my bones vibrate with it. The red flames of its ruined eye flicker, and for a heartbeat, I think we've turned the tide.

Theron seizes the moment. He lifts his sword high, arcs it down in a blow that would cleave a man in two. Steel bites deep into sinew and muscle.

Drusilla presses in, relentless.

But then—

The creature stops.

Still.

Too still.

Then its massive clawed hand reaches up.

And it rips the arrow from its skull.

Its ruined flesh pulls itself back together.

The fire in its eye burns anew.

And I know—we can't win.

"Jerrick."

I turn to Brennen.

He's looking at me. Really looking at me.

And his voice breaks.

"We have to go. Your life before ours."

I freeze.

Elena steps closer, her eyes shimmering with sorrow.

"Go, Jerrick. Your life before ours."

No.

The guilt chokes me.

I can't leave them.

Even thinking about running makes me sick.

I force myself to turn back—

Just in time to see Theron take the hit.

The tail whips around— a blur of force, unstoppable.

Crack.

Theron's body folds in half.

His ribs explode outward, bones jutting from his torn flesh like broken branches. His roar drowns out all other sounds, but still—

He tries to rise.

The creature spins.

Drusilla attacks.

Fast. Too fast for me to even follow.

She moves like a wraith. A flurry of blades and motion— dodging, striking, slipping through its defenses.

But it learns.

It adapts.

It moves in a sudden, terrifying burst—

Claws rake the air.

Drusilla jerks back— not far enough.

It clamps its jaws around her midsection.

Bites down.

Her torso separates.

Her legs hit the ground first.

The top half of her body follows a second later.

Her lifeless arms twitch.

The cavern goes silent.

"Nooooo!"

Brennen's wail shreds through me like a knife.

Elena steps forward, hands raised, her eyes locked on Theron's broken body.

Healing light gathers.

The creature turns.

And it sees her.

Everything slows.

"Elena, no."

It lunges.

One single, size-defying leap.

The claws carve through her.

Cleaving her in half.

Not just in half.

In pieces.

Her torso lands at my feet.

Her dead eyes stare up at me.

Why didn't you act?

Why didn't you act?!

She's dead because of you.

Just. Like. Your. Mother.

I gasp.

My stomach twists.

My vision blurs.

The air vanishes from my lungs.

Drusilla is dead.

Elena is dead.

I could have stopped it.

I should have stopped it.

"...NOW!"

I blink.

Once.

Twice.

Everything around me slows, the edges of reality softening, distorting, as if my mind refuses to process what it sees.

I hear the creature turning away from me, as if I no longer exist.

I glance down.

Brennen. His face is set, resolute, his small hands trembling as they clutch at my sleeve.

"We have to go now!" His voice is urgent, but there's a fragility underneath.

He doesn't think I'll move.

He's right.

I look up.

Theron is still fighting.

Bleeding.

Dying.

Elena's healing had barely begun before her life was torn from her.

I see the wound still gaping at his side, the ripped flesh, the dripping blood, the labored, gasping breaths as he tries to stay upright.

I should help him.

I should.

But I just stand there.

Watching.

Then, Theron falls.

The cavern rings with the sound of his body hitting the stone.

Lifeless.

Broken.

Next to him—Drusilla's remains.

Gone.

All of them.

Gone.

The creature sniffs the air.

It turns.

It sees me.

It charges.

I react.

A blast of force.

It hits. Dead center.

It knocks the creature back.

It doesn't fall.

It doesn't stop.

It doesn't even slow.

It reaches me.

Claws stretch wide.

Jaws snap.

Teeth bared.

I throw my shield up at the last second.

Slamming.

Tearing.

Scratching.
It rips at me.
Bites me.
Snarls.
It wants me dead.
Next to me, Elena's severed torso lays in the dirt.
Her eyes—
Empty.
Fixed on me.
Staring.
Accusing.
I had the power to stop this.
I had the power all along.
But I hesitated.
And now?
Now she's gone.
Just like my mother.
Oh, Mother.
I hear her voice.
"Run, Jerrick!"
No.
No, that's not real.
"Jerrick, please!"
Stop.
"Jerrick, do something!"
I scream.
My anger boils.
Surges.
Burns hotter than my grief.
It fills me.
Feeds me.
I let it.
I look up.
The creature is still clawing.
Still biting.
Still trying to take me.
But it won't.

It can't.
I won't let it.
I create a box of force around the beast.
Its jaws snap at the invisible walls.
It thrashes, howls, screeches—
But it can't escape.
Slowly—
So. Slowly.
I tighten the box.
Squeeze.
It wails.
It thrashes.
Bones snap.
Flesh buckles.
I don't stop.
It folds.
It crushes.
It implodes.
I let it go.
Nothing remains.
Not even a body.
Just black ichor and dust.
I drop to my knees.
And I sob.
Not the quiet kind.
Not the kind you can hold back.
Loud. Unrestrained. Violent.
The kind that tears out of you in raw, broken gasps.
I cry for my mother.
I cry for my father.
For Theron.
For Drusilla.
For Eldrin.
For Elena.
For Abby.
For the future she'll never have.
But most of all—

I cry for me.
Because I had the strength all along.
And it still wasn't enough.
The creatures come.
Dozens.
Maybe hundreds.
They snarl and claw, gnash their teeth.
They want my blood.
They bite at my shield.
But they can't get through.
Nobody can.
Nobody is stronger than I am.
And yet—
What does it matter?
Everyone I love is dead.
What future do I have?
What future does anyone have?
Maybe it's better if I'm not in it.
I exhale.
And I let go.
My shield drops.
The monsters rush in.
I welcome it.
Pain blossoms.
Bites. Claws. Teeth.
My vision fades.
The cavern melts away.
Darkness takes me.
And I do not fight it.

Chapter 18

Jerrick

I step out of the ceremony hall, the heavy doors creaking shut behind me.

The air is cold, biting at my skin—a stark contrast to the stifling, suffocating weight of the hall.

I don't realize how deeply I've been holding my breath until I exhale, my chest loosening as I take in the empty streets stretching ahead.

Unbonded.

The word clangs inside my skull like a dull, rusted bell.

I should feel defeated.

I should feel the shame, the weight, the finality of it.

But I don't.

Something else is gnawing at me, crawling under my skin like an itch I can't scratch. Something feels off. The city is eerily quiet.

I know why—it's been under lockdown for days, the Council ordering people to stay inside because of the tear.

And yet… I expected quiet, but not like this.

Not this unnatural stillness, this *absence* of sound.

I feel like I've walked into a place that has already died.

Instinctively, my gaze lifts.

The scar in the sky stretches above me, vast and terrifying, just as it always has.

A jagged wound, torn open by unseen hands.

I've looked at it a hundred times before. But this time—

Something is wrong.

Suddenly, pain rips through my skull.

A white-hot dagger of agony burrows into the back of my head, twisting, burning.

My legs buckle.

I collapse to my knees, gasping, clutching at my skull as if I can force the pain out of me.

A roar builds in my ears—a rising tide of something vast and terrible, a memory not my own but entirely mine.

Then—

Everything shatters.

Flashes.

A blade against my mother's throat.

The Keep, burning.

Little Abby's lifeless eyes.

Elena, reaching for me, her body torn apart.

Theron, broken and bleeding, calling my name.

I see everything.

Every failure.

Every death.

Every moment I stood powerless.

And then—

I remember.

My breath hitches, a ragged sound that barely escapes my throat.

I remember.

The time loop. The sacrifices. The hopeless fight.

I died.

Didn't I?

I remember the moment—

The creatures descending on me.

Tearing me apart.

I remember letting go.

I remember welcoming the end.

But I am here.

I am alive.

A voice erupts in my mind, a thunderous bellow that nearly crushes me.

NOOOOOO!

It shakes my bones, rattles my soul.

Why am I back here?! What are you doing, boy?!

Lathguard.

The voice of the beast that has haunted me, the shadow I have lived under—snarling, seething, enraged. And I—

I am not afraid.

I look up at the cascading Fog, pouring from the tear in the sky like a waterfall, unstoppable and endless.

The end.

That's what this was supposed to be.

But I am here.

I have another chance.

This time—

I will not fail.

I rise to my feet, slowly, my breath steady.

Lathguard rages inside my head, clawing at my thoughts, but I push him aside like an afterthought.

"What I should have done before," I whisper, my voice shaking not with fear, but with power.

"You will never walk this land again."

I channel.

A shield bursts around me as I launch into the air, the ground splintering beneath me from the force of my takeoff.

In seconds, I crash down in front of the courtyard, hard enough to shake the stone.

The guards flinch, their hands instinctively reaching for weapons.

I don't slow.

I don't stop.

I don't hesitate.

"Move."

One word.

They obey.

I tear through the courtyard, past stunned faces, through the back gate.

The door slams open.

I see them.

Two men.

One with a knife and a scar.

One with a stupid grin.

My mother—captive between them.

Just like before.

But this time—

I act.

The man with the stupid grin barely blinks before my arrow takes him in the chest.

The impact drives him back, his face frozen in stunned confusion before he crumples, lifeless.

The scarred man stumbles, turning—

A blast of force slams into him, hurling him back against the stone wall.

His head collides with a sickening crack.

He slides down, limp.

Dead.

For the first time in all of my lives—

I did not hesitate.

I acted.

I saved her.

I turn, chest heaving, breath coming fast, my hands trembling.

And I see her—

My mother.

Alive.

Alive.

Her eyes are wide, her lips parted, staring at me as if she can't believe what just happened.

And I—

I refuse to let her die again.

"Jerrick," my mother gasps.

Hearing her voice—alive, whole, unbroken—sends something inside me shattering.

She shouldn't be here.

She should be dead.

Her throat should be cut, her blood soaking the ground while I stand there, too weak to stop it.

But she's not.

She's here, and I—

I saved her.

I collapse into her arms, my body shaking, my breath coming in ragged, gasping sobs.

"Mom," I choke, clutching onto her like she might slip away if I let go. "I'm so sorry. I'm so sorry that I let you down."

She's stiff, startled—just for a moment.

Then she melts against me, arms tight around my back, like she's holding together something she doesn't even realize has been broken for so long.

"Oh, Jerrick." Her voice trembles, full of warmth, full of the love I thought I'd never hear again. "You could never disappoint me."

I try to hold onto the moment, burn it into my mind, but the urgency gnaws at my heels.

"Where's Dad?" I ask, desperate to lay eyes on him.

"They locked him in the back room," she says, her voice steadier now. "He wouldn't calm down. He kept trying to fight them."

Despite everything, I laugh, a wet, half-broken sound. "Sounds like Dad."

I don't waste another second.

I move toward the door, place my hand against the handle—locked.

A simple thing.

But nothing can stop me now.

I channel, grip the frame, and rip the door free as if it were nothing more than a loose board in my path.

I set it aside just as my father bursts out, pipe in hand, his eyes wild and full of fight—

Then he sees me.

He sees Mom.

He sees the two dead men sprawled on the ground.

His grip on the pipe loosens, his stance stiffens.

He lifts his brows. "Your handiwork?"

I nod, unable to force words past the lump in my throat.

Then he moves.

Wraps me in a crushing embrace, his arms strong, solid, real—

And Mom joins us, surrounding me in the only thing that has ever felt safe.

For a fleeting, precious moment—nothing else exists.

Not the Fog, not the battle ahead, not the terrible fate I left behind.

It's just us.

Just like it's always been.

A warmth spreads through me, not from magic, not from power—but from them.

From the love they have always given me.

From the foundation of who I am.

For a brief, blissful second, I let it hold me together.

Then Mom pulls away, studying me, her eyes searching—

"You're different somehow."

Her voice is quiet, but there's something heavy in her tone.

Like she's looking at me and seeing not just her son, but something more.

"It's as if a lifetime has passed since we saw you just a few hours ago."

I swallow hard.

Because she's right.

Because it has.

I square my shoulders, steel myself.

"I don't have time to explain," I tell her. "But I can end this. I can put things right."

Dad places a steadying hand on my arm.

"You found your destiny, didn't you?"

I nod.

And for the first time in so long, I know it's true.

I have never been more certain of anything.

The weight is still there—but now I know how to carry it.

I see the path laid before me.

I know what must be done.

"I love you both," I say, voice thick, heavy with the truth of it.

One by one, I meet their eyes.

"There hasn't been one day—not one—that I haven't been thankful for you. For the life you gave me.

Even when I got lost, even when I doubted myself… I found my way back.

And I'll forever be grateful that you're my parents."

Mom sobs, her shoulders shaking, her hands gripping my arms like she can anchor me here.

"Why does this sound like a goodbye?"

I can't lie to her.

Not now.

Not after everything.

I know now, more than ever, the importance of closure.

"What I must do to end the decay, to push back the Fog…" I swallow, forcing my voice to steady. "…it may cost me everything."

"Why you?" Mom's voice cracks, like she's trying to hold back something breaking apart inside her.

"Why must it be you?"

"Because it's always been my burden to bear," I say softly.

I don't flinch from it.

I don't fight it anymore.

I have accepted it.

Embraced it.

"I'm bonded with Lathguard. His bond is the key to everything. And I'm the only one who can use it to unlock the gate."

Dad looks at me, his strong hands trembling at his sides.

His eyes shine with unshed tears—tears I have never seen my father cry.

Then he nods, slow, deliberate.

"If it's what needs to be done," he says, voice thick with emotion, "and you feel—truly feel—that it has to be you… Then what more is there to say?"

He steps forward and places his hands on my shoulders, gripping tight.

"We love you, son."

His voice is steady now, as sure as I've ever heard it.

"We knew, from the moment you were placed in our arms, that you would do great things."

And just for a second—

I let myself be their son.

Not the bonded warrior, not the one who will change the fate of the world—

Just their son.

I breathe it in.

I hold on to it.

Because when I walk away—

I may never have this again.

"Your father and I are lucky to have you."

My mother's voice is soft but unshakable, each word sinking deep into my chest, settling in places I didn't realize were hollow.

"You're kind and loving. You're a hard worker and considerate. You're everything a parent could hope for, and more."

Tears spill freely down my cheeks, but I make no effort to wipe them away. For the first time, I allow myself to feel it—the love, the gratitude, the unbearable weight of goodbye.

Then I see it.

A shift in my father's face, his eyes going wide, looking past me.

I turn, pulse quickening—

And there they are.

Elena. Theron. And Branik.

Elena's eyes are red-rimmed, glossy with tears, and when she speaks, her voice is as fragile as a breath.

"We thought you'd be here."

I don't know what I expected her to say, but it wasn't that.

The guilt churns, twisting inside me, because I know what I have to do, but I also know what it will cost her.

I open my mouth, but only one sentence makes it past the tightness in my throat.

"I'm sorry that I wasn't enough."

Before I can say another word, she runs to me.

She throws her arms around me, pressing herself so close it's like she's trying to become part of me, to hold me together before I shatter completely.

"You've always been enough."

Her voice breaks—and so do I.

My knees almost buckle under the weight of her forgiveness.

After a long moment, she pulls away, wiping at her face.

She looks over her shoulder at Branik, eyes pleading.

"I found him and Theron on the way here," she says, sniffing. "He says he'll look after your parents."

I nod, swallowing hard, but before I can speak, my father's voice cuts in, sharp and indignant.

"Who says we need looking after?"

His tone is gruff, but I can hear the emotion straining beneath it.

I chuckle despite everything. "Nobody, Dad. It'll just make me feel better."

I turn to Theron.

He's staring at me, unreadable, arms crossed over his chest like he's trying to hold himself in check.

I take a step forward, then another—

And then I embrace him.

"I lost myself somewhere along the way," I whisper, voice low, raw. "Maybe I never knew who I was. Maybe I've always been lost. Whatever happened before, it doesn't matter. I'm here now. I'm your son. And this—all of this—ends today."

His body is rigid, a stone wall I can't break through—

Until, slowly, he softens.

His arms come up, and he holds me back.

Acknowledgment. Acceptance.

His voice is gruff when he finally speaks. "We don't have a lot of time. We need to get the Syphon and then—"

"There isn't time for that."

They all stiffen at my words.

Theron's brows draw together. "What do you mean?"

"The Fog was already touching Echomire before things reset," I explain. "With how fast it's pouring in now, we don't have time to retrieve the Syphon. We leave now."

Theron's lips part, eyes narrowing.

"But that means you'll—"

I cut him off.

"I already did. This time, I'll make it count."

"So, you've decided then?"

Elena's voice is barely above a whisper.

Her nose is red, cheeks damp, but her eyes—

Gods, her eyes.

She already knows what I'm going to say.

She just doesn't want to hear it.

I take a shaky breath. "I have. But don't think it was easy."

Her lip trembles.

I reach for her hand, hold it tight.

"I've loved you for years, Elena. I never thought I'd be telling you that. I was too afraid to act on my feelings, but not anymore."

I shake my head.

"If I don't do this, we all die. If I do it, only…"

She doesn't let me finish.

Her fingers press against my lips, silencing me.

Her tear-filled eyes search mine, pleading.

"Don't say it, Jerrick. You don't know that. It's not for certain."

She's wrong.

She knows she's wrong.

But I let her believe it anyway.

Then I do what I should have done long ago.

I kiss her.

Not a fleeting touch like before.

Not something half-hearted or hesitant.

I kiss her like this is the last chance I'll ever have.

Because it is.

She clings to me, pouring everything into it—hope, grief, desperation—like she can make me stay if she just holds on tight enough.

But we both know—

She can't.

I pull back just enough to rest my forehead against hers.

"If there is any way—any way at all—then we will be together."

She nods, biting her trembling lip.

I brush away a stray tear with my thumb.

"I don't want to die, Elena. But I'm ready to. For you. For them."

Her breath catches.

I step back.

She lets me go.

I turn toward my parents.

Their faces are etched with fear and love—a fragile, trembling mixture of hope and devastation.

They want to believe in me.

But they also know they can't stop me.

I meet their gaze, memorizing their faces.

One last time.

I won't let you down again.

I promise.

With each step away, the past peels away behind me—

The farm. The village. The boy I used to be.

All of it.

Gone.

There is no turning back.

Only forward.

I turn to Theron and Elena, offering them a small, knowing smile.

"Are you ready to fly?"

I don't wait for an answer.

I wrap us all in a shield, channeling with a force I've never wielded before.

And then, in a rush of air and Essence, We soar into the sky.

#

Theron

It takes a moment to adjust after the way Jerrick hurled us into the sky. My balance wavers, but the exhilaration of flight quickly overrides the disorientation. The land stretches below, broken and beaten, a world on its last breath. With my specialized vision, I see beyond the surface—deep into the veins of a dying earth, into the creeping rot that has claimed too much. But what strikes me more than the decaying world is the man flying beside me.

I don't recognize the boy I met all those lifetimes ago.

The Jerrick I knew—hesitant, unsure, plagued by doubt—is gone. In his place is someone forged in fire and failure, a man who understands what must be done and has accepted the weight of it. And it's *weighty*.

This isn't a fool's bravado. It isn't reckless determination or blind courage. *He knows*. He knows exactly what he's walking into, what it will cost him, and he's still *choosing* it. That is the greatest strength I've ever seen.

The sky above us is a monument to the fact that we are out of time. There are no creatures hunting us. No dark forces crawling from the shadows. The land itself has given up, resigned to its fate. And in a way, *so has Jerrick*.

But not out of surrender.

Out of hope.

He is going forward not because he expects to survive—but because he refuses *not* to act. He refuses to let fear or pain or loss keep him from doing what is right. And that… *that* is something rare. I've seen men with strength. I've seen warriors with the will to fight. But strength without the courage to use it for something greater than oneself? That's just *emptiness*.

But my son—

My son—

He is something different.

I wish I could say that fills me with peace, but it doesn't. Because as I watch him, as I see the way his jaw is set, the calm finality in his expression, a part of me is already mourning him. A part of me knows.

And I am terrified.

Not just for him.

For myself.

Jerrick has always been my tether—whether he knew it or not. He has been the single thing keeping me from slipping completely into the abyss. Every kill, every sin, every sacrifice I've made—I told myself it was for him. I let myself believe that one day, I would stand beside him and call myself his father. That he would see me and not just the ghost of a man he never knew.

But if he dies?

What am I then?

What kind of monster do I become?

I swallow back the fear, push it *down*. Now isn't the time for weakness. I look at Jerrick again. He is calm, unshaken, focused. Power hums around him like a storm barely contained, his presence vibrating with raw force.

I almost feel sorry for anyone standing in his way.

Jerrick is *terrifying* now—not because of his power, but because of the *man who wields it*. He is capable of destruction on a scale I can barely comprehend, but he wields that power with care, with precision, with a morality that would have crumbled in lesser men. I would fear anyone else with a reservoir dense enough to bond Lathguard.

But I do not fear my son.

I *admire* him.

And it crushes me that I have to let him go.

I used to think Jerrick was the best thing I had ever done. But I was wrong. The best thing I did was stepping aside and letting Thom and Abigail raise him. He is who he is because of them. Not me.

Yet, that doesn't stop me from feeling a pride so overwhelming that it nearly undoes me.

He looks almost… happy.

Jerrick, the boy who always second-guessed himself, the one who struggled to find his place, is finally found. He knows exactly who he is and what he must do.

And I hate it.

Because it means I have to let him go.

The island comes into view far too quickly. I wish for more time, just a little more, but fate is merciless. *This is it.*

Jerrick lands where we docked before, shields still wrapped around us. His voice cuts through the air like steel.

"Did you see them?"

"Yes," I answer. "At least fifteen SoulCasters. They brought even more this time. And twice as many guards. They're looking for a fight."

"Do we go back into the caves?" Elena asks, her voice small, barely more than a whisper.

Jerrick doesn't even hesitate.

"No," he says. "I go through them."

Something in the air shifts.

"I?" Elena echoes, frowning.

"Yes," Jerrick confirms. "I'm going alone."

She stiffens, her breath hitching. "But I can heal you, Jerrick."

And he just looks at her, his expression unreadable. But I know my son.

He isn't going to bend.

"We've been through this before," Jerrick says, his voice low but unwavering. "If you're there, I'll hesitate. I'll worry about you instead of what I need to do." He turns to Elena, and though his words are firm, I can hear the weight behind them. "I can't afford to hesitate."

I step forward, my voice rougher than I intend. "There will be more SoulCasters. They won't all be in robes. They'll be dressed as guards, waiting to gut you the moment you get too close." I let the warning settle. "Go in fast. Go in hard. No second chances. I saw white robes—they have healers. They'll patch up the wounded if you let them. But remember—" I meet his eyes. "—they can't heal someone if they're *dead*."

Elena stiffens, crossing her arms over her chest. "You're going to let him go alone?"

I don't flinch. "I didn't say that."

"I'm right here," Jerrick interjects, his voice sharp.

"I *know*." I hold his gaze, then turn back to Elena. "We'll be with him. But we'll hang back."

Jerrick exhales, the tension in his shoulders barely visible, but I see it. He isn't arguing. He isn't trying to be noble. He's resigned. He *knows* what he has to do, and for once, we aren't fighting him on it.

"Jerrick," I say, my voice steady. "You're not in this alone."

"We got here together," Elena adds, stepping closer, her expression unwavering. "We fight together."

Jerrick hesitates, just for a second, but that second tells me everything. He isn't afraid of what's coming. He's afraid of losing *us*. And not just because of what it would mean for the fight.

Because he's already lost us before. And he can't bear to do it again.

His throat bobs as he swallows. "I have a plan," he says at last. "I'm going to hit them hard. *Stay behind me.* I'll keep your shields up as long as I can. But it takes concentration, so if they fall, you run." His eyes flick to Elena. "*Do not heal me.* If I need you, I'll come to you. If I go down—" his voice tightens. "*Run.* Promise me."

Elena's lips part, but she shakes her head. "I can't promise you that, Jerrick. No more than you could promise me that."

I glance at her, feeling something close to admiration. Elena has always been gentle, but there's steel in her bones when it matters. When it comes to him, she won't yield.

Jerrick's sigh is slow and deliberate. But then something shifts.

His face hardens. His shoulders square. His hands curl into fists. And I see it—*the memory.* The weight of it slams into him like a hammer to the chest. He's remembering the cave. The screams. The blood. He's remembering how he *hesitated.*

Good.

Use it, son. Let it fuel you.

His voice is quiet when he speaks, but it rumbles like a storm gathering strength.

"…It's time."

We follow.

The north trail is eerily familiar, a path we've walked before, but this time, there's no uncertainty. There's no *guessing* about what we'll find waiting for us.

They're already there.

Brightly colored robes and gleaming armor stand out against the gray backdrop of the dying land. SoulCasters and guards, a solid wall of bodies ready for war.

And beyond them, *the Fog.* Thick. Churning. Only a hundred feet away, spilling like a sickness from the wound in the sky.

I count the robes. Blue. Red. Black. White. Yellow. Brown. *Too many.* This is more than Rorick sent before. He learned his lesson. He knows what Jerrick is capable of.

And he's scared.

But he should have brought *more.*

Jerrick doesn't slow.

He lifts himself into the air. Ten feet. Fifteen. Twenty.

The ranks below stir, voices rising in alarm.

"There he is!" someone shouts.

The words ripple outward, panic swelling in the crowd. They recognize him.

Jerrick's voice cuts through the chaos like a blade.

"This is your only warning. Stand aside or die."

There's a hesitation. Murmurs. Uneasy glances exchanged. But *no one moves*.

Wrong choice.

Jerrick exhales sharply, regret flickering across his face.

"You were warned."

And then—

Hell is unleashed.

He drops to the ground and *waves his arm*.

The air bends. Shimmers. Blurs like ripples in a pond.

Then it *hits*.

A shockwave tears through the front ranks with a sickening *CRACK*. Bodies are ripped apart before they even have time to scream. Blood spatters in the air like rain, limbs flung like discarded rags. The ones still standing are frozen in horror.

But Jerrick isn't done.

Twin spheres of gray mass form in his hands, pulsing with compressed force.

He hurls them.

For a moment, there's nothing. A heartbeat of silence. Then—

A guard screams.

His body collapses inward as if he's being sucked into a void the size of a fist. His bones snap like dry branches, his armor crumpling inward before he *vanishes* entirely.

Then another. And another.

One by one, they're *folded* into nothingness. Gone.

The battlefield erupts into chaos.

A wave of fire explodes from the side, rushing toward Jerrick, swallowing him whole.

I wince. Elena gasps. But the fire—

It doesn't touch him.

It parts.

Jerrick steps through the flames, untouched, shield shimmering around him like a second skin.

In a *blink*, he's standing face to face with a SoulCaster in red robes.

The SoulCaster barely has time to react before a wall of stone erupts between them, rising like a fortress.

Jerrick doesn't hesitate.

He waves his hand—

And the wall explodes.

Chunks of rock the size of *houses* rocket into the air before slamming back down, *crushing* anything in their path.

The red-robed SoulCaster is gone. Flattened beneath a slab of earth.

Screams rise around us. Guards stumble, slipping in blood. SoulCasters bark orders, desperate, frantic. But I see it in their eyes—

Fear.

They thought they were the hunters. That *we* were the ones being cornered.

But Jerrick?

Jerrick is a force of nature.

There is no mercy in his movements. No hesitation. Only the relentless, unforgiving storm of his power.

And it is devastating.

Screams. Chaos. Death.

The battlefield is drenched in the horror of what Jerrick has become. The few that still stand call out orders, trying to rally. Trying to fight back. But they're already dead—they just don't know it yet.

Jerrick keeps coming.

A force of nature. A harbinger of death. *The reckoning they never saw coming.*

He isn't fighting to wound. He isn't fighting to drive them back. There is no surrender here. No mercy. The healers, draped in white, stand frozen at the edges of the carnage, hands trembling at their sides. They came here to mend broken flesh, to bring back the fallen.

But there is nothing left to heal.

A gust of wind slams into Jerrick, knocking him to the side. Finally, a real challenge.

A woman in flowing blue robes rises to meet him, her red hair whipping around her face. A SoulCaster of air. She conjures another blast, sending boulders the size of wagons ripping from the earth, hurling them at Jerrick.

The first he obliterates midair with a flick of his wrist. The second hits him head-on.

Elena tenses beside me, sucking in a sharp breath. I grab her shoulder, steadying her. "He's fine," I say, pointing. "*Look.*"

Jerrick shakes it off. The way a man might shake off a raindrop.

The SoulCaster barely has time to react before he sends a ball of force streaking toward her. She moves—too slow.

The sphere rips through her cheek with the sound of splitting flesh. Her jaw shatters, a scream tearing from her throat before she spirals backward, blood trailing through the air. She disappears into the distance. *Maybe she survives. Maybe she doesn't.*

Jerrick doesn't wait to find out.

He turns back to the battlefield below, his presence alone enough to send men and women scrambling, trampling each other in their desperation to escape.

I've seen battles. I've seen death. But I have never seen this.

Guards slip in puddles of blood. Pieces of the fallen litter the battlefield. Even the SoulCasters—the ones who came here with power in their veins, certain of their place in the world—are running.

Jerrick is beyond them. He is beyond *all* of them.

He is relentless.

And as I watch, something tightens in my chest. Not fear. Not awe.

Grief.

This isn't who he is. He isn't me. He isn't a killer. He never should have had to become one.

But the land didn't give him a choice.

The island trembles beneath our feet. and the gate appears.

It isn't what I expected. It isn't some grand celestial structure. It isn't glowing with divine power.

It's small. Old. Wood and rusted nails.

It looks fragile. But it is anything but.

Jerrick lifts his hands above his head, his body a conduit of pure force, and then—

He brings them down.

The air warps.

A wall of pressure slams into the battlefield with the force of a collapsing mountain.

One moment, six guards and two SoulCasters stand in formation.

The next, they are gone.

Nothing remains but pulverized stone, splintered bone, and the blackened craters where they once stood.

The island groans beneath us. The tunnels beneath the surface collapse, swallowing the ruins whole.

And just like that, it's over.

Jerrick floats back down, his breathing heavy. His hands shake. But he doesn't try to hide it.

"…It's done," he murmurs, voice hollow. His eyes, once so bright, are haunted.

Elena steps toward him, reaching out. "Are you okay?"

"No," he breathes. His shield falls. His head bows. "I didn't want this."

"I know." She wraps her arms around him, as if that might be enough to keep him from crumbling.

I know what comes next. We all do.

But none of us are ready.

The voice comes like a dagger in the dark.

"Behind you!"

I spin.

I see the hand first. Black blade. A glint of steel cutting through the air.

The knife slides across Jerrick's throat.

NO.

Jerrick jerks back. His hand flies up to his neck—

But there is no blood.

His shield. The warning gave him just enough time.

The attacker is gone. A shadow. A ghost. One of the SoulCasters from the Order of Night. A man with no name, but a reputation steeped in murder.

A *cackle* drifts through the air. A whisper in the dark. Then—

He reappears.

Behind Elena.

Blade pressed against her throat.

I know this man. He is a legend. The kind whispered about in back alleys. The kind of nightmare that never leaves witnesses.

But he is looking at Jerrick now, and he is smiling.

"That was impressive, boy," he sneers. "Drop your shield, or she—"

He never finishes the sentence.

He chokes.

His body convulses. His eyes bulge as his throat begins to swell, his skin blackening and splitting from the inside out.

He stumbles, struggling to breathe, massive boils erupting across his arms and chest. Bone pushes through skin. His flesh over heals from the inside as he collapses to his knees, clawing at the air—

"Y-you're a—"

"I am."

Elena's voice is calm.

He chokes on his own bile before he collapses, spasming, melting in a pool of vomit and pus.

Dead.

Healers have always scared me.

And now I remember why.

For a long, silent moment, we just stare.

The body—if you can even call it that—still twitches, grotesque and unrecognizable. The air reeks of rotting flesh and bile, a nauseating cocktail of death. Even Elena, the one who did this, looks shaken.

Jerrick breaks the silence first.

"He thought he was grabbing the weakest of us." His voice is quiet, but there's something else beneath it—pride. He looks at Elena, and for the first time since we landed, his expression softens. "But he realized too late that she is quite the opposite."

From behind a jagged outcrop of stone, a figure emerges.

Brennen.

I see him first, of course—then Drusilla at his side, and behind her, Eldrin with his usual smirk.

But Brennen—he's barely standing. He limps forward, a bandage wrapped around what's left of his ear, his face drawn and hollow. His eyes flicker across the ruin Jerrick left behind—the bodies, the blood, the shattered ground—and then finally, they find Jerrick.

His voice is small. Trembling. "I was wrong."

It isn't an apology, not really. Just a truth that took him too long to see.

Jerrick says nothing. Just watches him.

Brennen swallows hard. He shifts something cradled in his arms, something small, something fragile.

I know before he speaks.

"I brought something for you," Brennen murmurs, almost too soft to hear. His fingers brush the side of his ruined ear. "When time reset… she was gone. She wasn't old enough to understand, so she reset along with everything else." He hesitates. "I went back to the Keep. I got her for you."

Then, he holds her out.

Little Abby.

Jerrick stares. For a moment, he doesn't move.

Then he takes her.

His fingers tremble as he pulls her close. She snuggles into him, small and trusting, and a single tear carves a path down his blood-smeared cheek.

"…How?" His voice breaks.

Brennen's breath shakes. "Watching all of you die… broke me." His jaw clenches. "I couldn't do anything but hide myself and walk away. When time didn't reset, I knew—I knew it was over. I spent a week making my way back to Aethel and my people."

He stops. His throat bobs.

"The Council declared martial law," he finally continues. "Those creatures stopped showing up. Apparently, they culled enough of you that the land stopped fighting back." His voice cracks. "A baby was born. Bonded with Lathguard."

A silence heavier than death itself falls over us.

Brennen looks at Jerrick, eyes dark with something wretched. "They brought him back," he whispers.

"Jerrick, Lathguard walked the land again."

The hairs on my arms stand up.

No one speaks. No one breathes.

Finally, I find my voice, but it's barely more than a whisper. "What happened?"

Brennen's expression crumbles. "Aethel reset things." A slow inhale, ragged and fraying at the edges. "But at great cost." His voice shakes. "He can't speak anymore. I think— I think he's dying."

The world tilts. Aethel—the one who made all of this possible. The one who held time itself in his branches. Dying?

Brennen isn't done.

"For me…" he breathes, "I was reset outside the Keep. One woman that was there that night… she…" his voice fails. He tries again, but his hands shake. "She had just given birth to a baby boy the day before."

He swallows hard.

"I…"

He doesn't finish.

He doesn't need to.

The words hit like a hammer.

Brennen's knees buckle. He falls at Jerrick's feet, sobbing. His shoulders shake. His fingers claw at the dirt, at nothing.

"I'm sorry," he gasps. "I'm sorry for what I did to you. I don't deserve your forgiveness. Please, Jerrick—please take it back."

Jerrick doesn't answer right away.

Instead, still holding Abby, he reaches down.

He grabs Brennen's arm. Pulls him back up.

And then—softly, simply—he speaks.

"You never needed my forgiveness."

Brennen freezes.

Jerrick's voice is calm, steady. Unshakable. "You did what needed to be done. You didn't know what the consequences would be." He lifts his chin, surveying the battlefield around him. "But in the end, it all worked out."

His gaze hardens.

"My parents are alive. I saved them because of you. Because of what you did, I had the strength to forgive myself."

His fingers tighten on Abby. "And now… I can do what must be done."

Jerrick turns away, breaking the moment. He steps toward Elena.

"If things go badly," he murmurs, "know this: I love you. Live your life, find happiness." His hand cups her cheek, thumb brushing away a tear. "And know that this is my choice."

She breaks.

Tears spill down her face, but she nods as he bends down, pressing a slow, aching kiss to her lips—then another, gentle, against each eyelid.

When he steps away, she isn't ready to let him go.

None of us are.

But Jerrick is ready.

He turns to Drusilla. "I feel like we were becoming friends." He smiles, something real in it, despite the weight of what's coming. "Despite that tough exterior, you have a big heart."

Drusilla crosses her arms, scoffs. "Don't get sentimental on me now."

He grins.

Then his face hardens. "You made a promise to me when I saved your life." He glances at Abby in Elena's arms. "I am no longer the recipient of that debt. She is."

Drusilla nods without hesitation. "It is done."

Jerrick turns again, eyes settling on Eldrin.

"This whole reset thing is weird, isn't it?"

Eldrin laughs, rubbing the back of his head. "Yeah. It is." He shrugs. "But it's given me another chance."

Jerrick nods. "You deserved one."

Then, finally—

He turns to me.

And I can't breathe.

My boy.

My son.

He steps closer, his gait strong, sure. His eyes pierce through me, full of truth.

"Dad."

The word slams into my chest.

There is so much in that word. So much weight. So much meaning.

"There is so much to you," he says, quiet but steady. "I wish we had more time. And who knows—maybe we will." He smiles. She's in that smile. His mother. Gwen.

"When I first learned the truth about who you were, it scared me." He breathes deep. "I didn't know what it meant for my future."

Then he grips my shoulder, his fingers solid, firm.

"But now I do. And I'm proud of where I came from."

My body trembles.

He keeps going. He's breaking me piece by piece.

"I know the pain you feel," he says softly. "But I was given a second chance. A chance to save them." His grip tightens. "A chance you never got."

His next words gut me.

"It's time to forgive yourself."

And then—

He steps away.

And I know.

I know I am watching him walk away from me for the last time.

I stagger as he steps away.

He's right. I know he's right.

But I've worn my guilt for so long, I'm not sure who I am without it.

I watch him walk toward the gate, my mind racing, spiraling through memories—what could have been, what I could have done differently.

Was it always going to be this?

I fought to keep him safe, but here he is, putting himself in danger.

I fought to protect him, but here he is, saving us all.

He doesn't look back.

He has made his choice.

And for that, I am proud.

Jerrick lifts his arms, fingers curling as the air warps around him, distorting reality itself. The pressure in my ears builds, a heavy, suffocating weight.

Then—

A blast.

The sound of shattered light.

The world erupts.

I can't breathe—air is sucked from my lungs, my vision swimming as my chest burns for oxygen.

Then, just as suddenly, it rushes back.

A deafening boom tears through the sky as the gate implodes, wood splintering, nails twisting inwards, shards of light exploding outward.

And Jerrick collapses.

Limp. Motionless.

I move before I even know what I'm doing.

I sprint toward him, my body not my own, my voice a raw, broken thing as I scream NO!

Over. And over. And over.

I fall to my knees, grabbing him, pulling him into me, pressing his too-light body against my chest.

I feel hands on me—Brennen, Elena, Drusilla—but they don't matter.

There is only Jerrick.

And he is gone.

His body is aged, his skin wrinkled, like he's been drained of decades in the blink of an eye.

This isn't real.

It can't be real.

What do I do now?

What am I without him?

For the first time in my long, brutal life, I let myself break.

I hold my son and I weep.

A sob rumbles from deep in my chest—so raw, so soul-wrenching, I feel like I might come apart.

A father should never outlive his child.

This is wrong.

This is wrong.

Then—

The ground rumbles.

The air in front of us ripples.

A force unfurls, stretching wide like the yawn of something ancient.

Something immense steps through.

A shadow looms, massive.

My heart pounds in my chest.

The Creator.

She stands over thirty feet tall, her bark-like skin dark and lined with the wisdom of millennia. Long, flowing black hair spills down her back, her dress woven from leaves and earth itself.

Her face is stern, but her eyes—her eyes are kind.

She gleams with power, her form haloed in white fire, like the first spark before the heavens were born.

I look up at her—desperate, raw, pleading.

"Please."

My voice is wrecked.

"Help him."

"Please."

The word barely leaves my lips, raw and desperate.

I lift my head, staring up at the Creator—this towering, divine being who stands untouched by the horrors that have unfolded before her.

My hands tremble as I clutch Jerrick's lifeless body. He's so light, as if whatever made him him has already slipped through my fingers.

"Please," I beg again. "Help him."

She gazes down at me, her face unreadable, and then—she looks away.

Upward.

Toward the tear in the sky.

Toward the darkness that still looms.

"I am grateful," she says, her voice low, eternal, carrying the weight of millennia. "But it cannot be done. His soul has fused with Lathguard's. He may not be himself any longer."

I squeeze my eyes shut, pressing my forehead to Jerrick's ashen skin.

I don't care.

I don't care who he is now.

I just want him back.

"Please." The word cracks in my throat. "I'll do anything."

But the Creator merely shakes her head.

"I already told you," she says. "I won't chance it."

Her gaze sweeps over the battlefield—the blood-soaked ground, the shattered remains of the gate, the sky still torn asunder.

"Time is short," she continues. "They will be here soon. And we are not ready."

She reaches out, touches the earth. A ripple of Essence hums through the ground, the air vibrating with something old.

"This place…" she murmurs. "It's broken. It's almost dead."

She closes her eyes, as if listening to something beyond us, beyond this world.

"I can feel him," she says finally. "Weak. But alive."

My breath hitches.

Alive.

But not as he was.

She lifts her hand, and light floods the space around her.

"I must go now."

And then—

She is gone.

No parting glance. No whispered comfort. No promise that this isn't how it ends.

Just gone.

The fog stops pouring from the sky. The land, for the first time, is still.

But the rift remains.

And Jerrick is still dead.

I kneel there, holding my son, surrounded by people who are as lost as I am.

Nobody speaks.

Even Elena—who never stops hoping, never stops believing—doesn't say a word.

Then, finally, she does.

Her voice is soft, broken. "What's next?"

I look at her.

Then at Brennen, Drusilla, Eldrin—all of them.

I hold Jerrick a little closer, and I force myself to stand.

My body is heavy. The weight of everything—the loss, the grief, the unbearable finality—it nearly crushes me.

But I stand.

And I say the words that will haunt me for the rest of my days.

"I'm going to bury my son."

Here ends Book I.

ABOUT THE AUTHOR

Nick Blade is a lifelong lover of epic fantasy, tragic heroes, and stories that hit hard and leave a mark. With a passion for deep world-building, morally complex characters, and gut-wrenching emotional stakes, Nick weaves tales that challenge fate, test the strength of the human spirit, and explore the power of choice.

When not lost in the realms of gods, warriors, and destiny, Nick can be found obsessing over battle strategy, crafting intricate lore, or questioning the very fabric of existence—usually with a cup of tea in hand.

The Rift and The Reckoning is the first book in a gripping high-fantasy saga that blends relentless action, heart-wrenching sacrifice, and an unflinching look at what it truly means to be a hero.

Subscribe to his free newsletter at **NickBlade.com** and become part of the inner circle with extra chapters, art, and to stay up to date with his latest books.

www.ingramcontent.com/pod-product-compliance
Lightning Source LLC
Chambersburg PA
CBHW071735110726
47908CB00006B/1589